THE BERLIN PROJECT

Also by Gregory Benford

Bowl of Heaven (with Larry Niven)

Bowl of Heaven

Shipstar

Foundation Universe: Second Foundation Trilogy

Foundation's Fear

Galactic Center

Across the Sea of Suns

Great Sky River

Tides of Light

Furious Gulf

Sailing Bright Eternity

A Hunger for the Infinite

Adventures of Viktor & Julia

The Martian Race

The Sunborn

Tales of Known Space: Man-Kzin Wars (with Mark O. Martin)

The Trojan Cat

A Darker Geometry

Jupiter Project
The Stars in Shroud
Shiva Descending (with William Rotsler)
Timescape
Find the Changeling (with Gordon Eklund)
Against the Fall of Night/Beyond the Fall of Night (with Arthur C. Clarke)
Against Infinity
Artifact
Heart of the Comet (with David Brin)
Chiller (also as by Sterling Blake)
Cosm
Eater
Beyond Infinity

Collections
The Galactic Center Companion, 2nd Edition
The Best of Gregory Benford
Mammoth Dawn (with Kevin J. Anderson)

Anthologies
Starship Century: Toward the Grandest Horizon (with James Benford)
The Mars Girl/As Big as the Ritz (with Joe Haldeman)

Nonfiction
The Wonderful Future That Never Was (with the editors of *Popular Mechanics*)
The Amazing Weapons That Never Were (with the editors of *Popular Mechanics*)
Deep Time
Beyond Human (with Elisabeth Malartre)

THE BERLIN PROJECT

A NOVEL

GREGORY BENFORD

SAGA PRESS

LONDON SYDNEY **NEW YORK** TORONTO NEW DELHI

SAGA PRESS

AN IMPRINT OF SIMON & SCHUSTER, INC.

1230 AVENUE OF THE AMERICAS, NEW YORK, NEW YORK 10020

Text copyright © 2017 by Gregory Benford

Jacket photograph copyright © 2017 by Thinkstock

Author photograph courtesy of the author

All photos and figures in this book are either from Wiki Commons, Los Alamos publicly available sources, or the author's family albums.

SAGA PRESS and colophon are registered trademarks of Simon & Schuster, Inc.

For information about special discounts for bulk purchases, please contact Simon & Schuster Special Sales at 1-866-506-1949 or business@simonandschuster.com.

The Simon & Schuster Speakers Bureau can bring authors to your live event. For more information or to book an event, contact the Simon & Schuster Speakers Bureau at 1-866-248-3049 or visit our website at www.simonspeakers.com.

Interior design by Hilary Zarycky

The text for this book was set in Adobe Jensen Pro.

Manufactured in the United States of America

First Edition

2 4 6 8 10 9 7 5 3 1

Library of Congress Cataloging-in-Publication Data

Names: Benford, Gregory, 1941– author.

Title: The Berlin Project / Gregory Benford.

Description: First edition. | New York : Saga Press, [2017]

Identifiers: LCCN 2016040114 (print) | ISBN 9781481487641 (hardcover : acid-free paper) | ISBN 9781481487665 (eBook)

Subjects: LCSH: World War, 1939–1945—Fiction. | Manhattan Project (U.S.)—Fiction. | Atomic bomb—United States—History—Fiction. | BISAC: FICTION / Alternative History. | FICTION / Science Fiction / High Tech. | FICTION / Historical. | GSAFD: Alternative histories (Fiction) | Suspense fiction. | Science fiction. | War stories.

Classification: LCC PS3552.E542 B47 2017 (print) | DDC 813/.54—dc23

LC record available at https://lccn.loc.gov/2016040114

To the Cohen sisters:
Martine, Elisabeth, and Beatrix

Cast of Characters
(in order of appearance)

Otto Hahn: German chemist; awarded 1944 Nobel Prize in Chemistry, 1944 but received award in 1945. Worked with Fritz Strassmann and Lise Meitner.

Karl Cohen (1913–2012): American chemist; PhD from Columbia University, 1936; Manhattan Project nuclear engineer; US Navy reactor program (under Hyman Rickover); director, General Electric nuclear power program.

Marthe Malartre Cohen: wife of Karl Cohen.

Rachel Paley: mother of Karl Cohen.

Irving Kaplan: American chemist, PhD from Columbia University.

Harold Urey: American chemist; awarded 1934 Nobel Prize in Chemistry, Manhattan Project; professor at Columbia University and UC San Diego.

Enrico Fermi: Italian physicist; awarded 1938 Nobel Prize in Physics, Manhattan Project.

Niels Bohr: Danish physicist; awarded 1922 Nobel Prize in Physics, Manhattan Project.

Edward Teller: Hungarian-born physicist; Manhattan Project.

Leo Szilard: Hungarian-born physicist; Manhattan Project.

Albert Einstein: German-born physicist; awarded 1921 Nobel Prize in Physics.

Martine Cohen: daughter of Karl and Marthe Malartre Cohen.

Rabbi Elon Kornbluth: fictional major Jewish figure in Manhattan.

Anton Paley: fictional Jewish refugee from Central Europe.

John Dunning: professor at Columbia University; Manhattan Project physicist.

Rudolf Peierls: German-born British physicist.

Ernest Lawrence: American physicist; awarded 1939 Nobel Prize in Physics, Manhattan Project.

Brigadier General Leslie Groves: builder of Pentagon; director of Manhattan Project.

Otto Frisch: Austrian-British physicist; Manhattan Project.

Moe Berg: American Major League Baseball catcher; United States Office of Strategic Services agent.

Elisabeth Cohen: daughter of Karl and Marthe Malartre Cohen.

John W. Campbell Jr.: science fiction writer and editor.

Sir Arthur "Bomber" Harris: head of RAF Bomber Command.

Frederick Reines: physicist; awarded 1995 Nobel Prize in Physics, Manhattan Project.

Luis Alvarez: physicist; awarded 1968 Nobel Prize in Physics, Manhattan Project.

Freeman Dyson: English physicist.

Sam Goudsmit: Dutch-American physicist.

Richard P. Feynman: American physicist; awarded 1965 Nobel Prize in Physics, Manhattan Project.

Paul Dirac: English physicist; awarded 1933 Nobel Prize in Physics.

Major General William Donovan: head of United States Office of Strategic Services.

Paul Scherrer: Swiss physicist.

Werner Heisenberg: German physicist; awarded 1932 Nobel Prize in Physics.

Admiral Wilhelm Canaris: chief of the Abwehr, the German military intelligence service.

Johannes Erwin Eugen Rommel: German army general, popularly known as "the Desert Fox."

Beatrix Cohen: daughter of Karl and Marthe Malartre Cohen.

Kaiser Wilhelm Institute, Berlin, 1938

When his office door slammed open, Otto Hahn looked up.

He stood, angry. "What?" The sight of scowling faces above dark leather coats and black uniforms shut him up.

The very mention of the Gestapo, short for the "Geheime Staatspolizei," elicited fear among the general population. Hahn was not so easily intimidated. He rose with dignity. "What is the meaning—"

"Sit, Herr Professor," said a major whose name SCHLICHER appeared above the pocket of his trim uniform. The Nazi party types always had the best tailors. Hahn could smell their strong boot polish. The major had a lean and hungry look, a glint in his eyes. "We are here to investigate the escape of your worker, Lise Meitner. She passed through the border to Denmark yesterday after leaving this laboratory."

"Did she?" Hahn feigned surprise. Two stiff-faced lieutenants stood just behind and beside the major. None were obviously armed.

"You knew she would." The major allowed himself a thin smile. "This woman's escape—and she was carrying documents—comes just as we receive word that you and Strassmann have found a new method of yielding vast energies."

"Yes. So?"

"You know Kurt Hess?"

"Of course. He is my fellow chemist here, and the head of the organic department."

"Also a loyal party member. He told us you aided this Meitner to escape."

So, an accusation. Hahn formally bowed. "She told me she was leaving. That is all."

"As a German Jew she should—"

"She is Austrian."

The major blinked, glancing at some papers he held in his left hand. Hahn took the moment to say mildly, "I gathered that your police generally wear civilian suits, in keeping with the secretive nature of your work."

The major shook his head in quick jerks. "There are strict protocols protecting the identity of Gestapo field personnel. When asked for identification, we operatives are only required to present this warrant disk"—a quick flip of a steel coin, then—"but we may wear the new provisional uniforms when making public arrests."

Hahn resisted his impulse to laugh at this marionette. "Of whom?"

"You, perhaps. As head of this laboratory you should have notified us of Meitner's escape."

"Kurt Hess already had, you said."

Another curt shake of his head. "I gather you published these results on a new energy source? In a journal?"

"In *Naturwissenschaften*, yes."

"I have glanced over it, and my advisers assure me it is important. This published document refers to Uranspaltung? The breaking apart of the element uranium?"

"Yes, we discovered that—"

"Then those who assisted in this are to be kept within the Reich, by order of my superiors. Meitner, especially. You should have known that."

Hahn spread his hands, shrugged. Perhaps he could defuse this insolent party man. "I could not keep an Austrian citizen from leaving the country. I am merely a scientist and have no civil authority. I gather from gossip that she left with ten Reichsmarks in her purse. You Gestapo are everywhere these days, especially at the border. She has somehow eluded you?"

Major Schlicher's mouth tightened. Before he could speak a call came from the corridor outside. "*Schnell!*"

The Gestapo men turned and ran out. Hahn followed them into the corridor, curious. A technician from his group was cowering against the wall. He was thin, pale, his eyes dancing anxiously.

Another Gestapo officer displayed a file of documents to Major Schlicher. "He was trying to leave with them."

Major Schlicher snatched the papers and glanced through them while the technician stood frozen. "These are about this Uranspaltung, I see."

Hahn smelled the acrid scent of fear. He said calmly, "This is one of my technical assistants, Georg Weissman. He worked on the isotope detection experiments with us. I expect he was merely—"

"Weissman, yes," Major Schlicher said as he peered at the technician. "Another Jew in your group. There seem to be many, too many. So this man was trying to escape as well, eh? Bearing documents on this energy source of yours. Like the Meitner woman. Probably all planned."

Weissman suddenly barked, "Lise was right! She got out! Bless her! I want the same!" He stepped back, arms waving, eyes white.

"Major, we simply publish the results of our work," Hahn said. "It is very important, I agree. There is true potential in this research to liberate energy. Of course, that means this energy could possibly be used as a weapon, but better, as a source of power. I suggest—"

"Enough!" The major pointed at Weissman. "Arrest this man, Lieutenant. We will see what we can get out of him." He gestured grandly, smiling.

Weissman hesitated, turned, and then bolted.

A lieutenant stepped forward, a black Luger in his hand. The shot rapped hard against the ceramic corridor walls. Weissman fell.

Karl Cohen

PART I

THE CURVE OF BINDING ENERGY

Life has two important dates—
when you're born and when you find out why.
—Mark Twain

1.

September 26, 1938

Not yet an hour on the ground back home in America, and already he was in trouble.

Karl Cohen had just passed through the immigration office with his new bride, Marthe, when the family descended. His tiny aunt Ida tossed off the cheerful accusation, "Where's your shiksa wife?"—somehow missing Marthe three feet away, perhaps because of Marthe's polished Paris look.

"She's not a goy," he muttered, voice low. Ida's eyes danced mischievously behind horn-rims. Karl kept his smile steady.

His mother, Rae, led the tittering inspection brigade, all eyes now on Marthe's tailored gray suit, fashionable hat at a rakish tilt, stylish brushed leather shoes, Paris fashion on parade. His aunt Ida embraced him, saying again, "She's my new goy greenhorn niece, eh?"

"She's *not* a goy," Karl said stiffly as his uncle Jack leaned in for a handshake, saying gruffly, "Name's not very Jewish, this Marthe. How do you spell it?"

Karl managed to ignore that as his sister Mattie rapped back at Jack, "The French way, damn it."

As Karl managed the leather suitcases in their dustcovers, he said, "She's as much a Jew as you, Jack." He couldn't keep a grating tone out of his voice.

In some official way that was true, though Marthe had converted from Catholicism only a week before, and gotten her tourist visa the day after that. Jack nodded and helped with the hatboxes, the toilet case that tinkled from the cut-glass bottles within, and another case for soap and cosmetics. The army of gear a woman carried! Karl had never known that till the hurricane-swept voyage over on the *Normandie*—pursued, a deck officer said, by a German U-boat. More drama than a honeymoon cruise needed.

They came onto the Pier 49 entrance along the Hudson River, the women afloat on their chatting, Marthe's eyes darting among these new relatives, her carefully lipsticked smile fixed, hand still clutching her passport with REPUBLIQUE FRANÇAISE stamped boldly on it. "I had to show them the check you kindly gave me, for a thousand dollars," Marthe said to Rae in her lilting fashion. The family brightened at this accent that made words flow like a liquid. "It is required, to show I am not an indigent. The inspector tossed my French francs aside as worthless." Bronx laughs greeted this.

Karl breathed in the peculiar scent of Manhattan, its crisp urban flavorings. He felt a gauzy lightness as his family chattered around him. He was back, they were safe. The New World.

A shortwave radio on a chair was rasping out a speech in German and Karl recognized it: Hitler, making his threatened ultimatum speech in guttural, barking stutters. The oncoming catastrophe was pursuing them, even here. Would the English and French let Hitler take the Sudetenland from Czechoslovakia? All signs at the Munich meeting said they would, or else there would be war.

Rae asked, "What will Hitler do next?"

"We decided not to hang around and find out," Karl said as they got into two cabs. A chorus of agreement, but eyes were still on Marthe.

Karl ended up next to Uncle Jack, who bore in immediately, his usual brusque business style. "You don't get the inheritance money from your grandfather Jonas, y'know, till I verify that your wife is . . . one of us."

Karl bristled but kept his voice level. "She is—here."

The certificate of conversion to the Jewish faith they got in Paris had gold script and flourishes. Jack studied it. "Just last week!"

"It's official. She had been meaning to—"

Marthe broke in from the window seat, "I had been attracted to the faith before, and Karl made me finally do it." She smiled, hands carefully knitted together in front of her. Karl noticed she wore her best leather gloves. "You will find my rabbi specifies the syllabus I studied."

Jack's mouth twisted, vexed. "You get nothing from my father's estate if I judge her not to be a Jew, y'know."

Karl softened his tone. "We have nothing to live on, Jack. I had to get her out before the war."

Jack scowled, turning away from Marthe, and whispered, "My dad felt we Jews should stick together. But this new gal of yours—"

"My *wife*."

"—she's a Catholic, just got some paperwork done, that doesn't mean—"

"Jack, I'm broke."

Jack frowned and worked his mouth around, as if tasting something sour. A short snort of frustration escaped his teeth. "I'll think on it."

Harold Urey

2.

Thursday, January 19, 1939

Karl's desk telephone rang for the first time. He frowned at the jangle. It had been installed just days before and hardly anyone knew the number.

"Mr. Cohen? I'm Armbruster at Bank of New York."

A curt, clipped tone. Karl could feel himself reddening. "Ah, I was going to come over—"

"With a check?"

"Well, no, I'm still running behind—"

"You're three months in arrears, Mr. Cohen."

Stall. "How did you get this number?"

"Your wife."

"You shouldn't call my home about this."

"Keeping it secret, eh? Wifey doesn't know you borrowed two hundred bucks to get by? Well, your home was the only number you gave us. Your short note is *due*, Mr. Cohen. I don't think I can delay much longer, and you know we dock you an arrears fee, don't you?"

"I'm not a simpleton."

"What happens next, that's simple. We attach your paycheck at Columbia University, Cohen. Pronto."

"I—I'll get it."

"You do that." *Click.*

He got up, paced. Making the first and last months' rent just to move in had strapped him. He couldn't bear the half-furnished look of the apartment they had just gotten into, so he'd let Marthe order a decent carpet. Plus, he couldn't go to work in the worn, sagging pants and shirts he had used for years. One of the Columbia lab techs had mistaken him for the janitor. He hadn't realized that the old adage, that two could live as cheaply as one, was flat wrong. So he had borrowed, and now he couldn't make the payments.

Uncle Jack's *I'll think on it* had turned into delay and paperwork, four months' worth now. So Karl had kept up a facade of thrifty prosperity but could do so no longer. He gritted his teeth. Harold Urey had told him the day before that his position here was uncertain, the money to run out in two months. Then what?

A knock on his door. Would the bank guy come here? It was only a few blocks away. He froze.

A fist hammered again. "Come on, Karl!" came Irving Kaplan's booming voice. "I know you're in there."

Karl looked at his desk, where he had been summing up his new calculation, using a fountain pen and lined paper.

The knock hammered again, louder. Karl finished the line, an equation giving a clear, simple result in deep-blue ink. He liked using a fountain pen rather than a pencil. This was a summary for Harold Urey, and he wanted it neat. Doing it in ink made it final. He liked the calculation's result. *Just as I guessed*, he thought. *No, not a guess. An intuition.* Not fascinating work, and at $125 a month, a married man couldn't get by, really.

When he opened the door, Irving hooked a finger at him. "C'mon. Big seminar, announced word of mouth. It's Bohr!"

Karl blinked and considered. He had gotten interested in all this nuclear business while touring Europe in the last few years. And Niels Bohr was the biggest theorist in the hot-topic field.

"Um. Bohr. I thought he was in Denmark."

"Just off the boat, seems like. Come *on!*" Irving was an old friend and could insist. His beanpole frame commanded attention.

Irving filled him in, talking fast on the way down the stairs from their twelfth-floor offices. The elevators were always in use and slow. Irving was not a man to wait. The Pupin Physics Laboratories were in a tall stack of overburnt brick with limestone trim. Karl was not athletic, slighter than Irving, and still getting used to climbing between stories in the largest building on the Columbia University campus. He had done his PhD work in Havemeyer Hall, a smaller and more comfortable building, though with poor lighting. It had suited his introvert nature well, since he could slip in and out without having to exchange small talk, which bored him.

When they reached the third floor, he saw no one coming up from the 120th Street entrance, so he asked, "Was this announced?"

"No time for it. Bohr appeared, surprise visit. Urey got the room, word spread."

It was a good idea to show up, then. Karl had been working for Urey only a short while, so far on calculations for a paper, "Van Der Waals' Forces and the Vapor Pressures of Ortho- and Paradeuterium." Not exactly a pulse-pounding subject. But it was solid science and Harold Urey was pressing him to finish and submit to the *Journal of Chemical Physics*. "It'll show my grant guy you can do things. I've got to get him to renew the two thousand for another year, and he's talking cheap. I can't guarantee your job for much longer."

Urey had a good sense for these things. He had discovered deuterium, the heavy form of hydrogen, and swiftly won a Nobel Prize for it. But Urey was interested in nuclear physics now and thought that chemists, who were the final authorities on identifying elements in tiny concentrations, could play a part. Here was a chance to get up to speed on the furiously competitive field, so far dominated by the Europeans like Niels Bohr.

Karl checked himself out as they walked. His overall gawkiness called attention to his hands and elbows, which often seemed to have minds of their own. He made himself stand straighter, walk firmly, head up. He didn't know many people here yet and had not tried to breach the perimeter of the nuclear physics group, small as it was. He spent his time pushing his pencil. Urey expected results quickly, because even Nobelists came under tightening screws when the only source of funding lay in private foundations.

Urey had built up a group finding how to isolate medically useful isotopes like carbon 13. His support came in grants from the Rockefeller Foundation, which was pioneering the new field of radioactivity for medical use. But Urey was growing tired of these utilitarian tasks, so he had turned down the Foundation's offer to continue the grants.

Karl normally did theory, using his mathematical talents, but lately, Urey made him move into the lab, where he had to do experiments. How far this would go was a mystery, though Karl feared for his future under the rickety funding of all research, in the gathering recession that now threatened to dip into a new depression.

As chance had it, Urey was the first person he saw as they approached the lecture room, hasty heels ringing in the corridor. He was sturdy and compact, with an air of compressed energy. The man who had discovered heavy hydrogen had a bantam energy, pacing impatiently. He hailed each approaching graduate student or assistant professor with "Hey, 'bout to start. Glad you could make it."

Urey grinned at Karl and Irving. "You're gonna like this."

Karl said, "Hope so," then added, "Sounds great."

This was entirely phony, but he owed Urey a lot. He had returned to New York from France in the fall of 1938 looking for a job, since his savings were vanishing and his mother could spare him only a paltry fifty-five dollars a month. Urey had not been on Karl's thesis committee, but he sympathized with those who suffered from the pervasive bias against Jews. Urey had sought a job for Karl, but the chemical companies didn't want a mathematical chemist, or a Jew.

Karl had growled at Urey then, saying, "They hire B students but not the best." Urey had shrugged, chewing gum, his shoes propped on his desk. These little habits had annoyed Karl when he'd looked for a thesis professor in 1933, and he saw now that error had major consequences. His own thesis professor, Miller, had been a classier guy but made no effort on Karl's behalf beyond the minimum.

Karl had become even more mathematical in Paris, by self-study, his preferred way to learn things. Now he might be facing unemployment within months, even though he would soon be Urey's last assistant; the others Urey had already let go. It was a good idea to be enthusiastic about whatever tickled Urey's nose.

He and Irving walked into the lecture room and sat near the front. About two dozen people were in the first few rows and Karl took a moment to look around, getting an idea of who was here. He studied the faces with care, thinking, *Kind of like Daniel looking over the lions when he strolled into their den.*

Enrico Fermi was talking to Niels Bohr, standing in front of the blackboard. Karl had seen a photo of Fermi arriving on the liner *Franconia* on the *New York Times*'s front page. He was the latest Nobel physicist, a fairly short man in a business suit, with an open, friendly Italian face and animated eyes. The *Times* had played up the intrigue of how Fermi and his family had left Italy to receive the prize in Sweden and then sailed off to New York, while the Italian authorities were readying a big reception for him back in Rome.

The Fermis had managed to get their household goods shipped, as if to a new home in Rome, but in fact to America. Their break with the Mussolini regime was sudden and shocking, making headlines. They were driven out by the new racial laws the Fascist government had instituted against Jews, copying the Germans. Fermi's wife was a Jew. Those Jews who could were streaming out of Europe, but most had no way to do so.

Karl studied the two. Fermi was frowning, Bohr gesturing, both talking— at the same time—and the seminar had not started. Karl sensed a tension rising: feet shuffling, a fretful murmur. By now there were maybe twenty people, all men, in the rectangular rigidities of the lecture hall, and Karl sniffed in the air a heady sense of something new, fresh, urgent. All without knowing what Bohr was going to say.

Others he knew because Irving had pointed them out before, but Karl had been uneasy about approaching them. The heavyset bearlike man in the front row was Edward Teller—one of the "Hungarian geniuses," as Urey had once described him. Teller spoke with animation, making his points with bushy black eyebrows that moved like a major feature of his dark face.

Another one sat beside Teller. Karl studied the scowling, animated face with thick lips and flat cheekbones, topped by thick brown hair, and groped for the name. *Ah yes, Leo Szilard.* Everyone in the front row wore three-piece suits in the European manner, though some were Americans. Urey was not a big "dresser-upper," as Karl's mother always put it, meaning people who used clothes to impress others. Urey was still playing host at the doorway, so Karl studied the rest of the crowd—

Then he saw it. Written out on the blackboard in a European hand was the reaction formula.

$$^{1}_{0}n + ^{235}_{92}U \rightarrow ^{141}_{56}Ba + ^{92}_{36}Kr + 3\,^{1}_{0}n$$

The formula spread across the blackboard was easy to follow. Slam a neutron into a uranium 235 nucleus—the lighter version of the element, Karl recalled—and you get out a batch of barium plus some krypton, with three more neutrons left over.

In his head Karl worked out the energy implications of the formula—and gasped. *People had done this. Broken a huge nucleus into two middle-size ones plus more neutrons. Germans had . . .*

The main point was that the collision gave off two hundred million times as much energy as an ordinary atom's reactions with other atoms. He was used to the low-energy end of science, the province of chemists. Now came this utter surprise, opening doors to—

"Good afternoon," Harold Urey said, coming to the front. "Thanks for coming on short notice. Professor Niels Bohr"—a nod—"arrived with major news, and I thought you should hear it from him."

Scattered applause, unusual in a seminar at the beginning of a talk. Bohr got distracted by some slide projector problem.

Karl could see the leading lights of the nuclear physics group lean forward intently—Isidor Rabi's team, and Eugene Wigner, up from Princeton. These faces he had learned from watching carefully in past seminars, but he had met none of them. They batted in another league.

Leo Szilard, the Hungarian physicist, sat with Edward Teller, who was scowling intently at the board. Karl had seen them in the halls, without ever speaking to them. He was a chemist fresh from his PhD and they were sharp, quick, well-known physicists with much experience. Their field was changing fast and he had picked up on some of it while in Europe, but as a chemist he seldom had anything to do with them.

Bohr made polite introductory remarks as he slid a slide into a projector. Urey pulled down a white screen and clicked on the projector. "I have done some calculations, somewhat based upon my own model, which treats a nucleus as a liquid, so the nuclear force is something like a surface tension. Here is a rough outline of that."

Karl had not seen the nuclear work summed up in such crisp fashion. It was all there, as the label made clear: CURVE OF BINDING ENERGY. The higher up the curve, the tighter a nucleus of an element held together. The

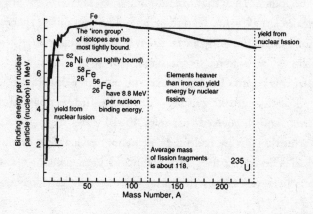

Curve of Binding Energy

curve had a maximum around iron, where the total number of protons and neutrons, the nucleons, was sixty. It fell off sharply for the light elements, and more slowly for the heavy ones, and uranium was highlighted at the far end, U-235. That was the less common isotope, less than a percent of the major one, U-238.

Karl had studied nuclear physics at the Sorbonne, but not systematically, and he had never seen this curve before. But he had read about bits of it in papers, while studying by himself in Paris—when he wasn't distracted by falling in love.

Bohr spoke carefully, slowly, in his Danish-accented English. "Two Germans in Berlin—Otto Hahn, a chemist, and Fritz Strassmann, physical chemist—have been following on Enrico's work"—a nod to Fermi—"by bombarding uranium with neutrons."

Karl had seen some uranium once, a dense, purple-black metal that had modest commercial use as a pottery glaze. Otherwise, worthless. But not any longer.

"So they worked away. After some slamming of neutrons into uranium metal, element ninety-two, they noticed something odd in their beaker—barium! They were startled! Like Enrico, they figured a neutron might hit a nucleus and chip off a few protons—make it into thorium, say." Bohr waved his hands, shrugged. "Thorium is element ninety. But barium!—it's element fifty-six. And iodine. They split uranium in two!"

And released lots of energy, Karl thought, but he kept quiet. That was what the equation said, but nobody in the room uttered a word.

Bohr slipped into some recent history, bringing the audience slowly toward what this meant. The Berlin experiments came directly from Enrico Fermi's work with neutrons four years earlier. He had bombarded uranium with neutrons and discovered that it produced dozens of radioactive substances. Fermi thought he had made elements heavier than uranium, and everyone had believed him. But Otto Hahn and Strassmann had now shown that the products were radioactive forms of much simpler elements, barium and iodine.

"So Hahn wrote to Lise Meitner on December 19, 1938—she showed me the letter—'Perhaps you can put forward some fantastic explanation,' Hahn wrote." He paused and faced the audience. "So she did."

Bohr was something of a dramatist, Karl saw. For this result, justifiably so.

Bohr turned to the blackboard, as if considering launching into the meaning of the equation there, and the curve on his slide—then turned back. "After Hitler took over Austria last March, her situation became desperate."

Karl thought, *Along with hundreds of thousands more left-wingers and Jews.*

Bohr shook his head. "Meitner was lucky to escape. Kurt Hess, a Nazi chemist, warned the authorities she was about to flee. Last July she took a train under cover to the Dutch border and some physicists argued her way across. She left Germany forever with ten marks in her purse. Before she got out, Otto Hahn gave her a diamond ring to bribe the frontier guards, if needed. Shortly afterward, the Gestapo killed a Jew who had worked with her. Apparently in a fit of rage."

A murmur from the audience. There were more stories like this all the time now.

Bohr spread his hands in apology. "I could not land her an appointment; there was no money. But she went instead to Stockholm, where she took up a post at a laboratory, despite the prejudice against women in science. There she established a working relationship with her nephew, Otto Frisch. They cracked the problem."

Karl thought, *So the Nazis drove out the Jew who really understands this. And those left behind . . .*

Bohr said, "Therefore, quite rightly, Lise Meitner and Otto Frisch ran an experiment over the holidays to test their idea—that the fragments would move very fast, spraying electrons and losing energy they could see with a Geiger counter. There it was!"

He turned to the equation and gestured to the curve of binding energy. "The energy yield they found fits the model too. They came to Copenhagen to tell me about it. Frisch calls it 'fission'—from the biologists' term for the division of cells." A final wave of his hand to the audience, coming to a stop when he pointed to Fermi. "And so I've come to tell you."

Fermi seemed to be calculating something in his head. Edward Teller's voice boomed from the front row. "Does it release enough neutrons to start a chain reaction?"

"We do not know," Leo Szilard answered in his quick, darting English, before Bohr could. "Never mind, Edward, I already gave the patent on this idea, of the chain reaction, to the British Admiralty." A decisive nod of his head. "Years ago."

"Why?" Fermi asked.

"To keep the idea secret, unpublished."

A silence fell as everyone thought this through. Fermi had been silent so far, his calm face showing no reaction. Karl knew something of what Fermi had done and saw a collision coming. Fermi rose and wrote some equations on the blackboard, musing. "In Rome we screened very carefully, looking only for alpha particles. . . ."

Bohr said, "The really energetic barium and iodine, they would stop very fast in a screen."

"So we missed them." Fermi sighed. "The screen we used, it stopped the barium and iodine from getting into the residues we checked."

Fermi turned to Bohr with weary eyes and a slanted smile, and shrugged. "So we thought we had discovered new elements. We even named them— hesperium, ausonium. Wrong! Mythical! They were ordinary old barium and iodine. We were careful—*too* careful." He grew more emotional as he said this, losing his mild manner. *Now, there's the Italian in him,* Karl thought.

Harold Urey said, "Recall Ida Noddack? She's a chemist—German, right?—wrote a paper, 'On Element 93.' About your experiments, Enrico. She suggested you'd failed to chemically eliminate *all* elements lighter than uranium, rather than only working down to lead. Barium, iodine—you missed those."

"We did not think it possible to make light elements from heavy," Fermi said.

"She didn't just point out the flaw in your chemical proof, though." Urey stood, walked to the blackboard, picked up chalk, thought better of it, and put it down. Karl had worked for the man a year now and he could see the slight jumpy energy in his gestures. "She suggested that the nucleus breaks up into several large fragments. All the way back in 1934."

Fermi said softly, "Noddack offered no experimental proof or theoretical basis for this possibility."

"So she was generally ignored." Urey's eyes danced with mirth. "Maybe because she was just a chemist—or a woman?"

Karl knew many chemists felt all the glory had gone to the physicists in the twentieth century. They had profoundly wrenched all conceptions of the world around them. Quantum mechanics undermined the small world of atoms, and relativity shook the larger cosmos, with its weird mechanics and models of the universe as a whole. But here in nuclear physics the chemists were essential, because they could tell what elements emerged from the disruptive experiments, which could now change one element to others.

There were a few chuckles, but otherwise the room was silent. The drama of Bohr's revelation could be seen on Fermi's face. His words came out cautiously, his features stern and still grappling with these ideas. Karl watched closely and saw a small tic in Fermi's left eye, as though the man was under pressures he did not want to show. His lips moved silently; he was deep in thought.

The others could see this reaction too. Fermi had just won the Nobel Prize for demonstrating the existence of new radioactive elements, brought about by slow neutrons. Quietly he said, "We entirely missed the big effect. The heavy elements, they split. The Latin is, they *fission*."

Karl already knew from corridor gossip that Teller was moody, tireless, given to fits of quick laughter and bursts of anger. But now he leaned back and said lightly, "Suppose Enrico had paid attention to Noddack, eh?"

Bohr frowned. "Looked for the lighter elements?"

Teller nodded energetically. "Maybe removed his shielding, too. Found this fission, could have."

"He would've gotten the Nobel even sooner," Bohr said. "So?"

"No, think." Teller wagged a scolding finger. "Germany, the Soviets— they take the military application of science far more seriously than these Americans. They would have started work on the obvious."

So there it was, out in the open. The obvious was a device beyond comprehension, a superweapon.

"Making a chain reaction go out of control?" Szilard nodded. "I thought of this in 1932, while walking to my office at Imperial College, London. To thus make a . . . bomb."

"They would be very far ahead, Germans, the Soviets. So Fermi's mistake was perhaps fortunate."

Another long silence in the room. "But not for long, not now," Urey said.

Urey's American speech style was more clipped, more direct than that of the formal Europeans. Karl thought about this through another long silence. American speech felt sawed off, forceful but less precise than the long, languid sentences of the Hungarians—Teller and Szilard, particularly. Karl was a mere twenty-six years old and these Europeans seemed vastly more mature, seasoned by millennia of war and trouble. It seemed impossible for him to imagine calling them colleagues.

Karl saw that for Fermi, the news came as a profound embarrassment. His somber eyes searched the floor, mouth turned down in a puzzled scowl. The elements beyond uranium he had partly been awarded the Nobel Prize for discovering had not been more massive than uranium; they came from fission.

Fermi was pale as he said stonily, "I must add a footnote to my unpublished Nobel Prize acceptance speech to this effect."

Bohr took this moment to quickly digress, ending up the talk with some slides of the data from Berlin he had just gotten from Lise Meitner. The talk concluded with curiously muted applause.

As the seminar broke up, Karl followed his instincts. He moved forward as the crowd dispersed, noting that three separate circles had formed around Bohr, Fermi, and Teller. Urey was in Teller's group, so Karl headed there. They were discussing details of the Meitner and Frisch experiments and he listened, picking up some of the physics jargon. He was fairly new to this subject and it was important to get the feel of it by the way people talked.

Then he moved to Bohr's crowd, about a dozen, and heard him expound on his model of the nucleus. Karl waited while some graduate students bombarded Bohr with questions. He could follow most of it but knew nobody else in the group. At a break in the conversation he said, "How sure are you of your model?"

Bohr blinked. Maybe Nobel laureates weren't used to being questioned? But Bohr just smiled and said, "At an eighty percent confidence level, as you Americans say."

"So why should a nucleus be like a liquid? Or the nuclear force something like a surface tension?" Karl kept his voice mild, no incisive cutting edge.

Bohr nodded. "Because there's a competition. The protons want to fly apart, the neutrons stir around and try to stop that happening. I made up a sort of simple calculation of that. It seems to give the curve of binding energy fairly well."

This struck Karl as remarkably honest. Considering that he hadn't actually gone through Bohr's published papers, he just nodded and resolved to correct that. He smiled and introduced himself. "I wondered how you reacted to Hahn's news, and Meitner's experiments."

Bohr chuckled. "I said, 'What fools we have been!'—because we were so blind. I never saw that the liquid drop could be shattered—like a water drop."

Karl was impressed with such modesty. He had seen plenty of lesser lights parade their arrogance around Columbia. To work among scientists entailed a burden. Everyone in the room had grown up through schools and universities where they learned they were quite often the smartest guy in that room. So when they reached upper levels of research, they carried the same unconscious angles of attack, a presumption of always having the right answer. Learning otherwise could shock them.

He nodded, thanked Bohr, and saw that Urey and Fermi were talking softly, heads tilted near each other. An opportunity.

Fermi said softly, "Why did you not tell me of these matters when you met us at the dock on January second?"

Urey shrugged. "Bohr said that the Germans were not yet published, so he kept it secret. They are about to publish in *Naturwissenschaften*, I believe."

Fermi said, "I can check their result quickly."

Urey nodded. "Good idea." Noticing Karl, he introduced them. Fermi murmured some pleasantries, but his eyes were distant.

Karl decided to go straight to the point. "Do you think a bomb is the only application?"

Fermi blinked. "Well, no, though Teller seems to jump at that. And Szilard. But any energy source can have many implications."

"To make electricity?" Karl guessed. "Use the excess heat to boil water, turn turbines?"

"Yes, very good application." Fermi saw this immediately, or more likely, had already figured it out. He turned to some others and said, "Let us get down to the lab."

In a moment the room was clear. Karl had a sense of anticipation, ideas swarming in his head. Urey took him by the arm. "Let me take you to lunch. We can talk this over."

This was a welcome gesture, including Karl the underling chemist. Urey seemed to know all the bars and restaurants near the Columbia University campus and led him to a narrow place packed with people. A white-capped short-order cook at a gas grill took barked orders from a cranky waitress who blew her hair out of her face after each sentence. Aromas of frying meat and grilled potatoes layered the air. Booths marked off tables with red-checked tablecloths. Ceiling fans turned languidly, stirring smoky air into a smooth blue-gray blur. There was no hurry in the place, a feeling of having been there all eternity, with only the faces changing in the pale winter light from the big windows. The waiters moved with quick, sure movements, delivering food that tasted exactly the same as when he was a boy in Brooklyn. His small, personal world was at least holding steady, while the larger world warped toward war.

In the hubbub and throughout the scattershot exchange of ideas with Urey, he still felt that the muttered talk nearby and the traffic murmur outside had a ring of the past, of history. And more history got made, every day. Karl began to think he could make some, too.

3.

Friday, January 21, 1939

Karl slogged through the film of crunchy slush over the sidewalks. Rain peppered him like cold spit. He had run out for extra supplies and a bottle of Bordeaux for what would be, *de facto*, the first Shabbat dinner he and Marthe put on—though nobody in the family really paid any attention to such Jewish rituals. The pocked heaps of dirty snow under a gray sky looked like refuse thrown out of passing cars. The world news was similarly depressing.

Two days before, he and Marthe had stopped at the Newsreel Theater on 68th Street to watch two hours of footage featuring the politicos and tragedies of Europe and Asia. There were clips of the Wehrmacht marching into Czechoslovakia, fruit of the Munich Pact. A speech by Neville Chamberlain, saying that England and Germany were "the two pillars of European peace and buttresses against communism." Right after, footage of Churchill saying in his ponderous way, "We have suffered a total and unmitigated defeat.... We are in the presence of a disaster of the first magnitude. ... We have sustained a defeat without a war, the consequences of which will travel far with us along our road." Then members of his own Conservative Party jeered him in Parliament.

Karl was still something of a Marxist, but in his soul he felt Churchill was right. Then the *March of Time* newsreel came on, showing scenes of Jews led away in Prague and speculating that the Nazis might spread out from the Sudetenland into neighboring territories. They were barely within their interpretation of the Munich Pact. Clips from Pathé and Paramount traced the rolling tragedies far away yet running right there on the screen in sharp black and white, immediate and insisting on his attention.

Karl shook himself. He had to lighten his mood for the party, a fest to welcome his family and friends into the bright new home of the newlyweds. In a flurry of work that day, he and Urey had finished the paper for the *Journal of Chemical Physics*. All to get ready for this party.

He crunched on along the sidewalks. Apartments crouched above pawn-shops, boozers, fly-specked lunchrooms cheek by jowl with poolroom bars and retail tabernacles. Some small diners had moved in, taking the place of other businesses whose memory persisted in ghost letters still doing service on abandoned signs.

They lived on the fourth floor of a building on 123rd Street, a half block off Amsterdam Avenue. It sported a pale brick facade, festooned with the requisite metal fire escape balconies and ladders. The sprawling, solid structure sorely needed a central courtyard, as the apartments were dark and the rooms cramped. From their apartment they looked down across the street on a pharmacy, University Chemists, their hanging neon sign coaxing DRUGS, LUNCHEON. It stayed open late and so drew happy but loud drunks. Even during the day, bums reeking of booze were fairly common, though harmless. Karl was starting to think of the neighborhood ambiance as "middle-class tenement," but it was what they could afford, and close to Columbia.

The entrance hall smelled of wax on ancient parquet tiles, glowing under incandescent bulbs like amber jewels. A hat stand with polished brass hangers pointed at the high dim ceiling, as if urging people up the steep stairs. Inside most of the apartments here, he knew from brief peeks through the doors of some tenants, every flat surface carried geegaws, doilies, vases, pincushions and shells, half-armed chairs that closed around you like a cloth hand. Styles from the Old Country still lived on in the furniture. He tramped up three creaky flights and keyed into a different world, a wonderland he thought of as Martheland, a tiny Paris in style.

She greeted him with a rich kiss, wearing the wide-striped dress he first saw in Marseille a year ago. When he had first met Marthe in Paris, right away his heart warred with his head, which said, *Too complicated to get involved with a French woman; you don't know enough yet to do that.* Or maybe it was his head versus a powerful voice lower in his body.

"I've finished the hors d'oeuvres," she said, gesturing to the dining room table, where an array of petite French sandwiches beckoned, each with the crusts carefully removed. "The turkey is in the oven, and I found chestnuts for the stuffing."

Karl sniffed, smiled, and said, "Other Jewish families would be looking for kugel, gefilte fish, chopped liver, sweet noodle casseroles, kishke. Instead, we'll feast on *dinde aux marrons*, crudités, lemon layer cake, and chocolate truffles. My family is not quite sure *what* to expect. This will raise eyebrows!" He liked the thought of his mother bragging about the food her foreign daughter-in-law, the French goy, cooked for them.

Marthe smiled. "What Americans think of as Jewish cooking is really Eastern European peasant food turned kosher. I think this will be a good start."

"I'll open the wine," Karl said as he started for the closet. "That'll surprise them too." He had just brought out the Bordeaux when their doorbell rang. "They're on time."

In came his mother, Rae; his aunt Mary; his sister, Mattie; and her husband, Lewis. Rae was an inch shorter than five feet and a classic feisty bantam hen. His times in France had given him enough distance to see her that way. Behind her was Mary, pale and muted as usual. Mattie was chatty. Lewis stood stolidly beside her, somewhat solemn and probably a tad drunk already, judging from his breath. The family was still getting used to Karl's marrying a formerly Catholic Frenchwoman, and not any of the perfectly good Jewish women his mother had pushed at him for years. He led them over to the makeshift bar on a small table in the densely furnished living room. He proposed an aperitif of Dubonnet with a festive small twist of lemon. The bottle was the last remnant of his fall trip to Europe.

"As the chemist in the family, I'll do the setups," Karl joked. "How do you want yours," he asked Rae, "on the rocks or room temperature?" He set about cutting the lemon peel. Older people liked Old Fashioneds, so he got out the oranges, sliced them, and set out cherries in a small bowl. Other cocktails would no doubt follow.

"Ah, martinis," he murmured, and trotted out the green olives to stick toothpicks in them. "Gibsons, no toothpicks," he muttered as he worked. For Manhattans he left the toothpicks off if the cherries had stems. Salt went into a shallow broad dish so he could just plant the already wetted rim down in it, then a lemon slice gashed at the end, all for a cocktail Marthe had learned about in Lebanon. He cut thick lemon slices for other cocktails and dropped ice cubes on them to keep them fresh.

His mother blinked. "Where did you learn to do this?"

He gave Rae a thin smile. "A chemist can acquire a lot in France." He had picked it up at International House, where he met Marthe, and alcohol was something like a competitive sport.

Rae frowned at this, and he realized she had not quite let go of the future she had imagined for him. He could have dutifully married one of the nice safe Jewish girls right there in Brooklyn, an easy walk for Rae. He could then aspire to the outer reaches of Brooklyn, with wood-shingled houses, screened front porches, neat lawns and strict shrubbery, and a cinder drive leading back to a one-car garage; a reasonable illusion of the salt-of-the-earth hometown America they all saw in movies. Not in a midtown Manhattan one-bedroom apartment, where honking cars and wailing sirens sang them to sleep.

Karl could almost hear Rae think about this, as he filled the aperitif glasses and remembered how he had let Sylvia down in a Paris café. It was partly Rae's fault. In a last attempt to stop the marriage with Marthe, she had encouraged the girl to rush over to Paris, to try to get him back. He had explained to Marthe that he needed a few days to show Sylvia the city, and when the "few days" seemed to be dragging on, Marthe lost patience and told him to choose one of them and be done with it. An ugly morsel appeared, way down in the bottom of his soul. A rational part of him felt relief.

He could strain for crocodile tears, but leaving Sylvia behind, back there in gauzy memory, was right. She was indeed a beautiful girl, but it had been an uneven battle anyway. His and Marthe's relationship had blossomed on two long train trips to the Mont-Saint-Michel she'd organized for her hiking group in 1936, and they'd kept in touch for almost a year with frequent, sometimes passionate letters when he returned home to job hunt. It wasn't just her looks that attracted him; she was a European intellectual—a sharp mind, well read, trained as a journalist, and with an unerring political instinct.

Rae took him aside. "I have at last gotten through to Jack. He sees your problem. He will release the inheritance."

Karl blinked. "That's sudden."

Rae gave a rueful chuckle. "I work slowly, Jack thinks even slower. Still, the sum is in a paying-out annuity. It will give you fifty-five dollars a month."

"Great! We can get by on that."

Rae gave him a motherly cheek kiss. He put all thoughts aside and was handing out the cocktails as three more people arrived, greeted by Marthe and Rae together.

Mattie came over and asked, "How's it going at Columbia?"

"Pretty well. Just heard about an amazing new source of energy."

"From what?"

"The nucleus of atoms."

Mattie looked blank. "If you say so, Karl. I hope it will be something big and you can profit from it."

"No idea." Karl had decided to say nothing about the ferment of discussions about fission. There might be a lot at stake.

He went to greet the new arrivals: his uncle Jack and his wife, Edith. A small child in tow, too, from a cousin. "Glad we got this inheritance thing settled now," Jack said, clapping Karl on the back as he shook his hand. "Marthe is a member of our so-called faith."

They both chuckled. The Cohens were divided over the issue of God. Karl saw it as a nonissue; he had no metaphysical complaint against the existence of death, the source of the big *why* in life—the major cause of religion, in his view. People all around him clung to their faiths as shelter against that *why*, but Karl did not. Science had stripped away whatever tattered religious garb he managed to assume at the larger family's occasional mitzvah celebrations.

He had found some comfort in an easy atheism and felt it grounded him in this world, the one that would end for him one day, but that he might alter for the better. He had read the whole Bible as a boy, and his skepticism deepened considerably when he discovered that among sexual behavior, forbidden were adultery, incest, and sex with angels. He sometimes thought that the right answer to the big *why* was just *why not*.

Unlike Uncle Jack, his father, Joseph, had been the only one of three brothers who, running a garment business, refused to change his name from Cohen to Colin. The rest of the family changed to Colin to get a sweet contract from the army for pants in World War I, out of fear that bureau-crats in distant offices would not give the nod to Jews. But Joseph refused to give up his birthright, the Hebrew name Kahana that an immigration officer changed to Cohen.

But the family's religious wing still had a real effect on Karl's life. Grand-father Cohen stipulated in his will that none of his unmarried grandsons would get anything unless they married a Jew. So Marthe had converted, tak-ing only a week to do so. That now brought Karl the extra fifty-five dollars a month now, much needed. For the first time in his life he felt flush.

Rae came over in proud-mother mode and plucked at his arm. "Play for us, son." He nodded and sat at the piano in the corner. He chose a piano version of a Mozart string quintet for her, quick and breezy, easy to play and not too long for the occasion. He preferred Bach, or Chopin preludes. He had deliberately practiced this earlier in the week, expecting Rae would show off her son this way to without being too obvious. Fair enough; she had gone through hard years after his father died and deserved a son's devotion, how-ever much she seemed obtuse and demanding at times.

Talk was rising now as people drank more and spoke over the music, so he shifted to a short, joyous Bach piece he knew well, one he had mastered when he was fourteen. The piece had some hard patches, where he had to leap from one part of the keyboard to another, then back, places he read through many times at the piano but had to go to his teacher to master. He knew even then he was laying a foundation with each learned piece for a lifetime of modest, private pleasures. The challenge was part of the pleasure too, a fact he learned from his hard-nosed teacher, Mrs. Feibelman, who when he asked, "How do I do this part?" answered, "Play it a thousand times and we'll see."

That had translated well into science and calculations. Do harder prob-lems over until you understand them, never take shortcuts because you know the answer anyway, and add more tools to your kit. Here he made an odd transition, into the sensual. That earnest method had worked with Marthe, too, the first time he had buried his face in her, realizing her body as a great work of art. An old lesson: you have to actually work the problem to know it.

He stopped playing when Marthe signaled it was time to eat. They crowded around the only table, some on chairs borrowed from a friendly widow on their floor. As he offered the Bordeaux and Marthe brought in the turkey, talk drifted to the war.

Rae waved a letter at Karl. "Some of my relatives, Paleys, were in the Sudetenland. Just heard! They got out when the Nazis marched in. They're near Prague. Your uncle Max got this letter at his firm."

Mattie and Lewis exchanged looks. "Just read it, Mother," said Mattie dryly.

Rae cleared her throat. "I'll just skip to the important part, and you can read the rest after dinner. It says, 'We sure Nazis take rest country soon. Want come America. We have very few hundred dollars in currencies. Need help to get there. Documents we pay for. Can America Paleys help?' Pretty desperate."

"I'm just starting out," Karl said. "Marthe and I are getting by, but—"

Rae nodded, but her lips were rigid, meaning she was going to stick to her guns.

"Maybe ten dollars a month for a while?"

Still the stiff face. "These people need it right away. I'm asking everyone in the family. If enough give, maybe in a while we can get something wired to them." His mother paused significantly. "Mattie and Lewis have already agreed."

Karl hesitated, thinking that both of them were employed, while his was the sole salary for two. He looked at Marthe, but her expression was carefully blank. All of her family was still in France, and everyone thought a German attack would come there first.

"Okay, ten a month. But not for long."

Rae beamed.

"Of course the firm is going to help, but it's not like the old days when we had the army contract," offered Jack. "Max told us about the letter a few days ago."

Rae went on. She was still frightened and furious about the Kristallnacht in Germany only two months before, with shops, synagogues, and homes smashed, thousands forced into camps, all by the National Socialist German Workers' Party government finally taking off the gloves.

"I got Marthe out in time," Karl said, "but I'm damn sure Hitler's going to go after the Jews more and more. That's what I heard everywhere I went in Europe last year." Rae nodded, head down.

Dinner went well, and when they came back into the living room, Walter Winchell was barking out his rapid-fire news on the radio. Several relatives hunched over it, listening to the notorious gossipy newsman with an audience in the tens of millions attack the Nazis, calling them "Ratzis."

Karl ignored all that. He had been a follower of Marx and Engels since his freshman year at Columbia, where it was the locally received wisdom. His Soviet tour, especially ten days on the train up along the Volga River to Moscow had vaccinated him against the disease of such politics. He had wanted to see the territory the original Paleys and Cohens came from in the Ukraine. But the tales of starvation carried out by the Cheka, and the summary executions against the walls of the Kiev city center, had cured him of Marxism. There was no better, original homeland back there for the Paleys and Cohens, and now he knew it.

Karl winked at Marthe, who went into the side room. Soon enough Walter Winchell's hectoring tone shifted to a dance band playing for the delight of the radio audience from the rooftop of yet another sophisticated supper club broadcasting from a midtown Manhattan hotel—a world he lived near yet had never seen, and didn't want to.

Rae was happier now that she had unburdened herself about the Czechoslovakian Paleys. She told a long joke that got a lot of laughs, about a doctor who mixed his laxatives and an aphrodisiac. In the corner the child ate her ice cream very seriously, spoonful by savored spoonful, in the slow, careful way children have. Karl admired how the little girl ignored the adult babble around her. He wished he could.

Then Rae came over to Karl and Marthe and gushed a bit about the "high French cooking." Karl did not point out that Marthe had had no culinary skills until after she had walked off the boat with him last September 26. Her ability to learn so much, so fast, was yet another endearment.

His sister, Mattie, edged over to where Karl stood against the wall and whispered, "Rae's trying to make up for opposing your marrying her. She still thinks it's maybe a mistake, but hopes you'll stick with it."

Karl smiled. "Some mistakes are too much fun to make only once."

Marthe heard this and beamed. She sidled up to him, looking out at the party. She patted his rear and gave him her signature sideways eye roll that always made him laugh. Such grace notes, especially near the end of a trying day, had made him realize for the first time that he loved her more than anything else in life.

A knock at the door. Karl answered. A messenger in uniform handed him a telegram.

"It's from Harold Urey," he said after tipping the man. "It says, 'Got funding for meeting Washington next week. Fermi Bohr will unveil fission experiments. Prepare for it. We go by train together.' Wow."

I'm in, Karl thought, and his pulse quickened.

Enrico Fermi

4.

Tuesday, March 21, 1939

Karl and Marthe arrived at noon sharp for the lunch at the King's Crown Hotel. Harold Urey had issued the invitations. Under pressure from his wife, Frieda, the wives were invited too. Urey greeted them with a broad smile, waved Karl to a round table and Marthe to another a few yards away. Karl now knew how to read Urey's round face, and this smile was a surface effect. Beneath that, beginning to show lines at his mouth and around the eyes, was concern.

"Ladies separate?" Marthe said with her lilting French accent, coming through her still wobbly English. Her mouth twisted just enough to convey displeasure.

"I imposed this upon Harold," Laura Fermi said as she rose from the ladies' table. She was a sturdy woman with a commanding manner; more so than her husband, Karl realized. "Please sit; I need advice on housekeeping."

Urey had turned away to greet others, so Karl sat beside Marthe for a moment, after introducing himself to Fermi's wife in the formal European way he had learned in Paris. He was beginning, with Marthe's help, to see that knowing the families of the men he wanted to work among was smart. Karl had attended the Washington meeting in January with Urey and was easing his way into the uranium work, a lesser figure among the big guys. *So be it, then.*

This meeting was unusual, away from Columbia and with wives present. Karl whispered, "I think Madame Fermi wants to know the other ladies, and Enrico wants a meeting with some privacy from Columbia, and this is the compromise." Marthe nodded, eyes calculating.

He reflected as Laura Fermi went on that the Italian accent always had a softening surplus of vowels, especially adding an *a* at the end of verbs. Laura and Marthe exchanged advice on the groceries, tearooms, dime stores, ladies' ready-to-wear, and hair salons in the ten-block zone between 110th Street and 120th Street, the "Columbia village" as she termed it. Laura Fermi said, "We are-*a* about to move to a furnished apartment—for-*a* of course we could bring no furniture from home, and so-*a* by the Fascists be detected—"

Karl let the vowels run by while he estimated what the purpose might be of this odd luncheon meeting. Szilard had just come in, with Irving Kaplan and the physicist John Dunning, even Bohr. Fermi, Bohr, and Szilard had their best suits on today. Something was brewing.

"We went on a canned-food spree in the shops," Laura Fermi said, "trying new foods. Pudding powders, even foods frozen—I have never seen!" Karl listened to her describe the Neapolitan and Sicilian dialects of the Italians in grocery stores, whom she had sought out until she found it was easier to understand their-*a* rich English. "Still," she said, "Enrico wishes to have a home where our children's knees carry brown dirt, not the gray city dirt here."

Karl caught Urey's signal to come join the physicists, as more arrived—a dozen around a big circular table. *Though I'm really a chemist by my PhD, they don't care,* he reflected, still surprised to be accepted. *Urey's a chemist too, but he has a Nobel.*

As they all ordered lunch, mostly sandwiches, Szilard hunched over, head bobbing, and introduced the meeting theme: money and secrets.

"Enrico has confirmed the fission process, the neutrons coming out—maybe better than two per splitting!" Szilard's voice rose expectantly toward the end of his sentences, like a salesman. "So there is energy to be had, if we can make a chain reaction sustain."

Fermi nodded somberly. "I would like to try that. The neutrons, though, they are-*a* too fast. They do not resonate with the uranium, I think."

"So we have to moderate them?" Karl ventured to ask, since he knew that physicists used "moderate" for "slow" for some reason. Usually he followed a minimal strategy—show up but shut up.

Around the table, as the sandwiches arrived, heads nodded. "Maybe water can do that?" Urey asked. Fermi considered, nodded.

Karl took a bite of his ham sandwich. It was nowhere near as good as the ones he'd had daily in Paris. Plus too much mayonnaise. New York had a lot to learn.

Between bites, a discussion began of ways to slow the neutrons. Bohr spoke slowly, as if thinking aloud, but now he sped up, catching the edgy excitement of the table. He thought that at higher energies the neutrons just plowed through a nucleus, maybe throwing off a few neutrons without shattering it. His liquid drop analogy to the uranium nucleus was controversial, and Fermi did not quite accept it. Karl did not know enough yet to have an opinion.

"Slowing neutrons is an old idea but tricky," Fermi said. "Paraffin, water—we know those work, from our Rome experiments."

"For what use?" Urey said mildly, and they all knew his point.

"To make heat, power," Fermi said. "That is my interest here."

Szilard cast narrowed eyes around the table. "This war that is coming—we do not have much time."

In a public restaurant, Karl saw, no one wanted to use the word "bomb." So as the discussion moved forward the men said "bang" or "critical mass" to describe putting together enough uranium so the neutrons would smack into nuclei, make them oscillate as the Bohr model said they would, spitting out lesser elements and several more neutrons. All that had to happen through maybe a hundred steps, each one doubling the number of neutrons in play, before neutrons started escaping through the skin of the uranium mass.

"So how big does this chunk of the stuff have to be?" Urey asked.

"To make-*a* power, very much," Fermi said.

"To make a bang, less," Karl guessed.

"How do we calculate this?" Urey asked.

"Surely we need to know more from experiment—cross sections for collisions, say, to start with," Bohr said. "Enrico, can you do that?"

"I will need more help," Fermi said, and they all knew he meant people and money. But being Fermi, he would lead the experiment and do a lot of the hands-on work himself. The man was a legend for his versatility, as well.

Karl said mildly, "How much metallic uranium—not the oxide, that's common—is there in the USA?"

Some puzzlement, then Dunning said, "Maybe a few grams, tops."

"How about Europe?" Urey asked.

With a dry, slow diction Bohr said, "A letter today says the regime in Berlin has established a new study center at Kaiser Wilhelm Institute on . . . uranium."

"So they'll buy up what they can," Urey said, blinking. "That's where Hahn and Strassmann are, so they—"

"Saw the obvious," Szilard said firmly. "My point, exactly."

Fermi turned to Bohr. "Niels, do you think they can make a power reactor?"

Bohr's mouth twisted in a startled grimace. "They will not bother. They will go for a more useful, more quick . . . device."

Still, nobody would say "bomb" in public. Karl said, "So what should we do now about publishing results?"

"Restrict it," Szilard said. "Agree to say nothing in print."

"Cat's out of the bag," Urey said. "Hahn and Strassmann have published, Lise Meitner and Frisch are about to as well."

"We can ask others to desist," Szilard said calmly. "I doubt the Germans will be saying anything in print."

Bohr nodded. "They have controls through government. Americans do not."

Karl could see a brimming conflict over self-censorship. To deflect an open dispute, he said, "First we have to have something to publish. Dr. Fermi, will you send your paper to a journal?"

"I might, to help the careers of my colleagues"—a nod at those around the table—"but it simply verifies the earlier German work. To do more I need money. I am starting up like a graduate student!" That provoked some chuckles. Then Fermi handed around a letter. "I asked George Pegram, your dean of faculty, who wrote-*a* to an admiral this letter."

When it reached Karl, he noted in the March 16 letter a phrase of introduction, Fermi's new professorship at Columbia, the Nobel, "no man more competent in the field of nuclear physics," and so on. But after stating that "uranium might be used as an explosive that would liberate a million times as much energy per pound as any known explosive," Pegram immediately backtracked. "Look," Karl said, "Pegram says, 'My own feeling is that the probabilities are against this, but my colleagues and I think the bare possibility should not be disregarded.' Some support!"

Fermi frowned, looking uncomfortable at this attention. Karl went on, "Plus, he mentions you'll be in Washington anyway to give a talk, so you will call his office to see if 'you wish to see him'—puts Enrico in a weak position, a supplicant."

Fermi said, "Ah, supplicant, same word as in Italian. Pegram was, you say, hesitant. Pegram said to me he hopes such explosives will be impossible, that he would rather gunpowder did not work either."

"How does he feel about the airplane or the tank?" Karl shot back.

"He did not say," Fermi said mildly, eyebrows aloft, and Karl saw he had overstepped his position.

"Sorry, but how did it go with the admiral?" Karl asked.

"We met. No result," Fermi said. "There is little proof, after all, that we are not pursuing a chimera. That is an English word?"

"Yep, it is," Urey said. "Did you show him the paper you and Dunning and the others published just this month?"

"He glanced at it," Fermi said, with a shrug that told how little the admiral thought of academic papers.

"So what can we do next?" Urey asked.

John Dunning said, "Understand how the neutrons propagate, that Enrico and I have now verified in detail. Then try experiments with U-235."

Karl knew him for the Dunning Optimism Factor, because he always minimized problems and stressed what was to be gained in an experiment. As the man went on into details, Karl saw that Dunning was a salesman, engaging everyone's eye as his gaze swept the table, emphasizing points with his hands, voice rising at the high points. He had dogged Fermi's work for years, finding new effects the Rome team had not. But Fermi won the Nobel. While Karl and Fermi and others were at the DC meeting, Dunning had shown that fairly slow neutrons came from hitting a uranium oxide disk with neutrons, driving some fission.

Szilard described the experiment for those who had not been there. "Unfortunately, the new cyclotron in the Pupin basement was behaving poorly. So we brought from the thirteenth-floor laboratory a radon and beryllium fast-neutron source—the type Dr. Dunning used for most of his previous work—and placed it next to the ion chamber containing a tiny speck of uranium. In great excitement, we saw about one big pulse on the oscilloscope every minute. The rate was so slow, we had doubts at first whether it was real or maybe a poor electrical connection. But when Dr. Dunning put the neutron source in a paraffin vessel—you Americans called it a slow-neutron 'howitzer', very funny—the rate went up to seven or so huge pulses per minute. We turned the switch and saw the flashes on the detector screen. We watched them for a little while and then we switched everything off and went home."

John Dunning said, "We understood the implications and consequences, too."

Szilard sighed. "That night, there was very little doubt in my mind that the world was headed for grief."

Fermi said, "Hitler has already made that inevitable."

Fermi had followed up on the experiment, refining measurements. Since then, three other American groups had verified the effect, and a first paper had appeared in *Physical Review* on March 1. The cat was out of the bag, but now the question was, how much more should anyone publish that the Germans would see?

"I prefer to try natural uranium," Fermi said. "The U-238 is over ninety-nine percent of the natural and may be the isotope that fissions." He leaned forward, intent. "These big energies, they tempt us. More moderate is to assume the common isotope, U-238, is the cause of the big energy results. Can we not agree?"

"I do not believe it is U-238," Bohr said. "My theory predicts it must surely be U-235."

"We will have a contest, then," Fermi said. "To see which it is."

Karl decided to push the issue. "Whichever isotope it is, a big result"—he raised his eyebrows to show he meant a bomb—"would require fission by fast neutrons, not slow. A chain reaction using slow neutrons might not proceed very far before the metal would blow itself apart, causing little, if any, damage."

There it was, out in the open. Urey looked around the table and cut into his steak. Fermi was having one too. The food had arrived without Karl noticing. He had fish and wished he had the courage to order a glass of white wine. But this wasn't Paris, and physicists would frown at anyone who had wine with lunch. Urey chewed and said deliberately, "So does a possible war take precedence, or a new source for power?"

Fermi relished his steak. "We cannot get such beef in Italy," he said, and then halted, perhaps realizing that it might be a very long time before he ever saw his native land again. Shaking that off, he said slowly, "The conservative thing to do is to play down the possibility of a chain reaction at all. We do not know it be absolutely true."

Szilard bristled, a spoonful of soup halfway to his mouth. "Surely Enrico, you must agree the conservative stance is to *assume* a chain reaction can happen, will happen, and so to take necessary precautions."

Fermi frowned, mouth twisted. "If a nuclear pile can work—we do not know this, only guess that we can slow the neutrons so the reaction is maybe stable—then perhaps we can understand these, well," he whispered, "these bombs. Pile comes first." A brisk nod.

Szilard pursed his lips in disagreement. "The war comes first, surely."

"We should not promise too much."

"There is great power here—we should seize it!"

"Do not advertise what we cannot deliver. Keep our work to ourselves."

Urey, Dunning, and Szilard blinked at this. "Secrecy?" Urey said. "In science? That just slows down the work. We need many minds focused on this opportunity."

Fermi paid attention to slicing his steak and then spoke with weight on each separate word. "Secrecy protects us all from undue speculation. I don't understand this statement. Yes? Data must rule. We must do experiment to guide us."

Szilard began, "Time does not allow—"

"Mistakes, yes, or improper speculations," Fermi said sternly, eyes on Szilard.

The two men stared long and hard at each other, two worldviews colliding silently across a table. In the background the happy chatter of the ladies sounded to Karl like voices from a distant land. Fermi came from Catholic

Italian farmers. Szilard's family was Ashkenazi Jewish. Karl was Ashkenazi as well, and he knew from comparing notes with Szilard that his parents were of the professional class who immigrated to Budapest and prospered. Szilard had good foresight. He had fled Germany, where he was doing research, immediately after Hitler came to power in 1933. He had gotten to America well ahead of the other fleeing Europeans.

"We will have to disagree on that, Enrico," Szilard said, the twist of his mouth making it clear he did not like to say it.

"For now, it is not an issue," Urey pointed out. "We have nothing more to report."

Silence all around the table. Fermi began talking about the ease of getting steak in America, plus many other things—even lemons shipped from Cuba—and the tension eased. Karl finished his fish and felt a whisper in his ear. "I have a doctor's appointment near here," Marthe said.

Karl saw nothing more would be said at his table, now that the ladies were breaking up. "I'll walk you over. But got to pay the bill first."

He and Marthe had debated coming to this hotel lunch because it was bound to cost at least a dollar each. "But you need to be in such discussions," Marthe had said firmly. She knew bits of what he was working on, and he had hinted a little at what might be at stake. Karl went to Urey and whispered an apology for leaving, then asked his cut of the bill.

Fermi heard this somehow and said to the entire table, "I invited all to this social occasion, and I pay."

Urey said, "Enrico, we could all—"

"The Nobel money is burning a hole in pocket—funny American phrase, I like it. No, I am host."

This brought smiles to all those around the tables. "See, I was right," Marthe said, "best to come." She darted a quick, moist tongue in his ear, and he beamed.

"What's this doctor visit about?" Karl asked.

"A feminine problem."

On the way over she told him the ladies had talked about domestic problems and hairdressers. Urey's wife, Frieda, had described how her father still rode a bicycle and had been hit by a delivery truck.

"How old is the father?"

"Eighty-one."

When he said quite reasonably, "The physics is not promising," he was startled at her laugh. She could always surprise him.

Once he had dropped her off, he walked the streets around 98th, where her appointment was in a stern gray granite building.

Karl had always walked to clear his mind. The March breezes carried blustery, welcome warmth. He reviewed the lunch discussions and decided to avoid the dispute over secrecy, to stick close to Urey. The work would have to show them what to do, not abstract theories about future risk. He savored the neighborhood, glancing in shop windows at washing machines and other appliances they might someday be able to afford. His $180 minus the ten dollars he was giving Rae each month, for getting the distant Paley relatives out of Europe, left them little room to maneuver.

As he walked, he slowly realized that the once familiar streets where he had grown up were now strange. They buzzed and honked in their restless energy, so different from the ambling avenues of Paris, where the humming car traffic did not dominate. In Paris, people eyed the swaying couples and odd, passing eccentrics, characters to be studied beneath leafy bowers. Here people walked fast and looked away, no eye contact, bound up in their whirring worlds. Everybody here was *getting things done*. In Paris, people were living.

How much more time would Hitler give the Parisia?

He walked back toward Columbia and past the granite monolith where Marthe had gone—and here she came out the entrance, smiling broadly. To his surprise, she walked boldly up and kissed him.

He chuckled. "Wow, did the doctor give you something?"

"No, you did."

"Uh, what—"

She gave a light, tinkling laugh. "In October we will have our first child."

A feeling unlike anything before rushed through him. He had gone from lover to husband to father in less than a year. Time was accelerating now, and the heady rush carried a surge of joy.

5.

Karl could not resist the show Dunning was putting on for the newspapers. He could hear the reporters' questions volleyed back in Dunning's booming tones. They echoed down the corridor and into his office. His cranny in the basement of Pupin Hall was next to Dunning's cyclotron lab.

He had taken a while to realize his desk was right in the cyclotron target field. On the other hand, he realized he would get little radiation, because Dunning's cyclotron was finicky and didn't run much; plus, he really preferred to work at home. He labored well after midnight and slept well into the day. Additionally, he and Marthe had discovered that making love in the afternoon had a warm resonance, to give way to sweaty languor when all around them New Yorkers scurried on their incessant tasks. It was very French, and he knew it also helped him avoid stray neutrons that might come through the wall.

So now he got up and went into the big cyclotron lab, where Dunning held forth before a swarm of reporters. Karl hung back and saw that Dunning, lit by a helpful big-beam light, was demonstrating the circulation of the blood, using radioactivity. He kept up a line of patter, chuckling, calling his grad students by nicknames, warming the room.

Dunning prepared a sample of sodium by irradiating a glass of salt water in the beam of the loud, humming cyclotron. Using a clicking Geiger counter, he first showed that some radioactivity was in the glass. He stretched out his hand with the Geiger counter at his fingertips: no activity. He then drank the glass of irradiated water.

Reporters didn't know the sodium spat out electrons that could do no harm to Dunning's cells. They murmured; wasn't this dangerous? Dunning didn't say. After some anxious minutes, the Geiger counter began to respond as the circulating blood brought more and more of the radioactive salt to Dunning's fingertips. Reporters scribbled all this down; flashbulbs popped. It was a great show.

The *Times* reporter described him as "a radioactive being," which drew laughs. Dunning's assistants hustled around, showing how a small toy subterranean mine collapsed, as they spun it up in a large centrifuge. Meaningless, but an opportunity for a photo the papers might use. The entire engineering lab was open for public walk-throughs. Karl took no part; it seemed a violation of the unspoken agreement not to let word of their fission experiments into the press.

He saw Harold Urey in the corridor outside. Urey had a big office upstairs but could not resist going to see the graduate students and experimenters in the dank bowels of the building. On any given morning he might burst into the office of a colleague, eager to talk. Seeing the colleague perhaps discussing current research with students, he would apologize and begin to back out. Of course, he was invited in. Urey would then rush to the blackboard and begin, "I've finally figured out . . ." and would soon be pouring out words faster than most could follow. "Does that seem right?" he would say at the end. Maybe one question or comment would emerge. Urey would thank the group warmly, again apologize, and rush out. The effect of this display on young graduate students was remarkable. They knew they were not such fountains of ideas, so quick and deft—and so their dreams of fame and Nobel Prizes faded.

"He's a showman, all right," Urey said, then shifted mood. "Now—we need to talk about what to do next."

Karl nodded, followed. "Y'know," Urey said on the way up the stairs, "during my stay at Bohr's Institute for Theoretical Physics in Copenhagen, Bohr didn't know I was a chemist. He thought I was a physicist. Helped me a lot. These physics guys think they own science."

Karl nodded. Chemists saw physicists as the undeserving wonder boys. "But learning from Bohr—"

"I got most of my physics in Copenhagen restaurants while dining with Professor H. A. Kramers, that's the truth. You got to know how to milk the essence out of these guys. Otherwise, it's all differential equations."

"I can handle those."

"Sure, that's why I hired you. Most chemists don't know enough math. My point is that to work with them, you gotta think like them."

They got to Urey's office and the Nobel laureate sat, put his feet up on his desk, and popped some chewing gum into his mouth. Karl recognized the rube style. Urey hadn't changed from years before.

Urey said, "Look, Bohr postulated that U-235 is the isotope that fissions. So let's go with Bohr."

"Fermi thinks—"

"The great Fermi is too cautious. Also wrong. Bohr's model says U-235."

"Everybody seems to think we should wait until Fermi's experiments show us which—"

"He'll burn half a year finding out Bohr's right. So look—separating the uranium isotopes is the obvious step."

Urey was the recognized world leader in isotope separation. Karl knew nearly nothing about it but had been reading the background papers on using a centrifuge to separate out the heavier U-238. Working with about a 1 percent mass difference made it tough.

"Look, did you read about that German-American Bund meeting they had in Madison Square Garden?" Urey pressed on.

"Uh, no."

"I had to see what morons these were—so I went. Cost nothing—somebody's footing the bill. Their leader denounced 'Franklin D. Rosenfeld' and called his policy the 'Jew Deal.' Unbelievable. This thing's gonna get worse, lots worse. That Bund is setting up training camps in Jersey! Training their people right here. Our own army is tiny. That National Socialist German Workers' Party running Germany has millions. We'd better have a knockout weapon."

Karl knew to just nod. Urey on a rant wanted no interruptions. Karl had heard of the Bund meeting but that evening took Marthe to see *The Wizard of Oz*, which she liked and he didn't. They had watched the crowds going to the Garden—mostly heavyset men with short haircuts and some bony women with intent faces. Some carried swastika flags, a shock to them both.

"So we—what?" Karl said. "Assume Bohr is right and find out how to separate out the U-235?"

Urey brought his feet down from the desk and sat upright. "You bet. We need money to do it and we've got to get some, to finance some experiments."

"How?"

"Go outside our usual routes."

"You have contacts with industrial people, sure. But why would they invest in a pulp fiction idea for a weapon?" Karl was honestly puzzled; he sat on the edge of Urey's big desk and noticed the Nobelist had worn a hole in his right shoe.

"Patents have lots of uses. I think the best hope for isotope separation is a high-speed centrifuge. Once we can separate the uranium, think what other isotopes we can get out. A lot of the radioactive ones may have medical uses, fighting cancer and so on. That guy Lawrence out at Berkeley is already doing plenty with that, using his cyclotron."

"So is Dunning," Karl said.

"Sure, we'll work with him. Dunning's not just a cyclotron man, he's inventive."

Karl knew a bit about these devices, all based on the same principle as the cream separator. Centrifugal force in a cylinder spinning rapidly on its vertical axis could separate a gaseous mixture of two isotopes, since the lighter isotope would be less affected by the action and could be drawn off at the center and top of the cylinder. A cascade system composed of hundreds or thousands of centrifuges could produce a rich mixture. "That seems more engineering than physics," he said.

"It needs some real analysis." Urey looked levelly at Karl. "You can do that." And Karl knew he could.

Albert Einstein and Leo Szilard, 1939

6.

Wednesday, July 12, 1939

Karl wondered why Einstein took his vacation down a lonely dirt road on Long Island. The man could go anywhere in the world and be greeted with glory and attention. *Well, maybe that's it,* he realized.

Teller was driving, scowling at the roads and muttering, with Szilard in the other seat and Karl behind. They had asked him to come along and deflect a French visitor who was with Einstein, and Karl's French was good enough to get the fellow away for a bit, they thought, so the two could present their idea. The aroma of the woods reminded Karl that he missed the easy presence of nature in Paris. Except for Central Park, Manhattan was all noise and smells. Maybe Einstein felt the same.

They got lost, of course, outside the small town of Peconic. Einstein's secretary at Princeton had said he was staying at a cottage belonging to a Dr. Moore, but nobody they asked knew where that might be. So Karl said, "Stop beside that small boy." Leaning out the window, he asked, "Where is Einstein living?" The boy snapped to, pointed, and directed them to a cabin at the end of Old Grove Road, a sunny prospect on a quiet blue bay. Even country boys knew the famous name.

No answer to a knock at the door. Karl walked around the cottage and saw the great man just tying up a sailboat at a small dock. They went down into the moist heat. Szilard hailed Einstein, introduced Karl, and got them herded back to the cottage porch. Einstein had an easy smile and told them about how he'd created confusion in a local department store, from his thickly accented request for a pair of "sundahls."

The manager interpreted this as "sundial," and some hilarity ensued.

"Mine atrocious accent!" Einstein showed off his new white sandals. "For a dollar thirty-five cents, it is." It turned out the French visitor had left that morning. Karl shrugged, not having a role anymore, and tongue-tied in the presence of the most famous scientist in the world. Einstein moved quickly with a muscular grace, though he was sixty years old and reeked of sweat; he had been sailing several hours. He was quite solid with little fat, sunburned, hair a windswept white halo.

Karl knew enough to stay silent while Teller and Szilard outlined the neutron experiments, plus some calculations they had made of how to build a U-235 bomb. They had reached the same conclusion he and Urey had—a simple slug of U-235 fired into a cylinder of U-235 would change about 1 percent of the entire mass into energy, before heating blew the entire thing apart. But that was enough to yield a bomb equivalent to ten thousand tons of high explosives.

"*Daran habe ich gar nie gedacht,*" Einstein muttered. Karl knew enough German to know he had said, *I never thought of that.* "These neutron experiments, I do not keep up as I once did. There was a time I could read all the papers on relativity. But now . . ." A shrug. "Kaput."

"We are sure of this now," Teller said. "Fermi has confirmed the basic process."

"A city killer," Einstein said simply, and sighed. "You want me to do . . . what?"

"I think it best," Szilard said, "not to involve the military quite yet. They will tie us up in red tape."

"I think higher," Teller said. "I think, to the president."

Einstein considered this, puffing on his pipe. "Not to people I know in Europe?"

"About a weapon?" Teller was aghast, already sweating through his white shirt, and tense. "It would not be seen well."

"I suppose," Einstein said, and turned to Karl. "You are native born, yes? You think your government would not like me to write to the queen mother of Belgium, who is an old friend?"

"Yes, don't." Karl said softly. "And I wonder if she has any real power."

Einstein chuckled. "Well, neither do I. And the Europeans will be fighting for their lives soon, as well."

"You expect another move by Hitler?" Szilard asked.

"Soon." Einstein had poured them some tea he kept in a thermos; now he sipped his. "He waits about half a year before making his next invasion. He took the rest of Czechoslovakia in March; it has been four months now. Another two, then."

"We would like you to dictate a letter we could work on, for your later signature," Teller pressed.

Einstein sat silent for a long while. Karl found it remarkable that the man of great fame would focus intently and, when Szilard said something, not respond, not seem to notice. A pause. Birds made their melodies in the distance. Finally he said, "Very well. You know, when I renounced my German citizenship, the Nazis took and sold my boat and land. They turned my cottage into an Aryan youth camp. Before I had even left the country in 1933, they circulated a booklet with a photo of me, labeled 'Noch ungehängt'—not yet hanged. Then they put a bounty on my head—twenty thousand marks! I did not know it was worth so much. So I suppose it is time to be sure they do not gain any more advantage against our cause."

"There is another issue," Karl said. "You know they are rounding up Jews everywhere."

"Ja, I have heard."

"If the war—and yes, there will be one, we all know it—is short, fewer Jews will die."

"Fewer everyone," Einstein said, nodding. "It has become obvious that our technology has exceeded our humanity."

They set to work on a draft, Einstein insisting on doing it in German, since his English was slippery. He joked about brushing off people who came up to him on the streets of Princeton by replying in German, saying, "Ich weiß nicht" to whatever they wanted. Pressed further, he'd say, "Pardon me, sorry! Always I am mistaken for that damned Professor Einstein."

Edward Teller

Karl did not get to see Einstein again, though he did work on the draft letter. Szilard presented Einstein with the polished letter to sign. Szilard had passed it through Urey, Fermi, and finally Karl for English issues, technical clarity, and persuasiveness.

When Szilard came back with the signed letter, he told Urey and Karl, "He agreed going to Roosevelt is the best course. Still, he wrote a lesser note, not revealing any physics, to the queen mother of Belgium."

"How's it getting to Roosevelt?" Urey asked, feet up on his desk.

"I asked Alexander Sachs, the banker and economist to carry it. He is a friend of Roosevelt from long ago." Szilard shrugged, as if this were a minor matter.

"You've always had a talent for getting to influential people, Leo," Urey said. "What about the State Department?"

"I have sent it to them also, asking them to reply within two weeks."

Urey said, "Very sharp. I hear from the secretary who typed the letter"— Urey tapped on a carbon copy Szilard had shown them—"that she was sure you were a nut."

Szilard sniffed, eyebrows raised. "Perhaps I am! She did not recognize the name Einstein at the bottom, either."

Karl saw this was a good time to bring up his idea. "We need support now—funds to move the research along. Seems unlikely this letter will lead to something right away. How about going through Sachs to reach Jews who would support us?"

They both looked at him blankly. "Huh?" Urey said.

"Einstein gets plenty of letters from Jews, reporting on what's going on in Germany and other places the Nazis already have gobbled up. Sachs may know someone who would like the idea of looking into the future, to weapons that might be crucial."

"That is a big leap," Szilard said. "How to tell non-physics people our ideas? Cannot be specific. We give away much that way."

"You have to give to get," Karl said mildly. "Harold and I have been working on using centrifuges to separate uranium. But that takes some engineering help—"

"And my research dollars are few," Urey added.

Szilard considered this, eyes on the ceiling. "I may know someone. A rabbi. You are Jewish, yes?" He looked at Karl. "We may go see him together."

"Bring that copy," Karl said, pointing at the letter. "Let him see it, especially this line."

The passage read:

> A single bomb of this type, carried by boat and exploded in a port, might very well destroy the whole port together with some of the surrounding territory. However, such bombs might very well prove to be too heavy for transportation by air.

"I'll bet we can make one lighter than that," Karl said.

Szilard's mouth twisted with skepticism. "You cannot know that."

"No, but I'll bet on it." Karl smiled, a trick he had learned to use when disagreeing with people senior to him. "Harold and I have worked on the mechanics. Pretty classical, just add a heat term from the fission reaction rate. That's the back pressure that stops a slug of U-235 from traveling to the end of the hollow U-235 cylinder. You can get the reaction rate from that. From that, a plausible explosive mass—and then the bomb mass."

Szilard blinked. Maybe he hadn't done the calculation in the simple-minded way a chemist turned physicist would. "I will think on that. I cannot ask Einstein to sign another letter, one without the passage about it being too heavy."

"Fine," Urey said, "get it out the door."

"That rabbi meeting, good idea," Karl offered.

"Very good. I am grateful to you for your illuminations," Szilard said. He straightened his waistcoat, worn even in summer, like the rest of the Europeans. Maybe that elegance helped him make contacts with Americans, especially the scientists, who wore ready-to-wear suits, baggy and gray, and wide, short ties. Nobody at Columbia looked like money.

Karl's family had been delighted to learn of Marthe's pregnancy. The parents-to-be went to Canada to jump through the hoops necessary to change her expiring tourist visa to a resident one, because Marthe wanted to work in journalism. Her January pregnancy ended her search for a job, which had proven fruitless so far anyway.

Every time they encountered his mother, Rae, they got bombarded with effusive plans for the "blessed upcoming event." They went to have dinner with her in Brooklyn, the three of them enjoying some brisket. After wine Rae pressed Karl to get a better-paying job than being Urey's assistant. He reminded her of how he was discriminated against because of his name. Rae's practiced outrage returned. She told an incident Karl had already forgotten, about his applying for jobs as an industrial chemist, in some cases going for job interviews. Once in Maryland he had overheard an executive refer to him in whispers as another from "Jew York," and the following guffaws.

Rae bristled. "Maybe that's okay in Maryland, but in Brooklyn we say, 'Go after the schlump.'"

Marthe smiled, a thin puzzled slice of rosy lips. "Catholics would perhaps say, forgive your enemy, but remember the moron's name."

"But my Karl has gotten himself into the center of this new work, right away," Rae said, beaming. "I want to hear how."

Karl shrugged but saw he would have to brag a bit; his mother wanted it. "I noticed an obvious feature of the weekly meetings the fission group holds.

The big guys always showed up. Going with Urey got me in. Anyone could ask a question, and when he did, all the audience paid attention to him. If there were several exchanges, all the better. And a questioner who caught the speaker in an error got rewarded with nodding heads and smiles from those around him. So I prepared—"

"He works at home a lot, stays up nights," Marthe added.

"—for them. Read the background papers. Read the competitors' papers as well. That always generates several questions, shows you know the literature. A question, innocently asked, can puncture a speaker's ideas like a stiletto."

"You turned into a physics mensch," Rae said. "Even though you're a chemist."

Karl shrugged this aside. "I began by calling out questions from near the back. After a few weeks, I moved forward. The senior guys always took the first-row seats, and pretty soon I was sitting only two rows behind them. They began turning in their seats to watch as I asked a question. Fermi, guys from Princeton, full professors from MIT, they began to nod to me as they took their seats. By now they all know me."

"So you've mastered a whole new field!" Rae was excited. "Physics, even."

Karl smiled; he always enjoyed his mother's compliments. "I was always more interested in seeing an analytic rabbit pop out of a higher mathematical hat than in a Broadway show."

"Yes, he has yet to take me to one," Marthe added, and they all laughed.

"This could mean a promotion, then?" Rae noodged him with raised eyebrows. Karl knew that putting her off the scent was the way to avoid conversational ruts, so he mentioned their unsuccessful efforts to get money for experiments, omitting that the work was about centrifugal separation of U-235 from U-238. He explained his idea, still unformed, to get Jews involved, since the Nazis would be the obvious target of such a weapon— though he didn't even mention uranium to Rae.

"Try that big deal rabbi I know," she said immediately. "He has big money contacts."

"He's high up?" Karl said to draw her out; he never kept track of the Jewish community, especially rabbis. He vaguely recalled some talk about one with eastern European contacts and who also knew the banking community. The European restrictions keeping Jews from owning land had driven them to be merchants, doctors, lawyers. If they yearned for money, banking was open to them. "Work with your head, not just your hands," Rae had said to him while he was growing up.

"A big Zionist, this Kornbluth is," Rae said. "If Hitler gets his way, there won't be any Jews to go to Zion."

Marthe said, "You think then like the Europeans?"

Rae said, "That there will be a war? Of course! That we should be in it? No."

"America could be the deciding factor," Marthe said, pouring coffee for her mother-in-law. Karl found fascinating the uneasy, delicate dance between the two women, pivoting around him. "As last time."

"The big thing will be Hitler and Stalin," Rae said. "They both hate Jews, so if they fight—and they will—it is fine with me. The only bad thing is, they can't both lose."

"Remains to be seen," Karl said, wishing this subject would go away.

"I have friends . . . who have friends," Rae said mysteriously. "I'll make some calls."

He doubted whether his mother could know much of the rich and powerful of Manhattan, but she had surprised him before. He shrugged and promptly forgot about it. He was focused on Marthe, while dinner-table conversation flowed around him. Slow, deep, muddy, but restful in its way.

They left early and took the subway back to 123rd Street. Even with her at his side, New York rankled him. After the gentle warmth of Paris and his sojourns through the rest of Europe, New York was a sudden cold shower. It struck him as immense, proud, rich, and ugly. At midnight you could buy a turkey, a morning newspaper, a car, a suit of clothes. Smells of gasoline, molding trash, rank steam from gratings—all swelled up around you. Arrogant skyscrapers—was there an uglier word in the language?—submerged people and their dwellings in shadows nearly all day, then trapped the traffic noise in sound tunnels to numb their ears at night. After the lilting vowels of French, he felt swamped by uncouth accents, slovenly pronunciation, tortured grammar. Faces seemed so various—thick-lipped, curly-haired, hook-nosed, almond-eyed, chicken-necked. People he had known well seemed like strangers. Why? Most were nonentities swallowed whole by their petty affairs. It disheartened him that if Rae had not been his mother, he would have nothing in common with her.

That's wrong, he thought, and resolved to do better.

So once home, he turned his attention to the one touch of France he could hold in his arms, Marthe's ripening body. It snared his attention every day when he came home. Marthe ran her hands down her dress, as if straightening wrinkles in the fabric that were not there, and he realized this was all show to distract him, enlist his male eye in her cause. Marthe's dress clung to her hips and thighs, her least movement animating its stylized cloth, setting it dancing with a body concealed but yet revealed through motion.

The talk of war had made this seem like clear, cool water in a scorching desert. At times, when they were locked in their eager geometry of *soixante-neuf*, she whispered her requests. Floating on rumpled sheets, they became pure bodies, not just heads trapped in lust, and the worries and words and their two different worlds evaporated into the mere vagrant fripperies they were. He thought of the coming war and yet desire seized him. Eros banished Thanatos.

Waking to morning sunshine, he found her arm draped over his chest and her head resting on his rib cage. If they had been wrestlers, she could rightfully claim a pin. She had pinned him to her moment.

The rabbi lived well. His apartment was in the upper Park Avenue luxury blocks where Rolls-Royce and Cadillac had dealerships. As Karl and Leo Szilard approached, Leo enthused about the atmosphere and Karl caught some of his newcomer enthusiasm. They enjoyed the scents of warm peanuts on street corners, bay rum and hair oil and Cracker Jack. A social scientist could have written a PhD thesis on the smells alone. Here parking spaces were as scarce as the cardinal virtues and the sidewalk rumbled by subway vents.

"I will do the technical," Karl said, "and then keep my mouth shut. You make the pitch."

"Your mother who will do the introduction—is that her?" Leo pointed.

Rae's long brown hair, styled in a bun, was tucked under a stylish dark felt cloche. She had never cut her hair, and when loose it reached all the way down her back. Her nose and cheeks and chin were discreetly powdered, and on her neat dark-blue wool coat was a large silver brooch. Dressed to the nines, as she had promised. She kissed Karl on the cheek and patted him with trembling fingers. Karl made the introductions and Rae peppered Leo with questions. She got it right; he had coached her to say *SIL-ahrd*. He carefully outlined their presentation plans. Karl added, "When we get to the money, the arithmetic of what we need, Mother—"

"I say nothing." She nodded. "Because it will be a lot."

Leo smiled. "We are very grateful for your arranging this introduction, Madame."

Karl saw she wanted to ask if this would mean a promotion for Karl, but she didn't. Leo had a suave charm that moved her effortlessly forward with gestures, eyebrows, his tilted head.

Rabbi Elon Kornbluth had an orderly brush mustache of thick gray hair, like iron filings lined up by a magnet. His apartment was large and muffled by thick rugs and burnished oak paneling. No Park Avenue traffic noise intruded. The living room had been color coordinated by someone with both money and taste, a rare combination. The only sign of what he did for a living was a seven-candle menorah and a scroll Torah open at the middle on a mahogany stand. Kornbluth made pleasantries, focusing on Rae at first with questions about her family. A woman, the rabbi's wife, appeared to deliver tea, eyes lowered to her task. Her hands were worn and cracked by work, but she poured the tea with a regal air.

Rae politely brought up the rabbi's support for Zionism. Karl knew little of this seemingly antique idea—that almost two millennia after their diaspora, Jews should regain Palestine. The irony was that secular Jews like him, who didn't believe in God, had cooked up the notion. His family were typical Ashkenazim of the socialist bent, who fled central Europe and knew nothing about the Middle East except what they read. Oddly, their very name held the acronym for the political socialist party that so hated them, the Nazis. This sore fact seemed to his Jewish friends to be so numbing that a friend had once called it pig irony.

The rabbi seized the bit Rae had given him and ran through an obviously polished little speech on gathering the Jews around such a cause in this time of peril. The rabbi's grand manner slipped a bit, and he began larding his sentences with words like "kvetch" and even "bubkes." Leo nodded as if believing every word, as did Rae, but Karl kept still.

"The Zion we seek, I have seen," the rabbi said grandly. "I have traveled through our ancestral lands. Between the seas—the Med, the Red, and the Dead. We can return, farm, build a Jewish state."

If there are any Jews left after this war, Karl thought. He wondered if the rabbi would bring out photos of Arab shepherds near the Wailing Wall next.

Then, without warning, Kornbluth signaled a new vector with, "So you have gained the support of the great Einstein, I hear?"

Leo Szilard then rolled out stories of Einstein, quoting the great man as saying, "People are like bicycles. They keep their balance only so long as they are moving." Then some Einstein funny remarks, building a picture of an ongoing collaboration between himself and Einstein, and by implication, Teller and Bohr, and with an artful nod, Karl. Onward, casually ingratiating, incidentally telling in soft focus the story of how uranium fission was discovered—"Though I must trust you to keep even the name of this element from your later conversations, as we are obeying a secrecy agreement"—and the prospects for both a power source and a bomb. Szilard was a master.

"Einstein and I, we have written to the president." Leo handed the carbon copy over. The rabbi read it raptly, eyes wide.

Kornbluth's eyes danced. "Ah, yes. Einstein must be right. Before studying the faith, I majored in physics at NYU. I have tried to keep up. I can perhaps follow these issues!"

"Einstein is very concerned about the fate of the many Jews who might fall under Hitler's rule," Leo said.

Kornbluth said slowly, "Yes, yes . . . Such a sad time it is." A canny pause. "You . . . mentioned this area as ripe for investment."

"Our work at Columbia, if funded properly, can yield patents shared by the investor," Leo said deftly. Karl was gaining an education in the light touch from him.

"And this could also lead to America having a future source of energy?"

"Money for Jewish scientists is especially hard to come by," Rae added.

Leo sped forward. "Energy, yes, if we hurry, yes. We are concerned that the original discovery was in Berlin. We recently heard that a special research group is now set up there to study uranium. They must have argued for its potential as a weapon." Leo had not told Karl this news, but it flowed into his argument easily.

Kornbluth pursed his lips and frowned. "What is the possible power use?"

Leo brightened. "This process will produce heat, eventually. We can boil water, make steam, drive turbines, make electricity. All those steps we use now, but the process gives us a million times as much energy per reaction as, say, burning coal."

Kornbluth smiled. "I like that. People—my investor friends—can follow that."

Karl felt obliged to say, "I think the weapon is more important. We have oil, but we do not have much military strength."

Rae added, "There is a moral issue, Rabbi. I believe, with all this war news and fears, we are too worried about what we may lose to care about those who are losing even more."

The rabbi took this with a scowl. "So with this nuclear thing, we can prepare for a war, and for a peace with a new kind of energy. And patents for both?"

This startled Leo. "I patented the basic idea years ago, of the energy release—and gave it to the British. I—"

"Why do that?" Kornbluth shot back.

"It is hard to patent a weapon, usually. The army likes to own those—"

"So they may buy such patents?" The rabbi leaned forward.

"Well, yes." Karl saw that Leo was reluctant to say this, but his salesman instincts quickly covered his momentary puzzled look. "But the eventual money will come from the electrical use, I would bet. There are details—"

Abruptly the rabbi clapped his hands on his knees. "I know enough. I will speak to my friends. They are interested in such avenues."

"Two avenues," Karl said. "The war will come before the electricity."

Kornbluth nodded gravely. "And soon. I hear every day, in letters and even telephone calls, pleas from people in Europe. You can give me some phone numbers to talk to these scientists? Fermi, Urey, Einstein?"

Szilard wrote some phone numbers, while Rae mentioned the fear of Germany on the march again. The men listened patiently, but Karl could see she had no effect. She lived in a world where people did things because they were good or bad. Karl lived in a gray world where people did things because they had to. Kornbluth inhabited a world where people did things in pursuit of profit. Few bulletins passed between those worlds.

They left with a good feeling. On the street outside, Szilard said, "He seems serious. I will alert Urey and Fermi for the rabbi's call. Einstein I know never answers his telephone himself."

"I was surprised he wanted those," Karl said.

Rae said, "Hey, boys—nobody tests the depth of the water with both feet." They all laughed.

Karl took them into a coffee shop for a little snack, glad that his mother and the rabbi had gotten through the meeting without using more typical Yiddish words like "gonif." Reform Jews had some intellectual pretensions, at least, beyond the schlepping tradesmen and kosher butchers. Nobody among their Jewish friends had beards, wore old-world-style clothes, or even skull-caps, except at temple. Karl couldn't read Hebrew lettering, never picked up the *Forvertz* Yiddish daily, and spoke in a clear, unaccented, East Coast tenor.

To Szilard, using Yiddish was a lower-class mannerism; best to not show any, then.

Karl knew he was still a very minor player in this. But the sum they had discussed, up to a hundred thousand dollars, was more than he had ever expected. A fortune, really.

PART II

THE URANIUM COMMITTEE

There is not the slightest indication that nuclear energy will ever be obtainable. It would mean that the atom would have to be shattered at will.
—Albert Einstein, 1932

1.

Friday, September 1, 1939

The knock at the door was a surprise. Even more startling was his mother's face as Karl impatiently opened it. Plus a man behind her. Not a boyfriend, much too young—

"Here's our Paley relative!" Rae said grandly, sweeping into the apartment. "Fresh off the boat."

Karl shook the embarrassed man's hand as he said, "Anton Paley, I am, yes, doctor, sir, yes, thank you for . . . your—" And there his English stalled.

"Welcome, happy you finally made it," Karl said, and introduced Marthe. "Maybe other Paleys can, too, later." He hoped his mother would not notice that they had just cleared away breakfast. It was nearly eleven a.m. He had worked late, as usual.

Anton's clothes were rumpled and worn, a gray cloth jacket with baggy pockets and a thin, inadequate shirt. They would have to buy him new clothes for the big city. Rae and Anton came in as Rae said, "There was something the newsboy was shouting about, down the block. About Poland."

"Oh?" Marthe straightened her dress with one hand and clicked on the radio with the other.

"—German troops reportedly have penetrated fifty miles beyond the Polish border, their tanks leading the way," a man's crisp voice said. "The British foreign office just issued a statement that this clearly violates—"

Karl switched it off. "So it's started. In Poland, not France." He needed to think now.

Rae looked at Anton with eyes narrowed and, to Karl's surprise, frightened. "You got away at the last minute."

"I am sor—sorry. Delay in Italy, took long. Had to pay." A shrug.

"After the German-Soviet Pact," Marthe said, "this is not a surprise. They will divide up Poland."

Karl did not want to talk about all this. The news did not even surprise him, but he felt a deep sense of dread begin. The pact of "nonaggression" between the Soviets and Nazis was barely nine days old. That had shocked most of the New York left wing out of their illusions about the Soviet workers' paradise. Friends of his had made excuses for Stalin, saying it didn't matter, just a maneuver in the struggle against Fascism. But quite a few had left the Young Communist League. Karl saw in this clash the real meaning of the ideals he had talked about through the 1930s. He had always leaned toward the kind of ill-defined socialism or Kropotkin-style, accent-on-the-commune, small-*c* communism. That now floated away like a cartoon fantasy. A symptom of his naive teenage years. Now the issues were hard, dark, immediate. He decided not to bring up this latest news with his other friends. These days, politics just wore him out.

Then Rae said, "But how could the Soviets agree to overrun—" She stopped, seeing that there was no easy answer to her question except the obvious.

Marthe offered some tea to Anton, ushering him to a chair. She moved heavily now and wore big housedresses to give herself easy movement around her growing belly. Softly she said, "We must introduce you to others in the, ah, Paley and Cohen families."

Karl was thinking hard but smiled at this, her steady way of integrating with Rae. "We must host a dinner," he said abstractly.

Anton had been silent but now sipped some tea and asked softly, "This war is, ah, to be worse, yes?"

"You bet," Rae said.

There were more people moving in next door to Karl's office, bangs and clatters, so he shut the door after Urey came in.

Harold frowned at the write-up Karl had made of his calculations. "Tell me what this means."

Karl knew by now that Urey wanted what he called "the straight scoop," not a whole detailed description of the work. "Your double-flow model, it works. I wrote down the basic equations and got analytic solutions."

"Closed form?" Urey leaned forward and looked at Karl's thick document, handwritten.

"Yes." Karl tried to keep pride out of his voice. Centrifuges had been around quite a while, and Urey was the world's expert on their uses. But nobody had tried to deal with the complex theory beyond useful approximations.

Urey scowled, mouth twisted skeptically as his eyes raced through the first few pages. He had a right to doubt. Generally, flow equations were notoriously hard to solve, so Karl had recast them for this case, using mathematics he had learned in Paris. He plunked down a drawing he had made to show the simplified problem. He had learned while writing his PhD thesis that showing a picture made for easier going before skeptical eyes.

Urey had devised the countercurrent idea and asked Karl to work out the equilibrium time equations for countercurrent columns. Uranium is a metal, but it could be locked up in uranium hexafluoride, a gas called "hex" by chemists. Fresh gas entered at the center of the rotor. Rotation then slammed it outward, where the wall forced it into a downward flow of gas at its periphery. Since inward rotational forces act more strongly on heavy than on light molecules, the concentration of the U-238 increased toward the outer wall of the rotor. Vents then took it away, keeping the U-235. That gas got recycled, on and on.

Urey studied the diagram. "Um. Didn't know you could draw. You left out the rotor, though."

Karl blinked. Indeed, he had. The essential element!

Urey tapped the inch-thick paper stack. "I'll have to read this one slowly."

Karl knew Urey was not strong at mechanics, so he said, "You worked with these fast rotors before. An electromagnetic motor drives it. How much can that be improved?"

Urey grimaced. "You put your finger on it. The bearings, that's gonna be the trouble. Plus—say, did you analyze the instabilities?"

"Some." They looked like trouble too, but Karl did not want to give away that fact. It might not turn out to be a fact at all, once studied.

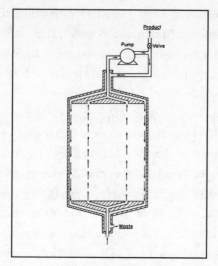

Two-Flow Centrifuge

"I mean, that's an engineering problem par excellence, as your lovely wife puts it."

"The perimeter will be spinning at about three hundred meters a second, pretty close to the speed of sound." *Which spells trouble.*

"Right. We need somebody like Jesse Beams down in Virginia to do that. I'll call him."

"How can we afford to do anything here?"

"I don't think we can!" Urey slapped his desk. "So we get Beams to use his Washington connections for it."

Karl smiled. "I like this grantsmanship you do. Never seen it before."

"The companies have more money for research than anybody else. We should hit them, too."

"I may have a lead into another . . . source."

Urey leaned forward. "So . . . ?"

"Working on it with Szilard. Private capital. Interested in patents with commercial applications."

To Karl's surprise Urey stood up, excited. "Exactly the right idea! There's plenty to be made in a good isotope separation plant. Lawrence, out in California, is using radioactive isotopes in medicine. But he has trouble getting them separated out. Some have short lifetimes, so it's important to grab them right away and get them to the patients."

Karl blinked. "I never thought of that. Can I get some references on that?"

"Sure, got some in my files, pretty fresh. To show who—?"

"Some people I know."

He took charge of Anton the immigrant for Rae, a man introducing another into a strange culture. Best to go with the Jewish angle, Karl realized, and show him streets with such shops. The Soviet invasion of Poland had darkened the Europe they both knew, and Jews were reportedly being taken away in large numbers, getting on trains to "camps." Karl took the young Anton's mind off that by helping him learn how to look for jobs as a clerk, and when he got one, Karl bought him a good working suit in gray gabardine.

So for a celebratory lunch, Karl took Anton to the Carnegie Deli for a corned beef sandwich. He suspected Anton needed some neighborhood gemütlichkeit—a word English speakers did not usually have, meaning warm good cheer. Instead of warm welcomes, the waiters yelled at you if you were confused. Anton struggled with the menu in English. An older waiter with a worn face addressed him in Yiddish, and that solved the menu problem. Anton had come to them through a family connection through Seymour Lipinski Paley, and young man had grown up in a shtetl far from Prague. His father drove a horse and wagon that carried baggage from the railroad station. The horse was such an important family member that he got the best place near the stove in winter.

"I have letter from friend," Anton said. "Others from home, Prague, escaped across river. German soldiers shot at them from a bridge. Water was cold. Drowned, some. Germans shot and laughed. Many did not make across river."

Karl sensed a pressure in Anton's fidgeting hands and compressed lips, and so let him talk about tales heard from other refugees. Of babies snatched away from mothers and swung like baseball bats, smashing their heads against a wall. Of men pitched out of high office windows onto the pavement below, sometimes crushing pedestrians. Of roundups taking whole neighborhoods and villages. Of bodies seen in fields, no explanation, witnessed by people hastily moving on, heads down. Of trucks seen on city streets, people standing mutely in them with fearful eyes, and never seen again.

After a while, as the pressure seemed to ease, he changed the subject to sports or politics, anything to get Anton away from the inward gaze these tales cast the young man into.

It took a while, but by asking leading questions, Karl got Anton out of his darkening mood. Anton's eyes began dancing, talking about his family, and in the middle of a story, a waiter yanked his plate away with some meat left on it. Anton sprang up and grabbed it back. Yiddish sprayed through the air.

When he got Anton settled back down, Karl explained, "You pay extra for the abuse. Reminds people of their origins."

Anton nodded, laughing. He had grasped that this was the charm of New York, brassy and true. Things got easier after that.

A day later Karl was back in the Carnegie Deli again.

"The rabbi will let us meet with them, yes." Leo Szilard's round face wrinkled with puzzlement. "But only after seeing about some engineering uses?"

"That's what he says. They want to be sure this is not just some professor's dream." Karl put down his tea and tried to block out the Carnegie Deli noise. This eastern European atmosphere had worked with Anton, but Szilard ignored all the atmospherics and everything but Karl's diagram of the centrifugal design.

"Then we must give them what we can." Szilard sat back, nodding decisively. "Though they should know these patents will most likely be classified."

"Maybe. Too early to tell."

A barking chuckle. "I know what happens when you assign a patent to a government. Nothing."

"That may not happen this time."

Szilard frowned, bit into his pastrami sandwich. "I think it must. But to go ahead we must, *ja*, we go back to the rabbi."

This time they did not take Rae.

Rabbi Kornbluth held a sheaf of paper, which turned out to be lawyerly assessments of the prospects Karl had shaped up, derived from Urey's sources. A convoluted chain, and Karl had no idea how this would turn out. Still, Kornbluth smiled.

"Thank you, Dr. Szilard, for sending by messenger those summaries. I have met with my several friends, and they assigned due diligence work on this to their assistants."

Szilard replied with questions about the feedback, and Karl stayed out of it. Just listening to them edge forward, gain a concession on a seemingly minor point, then pivot it to engage another issue—priceless instruction in the negotiating art.

Kornbluth leaned forward. "Are you quite confident that this method has applications beyond this armaments interest?"

"Commercially, yes. Particularly the medical." Szilard said this precisely, equal weight to each word, as though it were an evident fact. Karl wondered if cancer treatments would become so common, but he held his tongue.

Kornbluth nodded. "Then I believe the next step is a meeting between my investor friends and some of your Columbia people. They can do the contractual details of"—a delicate pause as he let them savor it—"a donation."

2.

October 14, 1939

Karl told Rae about this latest advance while they waited in the hospital for news of Marthe. She was in a long labor, and the nurses gave no news. Karl almost wished he had acquired the habit of smoking, to give himself something to do with his hands. They twitched and wandered, trying to express the anxiety he kept out of his frozen face.

"Don't worry," Rae said, "women do this all the time."

"But they aren't *my* woman, carrying my child."

"Go get us some tea, then."

When he returned to find there was no news, he brought up the good rabbi Kornbluth and the possibility of substantial funding. At least it was something to talk about. Rae wanted to know more and Karl tried to simplify it, failing. They went around in a conceptual circle, and he realized his mother had no clear idea of how things in the physical world actually worked. Everything was an unconsidered miracle to her, from chemistry to planets to atoms. When a nurse appeared, he sighed with relief.

"It's a girl," the brusque woman said. "Mother and child doing fine."

"What about—" Rae began, but the nurse was out the door.

Karl didn't care. He and Marthe had brought into the world another person, one who would see the world as fresh and bright and new, while to him now, it was quickly darkening.

To Karl's surprise, during the investor talks Urey and Szilard hit it off and worked well together. They came from vastly different backgrounds—Urey from Montana, Szilard from Budapest. But Urey had been chairman of the University Federation for Democracy and Intellectual Freedom and a champion of loyalist Spain. As early as 1932 he espoused an Atlantic Union plan for a world governmental federation. He often spouted antifascist rhetoric and militantly supported the New Deal programs. Like Szilard, Urey was a fountain of ideas but hard-nosed about getting support, too.

Karl was surprised when, in the middle of a strategy meeting on how to spend the investor money, Szilard said no more theory work was needed. "Karl's model is all we need. Now we need Dunning's team, this Beams fellow, hands-on people to roll up their sleeves."

Szilard was trying to pick up American slang, so he added, "We have the moxie now."

Urey liked this, but Karl slowly shook his head. He argued that they needed to figure out how centrifuges could work in gangs together: "To get the mass for a single bomb, we'll need to link together hundreds, maybe thousands."

Urey sided with Szilard. "This is a proof-of-principle program, Karl."

"Somebody's got to think how big this could get," Karl replied.

Szilard gave him a pensive look, then said, "There is evidence that the other side is thinking similarly."

"Oh?" Urey asked.

"A friend I left behind in Berlin sent me a letter, through another friend in Switzerland. Nothing addressed to me can escape Germany now. This friend, he says there are rumors at the Kaiser Wilhelm Institute of an *Uranverein*—a Uranium Club."

"Ah," Urey said. "With money from where?"

"The government. Another term has crept about. *Uranmaschine*—a uranium machine, perhaps a reactor."

"What agency is behind this?"

"The German Army Ordnance Office."

"And still we hear nothing from Roosevelt?" Karl asked.

"I will ask again my agent in this, Alexander Sachs." Szilard eyed them carefully. "I am not encouraged by your government's speed."

"Roosevelt is going for a third term, and he needs votes." Karl described the crowds he and Marthe had seen flocking to the German-American Bund rally. "Plenty of people don't want to even think about this war, much less jump into it."

Urey shrugged and sighed. "Our investors move faster than bureaucrats. It's the American way."

Karl used his same methods to work forward in the seminar room when the fission group met. With Fermi and the others in the front row of the regularly scheduled talks, there was plenty of reason to shut up. Generally speaking, you aren't learning much when your lips are moving. But now he was working on centrifuges and had genuine curiosity about how physicists dealt with the quickly expanding possibilities.

They still had to use chemical means to select out isotopes produced by neutron bombardment. Karl knew the pitfalls of these methods and pointed them out. Some hastily done experiments had missed nuances. The prime example of missing the point of an experiment was, of course, Fermi's not seeing the uranium fission phenomenon himself, through years of experiments.

Fermi himself recognized this, and in the seminars came to see Karl as a useful collaborator. He was working with two Nobel winners! Rae loved to hear about all this.

The Ureys helped the Fermis buy a home in New Jersey, just down the block from the Ureys'. Karl was delighted to get an invitation to a housewarming dinner party. Though the whole world worsened, Karl's world improved.

Harold Urey was studying the yard of the Fermis' new home as Karl and Marthe approached. He was bent over, frowning at the grass, hands on his knees. Then he sprang up with a grin.

"Karl! Marthe! I offered to help Enrico and Laura free their lawn of intruding crabgrass. They never heard of it."

"Very generous of you," Marthe said. "And . . . what is it?"

Urey waved his arms around. "This! Their yard is *all* crabgrass!"

That got a laugh repeatedly throughout the dinner party that followed.

Apparently crabgrass had no foothold in Italy, or, Marthe said, in France. It was an American irritant. So too were the steps the Fermis had to take to become American citizens—bureaucratic snarls. The Fermis felt they could not just get by on visas, as Columbia University had advised. If they were to help the fight for democracy, they had to get rid of their Fascist Italy ties, embrace their new country. This brought applause around the dinner table. "Bureaucracy is the crabgrass of government," Urey said.

They were enjoying a risotto Laura had prepared. They had not anticipated the ample baked haddock that followed as well, shimmering with fragrant butter and herbs. Yet no one turned it away.

"I hear that you and Leo have found a possible funder," Laura said to Karl, across the table.

"Possible. Never know until the check comes in." It seemed best to be guarded in open company.

"I am wondering when we will hear from the Einstein letter," Urey said, helping himself to a big chunk of haddock.

Laura Fermi considered this, her dark eyes flashing. "The letter your chairman Professor Pegram sent, asking in a weak way, for that admiral to perhaps listen to this man Fermi—recall it?"

Karl did. It had been passed around at the lunch at the King's Crown Hotel. He savored the delicious fish, had a glass of Chianti. The Fermis did not share his taste and served a red even with fish, but he was polite, too, and maybe Italians differed from the French. He sat back to hear what this smart, quick woman had to say. Laura Fermi shared a lot of qualities with Marthe. "I thought it a bit awkward."

Laura nodded. "That was, I suspect, the first time you scientists tried to form connections between science and government." She paused for dramatic effect. "Very American. I am not surprised that it does not seem to have worked."

"Why?" Urey asked, frowning with puzzled doubt.

"Why not work? Because you are-*a* new at it." Laura spread her hands, as if this was obvious.

"New?" Leo Szilard was puzzled as well.

"Europeans are used to the government paying for research, because we have so many authoritarian nations," Laura said. "Universities are government-controlled—in Germany, Italy, Hungary. That is where the money is! Americans, the money comes from companies."

Marthe said, "I see. Enrico went to see the admiral. A man just off the boat, who speaks like me with a thick accent, sprinkled with extra vowels— he goes! Those who wrote to Roosevelt to ask for help—Szilard, Einstein, Teller—all Europeans."

Urey pointed at Karl. "He had a hand."

"A small one," Karl said. "Tiny." He wondered if he was blushing.

Laura conceded, "Enrico has never learned to bang with his fist on a table." She leaned to her left and kissed him with a loud smack.

"In Italy, no foreigners would have succeeded, of course," Laura continued. "None! You Americans have not found your way out of your ivory towers."

Karl saluted her with his glass. "She is right. Americans are at a disadvantage."

It was embarrassing that he had never seen this. As talk ricocheted around the table, he saw that scientists in democracies had no strings to government at all, or maybe only long strands of red tape. A dictator decrees; a president asks Congress for permission to organize, then for cash. Hitler had the advantage.

3.

December 15, 1939

The next day Urey came into Karl's office with a letter in his hand. "Roosevelt's authorized an Advisory Committee on Uranium."

Karl rose from a desk covered with sheets of calculations. "Wow, great."

"Its head is a pretty old guy," Urey said, "must be sixty-five. It's a secret project too—a result of the Einstein-Szilard letter."

"Who's in it?"

"Me, Conant—here—" Urey tossed a sheet across his desk. "The usual crew."

"Physicists," Karl said, reading the list.

"I didn't tell you before because it's confidential."

"Uh, when did it happen?"

"October eleventh."

"That was months ago."

"Yeah. Really confidential. I just got our first money from it."

Karl beamed. "How much?"

"Six thousand dollars."

"*What?*"

"Roosevelt has to do it out of his hip pocket. No line items in the budget apply."

Karl slammed his fist on the desk, remembering suddenly Laura Fermi's remark about Enrico. "Bloody hell!"

Urey nodded sourly. "You've got to get back to your rabbi. We should be flying ahead by now, damn it. I'm stalled out, by crabgrass bureaucrats."

✦ ✦ ✦

The meeting turned out to be mostly a bureaucratic kerfuffle. The investors—all bankers in one way or another—wanted Columbia to sign over all patent rights, and Columbia wasn't quite that dumb.

Urey and Karl did what they could, but the investors wouldn't budge. Rabbi Kornbluth was solid with them too, his skeptical eye roving the room. Karl could sense they were on the edge, tempted but cautious with a wholly new area of science.

He now had more information leaked out of Europe, so he used it. Detailed letters and stories—of boxcars stuffed with whole families pressed in hard without food or water, whole villages raked clean, bodies tossed into ditches.

"They're rounding up Jews!" Karl cried to the investors, in a Fifth Avenue restaurant he would never have been able to afford. His audience just looked embarrassed. Misjudging, he pushed harder still. "They're taking away even rabbis."

That didn't work either. The investors blinked. This was news, but Karl had crossed a line. People didn't shout at them, no; they had money, after all.

But Szilard saw the thin wedge of an opening.

So days later Szilard brought Einstein into the Plaza—installed in a suite, no less. How Szilard had managed this he would not say. When Einstein came in by cab from the train station, the old man looked a bit tired. He was more than a bit bemused as the investors trooped in, five of them. They wore black business suits and white shirts and solemn ties, looking to Karl like morticians. Einstein had on baggy pants, a wrinkled white shirt, and no socks in brown loafers. But he was Einstein.

Silence in the room. The great man opened by handing around a postcard a friend had sent, "Years ago, when Germans could make fun of Hitler."

"It's you, with a glow behind you like a saint," Szilard noted. "And Hitler as a raving fool. I suppose the makers are now in prison?"

"Ja," Einstein said, shaking his head. Szilard spoke quickly, reviewing the chances of uranium leading to a bomb. The investors said nothing.

"Ja," Einstein said, "this could be a veapon of gross power."

"You believe it could also have industrial uses?" the more courageous of the five asked.

"I know not of this. I rely"—a nod toward Szilard and Urey and Karl—"on who know besser dan I."

"There is also the argument," another black-suit said, "that this can stop the Germans from killing so many Jews."

"By killing many Germans, *ja*. It may be so." A long, sour sigh.

To Karl, that seemed to say it all.

4.

April 1940

Harold Urey was as good a diplomat as any around, so Karl asked him to make an overture to Fermi. Karl simply did not have the courage to knock on Fermi's door and ask the great man to work on the basic centrifuge physics problems with him.

But a day later he did just that, after getting the nod from Harold. Fermi was a mild-mannered man, slightly shorter than Karl. Karl opened by asking about the Fermi team's experiments to find the number of neutrons emitted by the fissioning uranium. The results of these experiments were just out, published side by side in the April issue of the *Physical Review*. They showed that a chain reaction might be possible, since the uranium emitted about two more neutrons when it fissioned.

Fermi's office had tables stacked with scientific papers and bookshelves standing bare. "You did not bring your references from Rome?" Karl said to ease into the conversation.

"I-*a* have-*a* about four books, in all. One by my boyhood friend, Enrico Persico. I keep for sentimental. Rest are numerical tables, and your wonderful Rubber Bible."

This meant the *Chemical Rubber Company Handbook of Chemistry and Physics*, the CRC bible, which Karl had used since the 1920s. It was clear Fermi didn't need books. He worked out everything for himself. Just what Karl needed.

He had already seen that Fermi often raised an objection in a seminar and would not allow matters to proceed until the speaker had dealt satisfactorily with the objection. If the speaker couldn't, the seminar was over. "Fermi is a physicist with a capital *F*," Szilard had said, smiling.

Karl described the problem of the centrifuge mechanics and they set to work, calculating. At the rotor's bottom cap a heater turned uranium hexa-fluoride into a vapor. That condensed out on the top cap. The fast spinning drove the condensed vapor to the cylinder's wall. The heavier U-238 stacked up there and flowed down the walls, carrying just a tiny bit less of the U-235. Circulate the fluids thousands of times and the U-238 got richer in one chan-nel, the U-235 richer in another. Slowly, slowly, the isotopes separated out.

Fermi started to calculate on his own, saying nothing, and in a direct, simple way found the essential point. The ability of a centrifuge to separate U-235 from U-238 was proportional to its length and to the fourth power of the peripheral speed of its rotor.

Karl went through all this, fearing that Fermi would find an error. But he just nodded. Fermi squinted at the blackboard and said, "So double the speed, we get sixteen times the U-235. But rotor energy, it goes only as square of speed. So is more energy efficient than I expected."

Karl had taken a week to be sure this was true. Fermi had found his way through in ten minutes, a startling example of deft thinking. Karl saw that this stemmed as much from Fermi's appraisal of the art of the possible, as from his innate skill and intelligence. He simply saw into the physics and selected what he pleased.

Yet as he watched Fermi work at the blackboard, the equations marching on with no step skipped, he recalled that Fermi was modest to his core. He had heard many stories about the man's self-effacing nature, his dislike of pomp. When Mussolini had appointed him to the Italian Royal Academy, with the title *Eccellenza*, Fermi drove himself to the first meeting. Since Mussolini was to address the academy, the other Excellences had arrived in big limousines. Guards stopped Fermi in his old Fiat, their weapons drawn. Without pause Fermi said, "I am the driver of His Excellency Signore Enrico Fermi." The guards said, "Drive in, park, await your master." Fermi had waved to the guards as he left later, still alone in the Fiat.

Fermi came to a conclusion and reached for the CRC book. In a moment he jotted down some numbers and said, "A plausible rotation rate means . . .

ah . . . a linear speed at the end of the rotor of about three hundred meters per second. Steel or aluminum can handle that."

"Nearly the speed of sound in air," Karl said.

Fermi nodded, brushing chalk from his suit jacket. "And nearly the speed of a low-caliber bullet."

In an hour Fermi had redone what Karl had taken weeks to figure out. Karl burned with silent embarrassment. This was what genius looked like, up close—a casual speed and grasp, obliviously enjoying the work. But his quickly jotted equations had told Fermi one more point. "Ah, I see. The major difficulty with a centrifuge is that as the top speed of its rotor increases, it passes through various critical rotation frequencies."

Karl nodded. "That makes it vibrate like a thin rod. This clearly puts serious engineering demands on its bearings and damping mechanisms."

"Ah, so. *Si*. So let us attack that." Fermi's hands flew across the blackboard, the chalk clicking. He never talked while calculating, letting his hands speak for him.

It took two more hours, with Karl catching some small errors and adding a term to one equation. The windows darkened, lights came on. Otherwise this was Fermi's show, and he brightened as results came into clear view, fresh problems arose, got worked around, and they devised together some rule-of-thumb solutions.

"We have to speed up the rotor when it gets to those resonances," Karl said. "Just zoom through them so they can't rattle the rotor to pieces."

Fermi nodded. "Will take a lot of control. Very fast. You know, Pauli called this sort of thing *schmutz* physics. Dirt physics." They both chuckled. Pauli was one of the founders of quantum mechanics and a notoriously nasty critic.

A knock at the door, then Urey burst in without waiting. "I just got off the phone with that rabbi, Kornbluth. The investors, they're in for seventy-five thousand dollars."

5.

February 8, 1940

The program's first act was to get Columbia University to sign a contract with Westinghouse Research Laboratories. It paid them tens of thousands of dollars to develop a rotor of about eight inches in diameter, to be spun at five hundred revolutions per second. That rate limited the rotor's length to about forty-two inches, set by the expected vibration waves in a steel or aluminum rotor. The electromagnetic bearing had to be built to exact specifications, down to a hundredth of a millimeter.

Fermi devised a way to strengthen the magnetic field, too. Karl had not even thought of that element. The man was a quiet miracle.

They all pitched in, working with some Columbia and Westinghouse engineers. Fermi was at ease with these more practical men too. The design of the first major Columbia machine was finished in January 1940. Before Fermi, Karl had thought it would take far longer.

Soon enough, the arguments came.

"So *this* may well be the way to go," John Dunning ended with a flourish, a sweeping hand gesture at his projected slide. It showed all the methods for separating U-235 from U-238, as proposed by groups around the country.

> Electromagnetic mass spectrograph
> Liquid thermal diffusion separation
> Gaseous diffusion separation
> Gas centrifugation

John Dunning

"I'm for number three."

Dunning was a big, round man with a powerful voice that rolled over the Nuclear Seminar, as it had been innocuously named to seem just another tiny academic field. Yet they were all talking about making a bomb that could kill cities.

Karl kept quiet. He doubted that the diffusion methods would work well. Nobody had built even a prototype.

The first method, flinging uranium nuclei around with magnets to let the heavier U-238 fly outward, and so separate, looked really expensive. The last in Dunning's list was the centrifuge they already had working. Why list it last?

Harold Urey rose to object. "It's too early to pick a winner. Your number one, the mass spectrograph, that's from Lawrence in California. Sure, using his big cyclotron magnetic field to spread out the U-235 from the U-238 is physically clear—but what's the efficiency?"

Dunning nodded and waved his left hand as if he were batting away a fly. "I kind of agree, Harold. That's why I think a process I've been studying in my lab, number three, can do the job on a mass scale. We know diffusion pretty well. It's just quicker."

The crowd was bigger than Karl had ever imagined, in one of Columbia's biggest rooms. There were nearly a hundred men and a woman nuclear physicist fresh off the boat, too. Fermi had helped her and her husband, a well-known chemist named Joe Mayer, get out of Germany in time. Maria Goeppert Mayer sat just in front of Karl, nodding. She had easily followed it all, taking notes, though much of it had to be new to her. Her questions were clear, direct, and got at interesting parts of the problem Karl had not even thought of, such as flow turbulence.

The room murmured, everyone muttering an opinion on the choices.

That there were choices at all was news to Karl. He had been focused, ignoring all other issues and gossip. With Fermi and Urey he had worked to get the first fast centrifuge into operation. That meant going by train to the Westinghouse research buildings in Pittsburgh to shape the work, up to the first working device. He had missed that others at Columbia, Dunning's team especially, had been going along another track.

"I want to see some real separation data," Urey said, face firm. "If you have it. Not just some projections."

Karl decided to get into the fray, though he was still a junior member of this group. He said, "What membrane can stand up against the vicious bite of the uranium hexafluoride? Have you found one?"

Dunning was a big guy, and his body language showed that he was used to being in charge. He puffed himself up, adopted a thoughtful gaze, waltzed left, turned right, shrugged. Eyebrows up. "Not yet, no. We tried some simple filters and they blew apart. That U-hex is tough stuff."

Karl knew this already. As a chemist he saw that the cumbersome method of separating U-235 and U-238 was to push a gas of uranium bound to fluorine through a barrier, a membrane. The slightly lighter U-235 passed through a bit more effectively, so on the other side the residue got enriched.

Dunning dodged. "We'll see. Too early to tell."

Urey rose. "Too early to tell? But then you don't know it's gonna be the best."

Still, there was a logic to Dunning's argument. Apply high temperatures to the hex, put it under pressure, and the lighter isotope diffuses easier through a membrane, due to its higher speed. Karl knew that maybe a membrane of electro-deposited nickel mesh could do it. A big maybe, though. Since the mass separation ratio was quite small, a plant would need many stages. Each stage enriched the uranium of the previous one, just a bit more, before being sent to the next stage. The tailings from each stage returned to the previous stage for repeated enrichment. So a cascade of membranes, or of centrifuges, was the answer.

A huge industry. Nothing like it had ever been tried. Now they had to do it when the war loomed like a purple gathering cloud on their horizon. If the Germans got such a weapon, they could attack America, the whole world. Yet all these implications played out in a quiet academic seminar. He had seen paintings of surrealism, read some books—but this was the real thing.

"So this 'electromagnetic mass spectrograph' can do the job?" Karl asked.

"It's the brainchild of Ernest Lawrence, out in California." Dunning sniffed dismissively. "He calls it a calutron, and it's based on his cyclotron, which I've built a close copy of. It's all about the precise control of beams of charged particles. Like this."

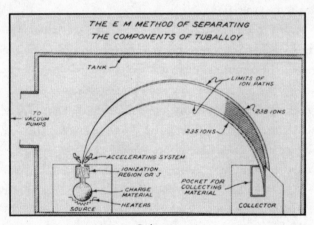

Calutron

"See," Dunning went on, in his element, "the technique is simple, but the scale has to be huge. You take a beam of ions, naturally occurring uranium, so it has U-235 and a hundred forty-three times more U-238 in it."

Dunning scribbled a quick equation on the blackboard. "Then pass it between the poles of a big magnet, so those two isotopes split into several streams according to their mass, one per isotope, each with a particular radius of curvature. Some charged cups at the ends of the half-circle trajectories catch the streams. Lawrence estimates—this is from a paper he sent me—he could enrich U-235 by about fifteen percent."

"So then you do it again," Fermi said from the front row.

"Right!" Dunning pointed at Fermi. "Keep refining it."

Fermi said mildly, "I respect Lawrence very much, but . . ." The room hung on his pause. "This-a seems very optimistic. The difference in mass is tiny between uranium 235 and 238. I would like to see data."

"I'm sure I can get some," Dunning said, turning away, smiling.

But Fermi was not through. "At the end of their arc, the ions of U-235 are more plentiful on the inside than on the outside of the beam. But the maximum separation even in the ideal case is small." He waved a small notebook, where apparently he had made a calculation during Dunning's talk. "There is only one-tenth inch for an arc with a diameter of thirty-seven inches—that is, ninety-four centimeters—which is the size of Lawrence's cyclotron. And actual beams are far from ideal."

Dunning drew back, gave the crowd a lopsided smile. "I never said it would be easy."

No kidding, Karl thought. He was not sure why he disliked Dunning, but that didn't matter much. Point was, Dunning was getting by on salesmanship, not physics. *But physics bats last.*

A few chuckles. Dunning's face fell. He kept on for a few moments, but Fermi had skewered his estimates. Leaving, Karl asked Urey, "Will this calutron thing compete with us for money?"

A shrug. "Sure. And Lawrence won a Nobel last year too."

Another Nobel in the field, Karl thought as he walked home through honking traffic. He was a mouse among dancing elephants.

6.

May 14, 1940

Karl lasted through the Pesach Sheni ceremony led by Rabbi Kornbluth, but it was a struggle. He thought about a calculation he was working on with Fermi instead of the rabbi's droning speech. This minor Jewish holiday was, Rae had informed him, exactly one month after the fourteenth of Nisan, the day before Passover. That in turn was the day prescribed for bringing a sacrificial lamb in anticipation of Passover. "Admittedly, I had to look it up," she'd said.

This was exactly the sort of arcane time wasting he had expected of religion, any religion. He had only once before been to temple with his grandfather Cohen and had been bored then, too. But that same grandfather Cohen had left Karl enough money in his will to let him go to Paris and discover Marthe, too. Time abounded in ironies.

He was here because his mother, Rae, thought it was canny to bring Anton and Karl to hear the rabbi, just to "keep lines of communication open" to the investors the rabbi had brought into Karl's world. This reasoning too seemed nonsensical to Karl. Investors, a few of whom he had now met, cared about results, not ceremony.

They were nearly free, almost out the tabernacle door, Marthe in front with the baby, when news came. The rabbi held up his hand and said solemnly, "Our enemies have invaded Belgium."

A rustle, and Karl got out the door ahead of Rae, who said, "I thought the Germans were going to hold off for summer."

Anton said, "They wait? Never. Already deporting many where I lived."

"They hit Norway and Denmark last month," Karl said. "Now they're headed for the main prize."

Marthe was already out of the tabernacle, he saw. She had bought a newspaper from the boy shouting the headlines on the corner.

HOLLAND, BELGIUM, LUXEMBOURG INVADED, it screamed. Marthe said, "You mean headed for France."

Rae said, "That's the way they did it in the Great War. Straight through Belgium."

People were already calling this World War II, Karl had noticed. Already it was bigger in scale, including the Japanese invasions in Asia.

"This one is going to be greater," he said. He decided to take them out to lunch. It might cheer them up a bit. Plus, he could write some calculations in his little notebook before the emotions of this day erased the idea that had come to him as the rabbi delivered his Hebrew wisdom, while the world burned.

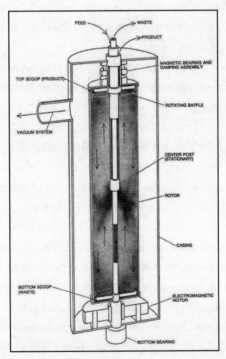

Centrifuge 2

Some obscure philosopher had said, *God is in the details*, Karl recalled. Now he was seeing that played out in tedium. Months stretched on.

The first centrifuge from Westinghouse had arrived, with some engineers to handle installation, so Karl had pitched in to set up the first trial runs. They got into a basement room once used for storage, now fitted with electrical and gas tube feeds.

The engineers dealt with the control systems, lots of wiring on racks, behind gray steel panels adorned with big dials. Ranks and ranks, like tiny skyscrapers. Everything had to be tried and tested. Karl dealt with the check valves and their monitors. All this he had to adjust and tune. Maybe the philosopher's saying meant that if you looked hard enough, God's fingerprints showed up somehow.

He had distilled some uranium hexafluoride, "hex," the real point of all this, but they would run with simpler compounds first. He used his chemical skills to do the rudimentary work of making isotopes of lighter elements, since they had a bigger fractional difference in mass. Now he wanted to see how the slim cylinder worked at high speeds. This was the first time he had seen his ideas shaped into solid hardware.

"All set up now?" Fermi asked at his elbow. They were in another newly cleared lab in the lowest basement of the Pupin Physics Laboratories, and he had heard that they were ready to run.

"Soon." Karl showed Fermi the diagram Westinghouse had supplied of the built machine and then took him behind the cowling that wrapped around it. There wasn't a lot of room left in the lab, after all the power and control apparatus got stacked in. Maybe universities weren't the best places to build and try such stuff. But that was where the people who had the imagination were, for now.

He forgot about Fermi as the trials started. The engineer team ran the centrifuge up and down, reaching interesting speeds, then backing off. The engineer team termed it a "spinner," calling out, "Spin 'er up!"

The engineers used the calculations Fermi had made, with some simple help from Karl. Maria Goeppert Mayer had done some insightful analysis that came in handy in the engineering too. Fermi had a clipboard and slide rule to keep track of the data. The man could do theory brilliantly, but he loved the grip of the real. They were near the resonances now. Fermi told the engineers to edge cautiously up into the danger area, and then accelerate through.

This worked on the first few of the whole-body resonances—vibrations that could shake the whole thing apart—he and Fermi had worked out, and some in the Columbia engineering department had improved. The spinner whined with an eerie, cutting tone. It rattled a bit as its speed rose, and then an engineer shoved the power on hard. The whine added a jarring, rattling sound, a peevish complaint—and then they were through, the whine quieter now.

They worked on, to higher speeds. Karl made up some impromptu earmuffs for himself and Fermi. That helped some.

They were trying for a speed of three hundred meters a second at the end of the rotor. Their predicted resonance was at 268 meters a second. They idled at 250 and Fermi nodded to the head engineer. Karl made a note in his own lab book and looked toward the steel cowling that surrounded the centrifuge. Its high-pitched cry rose.

The sound felt wrong. He jerked his hand up. A shrill note keened briefly—

Later, trying to recall the moment, he seemed to see his hand moving with languid, slow-motion grace. In memory, something had alerted his unconscious, lending the events a sliding grace.

Fermi's face seemed to smear and dissolve an instant before Karl had the sensation of somebody hitting him in the head with a baseball bat wrapped in goose down. No sound, just massive impact. Then he was weightless, buoyant, the world beyond a blur of soundless velocities.

No smack of landing. No sudden jar. But then he was lying in utter silence on a cement floor as cool as an angel's kiss, staring up at the high, ribbed ceiling far, far away.

He turned his head. Legs flicked across the milky foreground of this curiously flat, dimensionless scene. The disembodied legs seemed in a tremendous hurry for no apparent cause. Certainly he felt no great urgency himself. He turned his head again, finding it a great effort, the vertebrae going *rak-rak-rak* like a rusty crank-driven machine.

How had he gotten tired so fast? Steel sheeting lay curled next to him, its jagged edges glinting in the enamel light. The steel kiosk around the spinner was now a shredded box lying on its side.

It was odd, he thought, how wounded people looked like heaps of clothing, as if calamity was a confused fashion statement. They were somehow no longer people, just collections of their wrappings that had failed to protect them from the shrapnel weather here.

Pain started to seep into his elbows. His shirt was torn and bloody. Abstractly he noted the cuts and bruises where steel had peppered him. Metal was cold, so the icy threads he felt up and down his legs were steel. Logical.

The ethereal fog around him began to retreat, letting in movement—damp air, faces wide-eyed, their O mouths. Everything happened beyond the glass wall of silence.

He got to his knees in a gliding, soundless world.

He stood up shakily. Rubbery legs. Fermi was there with him in the silence, also getting up.

He saw an engineer with a deep shoulder cut wobbling out of the room, brushing past them, his seeping blood smelling like freshly sheared brass, startling and pungent.

God is in the details.

His hearing took a day to come back.

The doctors who tended to the injured—fortunately, none seriously—insisted they all go home for a day to rest up. Indeed, he felt little of what the "health syrup" advertisements on the radio called vim and vigor.

He got a phone call summary from Urey. The centrifuge had developed an instability, splintered, sprayed the lab with shrapnel.

Marthe cared for him, sending him to bed with a mock-stern face. That gave him a good time to play with the baby, whom they had given the mouthful name of Martine Claude Malartre Cohen. Snap pictures of the small, precious center of their lives. And think.

As he watched his wife move through the day, he realized that she and he had acquired important skills, almost without thinking about it. How to be vulnerable, how to set boundaries, how to listen, and how to speak up. They had learned the art of compromise and forgiveness and how to love someone, even when you don't always like them. Through practice and repetition, they were mastering this exquisite, complicated dance, cultivating wisdom and muscle memory that could be successfully applied to their future.

She now fathomed his earnest Jewish tribal loyalty, even though he was an atheist. She had laughed when Rae had described his family's reaction to first meeting her. "She's a looker," his sister Mattie had commented, and Rae herself observed, "So he's a goner." They had missed that for him, Marthe stood for Paris, style, beauty, Europe.

A deep wisdom flickered across her face, like light dancing on water. For him this was the finest sight the soiled world could give him.

These quiet victories would all vanish if the war now growing steadily like a cancer could leap the Atlantic and lay waste to everything he cherished.

Urey looked around the small seminar room, a week after the accident. "So where was the mistake?"

A burly Irish engineer said softly, "We hadn't secured the base enough. It ripped free."

Urey frowned, snorted. "That basic? Nothing fundamental?"

Fermi had a bandage on his forehead and hand but said mildly, "Apparently not. We should have checked more thoroughly. Engineers, we are not."

An actual engineer had sustained some eye damage and now wore dark glasses. "I take a dim view of all this," he said to mild chuckles.

God is in the details, Karl thought. He had a few bandages too, and the daze from the explosion had faded. Mostly he felt ashamed. "We've set the program back a lot. Nothing from the gear can be saved. It's all shards."

Urey grinned. "Think of yourselves as war casualties, gentlemen. And don't look dejected. We can go forward."

Karl demanded, "How? Our ideas can't be tested with—"

"I struck a deal with Westinghouse back when we ordered the centrifuge. Glad I did, now. They were complaining about the tight windings, about getting the fittings as accurate as we wanted. They had to make a model one to test their machining. So I made a proposal."

"Ah!" Fermi said. He was always the first to grasp implications, Karl knew, but what—?

"I had extra cash from our investors—sorry, donors—so I cut a deal. They made a second one, from the model they had to build anyway, and"—a dramatic pause, which Urey relished—"since I give them an extra ten thousand dollars."

Everyone laughed. "There's a second centrifuge?" Szilard asked, startled.

"They need to shape it up, sure." Urey stood, preening just a bit. "But it'll be here from their plant in a week. About the time you guys' wounds heal."

PART III

ANOTHER DAMNED ELEMENT

1.

May 11, 1941

Karl had never played soccer before, and now he knew why.

Anton had urged him into it. "Exercise, you need." With a wry smirk, just a heavy-browed touch of a man-challenge.

Now Karl was bent over, getting his wind back in big gasps as fleet-footed foreigners raced away down the field in pursuit of a dirty ball. Bright day, cotton clouds, and he was staring at mud. The sharp spring air seemed to cut in his throat. He would rather be home with Marthe, taking photos of their baby and getting some much-needed rest.

He was feeling somewhat human when he glanced up, still panting, and saw the teams bearing down on him. *Like they're chasing down a bouncing rabbit.*

The ball came plunging toward him out of a clear blue sky. Without moving a step, he launched his head at it, the way he had seen others do. It hit, knocking his glasses off into the mud—and the ball shot back downfield.

"Is great!" a player called downfield, waving Karl into the gang now rushing away. The ball bounced among a scrum of players, and his side got control. Karl snatched up his glasses and strolled that way, knowing he was no good at the tricky foot maneuvers these European players had, like gazelles dancing as they ran. He watched a big, burly Hungarian slap the ball into the goal with a hard kick. Cheers.

"Is time!" a voice called. Game over, he gathered. The clock had run out, leaving Karl dripping with sweat. He turned to see Marthe waving, their daughter standing with a wobbly grace beside her.

Anton came pounding up, hardly panting at all, and clapped Karl on the back. "Head shot, first game! You a natural."

Karl decided to bask in this approval as they walked toward Marthe. He had simply reacted instantly, without thinking. "We won!" Anton called.

Marthe bent over and whispered to the tiny little girl, who then clapped her hands, grinning. More men hailed him, and Karl realized his sudden move had led to their score. He was an utterly accidental hero.

"Meet Yusov." Anton gestured. "Scored point."

The Hungarian shook Karl's hand. "Engineer, I."

"Just off boat," Anton added. "Needs job."

Karl was getting used to this by now. "I'll put you in touch with hiring at Columbia."

"Ah, thanks!" A clap on the back from his fellow soccer buddy. Maybe Anton felt that was the real point of this game? There actually was a steadily growing demand for technical people, and Columbia did pass on applicants to other places that were hiring. Refugees would fit in.

As they walked away, Anton said, "Yusov got out, go through Turkey. Family was taken away but he was on trip, so slipped across border."

Another story getting familiar. "Was everybody on our team Jewish?"

"Yes, is so. Also other team." A shy glance. "Just off boat, some of team. Need jobs too."

So it had been something of a setup. Not a bad one either. He now had enough contacts in the growing nuclear effort to help them, and somehow they knew that. Karl slapped Anton on the back and laughed at the sky.

May 23, 1941

Karl had heard Fermi refer to Leo Szilard as an "intellectual bumblebee," for nurturing and enriching science freely and broadly. Quite right—Fermi and Szilard were opposites. Fermi was conservative, careful, methodical. Szilard was imaginative, flamboyant. Fermi seldom said anything he could not demonstrate. Szilard seldom said anything not startling and new. Fermi was humble and self-effacing. Szilard could not talk without giving orders. Urey remarked that they were "antiparticles" of each other, in the sense of Paul Dirac's theory of electrons and antielectrons.

"They need a mediating particle, Karl. Why don't you take the job?"

"I'm not qualified."

"You'll learn. More important, nobody else wants it."

Fair enough. Szilard had pushed through Einstein's letter to the president, after all—a brilliant move. So he spent more time trying to mediate between the two. The most effective way was to simply keep them apart. But Karl was unprepared for Szilard's bursting into his office, brandishing a rather lurid cover on a science fiction magazine, saying, "This is important!"

It was *Astounding Science Fiction*, the May 1941 issue, featuring a garish painting showing a man with two heads. Szilard quickly turned to a story by Anson MacDonald, "Solution Unsatisfactory." Karl eyed the illustration and grimaced. "I didn't know you read fiction at all. I don't."

"Is full of ideas, like me. I find in this story prediction of just such a nuclear program as we are in. Then works out that each side will have them, so stalemate follows. Only difference is, the weapon is spreading radioactive dust. To pollute, make use of a territory impossible—not using as explosive."

"Wow." Karl read the first few paragraphs. "Can I borrow this?"

"Do. I went and bought five copies after I read it last night."

"What do you think we should do about it?"

Szilard paced, face skeptical. "I do not treasure the intelligence services of any government. So just discuss this among ourselves."

"I never thought of just contaminating an area, to deny it to an enemy."

"I either." Szilard rolled his eyes and screwed his mouth around with distaste. "Horrible, this idea. Cities, countryside. This could be quicker way to use radioactive substances."

"Nasty. Do you think we or anyone would do that? The poisoning would last for years. Until it got washed away."

"I know some Germans get this magazine."

"Jeez."

A day later Karl attended a small meeting of everyone Szilard had given copies of *Astounding Science Fiction*. He felt out of place, not a fiction reader at all. He had spent an unpleasant half hour reading the story, in which "atomic" bombs—a strange term, since the energy came from not the atom, but its nucleus—get developed by the United States and the quasi-Soviet "Eurasian Union." A brief atomic war breaks out that the United States wins. America thereafter has to impose a military dictatorship over the rest of the world to prevent future nuclear warfare. But the Eurasian Union has the weapons, too, so this stalemate is a disagreeable equilibrium. That was a solution to the nation-state warfare problem, but unsatisfactory, since the free nations did not win out.

It was an unsettling idea. By now the brutal grind of the war had shown them that targeting civilians was no longer a despicable crime in the eyes of the world. Everybody bombed civilians. Millions had died, many in their own homes. Using radioactives to pollute a broad area seemed somehow worse than just blowing up a city.

"This is why we need more secrecy," Szilard said as an opener. "This new idea should not be in a magazine."

"Cat's out of the bag," Urey observed wryly.

Szilard saw he was losing his audience. He responded by citing his own experience. He had met H. G. Wells in London in 1929, and in 1932 read Wells's *The World Set Free*, written in 1913 about a worldwide atomic war in the 1950s.

"I went to see Wells. He feared such a war. He speculated that the only way for humans to escape Earth to visit other planets was if they were powered by 'atomic' energy, he called it. I said was really nuclear, since would not come from the electron orbits that make atoms work. He ignored that, liked atomic better. Arh!—novelists!"

"He did have the idea first, though," Karl added.

"Yes! But how to do this atomic bomb? And now, how to use that to win a war before the Germans?"

Fermi said, "This-*a* war will use such weapons—probably to end it."

Edward Teller nodded furiously. "The Germans are ahead of us. When they read this story—ah!" He shook his head, face dark.

Szilard paced anxiously. "Even the possibility of such weapons means we need a new set of holy commandments. Instead of 'Thou shalt not kill,' we need 'Do not destroy what you cannot create.' Such bombs are too big in impact to use against civilization. They will destroy everything! So I think we need international control of such weapons."

Karl saw where this was going. These were brilliant men, fast thinkers, quite sure they were right—an occupational disease of physicists, he had learned. He felt humble among them but stood taller and made himself say, "By whom? The nations that are fighting? That's over a dozen already."

Szilard's face relaxed. "You all know I tried, by sending cables—ah, so many!—to get Joliot-Curie in Paris *not* to publish his estimate of how many neutrons come from a uranium fission. I failed. Frenchmen! Damn! Joliot published, as did"—a nod—"Fermi's group."

Fermi smiled wryly. "So it became a matter of general knowledge. We research, we publish—that is science." An expressive shrug. "That made the possibility of a chain reaction appear plausible to most physicists. Everywhere. We are not politicians."

Karl said, "The Soviets, the Germans—hell, even the Japanese—all know now how many neutrons shoot out of a fissioning nucleus."

"So we need complete secrecy *now*," Szilard said, stamping his foot.

"Secrecy will slow down our work," Teller said firmly. "I oppose it. The Germans are the best scientists in the world—and probably well ahead of us."

Urey said, "The army's getting assigned the management. So we're gonna get all the hush-hush rigmarole."

The faces around the room told Karl this was not good news to anyone except Szilard.

A few days later, Harold Urey looked vexed. "There's an Englishman who wants to talk to you."

Karl nodded and put down the distillation glassware he was assembling. He was refining the hex the centrifuges needed, and it was tedious work. "He's here?"

"No, they want you to meet him at LaGuardia."

Karl frowned in disbelief. "He's flying in, with the Germans keeping their cap on England's airspace?"

"They think it's important enough, so this guy has hitched a ride." Urey sniffed the air in the crowded basement lab. "What's that?"

"Some fluorine escaped. Who is this guy?" He thought it better not to ask who the mysterious "they" might be.

"Funny name for a Brit—Rudolf Peierls. Used to be German. Turns out he was at Cambridge University when Hitler came to power, and he switched citizenship. He got a gander at your calculation of the countercurrent rate, says it's wrong. And the method is unstable."

"I saw that, sure." Karl went over to a bookshelf and picked out a thin typed paper. "Irving and I got his paper and we wrote this." He held up their paper so Urey could read the title: "The Correct Equilibrium Time of a Cascade."

Urey laughed, slapping his knee. "Right, saw that, haven't read it yet. He says he wants to talk it over."

"For that they fly him through the German air cover?"

"We have planes coming back anyway, part of Roosevelt's Lend-Lease program somehow. He got a lift. Lands at LaGuardia in an hour."

"I'd better go. Say, who's the 'they' who wants this?"

"People in Washington. The Uranium Committee has people from the War Department sitting in with us now."

Karl didn't much like the sound of that. "So it's like that now."

"Red tape comes with the money. No blank checks."

Rudolf Peierls looked, as Karl's mother used to say, like something the cat dragged in. His wife looked worse. She had a set, aggrieved frown and pursed lips, gazing around at the airport as if inspecting it for rats.

Peierls shook Karl's hand, and so did his wife. They both gratefully sank into their chairs in the LaGuardia restaurant. "Ah! Soft. The seats coming over, they were buckets," Peierls said.

His wife, Genia, who had been silent, spoke in a German accent similar to her husband's but overlaid with Russian notes. "Unheated. Horrible WCs. In fact, from Newfoundland, no water left at all. Was hole in floor." She gulped down the large glass of water as soon as the waitress arrived. "Worst thing for health is to be idiot."

Karl saw that since the definite and indefinite articles did not exist in Russian, she considered it was also superfluous in English. He was feeling flushed, successful, and these ragged two looked as if the war was taking a heavy toll. "Order the steak."

"We cannot afford—"

"I'm paying. Beef is lots cheaper here anyway. Might as well get some protein into you." Both the Peierlses were drawn and pale, hands jittering. "Lay off the coffee, though."

"It was all they had to drink aboard," Rudolf said. He bit off some of a dinner roll and glanced at it. Karl preferred European bread and figured that probably Rudolf was startled by the quality difference. "I had time to go over your calculations, the ones with Irving Kaplan. I came because I thought they were in error."

"The error was in *your* earlier paper. You were off the separation rate by a factor of five."

Peierls seemed startled at how quickly the shrimp cocktail salad arrived. Karl had ordered three when they came into the restaurant. He had heard that the English were low on vegetables, and he was certain they couldn't bring in lettuce.

Rudolf stopped eating and said carefully, "It was a long flight. We stopped in Ireland to refuel, then Newfoundland. Terrible food. So I had time to review my calculations . . . and I found an error. Mine. Ironic, isn't it? The MAUD Committee sent me to straighten you Americans out." A shrug, a sigh. "And I found it was we who needed straightening out."

"You found the factor of five."

A rueful smile, arched eyebrows. "Indeed. And I was wrong in saying that the method is unstable."

The perfect moment for the steaks to arrive, medium rare. The Peierlses gazed at the big, thick rib eyes, Karl thought, with something resembling religious awe. Rudolf and Genia dug in eagerly, and after a few moments Karl ordered a bottle of a decent red wine to go with the steak. He might learn more if they were lubricated a bit.

"What's this MAUD thing?" Karl hated the rising use of acronyms.

"It stands for Military Application of Uranium Detonation. Our report includes cost estimates and technical specifications for a large uranium enrichment plant. James Chadwick read it and said he realized that a nuclear bomb was not only possible, it was inevitable. He had then to start taking sleeping pills. It was the only remedy."

His wife spoke up, about enduring the Blitz and how air raid sirens kept them up nearly every night. They were in Birmingham now, an industrial city pounded daily, but there were air raid shelters. The wine arrived, a decent red *vin ordinaire*. Karl had been surprised that an airport restaurant had a wine list at all, even though it was just two, red or white. It was barely midday but Karl could see they all needed it, and he wanted to celebrate. A British physicist had been wrong about a calculation by an American chemist. Hooray, indeed.

Genia had two quick glasses and then began to talk about the war, not as it was for them, but for the Soviet Union. "You Americans must come in, you must open second front with British."

Karl recognized this as the new party line. The Germans had launched their blitzkrieg against the Soviet Union on June 22, blowing open the treaty that had let Hitler and Stalin divide up Poland. The Soviets had gobbled up Latvia, Lithuania, and Estonia as well. Now their 1939 ally was their 1941 enemy. This latest news had taught Karl that dictators were all alike, in the end. But not so Mrs. Peierls. "Your soldiers, they have to get"—she struggled to find something ridiculous, he could anticipate—"a *grapefruit* every morning, to fight at all!"

"I doubt—"

"The Soviet people can fight with empty bellies"—her voice rose—"and they are!"

"The sentiment here," Karl said, "even among my friends of the collectivist persuasion, is to let these dragons fight it out."

"But a second front would help England, too," Rudolf said.

"Help them die faster, yes. I favor letting Stalin take a beating for a while, not more for Churchill. Or for you."

This put a pall on the conversation. Karl reflected that he had never learned to mute his views, and plainly was never going to. Genia, whose blouse sported a hammer-and-sickle pin, gave him a glare as she cut farther into her steak. Karl wondered how much Rudolf had told her about the nuclear work. He had learned not to challenge hard-line Communists, and instead said softly to Rudolf, "I heard you have calculated with Otto Frisch the minimum mass for an . . . explosive."

This was neutral ground, so Rudolf gratefully took it up. "Yes, he got out of Europe. Here, I have our memorandum."

Karl looked at the carbon copy and scanned its abstract and raised his eyebrows in surprise. "You estimate just a single kilogram of U-235?"

"Perhaps a bit more." A shrug. "But not much more."

"That makes it a lot easier. We've been thinking it's many tons."

"How to get the U-235, that is the question."

"Centrifuges look good."

"Our MAUD Report dismissed all but one method, including the centrifuge. We recommend gaseous diffusion of uranium 235 on a massive scale."

"I think we can change your mind about centrifuges." Karl spoke carefully because he was surprised that Peierls was so openly discussing this with his wife present. Karl had chosen a table far from others so he could be open, but the wife worried him. "And that diffusion method—found a membrane that can stand up to uranium hexafluoride—the hex, we call it—yet?"

"Um, no. That is an engineering detail." Peierls sniffed disdainfully and leaned forward. "More important, since spring 1940 a large part of the Kaiser Wilhelm Institute in Berlin has been set aside for uranium research. Our agents are tracking that."

"So your MAUD Committee wants to work with us?"

"Yes. Soon. We may have to move our physicists here for that. The bombing is flattening much of our industrial base."

"You should go to Washington, DC, for that."

"So I will. You think this work could move so quickly as to change the outcome of this war?" Rudolf asked intently.

"If we focus, yes."

"On what?"

"Getting something that works. Fast."

"Quickly enough to open second front?" Genia leaned forward.

I wonder if she'll keep the Soviets informed about this, Karl thought. *Better tell Urey . . .*

"There might not even need to be one," he said.

♦ ♦ ♦

Later that day Karl went to a seminar that proved to be a John Dunning sales pitch. He had to admire the verve and showmanship that went into the slides that paraded on as Dunning detailed how his group had heroically grappled with the problem of diffusing the hex through a membrane of various metals. Hex was highly toxic and reacted violently with water. It was corrosive to most metals, so they had to replace membranes often. But Dunning strode through these problems with jaunty self-confidence.

At the seminar's end Karl noticed Dunning introducing several men at the front of the room to Urey. Minutes later Urey appeared in his office. "Those guys up front, they were from Washington. They're part of the Uranium Committee, on the engineering end. Dunning wants all the development money the committee has to go to him."

Karl blinked. "How can we stop that?"

"Faster progress. I want you to work out how to gang all the centrifuges together."

"We've only got the one from Westinghouse—"

"And I'll go to DC to get us some money for more. But first, I want to put you to work at Kellex Corporation. They're doing the study on what method we should use to separate out U-235."

"I don't want to leave Columbia."

"I'll get them to pay you more than I can."

"Look, I'll go talk to them, that's all."

The next day, as Karl stood outside at 223 Broadway, the Woolworth Building loomed large. Covered in veined marble, it was one of the first skyscrapers— an ugly term Karl hated. Inside, he studied the ornate, cruciform lobby ceiling, framed by mosaics and stained-glass illuminations brimming with light, all of it setting off thick bronze fittings. Ugly name, but beautiful interior. Over the balconies of the mezzanine murals depicted earnest LABOR and COMMERCE. The Kellex private offices on the thirty-third floor boasted more marble and a snooty secretary in high heels, who ushered him into a meeting room.

He was back out in thirty minutes. He took the subway uptown and marched into Urey's office. "They want me to work on how to scale up a gaseous diffusion plant, not centrifuges."

"Ah. So Dunning's already sold them?"

"Looks like. They're starved for technical people, but they won't even consider anything but Dunning's work, the British stuff, and something from Lawrence in California."

"Ah, that hyper-cyclotron idea. Calutron, they call it. Where is Kellex getting their people?"

"No idea. Maybe they don't know either. They opened by asking if I knew anybody else they could hire. Your committee must've gotten a good chunk of money for them."

Urey nodded. "It was an insider deal, with help from the War Department. Plus that Brit guy Peierls."

"Really? He didn't say anything to me about it." Karl wondered how a guy with a loudmouth wife could be involved in diplomacy.

"Seems Peierls brought with him a letter from Churchill. He went straight to the White House with it, turns out. That got 'em this extra money. Plus, he offered to ship us some good people to help. Some are Germans, even, who got out in time."

"Like who?"

"Never heard of 'em, but he said one was really sharp, could come to Columbia."

"I want to stay here too, and push the centrifuges. Nuts to this California idea, and diffusion. Okay?"

Urey smiled. "Glad you didn't like 'em at Kellex. I had to send you for an interview, part of the deal. The German? Name is Klaus Fuchs."

2.

October 15, 1941

Karl walked from the train in the lush, fragrant air of the old South. The bus station right beside the tracks had a long gray bus idling and he noticed the whites were in front, the blacks in the rear. He could sense a difference already in the very air of the South, a region that deserved its capital letter.

A ticket taker told him the university was an easy walk, so he strolled down a street of old brick buildings and small diner-style places wedged between, smelling of fried food. The movie theater was showing a Laurel and Hardy, *Great Guns,* with big posters. Admission, forty cents. Below the sign was a smaller one: COLORED ADMISSION, 20 CENTS, SEATING UPSTAIRS.

The University of Virginia had a grand prospect laid out by Thomas Jefferson, a reminder of a greater past. Arcades connected buildings around the vast sweep of the central lawn, embraced by curving brick walls that surrounded the campus, giving a reverent hush to his approach to a pantheon-like rotunda. He wondered if the looming, independent pavilions, formally arrayed in a neoclassical composition, were an analogue for the federal union as Jefferson saw it—self-governing states working together for the common national good. In any case, it set him at ease.

For two days he had been down to Oak Ridge in Tennessee to get an idea of the electrical capacity there, and how to arrange a huge centrifuge array. It was a nexus of the Tennessee Valley dams FDR built to invigorate the area. Now he looked forward to seeing some results from the lab here, also funded by the Uranium Committee. He had joyfully called home to wish Martine a happy birthday, her second. Her tinkling laugh rang through the fuzzy telephone connection.

Karl made his way along quiet walks shaded by oak trees, savoring the birdcalls and soft rub of moisture. All this calm jerked away when he saw men pacing around the Engineering Department lab in blue-gray uniforms, carrying old World War I rifles with fixed bayonets. Karl approached close enough to see that their arms carried Virginia Protective Force badges, some kind of state guard. He stopped, wondering what to do, when a big man came out of another Engineering Department building and hailed him. Karl realized that in his suit he was conspicuous among the casually ambling undergraduates.

"Hi there—Karl, right? I'm Jesse Beams. Got your questions. Good ones. Got some answers, too." The broad-shouldered man was affable, relaxed, but not when he discussed his first love—centrifuges.

"We're sure happy your Dr. Urey handed us the money to try out my ideas. Mighty glad to get it, I assure you." Beams's eyes were quick, analytical, belying his soft, rounded vowels. "I couldn't get enough industrial support to do this magnetic suspension idea the right way."

They went into a big, barnlike laboratory made of broad wood planks. Beams brought out his staff and students, who formed up in lines like soldiers. Perhaps they already knew more than they should, and thought of themselves as in the war effort. Maybe beneath these broad oaks they sensed the immense carnage sapping lives every day.

Karl had learned to keep quiet when engineers threw their chests out and launched into their birdsongs. Normally inarticulate, they would trill and soar when singing of their dreams. Beams had designed a strong magnetic field to serve as a frictionless bearing, to let centrifuges spin faster.

Beams introduced his students and staff and showed Karl a cross section of the bearing, standing in air. The steel spindle stood on its invisible magnetic base, secured at the top with a twin magnetic clasp. Beams urged Karl to touch it, and he could not budge the steel rod out of place. Then Beams hit a switch and the vertical spindle spun up, hurling its crossbeam rotor around at such speeds that it was quickly a gray blur.

"Impressive," Karl said. "How about in a vacuum?"

"Gotcha!" Beams smiled. He flicked another switch as his staff watched, faces alive with anticipation. Karl realized he was the visiting bigwig, representing Urey and the Uranium Committee, their funding source.

A tall centrifuge he had not even noticed began spinning up with a high, shrill whine. It was inside a bigger metal cylinder with windows into the lit interior. A vacuum pump labored away to keep air out. They had the rig properly shielded by big stacks of sandbags. The story of the Columbia explosion had spread. Beams asked him about that as they followed the big centrifuge's spin-up on an oscilloscope. "How bad was it?"

"Knocked us down pretty well," Karl said. Southerners tended to clip the articles off sentences, and sometimes the subjects as well, so he followed suit. "Ended up on the floor, some cuts, no hearing. Deaf as a post for a day or so."

They all nodded sagely. Karl had brought a report from the big-time battlefield of science.

The centrifuge was running now with a thin, cutting sound that he imagined was like a million screaming insects. That image came to him because in Jesse Beams's lab there were pesky flies that buzzed by his ears and pricked at his neck. He focused on the oscilloscope and saw that Beams was running the rotor at speeds a lot higher than the Columbia lab had managed. This "spinner" was broader, taller, and had none of the little rattles he was used to.

"Can you try hex in it?" Karl said mildly.

"Got to do that, yes. I'll be glad to! We can talk over all the connections and joints, the flow points—you sent a pretty big set of requirements."

Talk they did. Beams had a natural feel for engineering that Karl could admire but never copy. He had picked up some skills from the Columbia engineers, but their worldview was not his. Intricacy, detail, pattern were second nature to him. He was somewhat hands-on in a chemical lab and could frame a decent differential equation, but the spiderweb of tradeoffs in making a working machine was another country, with a language all its own.

He had a long, lazy dinner with Beams and his large, somewhat raucous family. There was cool bourbon and branch water before, southern fried chicken for the main course, and pecan pie to finish. Somehow this first immersion in the soft southern style reassured him that these people could solve the puzzles of fast spinners. He knew there was no logic to this, but he could read the competence of the Beams group through the many little details that made all the difference.

Over an after-dinner drink, he told Beams that Westinghouse and now Union Carbide stood in the wings to build hundreds of them, if not thousands—centrifuges that could spin hard and fast for weeks and months and years if necessary, ganged together. All to harvest a dark black metal that until now had been mostly used to color ceramics. Assemble the rare kind, the U-235, into a sphere weighing as much as a small woman, and it could flatten a major city.

At his small hotel he got some follow-up details from Urey in a tightly worded but long telegram. He read it before falling asleep.

The British effort proved to be ahead of the Columbia work, plus they had the Churchill letter to spur FDR. The president had somehow gotten the uranium work in under the Lend-Lease funding, though it made no logical sense; but much in Washington, DC, these days didn't, Karl thought.

The Uranium Committee was now reorganized. A new Office of Scientific Research and Development was created by executive order of the president as the center for the application of science to national defense. Urey was a member of its Section on Uranium, given responsibility for uranium isotope separation by any methods that worked. He still had to compete with Dunning, though, who favored pushing the hex through some hypothetical membrane that could stand up to the punishment.

Karl got up in the morning and worked with Beams through the day, liking the man and his deft, sure methods. They had pork chops with a luscious brown gravy for lunch, with a mellow zest he had never tasted before. He got on the train at five p.m. to head back home and the ticket taker whispered to him, "Get on back, now, to Jew York."

The man was thin, maybe in his fifties, a scarecrow in his worn uniform. The eyes were narrow, black, the face hard.

The man's slithering, thin voice slapped him back into the real world. Millions like Karl were facing this all over Europe and Russia now. Karl sighed and cast a dry gaze at the ticket taker. "Grow up."

◆　◆　◆

Urey filled Karl in later on the British angle. He had gone to Washington to ferret out the story. Dr. and Mrs. Peierls were the second ones to come. Next a Marcus Oliphant flew to the United States, ostensibly to discuss a radar program, but actually to find out why the United States was ignoring the MAUD Committee's findings.

"What the hell?" Karl fumed.

Urey leaned back, feet on desk, a hole in his shoe sole again, and said, "The minutes and reports had been sent to Lyman Briggs, the director of the Uranium Committee, and Churchill was puzzled to receive no comment. Marcus Oliphant called on Briggs in Washington, only to find out that this inarticulate and unimpressive man had put the reports in his safe and had not shown them to our committee. So he went back, amazed and distressed. Churchill sent an outraged letter to Roosevelt's people—all out of official channels. That shook up things plenty."

Karl found this hard to believe. Urey said, "Welcome to reality. The Brits sent us a later report too. Their intelligence people say there's talk at the Kaiser Wilhelm Institute of a new term, *Urantrennarbeit*. It means how much uranium they can get from a practical working machine."

"I have suspicious about Mrs. Peierls."

Urey nodded. "So do others. They'll keep watch on her."

"So the Germans are sprinting ahead. We don't have a working machine, not yet."

"We will. Back to work." Urey waved him away. Karl was relieved to have brought up Mrs. Peierls, only to find others had it covered. He did not like suspecting people. Maybe Americans were more innocent about others than Europeans?

Anton waved at the field of the Yankees and said, "So explain. I want understand national pastime."

"The Red Sox hate the Yankees," Karl said, "and that's why the noise is so loud. It's mutual." Then he detailed the rules as the Yankee pitcher struck out three Sox in a row.

When the Yankees were up, Karl said, "See the Sox catcher? Name's Moe Berg. One of the few Jews in baseball, and he even played on an all-star team. Can't hit well, though." He sat back and waved to the hot dog guy, having exhausted nearly all the knowledge he had gotten from a guy in the Columbia machine shop the day before.

"Your Babe Ruth was Sox once, I hear?"

"They traded him to the Yankees before the World War and haven't won a series since." There went the last of the lore he could remember. He handed Anton a hot dog slathered with mustard. When he bit into his, the greasy joy of it reminded him of boyhood and long, lazy summers with his father. That brought a pang; he seldom recalled his dad now as he moved through his focused days. He had been gone over a decade. Karl wondered what Joseph would have thought of these terrible days.

Anton's smiling immersion in the national pastime brought a joy into a part of Karl he had not felt in years. Something beyond the simple pleasure of family. Anton had become like a son.

Moe Berg came up to bat two innings later and struck out. The crowd around them, Yankee fans, cheered. Moe threw a scowl in their direction, then removed his cap and bowed. That got a laugh.

One morning, walking to work, Karl saw Leo Szilard coming out of the entrance of the Pupin Physics Laboratories. The man who had first envisioned a sustained nuclear fission reaction came striding toward him in short, stabbing steps. Szilard was half a block away on 120th Street, making for Broadway, head down and apparently thinking. He wore a steel-gray three-piece suit. Karl noticed a man in a brown suit and broad-brimmed hat step out of an alcove and quite deliberately fall into step behind Szilard, twenty meters back, making a note in a small book as he set off. Karl was a block away and instinctively stepped into an alley. In the purr of traffic, nobody noticed him.

Szilard went by, still ferociously staring at the pavement, and his tail man followed, eyes on Szilard's back—until Szilard whirled around, arms spread. Karl was close enough to hear Szilard say, "We meet again! Let's have a coffee, yes?"

The tail stopped, startled. Szilard stepped up, shook the man's hand. "I know you follow me, see what I do. Why not I fill you in, as you Americans say, so your notes will be better?"

The tail stood paralyzed, then slowly nodded. They went off to a coffee shop. Karl admired Szilard's open audacity with the security blanket that had fallen around their work. He started back to the Pupin Labs, smiling at a story he could tell Marthe.

"Rabbi, Columbia University does not take any 'commission' for negotiating these patents," Szilard said carefully. They were sitting in Rabbi Kornbluth's study, genteelly sipping tea. The chairman of physics, George Pegram, sat beside Karl, eyes a bit puzzled but staying quiet, letting Szilard carry the ball.

"Then why this ten percent fee?" Kornbluth demanded. He was proving a hard-nosed negotiator, Karl thought.

"Those are legal fees, one time only." Szilard cast an appealing look at the chairman of the physics department, but got no help. "If the program goes to full production of centrifuges, using the patents the Fermi team and this Beams fellow developed—well, naturally, you will get further royalties."

Karl felt out of place. He sat beside Rabbi Kornbluth because he had helped interest the man, but he had no great concern about the first payoff from the scheme. "I should point out that with the Beams team results, this magnetic ball bearing, the efficiency has greatly increased. You profit from *all* uses of that. All."

Kornbluth cast his skeptical gaze over all faces in the room, a tactic Karl had noticed worked well. Everyone seemed to sit up a bit straighter when the rabbi considered them. "I want to be sure civilian industrial methods are being pursued too. My investors did not really contemplate just war work."

"The money is the same, I would think," the chairman said.

Kornbluth gave them his measured scowl. "These documents just incidentally allow Westinghouse and Union Carbide to make as many of these spinning machines as they like."

"You implicitly agreed to that in your original funding," the chairman said.

"We never thought—"

"It could move so fast?" Karl said quickly. "But that just means you get royalties sooner, on what we might as well admit is a very good payoff for your group."

"I am obligated to protect their interests," Kornbluth said mildly, giving Karl a gimlet eye that seemed to say, *Support me, you're a Jew.*

Karl had always disliked that kind of clannishness, but he compromised by staying silent.

"Believe me," Szilard said with a reassuring pat on the rabbi's knee, "this could be a very good thing for your group. We are considering building large plants, filled with these devices."

And you might just save millions from the Nazis, Karl thought. But as usual, it was smarter not to get out ahead of the parade. But how else to lead it?

Intelligence knew that the center for some nuclear work was the Kaiser Wilhelm Institute in Berlin, founded by Peter Debye, a famous physicist, as director. The Nazis kept pressure on the Nobelist Max Planck to oust Jews who worked there. Word about this got out through Switzerland.

Szilard told the story. "Debye was naive, but he was smart enough to get out in 1939. So Albert Speer, Hitler's can-do man, turned to Werner Heisenberg to oversee the project. Heisenberg is an easy target for the Nazis, with a big ego and the insecurity that hides behind it."

"You know these people well," Karl said carefully.

"Well enough to know their limits, yes." Szilard smiled without mirth. "Planck feels he has to carry on his duty to Germany, so he takes some nominal interest, though it is not his field. Once at an official gathering he had to try three times before he could force himself to say 'Heil Hitler' in a whisper. The Nazis wanted Debye as director to rename the institute, but he knew they wouldn't approve of giving it Planck's name. So he had 'Planck' carved into the stone over the entrance. The Nazis didn't like that, either. Ordered to remove it, Debye covered it with a wooden plank—a pun that works in both German and English."

3.

December 7, 1941

"You're working too hard," Marthe said while she cleaned up food their burbling daughter had spilled. Martine babbled in her wobbly French. They had elected to introduce English in a year or so more.

Karl looked up from his notepad. He had stayed up late working again. They had finished breakfast at noon, but now the baby demanded more, a good sign. "I think well at night, but sometimes I dream up new calculations, so—"

"You take Sunday morning to work them out, yes. I know there is more pressure on you. These military people, they demand more and more."

"Mostly more paperwork. Every day brings signs of the program moving from research, straight into the engineering and construction phases. So I squeeze in some thinking on weekends."

Their attempt to arouse the government to the military potential of uranium fission had finally succeeded. The chain reaction group at Columbia, headed by Fermi and Szilard, was moving to the University of Chicago. Karl would miss working with Fermi. Szilard was staying, though.

"It is affecting our love life."

"You didn't think so"—he paused; how long had it been?—"last . . . Tuesday."

"That was the week before last," she said dryly.

"Oh. Uh . . ." A knock on their door saved him from his own confusion.

Marthe gave him an eye roll and a wry twist of her well-lipsticked mouth—she had planned romance when Martine went down for her nap, he saw—and flung open the door with impatience. "Ah! Rae!" His mother's mouth worked, eyes anxious.

"I came right over to see what you thought of all this, Karl."

"Uh, what?"

"Don't you listen to the radio?"

"Slept late. What's up?"

"The Japs have bombed Pearl Harbor."

Karl rummaged through his geographical memory. "Which is . . ."

Rae shot back, "In Hawaii! They've bombed *us!*"

In the next hour the radio played Roosevelt's short speech over several times, followed by excited coverage of the damage from a broadcaster on the ground near the navy docks. Marthe observed wryly, "And after we shipped them all that oil and scrap iron too."

Karl caught her sense and laughed. "You're always ahead of us on politics."

Rae frowned sternly. "This is war, not politics."

"War happens when politics fails," Marthe said.

Rae sighed. "So now we're in for the whole *tzuris.*"

They spent the bulk of the afternoon walking, witnessing the aimless energies that ricocheted in the streets and the parks. Excited chatter, cars grinding gears, boys running underfoot, blustering hot-eyed arguments on street corners, plenty of noisy business in bars reeking of sawdust and beer. Everyone wanted to *do something*, but Sunday was a day designed for leisure. Nobody could volunteer. They watched an argument between two young black men about the army versus the marines that turned into a fistfight. The stench of burning oil somewhere blended with a smell of anxiety. Some knots of men were even smiling.

Once Rae had gone and Martine was asleep, Karl talked to Marthe about what this might mean. He described how the centrifuges were proceeding, how he might have to travel more.

"You are not tempted?" Marthe asked hesitantly.

"Uh, by what?"

"Volunteering."

Marthe's father was a French army officer, now staying on a farm in the south of France, out of the action. Marthe's infrequent letters from her parents made it clear that her father disliked de Gaulle and would not work for Vichy, either, so he had opted out. Still, her upbringing was in the military culture.

"Not really."

"My father was at Verdun in the Great War."

"And nearly killed, as I recall."

He thought. Millions of Americans would soon march off for foreign ports they could not find on a map. No rifle would lie idle, no gap in the ranks, if he did not volunteer. He was more effective against the Germans and Japanese with a slide rule and a pencil than he would be with a rifle. *Just look how you did in that soccer game. . . .*

"It could be a great adventure for you." She said this slowly, as if thinking it through for the first time. "Men like war. You heard the excitement in the streets today."

This surprised him. He had never thought of war as adventure, but maybe he should. He paused before saying, "When the bugles blow, the drums play. . . . Nope, this is a panzer war, a technology war. I'm more good here."

He had expected a flicker of disapproval, but instead she beamed. "Before Rae came through the door, I was going to say that Martine and I need more of your time. We'll get none if you go off to war."

"Then why ask . . . ?"

"I reverted to being my father's daughter. Support the fighting man—I got that from my mother. But I am not that now. I am your wife. A woman with an odd husband."

In the end, he knew, this was not a matter of rational calculation. It was about what felt right. A small part of him sent a sardonic thought. *About my feelings, my emotions—me, me, me?* But he suppressed that, too. "How odd?"

"Always thinking, calculating. Feeling, yes, but not speaking of it."

He tried to rescue this day with a mathematical joke. "I'm pretty complex, but then most are. Maybe I'm odd, but at least I'm not a square. I'm rational, positive—"

She put a hand on his open mouth. "Stop. *Arrête.*" And kissed him.

4.

February 3, 1942

Ernest Lawrence had made the trip from California with big news. He was known worldwide for his "atom smashing" particle accelerators and had snagged the 1939 Nobel Prize for the work done at his UC Berkeley Radiation Laboratory. He was tall, with a subtly commanding bearing that made you listen to his flat, midwestern voice. Karl watched him unveil a new element, with slides, data, equations.

They had built up the brand-new element by bombarding the element neptunium, heavier than uranium, with neutrons, hoping they would stick. The neutrons did, and then threw off an electron, leaving a new thing on Earth, element 94.

"I remind you that uranium was named for the planet Uranus, and the next element up, neptunium, for Neptune. We considered the name 'plutium,' but later thought that it did not sound as good as 'plutonium.' We chose the letters 'Pu' as a joke—you know, the sound you make when something stinks."

Lawrence paused, but the joke fell flat. "Okay . . . Alternative names we considered were 'ultimium' or 'extremium' because we think maybe this is as far as anybody can go in building new elements, just by hitting them with slow neutrons, the way we did."

He showed slides of plutonium's nuclear decay modes, and Szilard asked, "You are to publish this?"

"I didn't do the primary work here. The guys who did—well, they decided to call back their paper from *Physical Review*."

A stir in the audience. "Because of security issues?" Urey asked.

Lawrence nodded. "They already had it accepted, but the phone rang. It was the government, the army. A general, no less."

"This plutonium," Karl asked, "you're sure it decays like uranium, spits out enough neutrons?"

"Like you guys found with uranium? You bet. That's why we're not talking. Except to you guys, of course."

"So there's another path to a bomb," Szilard murmured. Everyone in the room found this encouraging, Karl saw. Smiles and congratulations all round.

He didn't feel that way. *Another damned element!* This new fissionable nucleus could split their effort, slow the hard-won momentum of the program. But the physicists found such discoveries inherently exciting. He realized that most of this audience, men and women alike, was focused on the physics. He was focused on the war.

Edward Teller stopped Karl in a basement corridor and thrust a paper at him. "Look, Bohr sent this by courier."

It was a rough drawing of a rectangle. There were round cylinders partly embedded in the rectangle. An arrow showed that the cylinders could move in and out.

Teller said, "Bohr says that Heisenberg showed this to him, on a visit to Denmark. What do you think?"

Karl had worked with Fermi enough to see that it was a sketch of a nuclear reactor with many control rods. He said so.

Teller's mouth twisted, his eyes narrowed. "What did Heisenberg intend to say with this?"

"Maybe just 'Look, this is what we're trying to build. You'll recognize that this is a reactor, not a bomb.'"

Teller considered this, shuffling his feet. "If so, he overestimated Bohr's knowledge of atomic power. Bohr says he doesn't know what it is, wonders if we do."

Karl studied the sheet. "Pretty crude. Maybe he was trying to get Bohr to be a messenger of conscience?"

Teller gave an exasperated snort. "Szilard said that when I showed him. He thinks Heisenberg wanted Bohr to persuade us to refrain from working on a bomb."

Karl chuckled. "Send it up the 'command chain,' as they call it these days. Then forget it. Nobody's going to stop this, now that we've got some momentum. Plus more money from Kornbluth's investors."

Urey paused outside the apartment of Rabbi Elon Kornbluth and said, "Look, pretend you don't know what's going on. These guys, the investors, they had to sign off on the patent payoff, so they're grateful. But they don't know why they're getting rich."

"Rich?" Karl was mystified.

"Their attorney held out for a lot of money to let Westinghouse make full, free use of the centrifuge patents. Plus, Columbia was in on the deal and saw their chance. The military, they needed to work with Westinghouse and farm out some centrifuge work to other companies. Big kerfuffle. It got messy, so the army solved it by buying the patents outright."

"That's what this party is about?"

"They want to thank you. They want to know what's up, who needs centrifuges this much, and they'll ask you. Say nothing."

"That's easy. I know nothing."

They went in, and six men in tailored business suits rose to greet them, clapping their hands. Karl was startled; Urey beamed. Rabbi Kornbluth pressed glasses of sweet wine into their left hands as they used their right hands to shake those of the investors, who peppered them with compliments. Kornbluth now sported a beard to match his brush mustache of thick gray hair, giving him more authority as he swept through a tribute to the vast financial insight of one Karl Cohen.

For the next hour, amid the thick rugs and burnished oak paneling, they plied Karl and Urey with darting questions. How had Karl known there would be such a demand for industrial centrifuges? It must be related to the war, yes? Maybe a new way to make food for the troops? Or something more . . . important, say?

Karl hated the cloying sweet wine that somehow managed to be worse than the horrible Manischewitz. He managed to look like he was sipping it as he nodded, smiled, and dodged questions. Urey artfully got them to believe in the food idea, complimenting the astute businessmen on their insight. Karl found a way to hide his wineglass behind the Torah scroll open on its mahogany stand. Soon they were back on the street.

"How much did they make on the deal?" Karl asked as they headed for the subway amid honking traffic.

"Better than ten to one," Urey said merrily. "A million! Your tax dollars at work."

"Seems like war profiteering."

"Hell, I'd have put some of my leftover Nobel money into it, but it would be a conflict of interest."

Karl thought, *So going to Kornbluth, the Jewish money, may have made all the difference....* "Something's up, isn't it?"

Urey stopped at a newsstand to buy an afternoon edition of the *Times* and some chewing gum. He was a demon for war news. "You bet. They've decided upstairs"—a lift of eyebrows to mean Washington—"to go hot and heavy with centrifuges. It's cheaper in the long run to own the patents, then do more engineering to improve on them. Don't have to go back to the original patent holders that way, every time you want to add a grommet."

Karl stopped walking. "What happened?"

"There's a military head of the whole thing, now, about to get officially crowned. He listened to all sides, in a big meeting we had about which paths to follow. He mulled it over, decided. He's a quick type."

"He should be. The Germans have surrounded Stalingrad. If they—"

Urey held up his hands. "I know. Look, Karl, I can't tell you what the big guys above me are thinking. But your little speech at that Dunning talk helped."

"How?" Karl could barely recall that.

"There was a guy who liked your points."

"The one in the back. Big guy."

"Yep."

"Who is he?"

"You'll meet him in time." Urey chuckled and went down the subway steps.

PART IV

THE MANHATTAN ENGINEER DISTRICT

Leslie Groves's ID

I'm very well acquainted, too, with matters mathematical,
I understand equations, both the simple and quadratical,
About binomial theorem I'm teeming with a lot o' news,
With many cheerful facts about the square of the hypotenuse.
I'm very good at integral and differential calculus;
I know the scientific names of beings animalculous:
In short, in matters vegetable, animal, and mineral,
I am the very model of a modern Major-General.
—Gilbert and Sullivan, *The Pirates of Penzance*

1.

November 22, 1942

Oak Ridge was a sea of mud.

Sticky, rank, turd-brown. The entire valley had been churned up and buildings slapped down in hasty fashion. On good advice, Karl had worn heavy rubber boots, and so made his way down slippery pathways to the construction shack center, a series of Quonset huts with rippled galvanized steel skins. He paused outside one, sniffing smells new to him. This was another part of the old South, leafy and hilly, awash in fragrances of rich loam. Teams labored to tilt up walls of fresh nailed pine, trucks and tractors roared. The war was pulling people out of their comfortable niches and thrusting them into the world. Maybe that would have a good effect.

Plywood walls sealed the ends of the tubular huts, and the floor inside was pressed wood smelling of adhesive fumes. Inside, Karl caught inquiring glances from men who were taking their seats in the pocket auditorium.

On the report board was a single name: BRIGADIER GENERAL LESLIE RICHARD GROVES JR. The man himself was pacing on the platform, impatient to get started.

Karl stopped, staring. It was the man who had sat in the back of a Dunning seminar. He was big, his khaki uniform fresh, muscular in shoulders and stomach, face stern and focused. Karl recalled that Groves's experience overseeing the building of the Pentagon had led to his getting this project leadership.

Karl and Marthe had read about the appointment in the *Times*. There had been a picture, but somehow Karl had not made the connection. Now here the man was. When she read about Groves, Marthe had said, smiling, "So you're not in the army but are working for a general anyway." Karl had not even chuckled.

Karl took a seat, and Groves began the meeting at ten a.m. sharp. Then the general sat beside a card table with something on it, beneath a draped cloth. Karl ignored the first logistics discussions droning on in jargon-packed sentences from some colonels. Minutes crawled by. Logistics did not bear on why he was here—to see the first big centrifuge plant. The Uranium Committee was now cryptically called S-1, a disguise for security purposes, with a pyramid of offices and executives—meaning, layers of paperwork. Karl tried to keep his distance from all that.

The eighty million dollars allocated focused on Oak Ridge's sprawl, under construction now. The project's goal was a hundred grams of U-235 a day. That would take a year to attain, Karl estimated, since the first building was just now lurching into operation. He and Urey had worked through the complicated network necessary to make a kilogram of highly pure U-235, long weeks of work—and found it demanded forty thousand centrifuges, at a cost of about a hundred million dollars. "A lot of battleships," Urey had remarked.

Then Groves rose and in a flat baritone said, "The president pressed this job on me because I built this in less time than anybody thought." With a quick turn he snatched the cloth from the table, revealing a huge cake with white icing. Everybody rose to get a view. Karl saw it was shaped like the Pentagon. *Something of a showman . . .*

"My staff just gave me this, kind of a tribute, I guess. You guys can have it after this meeting. Me, I don't much like cake."

This got a laugh and everyone relaxed, and sat back down. Groves said, "We're calling this project S-1, but informally, in-house, it's already got the name of Manhattan Project. But I'm headquartering it here, where the heavy lifting has to be done."

Well done, Karl thought ruefully, *since the right path started in Manhattan. . . .* And now the work at Columbia outflanked the methods the British thought would work better.

Groves discarded his brusquely jovial face and put on a scowl, hands on hips. "I have already participated in the selection of sites for research and production here at Oak Ridge, plus others to come in Washington State and New Mexico. I shall direct the enormous construction efforts there. I made the critical decisions on the various methods of isotope separation as well—hence this centrifuge plant, with more to come. The Tennessee Valley Authority is the best site, with under-used electrical power capacity. All this we will call the Clinton Engineer Works, period—nothing to give away what we're doing."

Groves paused, eyeing the officers. He held them just long enough to let some tension build; then his face went stern.

"This is *not* a standard army project. We're building something, but we don't have a blueprint. We have to work with the scientists—not a disciplined bunch, I can tell you." This brought a wave of laughter. Karl smiled. Groves ignored the laughs, though he smiled. "Get this straight. I shall direct the acquiring of raw materials, especially uranium. As well, I will supervise the collection of military intelligence on the German bomb program, which seems well ahead of ours. We've got to keep this tightly secret! We will also take countermeasures against their intelligence gathering. All these are my charge, gentlemen, directly from the president. Questions?"

"What's going on at the other places?" a voice down front called.

"You will learn that only on a need-to-know basis," Groves shot back. "Let me be clear about the size of this project. During the first week that I was on duty here, I could not walk out of my office and down the corridor without being assailed by officers, or worse, by civilian engineers with liaison responsibility for various jobs. It is no exaggeration that during this period decisions involving up to five hundred thousand dollars apiece were made at the rate of about one every hundred feet of corridor walked."

This got a loud laugh. Karl joined in as he realized that the day-to-day decisions Groves faced would go beyond the abilities of any scientist he knew, easily. Groves went on, "This job will get still bigger—and fast. Through it all, I will ruthlessly protect the project from other government agency interference."

"What's this we hear about New Mexico?" Same questioner.

"That's a possibility for a different aspect of S-1." Groves gestured to a man in the front row, who stood. He was thin with a crew cut and was smoking a pipe. "Dr. Oppenheimer and I are taking a train right away, to scope it out."

"He's a theory guy, right?" someone called.

"Yes, I think it's smart to have at least one guy who understands this stuff."

This fetched general laughter. Oppenheimer bobbed his head modestly and sat as Groves boomed out, "We're pursuing a couple different ways to do this. The stuff about 'atomic piles' is maybe right, and we can produce the—well, let's call it the 'bang stuff,' because there are different things that can make a bomb. Different things you slam together, I mean. Oppenheimer will look at those, see how to get it done."

Karl stood, and Groves looked toward him. "Sir, can't we focus on the project running here—the centrifuges? We can concentrate our work, not let it get spread out."

A military man expected the "sir," Karl knew. Groves blinked, thinking this through. "With two approaches, we can maybe find the least expensive way to do it, see."

"What does the war cost every day?"

Groves was not used to this kind of question, Karl saw. He said slowly, "I hadn't thought of it like that. We finish fast, we save money."

"Lives, too," someone said.

Karl knew that every day now the war was burning what this whole project might cost, in total. He had made the estimates from standard economic data and federal budgets. Nailing a fact like that to Groves's chest was not smart, though. Let him think it through.

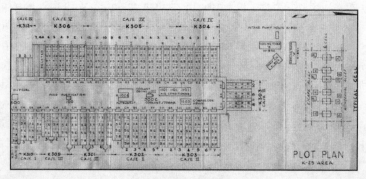

Plot Plan K-25

✦ ✦ ✦

Detailed talks came next. Karl sat through the lamp-lit visuals of the even bigger centrifuge plants to come. The largest was to be called K-25, in keeping with the project-imposed subterfuge of meaningless numbers and letters. Each little square was a coordinated suite of centrifuges, with myriad pipes and wires.

The complexity of it all numbed the mind. To Karl these were like neurons in a monomaniac brain, perpetually thinking whirring thoughts and spitting out steady streams of U-235, "tube alloy" in security-speak, measured in grams per day. Drudge work.

K-25 would be the world's most gargantuan building when fully built out, covering fifty acres and strumming with the high-pitched shrieks of tortured metal all day, every day, through the year or more that a single warhead would take. Artillery shells demanded mountains of copper, so K-25's wires were of silver, over ten thousand tons (kilotons, as Karl had learned to say) of it, straight from Fort Knox. This fact, too, was an ever deeper secret, to prevent pilfering of the wiring.

The tour of the world's very first centrifuge plant drew few from the meeting. They had mostly seen it and all had heavy workloads, and so scurried back to their offices. Karl was here, sent by Urey, to observe and advise, so he walked a few paces behind General Groves and kept silent.

The trim steel walls and thick power lines stood out among the green Tennessee hills that soon enough would be covered in housing for the thousands about to pour in here. All around these sleepy valleys, US marshals were tacking notices to vacate on farmhouse doors, and construction contractors were rumbling in.

Inside the long plant, centrifuges were running in gangs of twenty, their shrill whine unnerving. Everybody wore earplugs. The whirring centrifuges were nearly man-size cylinders, with tubes running out top and bottom, sandbags stacked on top to dampen vibration, water running down the sides to cool them. Karl knew the layout by heart, had worked on blueprints and fluid lines for months, but seeing it in its noisy majesty was still a thrill.

"You're the centrifuge guy, right?"

The question came out of nowhere for Karl, who was tracing the complex weave of piping around the centrifuge racks. He turned to see the question came from Groves, with other officers standing behind the big man, whose belly bulged over his belt.

"Uh, yes. I'm with Urey at Columbia." He started to put out his hand, thought better of it, and said, "Karl Cohen, sir."

"Sharp question you just asked in there. I saw you do that at Columbia, too." A quick smile. "Helped me make up my mind. Gave me ammo to use in meeting with the higher-ups, the experts."

"Why didn't you identify yourself then?"

"I had the job, General Marshall gave it to me. I wanted a combat command; he said no, since I'd just built the biggest building on this continent. But—I wanted to wait until my promotion to brigadier general came through. I figured you scientists would have more respect for a brigadier than some recently promoted colonel."

Karl didn't know the import of this and doubted that people like Fermi and Teller did either, but he suddenly understood that Groves lived in a hierarchy that respected order and clarity. Rank mattered. Direct talk did too. This opening moment might be his best chance to make an impression and give advice that mattered. Groves liked plain speaking. So Karl ignored the tightening in his belly and said, "Ah, so you liked my money versus time argument back there?"

"Sure. Because, see, I've got a budget. It's about half what I asked for."

"The spinners here"—Karl swept his arm out—"are working pretty well. We'll know after the uranium has gone through a few thousand processing steps."

"You mean, know if we can get weapons-grade stuff out of it?"

Karl had never heard the term, but he nodded. "Once we know what that number is, precisely."

Groves snorted, eyes sharp beneath his scowl. "That's what I want to know. How to build the damn thing too, once we've got the U-235."

Karl spread his hands and gave a wry smile. "Sir, cost is one way to look at this, sure—but getting a big killer bomb to use against the Germans is more than that. They're slaughtering countless people every day."

Groves raised an eyebrow, as if already judging Karl's response to his next sentence. "People are madder at the Japs."

"They're small fry. The Germans are the deep enemy. They were well ahead of us in nuclear physics before the war started. Probably are now, too. This is a race."

Groves turned to his officers and gave them a quick, short nod. "So it is. But we've got to try any method that looks good."

"Why are you bringing in Oppenheimer? To do bomb design?"

Karl could see this direct questioning was not what a general was used to. Groves blinked and beckoned to him with a crooked finger, waving his officers aside, and the two of them walked together to a quieter part of the plant. Here, pressure gauges told of the innumerable pumps driving the system, watched by teams of mostly women wearing sensible pants and blouses, whose eyes never left the dials. Other attendants were working all along the production lines, and they stepped aside for the general. Some glanced at his rank and stiffened.

"Look, I don't want staff to hear all this," Groves said gruffly. "Don't like gossip in a command. I know you've been in on this from the beginning—I got dossiers on all you scientists, tryin' to figure you guys out." A chuckle, shaking of head. "I want Oppenheimer to see if this plutonium idea will work out. And how to build a bomb, sure. He's arguing for a place in New Mexico, some boys' school, wants me to go see it with him."

"A desert is a good place to test a big bomb."

"So I figured."

"The money you spend on plutonium—hell, we don't have enough of it to even see with the human eye now!"

Groves let his mouth relax into a wry curve, as if amused at this scientist who kept poking at him. "I know. Oppie says plutonium might be easier to make in Fermi's reactors."

"So you're building those, too?"

"You get right smack to the heart of things, don't you?" Groves gave Karl a skeptical look. "Yeah, the reactors we're putting out along the Columbia River. Big, expensive things. Modeled on the small one Fermi built in New Jersey."

"You're spreading the work all over the country?" He felt his stomach muscles tense. Groves seemed the sort who could turn against you if you questioned his assumptions. But it seemed the only way to tease out the man's thinking.

A shrug with raised eyebrows. "Plenty of electricity from the dams along the Columbia, like here. Plus room to build, like here. And senators sure like to hear about big new projects going into their state."

"I urge you to pour your funds into these spinners, sir. They're simple, we understand them. Plutonium—that's a multiple-miracle problem."

"Meaning?"

"Fermi's reactors have to work well and make plutonium, by banging neutrons into the U-238. Make a lot of it. Then plutonium has to work in a bomb. Three miracles, with the clock running."

Groves leaned against the plant's outer support wall, and Karl saw the man was tired. "I heard from a little bird that you and Urey put the kibosh on that guy Dunning's idea. What was it again?"

"Letting uranium diffuse through a wall, so the lighter U-235 gets through a bit faster."

"Huh. Sounds not so clean as your spinners out there."

"It's not. Nothing we know can stand up against the hex, either. That stuff eats up everything we've tried."

"Ummm . . ." Groves sighed, and for just a moment Karl felt for this man, besieged by bureaucratic pressures. With two stars on his shoulders, he probably didn't get much advice he could take as untainted by influence.

Groves straightened, threw back his shoulders. "Y'know, I wanted to command a division. Hit 'em in Africa, Europe. I wanted to *be* there. Once you go into the Army Service Forces—hell, no getting out."

Karl saw now the cracks in Groves's facade. The general snorted ruefully and peered at Karl. "The head of Service Forces Somervell, his appointment letter to me said, 'If you do the job right, it will win the war.' You think so?"

Karl nodded. "Einstein told me he thought it could be decisive. He understands the war better than most. Einstein told me he even saw Hitler once. Some Nazi party parade through Berlin. Einstein was coming home from his university office. The Nazis always stage their big public events in the dark, when every advertiser knows people are more easily persuaded. So Einstein looked at Hitler and vice versa, they both recognized each other. Hitler gave him a look of pure rage. Einstein was the most famous Jew in the world, and he lived in the same city as Der Führer. That's when Einstein knew he had to get out."

132

Groves frowned at this. "Wow. Really."

"So later, Einstein wrote the letter to FDR that started this. I know—I was there when he and Szilard went over the wording."

"Einstein's in on this?"

"Not really. Turned out he knew nearly nothing about nuclear physics. But he got the point."

"Really?" Groves goggled. "Einstein?"

"Scientists specialize." Karl knew he was winging this, letting his emotions out, but he could not stop. Not now. "We have to. FDR got the letter just a day after the USSR invaded Poland. The other part of the Nazi-Soviet deal. They united with the German army, about halfway across the country. That made it clear that the huge, heavily armed dictators were chewing up Europe. Roosevelt made the connection. If anyone develops this weapon, it should be the democracies. Us."

Groves stepped back, surprised. "I never heard about all this. I was busy building the Pentagon."

"Wouldn't it be nice if we knew Hitler was at home in Berlin, and we dropped a bomb so big it couldn't miss him?"

Groves brightened. "You bet. But . . . who'd be left to surrender?"

The general gazed off into space and then shook himself. He swiveled sharply and led them back into the spinner noise. Groves gestured to his officers, who were slouching around, looking at the complicated spinner arrays in puzzlement. "Attention!" The officers jumped, stood up straight, hands flying up in salutes. "This is Cohen, Karl Cohen. He and the Columbia gang worked out the plans for this plant. You got questions, ask him."

Groves turned back to Karl. "Still, Cohen, you've gotta remember in all this, an old army rule: brass outranks brains."

His men laughed, but Karl didn't. He thanked Harold Urey, who had taught him how to speak up when he really felt something. Another lesson he could carry forward.

Groves poured a water glass half-full of amber fluid and handed it to Karl. "You look like a bourbon man. Try this."

Karl sipped it, judging the mellow, heavy taste. "Um . . . smooth," he said diplomatically. He was a wine man, really, and once again knew why.

"Made locally, not legally." Groves grinned, gestured to an ordinary stiff-backed chair. The small cabin smelled of tart pine sap and odd oily fumes. Groves sat just a foot away in the bare living room of the one-bedroom shack.

"Couldn't they give you—"

"Better quarters? Sure, but people think I'm enough of a blowhard already." Groves winked, slugged back half his glass. "I thought I'd have a sit-down with you, show you this—"

He pitched a transparent plastic envelope from a side table into Karl's lap. Inside was a flat lump of yellow clay.

"That's from a mine in the Congo called 'Shinkolobwe.' It means 'the fruit that scalds' in whatever language they use there."

Karl felt heat on his thighs and tossed the envelope to Groves. "Yellowcake—so rich you can feel it!"

Groves laughed. Karl guessed this was not the first time he had played this trick. Still, he managed a grin. "So that's the source of our starter uranium?"

"Got it! Sixty-five percent uranium—best ever found." Groves snapped his fingers and a broad grin spread across his face. "Those Congo guys painted their bodies with it, did ceremonial dances—never knew they were getting a dose."

Karl sat back. "How did we get—?"

"Turns out, it was Einstein. He wrote to the queen mother of Belgium, for Chrissake!"

Groves got up, added bourbon to his glass, and gestured to Karl, who shook his head. *Best to just listen here. He wants to talk.* He recalled Einstein saying something about the queen mother, and Urey had mentioned that the Congo was the world's best source of starter uranium. The world was moving all around him, forces aligning, from the genius to the poor men who worked a mine that poisoned them, all in a looping chain of ever-greater complexity, a spaghetti of timelines....

"So Einstein sets it up with one goddamn letter! Gotta admire that guy. So that's how we locked up the Congo supply, bingo. We're flying it in on Pan American Clippers, the only air service there."

Karl thought as he waved away Groves's next offer of the bourbon bottle. The Pan Am Clippers hearkened back to the nineteenth-century clipper ships and were the only American passenger aircraft in intercontinental travel. To compete with ocean liners, the airline offered first-class seats and flight crews of formal attire. No leather-jacketed, silk-scarved airmail pilots, the crews of the Clippers wore naval-style uniforms and adopted a set procession when boarding the aircraft. "Sending uranium freight on a passenger plane?"

Groves nodded, frowned. "Security. The Krauts have plenty of agents in Africa, and they have the Belgian company, Union Minière, with a gun to its head. But that's in Europe. They've got nobody to enforce their rules in the Congo, so they're getting their pitchblende yellowcake uranium from Czechoslovakia."

"But—on a *passenger* plane?"

"We keep things quiet that way. The Belgian Union Minière guys, they pack it in suitcases, check it through. It's down below the passengers, and the bags have heavy lining. No real radiation risk there, minimal dosage."

Karl sat back and let warm bourbon flavor swarm up into his nostrils. "But . . . as baggage . . . ?"

"There's a war on, y'know. Here, have another."

On the train back to New York, Karl sat with Fermi. The Italian had been here advising another group at Oak Ridge, working on how to build reactors. The simplest way to make the new element, plutonium, was to put uranium ore in a box and let the decay deliver neutrons, making some plutonium, proving the method.

Fermi was tired, but together they relaxed and sipped some of the Groves bourbon he had bestowed on each of them. Wistfully, Fermi recalled doing, just two years before, the hard manual labor of assembling carbon bricks for a test. The physicists on the seventh floor of Pupin Laboratories started looking like coal miners. Their wives wondered what was happening.

"We looked like honest laborers," Fermi chuckled, "real working men."

To measure how well neutrons diffused through graphite, Fermi had gotten Columbia to give him a very big room in Schermerhorn Hall. They built a big pile of graphite, which is black, and so is uranium oxide. Handling many tons of both makes people very black. Fermi asked Karl to help, and Karl did his best, but it wore him down. He couldn't think by the time he got home, so the evenings, when he often did his best work, were lost to him. It was harder to believe in serene mathematical beauties when you have dirty hands. Marthe got irked too, at having to launder his clothes just to get the black grains out. "Impossible! *Dégueulasse!*" she cried in severe French. He had to ask and learned that *dégueulasse* meant disgusting.

Then the sciences dean had noted that there was a football squad at Columbia with many husky boys, who took jobs by the hour to get themselves through college. So why not hire them? Soon Karl found himself working beside undergraduates who could lift fifty pounds without blinking an eye. They would come in after football practice, wearing their sweaty uniforms. Columbia footed their laundry bills as well.

Fermi laughed as they reminisced. "Good work. We found how many neutrons a fission spits out, about 2.3, and how far they go. Crucial information, all classified, of course. That seems like a very long while ago."

They were riding in a nearly deserted carriage, so Karl leaned forward and said softly, "How do we build the 'gadget'? Groves has Oppenheimer looking at that, but I want to think ahead, see if there's some simple way to do it."

Fermi nodded. "I have been working on building the reactors. I do not think-a, if we get plutonium from them, detonation will be simple."

"Why?"

"Plutonium reacts quicker than uranium. It will fizzle unless assembled very fast."

Fermi gave him a significant look. There was more to the issue, but Fermi could not use technical terms in a public place—even though the nearest person was a soldier sprawled asleep two seats away.

Karl nodded and thought. It had taken him weeks of working through nuclear cross-section data, then using differential equations, to explore the intricate dynamics of colliding chunks of radioactive atoms. The U-235 spit out neutrons that raced ahead of any slug driven by explosives. The angry energies housed in the U-235 communicated with each other as if you slammed two blundering masses together. They could get to a critical mass as they approached each other.

For the mechanics, he had brushed up on old courses taken while he was a rather puzzled undergraduate. He had spent endless hours with his "slippery stick" as Marthe called it, the Keuffel & Esser slide rule that was the best at scientific calculations. They were not made by earnest German engineers and craftsmen, as he had at first thought, but rather came from a factory in Hoboken. Somehow it felt better to work with a Jersey product than a German one. Once he had the principles straight, the equations worked out and double-checked, the numbers tumbled out.

Karl leaned over and in a whisper said, "I calculate that with a slug of ninety percent U-235, you could make a simple 'shotgun' bomb. Shoot a plug of U-235 into a hollow cylinder of U-235, force fast neutron production. Maybe even one percent of the bomb could convert into energy—the equivalent of tens of thousands of tons of TNT, going off all at once."

Fermi frowned. "*Si*, a 'shotgun' assembly, simplest. The Berkeley gang—Lawrence and Oppenheimer, mostly—want to use plutonium in them. Is too much of a good thing."

Karl felt the clacking train accelerate, giving them more background noise to cloak their words. "Certainly plutonium has more energy per nucleus, but what happens to it during the microseconds while the 'bullet' goes through 'the barrel' at the center of a plutonium cylinder?"

Fermi's eyes roved to the ceiling as he thought, remembering. "In my lab, we did this experiment. Take a few milligrams of plutonium and expose it in our atomic pile. I stood nearby while the operators at the big cubic atomic pile slid the exposed plutonium back out. The sample was behind lead shields, but the Geiger counter mounted on a wood table told the tale. The pile-exposed plutonium had 'seen' the uranium fissioning inside the pile, and now was spitting out alpha particles, electrons, neutrons. *Mama mia*, the entire radioactive zoo."

"That strongly?"

Fermi nodded. "It'll do that the first microsecond it charges down the barrel. The heat will stop the plutonium bullet and the whole assembly will blow apart, before we get critical mass. Of course we do not publish this."

"Damn," Karl said. "I figured that it would be a major issue, but—"

"We can make a quick shotgun device with uranium," Fermi said. "Plutonium, we'll have to be maybe a hundred times faster."

They both pondered this in silence.

Fermi said mildly, "We also had something of a scare, at a meeting with Teller and Oppenheimer and the theory gang. We were just tossing around ideas."

"Scare?"

"We were discussing whether a fission event could then give us the neutrons and energy to make hydrogen burn together—to fuse."

Karl recalled that diagram that started it all, when Bohr spoke—the curve of binding energy. At the left side, the lightest elements had an energy gain if you could slam their nuclei together. But— "That takes a hell of a high temperature."

"It does." Fermi pursed his lips. "But it could happen. Coat a fission core with heavy hydrogen, we calculated, let the fission heat it—and that could make a far more powerful weapon."

Karl was stunned. "Let's stick to just fission."

"I agree. But then Teller said, so hydrogen could work. Then why can't a fission event ignite the nitrogen in our air?"

A cold sensation swept over Karl. "Could . . . could it?"

Fermi chuckled. "We calculated it together. The large electrical repulsion between the nitrogen atoms makes it not work, after all."

Karl felt a kind of conceptual vertigo. "Thank God."

"I thought you did not believe in God." Fermi nudged him.

"I don't . . ."

"Neither do I. But I believe in the devil, and his name now is Hitler."

Karl sat in silence. *So this bomb we're working toward, it's just the starter kit for . . .* The rich southern land slid by outside as he gazed into an abyss. Fermi too caught the mood, and they sat staring into the distance.

"You are Fermi and Cohen, right?" a tall blond man said. Two men in suits had appeared and stood in the aisle, looking at them. Both were bulky, solid.

Karl and Fermi said yes. "Got ID?" the tall one asked, and the scientists showed theirs. Only a few years ago, Karl thought, he would have been insulted by such a demand.

The tall one said, "General Groves has assigned protective security to about a dozen of you key scientists. We're your team. We got on at the last stop."

Karl and Fermi were stunned. The tall one said, "We spotted you because you were using technical words. Maybe not the best place to do that talking."

Karl and Fermi nodded, reproved. The second man said to Fermi, "I am your bodyguard, Johnny Baudino. I gather your title is Excellency Fermi."

Fermi laughed. Karl was vexed. "Why this?"

"General Groves fears that assassination-as-sabotage is a real possibility, sir," the tall man said. "I'm your guard, Dr. Cohen. Eric Thompson. We're with Military Intelligence."

Karl sighed. More procedural trouble that would burn up time. He held on for another moment to what he felt now, a touch of dizzy revelation. The war had changed, off on a path few knew, but one that could be decisive. This was no longer the grinding, big-battle war the endless commentaries expected. Maybe, just maybe, a decisive weapon could end it quickly. This territory was the unknown.

So much for the freewheeling exploration of the early days. With huge stacks of money came controls, paperwork, and now guards. At least Marthe and Karl's mother would get a laugh out of this.

A week later the laughs were gone. The rules General Groves had set could have been chosen by an old-world mother for her teenage daughter.

Enrico was not to walk by himself in the evening, nor was he to drive without escort to the newly built Teaneck Laboratory twenty miles from home. Fermi had resisted efforts to move the big reactor pile to Chicago when he learned the Manhattan Project wanted him to set it up in a squash court, inside a football stadium. So the pile got built in New Jersey. It became the model for many more in Washington State. Fermi often introduced Baudino to his fellow scientists as "my colleague," saying, "Soon Johnny will know so much about the project he will need a bodyguard too."

Karl had to endure the tall Eric Thompson, walking with him going to and from work. Eric spent most of his day playing cards with Urey's bodyguard. It seemed a waste of manpower to everyone. Szilard's guy didn't like cards and instead spent his days studying for a degree in mathematics; he was a Hungarian. "I want to get something out of this war, see?" the man said.

2.

March 22, 1943

Walking home one somber day, with the wind still bitter, Karl thought about how he had gotten here. Rabbi Kornbluth's insider ability to find a hundred thousand dollars or so among a half-dozen investors had been crucial.

That sum was nothing now, but it had been critical when he and Urey had nowhere to go for even ten thousand bucks. They built from that small foundation. A decent sum for the work of the Beams team in Virginia, and more for Fermi's work, through Urey's crafty grantsmanship in Washington. Now Groves came in and decided in their favor, settling a half year of disputes among the high committee that ran the whole shebang.

And now German tank forces were advancing around Kharkov, but the Brits and Americans had overrun German tank divisions in Tunisia. The war ground on, pluses and minuses every day.

He was lucky to be in the thick of things that mattered. If he hadn't just gotten back from France with Marthe when Urey needed help, he'd now be at some chemical company, doing quality assurance or devising better industrial processes for explosives. He was a lucky man. Life was contingent, undetermined, and the big things you never saw coming.

As he came into their apartment, three-year-old Martine came squealing into his arms. He whirled her around, showered with shrieks, and they did a little dance for her to show off her footwork, better every day now. Marthe sat, heavily pregnant, enjoying the floor show and very carefully opening an onionskin letter. He went over, kissed her, nuzzled a bit. The letter was written in her mother's thin handwriting, from occupied France. Her family referred to Marthe's parents as Rama and Ripou. Ripou was a colonel in the French army, now sent back to Marseille in June 1942. He left the army, joined his wife. No word since then, an alarming silence.

"He has refused to command a prisoner compound," Marthe said. "Doesn't want to serve with the army or the Free French, either. They've gone into hiding."

"In France? How?" Karl was astounded. He had gotten on passably with his in-laws, even when they tried to block Marthe's returning to Paris from Lebanon to join him. Ripou was a stern, hard-line military type, a bit beaten up by running occupations in Lebanon and Syria. But that had kept him out of the collapse of the French in May 1941, and possibly had saved his life.

Marthe said, "By 'going to ground,' as you say in English."

"Where?"

"Grasse, just inland from the Riviera. The Vichy government is looking for him—he's a traitor in their eyes."

"What? They could try him for refusing an order?"

"No one knows what, I gather." Marthe frowned. "These Red Cross messages, only twenty-five words! But Rama wrote around in the margins."

"So they're holed up?" Somehow living on the sunny Riviera seemed not so bad, but he kept that to himself.

"With a vegetable garden, Rama says." Marthe frowned. "She says she may have tuberculosis, too."

"Damn! Anything we can do?"

Marthe gave him a wan smile. "Send a Red Cross package, perhaps."

"Hell, send them ten!"

Bureaucrats now called the program the Manhattan Engineer District, apparently to make it sound dull and discourage speculations about where so much effort was going. The name stuck, although Groves moved most of the work from Columbia and his office at 230 Broadway to Oak Ridge, and later to big reactors outside the small town of Hanford, Washington, along the Columbia River.

Eric the bodyguard was always there at Columbia University. Levels of administration grew, though mostly at Oak Ridge. The pace accelerated. Improving the centrifuges became Karl's focus.

Insights and observations from many scientists now passed before his eyes. He gave talks to larger and larger audiences of scientists and engineers. He learned to blend together work from many minds—ideas that had long since been field-stripped, sorted, and stowed in the toolbox with the serial numbers filed off. His world became one of low-leakage seals for rotating equipment, mass spectrometers for process analysis, leak detectors, circuit boards—all needed for both laboratory research and plant construction. This was not dispassionate science, no search for truth, but rather a new beast in the world—a targeted gamble to change the basic rules of warfare, by accelerating the damage levels to astronomical heights. And stop the Germans, who must be well ahead of the Allies. They had set up an entire group in Berlin when the USA effort was a dozen people at Columbia, with a budget measured in thousands of dollars.

The beginnings of all this now seemed to lie far back in the past, in a rosy, cozy world when he and Marthe had wed and the war was still only a haunting possibility. That age was gone. Now Karl worked long hours but took care to stay close to his family. He even pretended interest in Marthe's joining a knitting group that made clothes for soldiers.

Amid the steadily rising din of Manhattan, he had done well. Urey gave him a raise, and shortly after he gained the title of director of the Theoretical Division at Columbia. The title covered only the centrifuge work and Karl knew it was because Fermi didn't want to run the group. With the money he bought nine acres of mostly forested land far out in the boonies, mid-Long Island, beside a potato field. The land cost $550, and they bought it in ten installments. It frustrated him that they had to buy it under Marthe's maiden name. The Realtor had hinted strongly that this would be far easier, both with the banks and the county offices, than for a Cohen.

They spent weekends there and Eric the silent guard dutifully came along too, pitching a tent nearby in the woods. He even enjoyed it, camping and swimming when it was warm. Karl bought an old black Plymouth and used carefully hoarded gasoline ration cards to get them there. They had a log cabin brought in and planted in the middle of their plot, and a well dug. Karl had to pump the water with the manual lever, hard work, so Marthe used every drop three times: drinking and dishes, bathing, and finally, washing the floors. They used kerosene lanterns for light, as there was no electricity for many miles. The iceman came weekly with huge blocks of cloudy ice for the icebox. Still, they all liked it, a small garden oasis far from the ever-noisier concrete canyons of Manhattan.

So much destruction had descended on the world now, it echoed through every hour. At times the world seemed to be insane. The 1930s had been crazy enough, certainly; there had been wars where people could take a streetcar to the front. Now the scale was enormous and the countless dead strewn across Europe and Asia were merely the Not Present on various roll calls, their voices forever stilled. Only their deeds testified to them now. The outcome of this monstrous war was still quite unsure. The only certainty was the death count, well into the millions, and accelerating by the day.

Security worries rose steadily. General Groves was startled by a piece in *Time* magazine titled "Science Hush-Hushed," and called Karl in:

> Exploration of the atom—chief interest of physicists—has come to a stop. . . . Such facts as these add up to the biggest scientific news of 1942: that there is less and less scientific news. Technical journals are thinner by as much as 50%, and they will get more so: much of the research now published was completed a year ago before the conversion of U.S. science to wartime uses had reached all-out proportions. A year ago one out of four physicists was working on military problems; today, nearly three out of four. And while news from the world's battlefronts is often withheld for days or weeks, today's momentous scientific achievements will not be disclosed until the war's end. . . . Pure research is not secret now. In most sciences it no longer exists.

Groves tossed it on his desk. "Do you think this is a leak?"

Karl studied the story. "Just a smart reporter putting facts together." He smiled. "It's still a free country, even in a war."

The *New York Times* headline was stark:

PAN AM CLIPPER CRASHES AT LAGUARDIA
Mysterious Yellow "Dirt" in Debris
A Pan American Clipper on the African route broke open on landing at LaGuardia Field yesterday, spreading suitcases and an unidentified yellow substance across the runway.

Karl handed the newspaper back to Groves. "So the yellowcake shipment got out of hand?"

"Dummies in the Congo put it in ordinary leather suitcases." Groves grimaced and fingered his curly chestnut hair. "Uranium is heavy as hell. Screwed up the balance of the plane. The Clipper came in low. When the rear wheel came down it blew, the whole assembly fractured—blooey! Popped the whole compartment open, the plane slid all the way in. No fire, thank God. Passengers okay, but it spread luggage all over the landing strip. Ripped up the luggage. The yellowcake got out."

"How radioactive was it?"

"Recall that cake I tossed into your lap?" Groves paced his Manhattan office, his belly protruding over his brass belt buckle.

"Warm stuff, then. How many were exposed?"

"Pan Am got them off the field pronto. "Undetected, pretty much, until some-damn-body wondered why there was so much yellow everywhere. And why the army sealed off the area, scraping up the stuff. About a ton of it." Groves grimaced.

"I didn't read about that."

"The cheaper papers nailed it. We asked the *New York Times*, sure, but word got out on the newswire."

All this had escaped Karl. "What were the Geiger counter readings at the airfield?"

Groves scowled, sat back down. "Pretty bad, if we'd left people to work around there."

"So word didn't get out about what it was?"

"Not so far. We had to hose down the whole airfield to get the dose count down too. People noticed, for sure."

Karl paced, thinking. "The Germans can get the *Times*, right?"

"Yeah. So we've got to float some cover story. Any ideas?"

"Say it was a mineral used to make paint. Not really untrue, either."

Groves considered. "Sounds right, yeah. I had a team with Geiger counters cover the area. Some residual radiation, nothing big."

"It's supposed to rain tonight. That'll wash it away."

"If the *Times* gets word it's radioactive, there'll be plenty more coverage."

Karl nodded. "So ask them not to cover it."

Groves looked startled. "You think they'll do it?"

"Maybe."

"I don't like alerting newspapers that we have something vital going on here, see?" Groves shook his head. "Let's hope it dies down."

"The Germans might suspect, though, just from this story."

Groves sighed. "A chance we gotta take."

The war intruded everywhere.

He and Marthe went to see newsreels but few dramatic movies. The news was shocking, and sometimes they had to look away from the screen. But at least it was real. Hollywood had gone for patriotic schlock. Sherlock Holmes and the Invisible Man were updated and turned into Nazi hunters. Staged combat films always showed that Democratic Man was superior to the jackbooted automatons that tyranny creates. Since California had beaches, there were plenty of navy and marine assault movies. It felt odd to watch a film about this, when on the same day newspapers headlined amphibious assaults on islands hard to pronounce. Occasionally a gem came through, as when the film *Casablanca* appeared in November, just when the USA made its first direct attack on German forces with troops landing at Casablanca, North Africa. In the movie Bogart fought with quips, and in the real North Africa the US Army used tanks.

Karl had to admit the film was good, beyond its propaganda. Somehow scenes that seemed cliché nonetheless worked with quick humor and sounded sardonic notes. Marthe loved the Paris scenes, though of course they had been shot in Hollywood.

The country was changing, and they all felt it in the air. Loafing on the job had become synonymous with treason. Engineers were in more demand than infantry. Karl pledged to buy ten dollars a month of war bonds. Everyone feared the Germans were far ahead of the Manhattan Project. Fermi entertained a dinner party with a dirty physics joke he had invented. "Heisenberg, you see, he is a terrible lover. If he has the right position, he doesn't have momentum." The physicists laughed and their wives looked puzzled. Fermi went on, "And when he can find the energy, *pffft!*—he doesn't have the time."

When Karl explained this to Marthe, on the way home, she laughed dutifully. "So *this* is how you men learn your physics, eh?"

A week later Marthe was incensed. She held up a thin letter. "My cousin Pierre Malartre is in prison camp. His letter took three months to arrive—sent in January."

"From where?" Karl ran his eyes quickly over the lines, in French, on onionskin paper.

"Germany—and look." A big white sticker at the envelope's end: INSPECTED BY 8349. "They're reading our mail."

"From a war zone, an enemy country."

"I do not want them to!"

"It's a war. Better they tell you about it, at least. What's he say?"

"They had a terrible cold winter." She paused. "I wonder if we can send him food through the Red Cross."

"I think so. Look—he's alive and out of immediate danger. Sounds like good news to me."

"I hear so little from my family in France now."

He sighed. "And a big hollow silence from so many of our distant relatives, scattered across Europe."

"Jews."

"Yep."

Maria Goeppert Mayer came into Karl's office waving a newspaper, eyes dancing. "What means this?" Her English was getting better but when excited she reverted to German sentence structure. Karl looked at the *Daily News* headline.

ROOSEVELT DENIES URANIUM IS FOR BIG BOMB

Yellow paint materials at LaGuardia not part of military program

"Damn!" Karl said. "How did this get out?"

Maria said, "A reporter got some yellowcake, had a chemist look at it. Some physicist I never heard of guessed it might be part of some bomb. A reporter got a question about it into the White House." She looked a bit bewildered by how complicated news stories were in America.

"Crazy for the president to even answer this," Karl said. "What a price we pay for a free press!"

Maria nodded. "*Ja.* Better than not free, still. But ... this will send a signal to Heisenberg, for sure."

"You're sure Heisenberg is running the German bomb program?"

Maris sighed. "He is the obvious one. And smart enough to make it work, if the Nazis get out of his way."

They stared at each other speechlessly. Karl resolved to definitely not bring this up with General Groves, at all. Best to stay away from him for a good long while.

More physicists flowed through Columbia. Many were Brits headed for Oppenheimer's growing Los Alamos lab in New Mexico, devoted to figuring out how to make a plutonium bomb. Karl thought that was a waste of time. "Sure," he told Teller, "if they get enough out of the reactors we haven't built yet. But can they handle this new element we know nothing about?"

Teller scowled. "Oppenheimer thinks they can calculate ... Um, yes."

"We have uranium coming out now—not fast, but Oak Ridge is scaling up. We *know* how to build a U-235 bomb. We won't even have to test it!"

"You think not?" Teller looked worried. "Drop on some target, the Germans find it—if it doesn't go off, we give our hand away."

"It'll work," Karl said more firmly than he actually believed. He had never designed a bomb before, and neither had any of the brainy bunch working seven days a week to give birth to one.

Still, through innumerable meetings and coffee chats and blackboard arguments, a consensus grew. Their early estimate of a one-kilogram bomb was wrong, because the nuclear burn wouldn't really be efficient. A somewhat enriched bomb of U-235 could weigh sixty kilograms—a cube six inches on a side—and burn up only 1 percent of its mass, yet still flatten a city. Karl calculated that he could hold an ounce or two in his lap for a month without any health risk. But assembled swiftly, neutrons would spit from one disintegrating nucleus to the next, and the whole cube would heat and explode.

The group had to produce neat visuals so the military could understand the major issues. Karl found himself using slides that reflected more confidence than he actually had.

They staged a demonstration of the shotgun assembly method, whose cover illustration was:

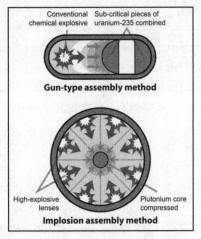

Assembly

Oppenheimer's guys—it was all guys except for the secretaries—thought it better to make plutonium in the reactors being built along the Columbia River and slam it inward, in a spherical collapse. This idea too had a detailed report with a cover illustration senior officers could understand at a glance.

Following Oppenheimer's talks, Karl stood to say many times, "Implosion is trickier. Much faster, sure. But we don't know how to do it right now." He learned that you had to hammer arguments home again and again. It was like framing a house, one patient nail at a time. At times the talking blotted out the physics, robbing him of what he most liked to do.

Karl argued before countless panels, "Remember, this has to be an actual bomb and will have to weigh a *lot*. It may yield a bigger bang, but the bomb will be so big we maybe can't get it into any existing bomber."

He had become privy to classified plans for the British Lancaster bomber, a big four-engine workhorse. The USA didn't have any plane of that capability yet. The big Lancaster bomb bay could accommodate a shotgun bomb, just barely. The British adviser on aircraft called it an "A-bomb," as even scientific reports did, copying from the old H. G. Wells story that confused nuclear and atomic processes. The shotgun nuclear bomb would have to fly in a Lancaster, so the British had to be brought in.

They had started to think about how to deliver a bomb, whose mass and size they were still quite uncertain about. But it would be bigger than any bomb ever used, that was clear.

General Groves was there, sitting in the back. He barked out, "Bring some pilots and engineers in on this. Guys who've actually flown those birds. We've got American pilots working with the Brits—get them."

Then Groves left, hat tilted at a jaunty angle, striding out powerfully and not looking back.

PART V

MORAL CALCULUS

If you chase two rabbits, you catch none.
—Confucius

1.

November 1943

Karl inhaled the moist aroma of Washington Square with a sigh, glad to be back in his familiar New York. A week at Oak Ridge had worn him down with its endless details of the ever-larger centrifuge networks, the monotonous ferreting out of minor flaws—all to enhance the efficiency of capturing specks of U-235.

He had been encouraged to see that Oak Ridge was now a sprawling complex, a dizzying mix of accents. He was only momentarily startled when a man at the small cocktail party General Groves put on asked, "Would you like some ass in your drink?" It turned out the bartender was from Texas, a land Karl knew not. Ice did indeed improve the bourbon.

Oak Ridge's busy hustle he had found tiring. Machine shops, transformer stations, test sheds, assembly lines, slapped-together plywood warehouses right next to barracks and cafeterias. Black Bakelite instrument panels, patchboard electronics, flickering oscilloscopes. Karl liked problems, but not the stale routines of squeezing every tiny improvement out of a running, ever-larger regiment of whirring centrifuges. Even his small discoveries came with the need to get some stiff military type, an officer with scrambled eggs on his hat, to sign the right paperwork.

Now he was headed to another meeting with Groves, cutting across Washington Square beside a pickup jazz combo playing for pocket change to an audience of NYU students and bums. By the big fountain splashing at the center, black boys did gymnastics for an earnest-faced covey of housewives holding shopping bags. Dogs capered and barked their pack signals near the chess hustlers crouched over the outdoor tables, waiting for naive prey to give them a little money.

Government regulations had limited fabric lengths, banished pleats, and forbade having more than one pocket. Men now had a slim trim in the pant legs and women looked more military—gray flannel suits, low-heeled shoes in polished fake leather, shoulder-strap bags, berets and felt cloche hats. Short skirts, too, which Karl enjoyed, and long-sleeved blouses with deep décolletages, often of rayon or cheaper stuff.

The war had seeped into everything. People listened to the news that ran in tinny, excited voices in bars and lobbies and even street corners. Chewing gum now came in cellophane, not tinfoil. Food and gasoline were scarce. A company marketed toilet paper with WIPE OUT HITLER and a sketch of Adolf on every tissue; it sold out everywhere.

The news was an anthology of disasters. Himmler had ordered Gypsies into the same camps as Jews, since they were an "under-race." The marines had landed at an island nobody ever heard of, Tarawa, and took it with heavy casualties. The Soviet front was a slaughterhouse. Still, British bombers had hit a power station in Norway, and the fight in North Africa was going well.

Karl entered the elderly-looking, vaguely Moorish Hotel Earle. A liveried doorman directed him to a clanking elevator. Groves himself opened the door on a rather grand room where a tall, blocky man with a dark complexion sat in a high-backed chair, reading an issue of *Le Monde*. A *Le Figaro* lay on the broad arm of his chair. This seemed an expensive affectation to Karl, who noted the way the big man nonchalantly displayed them. He glanced at Karl, then back at his newspaper.

"C'mon," Groves said in his bulldog growl, "other room. Where's your bodyguard?"

"Called in sick," Karl said. In fact, Karl had slipped away from Columbia without telling Eric Thompson at all. He didn't like being "chaperoned," as he called it.

They went into an office setup, a desk and files. A Colonel Ken Nichols, according to his name badge, sat at a desk covered with papers. Groves unbuttoned his wrinkled tunic, took it off, handed it to Nichols. "Take this, find a dry cleaner, get it cleaned right away." Treating a colonel like an errand boy was part of the Groves way. Nobody should ever doubt who was in charge. Or as Groves had put it after he had a few bourbons in him, "Ass— kick it or lick it."

Groves shut the door. "Don't want Nichols hearing this. How's things going at Oak Ridge? I get my reports, but I like to hear it from somebody who runs the numbers."

"We're going better. Could have a critical mass by spring."

"Great! I want to see it tested."

Karl masked a flicker of irritation. "Our production rate now will give us a new warhead maybe every three, four months. Testing it will make the war run longer."

"Uh. But to be sure it works—"

"Fermi's sure. That's good enough for me."

Groves frowned, paced. "Fermi's not a weapons guy."

"Neither am I, or Urey—but the physics is damned simple."

"We'll decide that later." Groves waved the matter aside, shook off his mood, and pointed. "That guy sitting outside, recognize him?"

"Um, sort of." Some dim memory nagged at Karl.

"Moe Berg. Until he's finished reading a paper, he considers it 'alive' and refuses to let anyone else touch it. When he's done, it's 'dead' and anybody can read it. Says he wants to integrate everything from various papers, get a picture—every day."

"Then he's—"

"Yep, from intelligence. I want to bring him onboard for some espionage work."

Karl felt a memory tug at him. "There's something else about him. . . ."

"You a baseball fan?"

"Not really."

"He was a major league catcher for the Sox."

"Ah! I saw him at a game." The only one he had ever seen, with Anton— who had become a big fan. Karl recalled Berg crouching behind home plate like a bear.

"Casey Stengel said he was the strangest man ever to play baseball. Got a law degree, went to Columbia and Princeton."

"Strange?"

"The Dodgers scout summed him up as 'Good field, no hit.' And a guy from the Senators speaks seven languages—and he can't hit in any of them."

Karl laughed dutifully, as he knew Groves expected. "The languages will help in his espionage, right?"

"Should, sure." Groves frowned, as if reviewing things he would not reveal. "I want you to brief him on the physics. He's going on a mission to find out what the Krauts have been doing."

"Where?"

"Italy first. Then France." Groves looked pensively out the window at Washington Square.

Karl studied the high ceilings bordered by elaborate moldings, the casement windows with leaden mullions looking grandly out over a huge elm tree, rippling in the soft wind. "That's the oldest tree in the city, the hanging tree—used for executions around the time of the Revolution."

"Um." Groves was not interested in tourist talk. "Wanted to tell you about that heavy water plant in Norway we bombed. The catcher found it—Moe. He went in secretly and located it precisely in a gorge. I asked for a bombing raid, and the Royal Air Force nailed it." Groves smiled, puffed up a bit by having a battlefield role.

Karl sighed. Heavy water was a good neutron moderator. "So the Germans are building a reactor." *Like Fermi's. And Heisenberg let Bohr know with that sketch he casually made.*

"Yep! I want to know how far along they are. That's Moe's job. He's the best. But he needs to know a lot of the physics, how to discuss it with Italian and French scientists. That's your job—teach him. And quick."

"So he can look for signs of the right interest areas?"

Groves looked around impatiently. "Yes. Look at this hotel! He knows how to live right, the catcher does."

"Berg can afford this?"

"The Office of Strategic Services has a fat budget. They assigned him to me. Let's see if he's through with those damned newspapers."

They went to the larger room, where Berg was standing in shirtsleeves, looking out the big window. Karl could see the broad, muscular shoulders and thick arms. He had paid no particular attention to this man when he was a catcher at the one game with Anton, and now, in the strange currents of war, their paths crossed. Moe's blunt, sunbaked face seemed pensive. Karl introduced himself and stood studying the big man who said softly, "Nice view of the hanging tree."

Had Moe heard them talking in the other room? But no— "I always take this room for its view of the tree and square. History!"

Groves said, "You two start talking."

Moe turned and gracefully folded himself into his deep chair. "You got a law degree, I hear?" Karl began.

Moe grinned. "I'd rather be a ballplayer than a justice on the Supreme Court."

"The general said I should walk you through nuclear physics."

"Right. Details matter—technical terms, names, stuff that might slip in conversations. Espionage is more like archaeology, dogged digging and sifting. You gotta look for little things, clues."

Groves had gone back into the office, perhaps understanding that some personal nose touching had to happen to get the two of them to work together. Groves wasn't all bulldozer manners after all.

"You speak French and Italian?"

Moe lounged back, crossing long legs. "Having been acquainted for years with that beautiful creature known as Latin, I try to savor its ornate, loquacious offspring. Yet the French accent eludes me."

Karl smiled. Somehow this big guy with an easy, sliding smile and precise diction made you like him. *Presence, that's it.* "My wife can help you with that. Have dinner with us."

Moe Berg

Moe Berg appeared exactly on time at their new address at West 121st Street, seven p.m. He brought a bottle of good Burgundy, presenting it with a flourish. Karl wondered how Berg had gotten it but thought it better not to ask. Marthe had sent word she would prepare one of her fragrant goose cassoulets, whose aroma filled their apartment. Somehow she had bargained her butcher into getting her a big goose, despite all the rationing.

Karl had spent days teaching Moe the basics of uranium, fission, centrifuges, reactors. He was a quick study. Along the way he asked if the Japanese had a similar program, and even asked Groves about it. Apparently not. Groves had told Karl that Berg had been on the 1934 all-star team that toured Japan, even though his batting average was in the high 100s. The Department of War had pressured the baseball mavens to include Berg, and he had faked his way to the top of a tall hospital and taken movies of the Tokyo skyline without being observed. Jimmy Doolittle used those pictures to plan the raid of Tokyo. Karl had seen the movie about that raid and found it stirring, just what the country needed in the year after Pearl Harbor.

Marthe was impressed with Moe, murmuring to Karl that he was "graceful for his size." She liked their new, rather more stylish, two-bedroom apartment, a clear step up in status, under the Columbia social umbrella that stretched for blocks around. This was their first dinner party, and she beamed.

Marthe started addressing Moe in French. Moe responded readily. He displayed an oddity, gotten from "one of my contacts," he remarked casually.

Karl and Marthe held the embossed card gingerly. It was Hitler's 1941 Christmas card, a photo of the Winged Victory of Samothrace, an ancient Greek statue the Wehrmacht had taken from the Louvre. His greeting was printed: *Our Winged Victory*. Beneath that was a scrawl with only the *A* and *H* legible. "He . . . touched this," Marthe said. Her hands shook, nearly dropping the card.

"Somehow, this makes the war more personal," Moe observed. "We have to get Winged Victory back."

Martine danced around the visitor, breaking the mood, welcoming him in her sprightly French. Marthe brought wineglasses and they sat, Marthe holding their youngest, Elisabeth, who watched Berg with wide, wondering eyes, as though his size made him a member of another species. Martine spoke her excited girl's French and Marthe joined in, exchanging small talk.

Berg studied Marthe's face carefully to see how the slippery words should be shaped. In American-accented French, he said, "I learned French at Princeton. Not much speaking in class, though. Never joined a dining club— what they call a fraternity—so I had time to study."

"Get any invitations?" Karl asked. He had a certain amused curiosity about the stuffy clans of the Ivy League.

"One, the only Jew in my class to get one. I turned it down. I didn't think I could put away that much booze."

Marthe laughed and Martine looked puzzled. Karl whispered to her, "Drinking alcohol, like wine," and tipped his glass.

"Between playing baseball and studies, that was it for me." Berg shrugged. "I caught on that my fellow students just memorized some Latin abbreviations such as QED, e.g., and i.e. For most of them, these are all short for 'I speak Latin, and you don't.' I hated those types."

Karl helped Marthe set the food just as Anton arrived. He was well dressed and in wide-eyed awe of Moe Berg. Since that one game Karl took him to, he had become a rabid Dodgers fan—but any pro player was a god. Berg tolerated Anton's fan talk through the salad, telling a few stories about split-second double plays and inside gossip about icons like Lou Gehrig and Babe Ruth. Anton said, "But why you retire? You had over a decade in the game."

"Well, there's this war thing," Moe said, and left it at that.

Anton shrugged with a lopsided, knowing smile. He had learned that, as with Karl, there were questions you shouldn't ask.

Moe told Anton how he had started in the minor leagues after Princeton. "You like university more than baseball?" Anton asked, incredulous.

"Of course. As I settled into the first Princeton semester, my heart was beating like that of a boy with a pocket of heavy change as he walks through the door of a candy shop. It was bliss, I thought, to fill in my ignorance of literature and language, poet by poet, guided by tenured wizards, in classrooms from the colonial era. I would look out at the drooping golden-leaved elm branches shivering in the sunlight, outside in the Yard—then go to baseball practice."

This reverie impressed all the Cohens. Moe dug into the cassoulet with trencherman vigor. Marthe had made two, anticipating that a big athlete would need more. She was right. Moe regaled them with tales of his baseball life, travels, friends. He was smooth, funny, wry. Karl noticed he gave very little away about his personal life, probably a useful skill for a spy—talk much, reveal little. That he could do this in French, which Martine could follow now at age six, was even more impressive. Moe asked Marthe to correct his pronunciation and carefully repeated each word he got wrong. Karl learned a lot from this, though he had lived in France for many months.

"Tell me about how you learned physics, Karl," Moe said over dessert—a luscious crème brûlée. Karl dutifully trotted out his career arc, the incredible bit of luck he'd had when Urey hired him and the Manhattan Project began. Anton got restless at this, since his French was weak and physics was not baseball.

Moe saw this and leaned back lazily, saying in English, "Y'know, Anton, mastering an academic discipline is an exponential domain—and so is baseball. You have to learn the basics over years, before you grasp the structures of the field. Then you can begin to play creatively with the concepts, with the moves—like, say, how to pick off a runner who takes a long lead from a base. Ice hockey is an exponential activity too—it takes years just to skate well enough. Karl did this with physics and chemistry. You can do it with—say, what do you do?"

Pleased with this attention, Anton looked around the table significantly. "I have changed jobs, or will soon. I volunteered for the navy."

Stunned silence. Marthe bit her lip. Martine looked puzzled.

"I want to *do* something to defend this country," Anton said with a jutting jaw. "They are killing my family in the Ukraine, murdering Jews everywhere. While I sell things in a store!"

Karl said, "You're right. We have to do something."

He glanced at Moe. Berg was the sort whose silence was more eloquent than his words. Anton didn't know what Karl was doing, of course, just thought he was teaching classes at Columbia—which he wasn't. Marthe joined in with a murmur of approval, but Karl could tell she was dismayed. She seldom heard from her parents hiding in the south of France, and nothing at all from her other French relatives. Karl felt a sudden lift, a strange joy. The urgency in Europe and across Asia needed the cheetah's sprint, not this turtle's plod. He had to do as much as he possibly could.

"Anton, you're doing the right thing," Moe said.

Anton smiled and looked around the table, basking in the praise. It was as if a beam from heaven lit his face.

Karl tried to look happy.

3

Theory could only go so far. As director of the Theoretical Division of the Manhattan Project at Columbia, Karl found it hard to keep a grip on the many multiplying threads of the effort.

To find out what was needed in what the security people insisted they call the "Tube Alloy" project, he decided he should show up to help with the next essential job. Fermi had built a small reactor in Teaneck, New Jersey, and the sprawling sheds around it were now an impromptu experimental group, trying to design the eventual bomb. Otto Frisch, the leader of this Critical Assemblies group, was trying to accurately determine the exact amount of enriched uranium required to create the critical mass, to sustain a nuclear chain reaction.

Otto was a stately Austrian with great skills as an experimenter. He had left Austria shortly after Hitler rose to power, and taught in London. He had met with his aunt, Lise Meitner, while on vacation, just after she got word of the Berlin results. Together they figured out that fission explained those 1938 Berlin experiments. Otto had quickly isolated the fragments produced by fission reactions, and urged the British to start a bomb program. Now he was leading the bomb builders.

"A job I never thought I would do," he told Karl. "In fact, we are in the middle of a trial right now."

Otto led Karl into a big room full of experiment gear, all centered on an array. Above them hung half spheres of enriched uranium hydride centered on a steel rod arrangement, with motors to move them. "We bring those uranium hemispheres together, to measure rising neutron activity, as we approach critical mass, see?" Otto thumbed the motor control and worked the assembly farther apart by a centimeter or two. "The metal bars scatter some neutrons away—and so increase the time that the reaction requires to accelerate. Nothing to reflect neutrons back into the uranium."

Godiva

Karl was nonplussed. "While you're . . ."

"Over here, behind this steel shield."

"Ah, good." Otto's team was already behind the shield, working before a board of dials and levers.

"There are no reflecting surfaces nearby." Otto gave him a thin smile. "So we call it the Lady Godiva assembly."

"Cute."

A low gong sounded. They clustered behind the shield. "One day," Otto said, "I almost caused a runaway reaction. I was adjusting a coupling while leaning over the stack. I'm mostly water, plenty of hydrogen—so my body reflected neutrons back into the stack. Out of the corner of my eye I saw those little red lamps"—he pointed—"flickering. They do that when neutrons are being emitted. They were glowing continuously!"

"My God." A sliver of fear arced through Karl.

"So I quickly scattered the bars with my hand, whoosh!"

"What was your dose?"

"Later I calculated it." A shrug. "Quite harmless, a full day's permissible dose of neutrons. But if I had hesitated for another two seconds—the dose would have been fatal. Tickling the dragon's tail," he said, and laughed. Karl did not.

"Starting!" a crew member shouted. The gong rang hollow in the big room. Even in the spare, high room smelling of dust and warm electronics, a silent tension layered the air. On the dials Karl could see the neutron count grow as the engineers carefully brought the uranium hydride closer together. Otto calculated as the experiment ran, until—"Halt! Close enough."

The team broke for lunch, but before Karl and Otto joined them, Otto finished a calculation. "Confirms our previous data, *gut*."

"Have you used this in the shotgun bomb design?" Karl peered at the pages of calculations, not following Otto's handwriting well.

"I think about seventy kilograms, using that new gun design. That's two critical masses, a safety factor to be sure."

Karl nodded; he had done a similar calculation and got about two hundred kilograms. Otto's data was better. "Good news. We can get bombs faster, then."

"The centrifuges, they are running well?"

"Pretty well. Ernest Lawrence's calutron helps—he can improve the purity of the centrifuge U-235. It's still a while, months probably, before we can get the first bomb."

"*Sehr gut*."

They ambled away, discussing how the uranium gun-type weapon was straightforward, almost trivial to design. "You think the Nazis cannot develop a plutonium bomb?" Otto asked.

"Out at Hanford they're trying to make enough in those big reactors, but it's slow work. Plus, this new isotope they found turning up, Pu-240, is a fast neutron emitter. It's too fast to use in a gun—the whole thing will explode from thermal heating before we slam together critical mass."

Otto blinked, frowned. "So the gun-type design must work with enriched uranium only? Can we fit that into our bombers?"

"The engineers think so. Say, I saw no light come from the experiment—

neutrons can't light up air?" Karl knew the answer, but something made him fill the silence with words.

"No. But when the bomb goes off, the X-rays will heat a fireball."

Good old $E=mc^2$. Mass wants to become light, Karl thought. Einstein had first said that, and now would see it done.

4.

Groves paced behind his desk like a bear in a cage. He had a sizable office in a new building at Columbia University, amid undergraduates. He and his staff stood out like toads on a birthday cake.

He grumbled and growled to himself and then abruptly turned and said to Moe Berg and Karl, "Look, I just got a briefing. Our secret war research is now under the Office of Scientific Research and Development, OSRD, headed by Vannevar Bush. It divides work among divisions on radar, rockets, nuclear, and so on. You guys should know something they figured out. Near as we can tell, the Germans have no such overall organization, because the Nazis are antiscience. Our agents and intelligence guys say they don't believe in a clear connection between science and military power."

Karl sat and waited, knowing by now not to interrupt Groves when he was venting. "They've been sure they can win it, so no need to do research. They draft their scientists, too. There's a Führer's List that exempts men from the arts, movies, even an astrologer—but no scientists."

Karl put in, "Sounds like good news." Moe just nodded.

"Well, I don't buy it!" Groves smacked his hand on his desk, making a pen roll off and clatter on the floor. "I think they've kept the atomic work secret." He picked up a folder with CLASSIFIED across its cover in red. "Uranverein— Uranium Club. *Uranmaschine*, U machine, reactor, German Army Ordnance Office. These terms keep turning up in intelligence reports, but with no detail."

"They started that work at the Kaiser Wilhelm Institute in Berlin," Moe said mildly.

"I know," Groves said. "I had it bombed. Photos showed we got a lot of it. So they've probably moved their *Uranmaschine*."

"If they have big buildings full of centrifuges, like Oak Ridge, we might spot them," Karl said. "They'll need plenty of electrical power, so maybe near one of their dams."

Groves brightened. "I'll get the air boys on that. There's something more, though." He flipped open the file, scanned it. "Intelligence operations in Denmark have spotted bigger rockets than the 'flame-tailed airplanes' they had seen earlier, now called buzz bombs. Some of these fell into the North Sea, big bullet-shaped things. These seemed large enough to carry a nuclear warhead of the shotgun type, I'm told. So, Karl, is that why they're developing this?"

Silence. Karl wondered how anybody knew the tonnage of a bomb they hadn't designed yet.

"There's more." Groves flipped to other pages. "There's something called 'Vergeltungswaffe 2,' meaning Vengeance Weapon 2—V-2 for short. It's real, nonpropaganda name is the A-4, or Aggregat 4. Meaning an aggregated weapon, many parts. We broke a coded message that says, 'Lessee . . . *A-4— die Typenbezeichnung der ersten funktionsfähigen großen Rakete in der Welt mit Flüssigkeitstriebwerk*.'"

Karl mustered his spotty German. "It says, the A-4 is the type designation of the world's first functional large rocket with a liquid engine."

"The buzz bombs were gasoline fueled, lit by a fast spark plug, right?" Groves stood, fidgeted in his pockets, took out some chocolates in paper wrap, and popped them into his mouth. It was a seemingly automatic gesture, and he munched them down, eyes distant. Karl had noticed that Groves's girth grew under the pressures of his task. "So they're building this damn rocket, and fast. If they can put a nuclear warhead in it, that's considerable 'vengeance,' all right."

Moe said mildly, eyebrows raised a bit, "So you consider the lack of leads to their uranium project a clue, General?"

"I don't want to be snookered by that, yes. Point is—could they use an A-bomb against the French coast landing everybody knows we're planning?"

Silence again.

✦ ✦ ✦

Harold Urey looked worn, gray, tired. Even his suit was wrinkled. "Karl, I've just gotten new data on plutonium. They're making tiny bits of it out at Hanford, following Fermi's plans. Enough to get a look at how it reacts to neutrons."

Karl sat in a stiff-backed chair beside Urey and they worked through the papers, stamped SECRET in red on every page. "The bottom line is, plutonium reacts fast, spilling out neutrons."

Karl sat back, mouth aslant. "Most people seem unaware that if you have separated U-235, it's a trivial job to set off a nuclear explosion. If only plutonium is available, making it explode is the most difficult technical job I know."

Urey got up, picked up some chalk at the blackboard, jotted a few symbols, apparently thought better of it, turned back. "That's my conclusion too. But Groves likes those big reactors. Thinks plutonium production in them is a good backup, in case we don't get enough U-235."

Karl remembered when Fermi's team had gotten the first reactor to work in September of 1942. An observer had called Urey, saying obliquely, "The Italian navigator has landed in the New World." Urey asked, "How were the natives?" and the observer laughed, saying, "Very friendly."

Karl pointed to a plutonium reaction time. "You'll get a fizzle if you use a shotgun bomb. I'd bet that to make plutonium work, we'd have to implode a shell."

Urey went to the blackboard and started calculating. He and Karl worked out a basic implosion equation, both trying to imitate Fermi, who famously made simple estimates to get a grip on a problem. Maybe when Fermi was young he could jot ideas of surpassing insight on cocktail napkins, but Karl had no such gift. Process led to progress. Solid, steady systematics were the path. But he joined in as Urey sketched out a way of estimating how symmetric an implosion had to be, to crush plutonium to a critical mass, without getting so asymmetric that the heating metal would make lopsided jets jutting out, and spoil the burn—a fizzle.

After a half hour, with missteps and puzzles resolved, Urey said, "Hell, we might have to synchronize the implosion to an accuracy of a microsecond!"

Karl said, "That's very hard, right?" He knew little about advanced electronics.

"You bet." Urey collapsed into his chair, scowling. "We'll have to persuade

Groves that U-235 is the way to go, and all our money should go into more centrifuges."

"That guy Oppenheimer, with the team he's shaped up down in Los Alamos—he must know this."

Urey's mouth twisted into a canny, cynical curve. "Sure, but he's keeping quiet. They'll have to work hard to beat this implosion problem."

Karl considered. He hadn't told Harold about his meetings with Groves and Moe Berg, because of Groves's strict security rules. The research organization at Columbia University under Urey's direct supervision had been growing rapidly. In 1942 and 1943 Urey had attracted many eminent scientists from academia and industry to assist in the centrifuge work. There was Columbia work, but most of the effort was at Oak Ridge. A small team was trying to make U-235 by gaseous diffusion through barriers, with little progress. By the end of 1943 Urey had about six thousand working on centrifuges, mostly the women who ran the ganged groups of "spinners," as everybody called them. These were crucial, because men were terrible at keeping careful track of the ebbs and flows in the vast system. It had turned out that ordinary women from farm country had the focus and fervor to further this tedious war work. They easily outperformed the PhDs, though they had no idea what it was all about. In all this, there was also the calutron, a big mass spectrometer separating uranium by brute magnetic force.

Details and paperwork galore. But Urey had little taste for administration, and the burden weighed heavily on him.

A sigh. "Karl, how'd you like my job?"

"What?!"

"Groves doesn't like me. He puts off seeing me, even about urgent business."

"Uh, so?"

"He likes you better. I'll bet he'd like to see you running this whole swamp I'm in charge of."

This rocked Karl. "I'm not qualified."

"Sure you are. You can fill out paperwork with the best of 'em."

He decided to treat this as a joke and laughed dutifully. "Ah, but paperwork gets more attention if a Nobel winner's signature is at the bottom."

Urey sighed. "You're right. You're sure having more fun than I am."

✦ ✦ ✦

Karl distracted Elisabeth and Martine as Marthe spread the letter from her mother out in full, its thin pages crackling like cellophane. Her eyes raced over it, eager for news.

The normal letter exchange through the Red Cross, often with side trips through Geneva, took about eight months. You got only twenty-five words on a Civilian Message Form. Marthe had sent *Elisabeth born April. Karl, Martine, baby, I, in best health. Everything all right. Hope you keeping well until reunion. Regards to family. Answer through Red Cross.*

That had been dated April 19, 1943. The reply came on December 6, 1943. *Welcome Elisabeth. Happy good news. Family and we good health. Madeline 2 boys. Living well with garden. Will live after war 2 apartments. Affectionate sentiments.*

This latest letter had arrived with stamps along the way from Geneva and Washington, DC.

Marthe sighed, buried her head in her hands. Karl put a hand on her shoulder and felt her weeping silently, not to disturb the children. Karl could see the pages were nearly black. This latest Civilian Message Form letter said, *Times hard here.* The rest had been censored out.

5.

March 7, 1944

Harold Urey held up a report. Karl saw it was yet another TOP SECRET mimeographed data summary. "They've got a new estimate of the 'crit,' the latest value for a critical size of U-235: about fifteen kilograms."

"We'll have that much in about three months from Oak Ridge," Karl said. "But I think we should overshoot some, maybe even by a factor of two."

"Then the yield, Oppenheimer says, should be five to ten thousand tons TNT equivalent."

Karl went to the blackboard, made a few notes. "Sounds right. So maybe we can hit the Germans before the Allies go into France."

"Barely possible," Urey said, sitting back in his rocker-style wooden chair.

"If we just had more spinners—"

"I know. Prob'ly shouldn't tell you this, but our budget won't get expanded. This radar program at MIT is soaking up all available cash."

Karl said, "Damn! Don't they understand this can stop the war?"

Urey stood, patted Karl on the back. "Look, a half-perfected radar is still useful; half-perfected atomic bombs don't work."

Karl nodded ruefully. A knock at the door.

"Dr. Urey?" the ordinary-looking man in a business suit asked. "I'm Arthur Riley, an investigator from the Counter Intelligence Corps of the War Department." He flashed an ID. "I need to ask about a suspicious occurrence."

Without pause he put a magazine with a gaudy cover on Urey's desk. "Note the passages I have marked."

Harold and Karl read them, heads together.

"U-235 has been separated, in quantity easily sufficient for preliminary atomic-power research. . . . They got it out of uranium ores by new atomic isotope separation methods; they now have quantities measured in pounds. By 'they,' I mean Seilla research scientists. But they have not brought the whole amount together, or any major portion of it. Because they are not at all sure that, once started, it would stop before all of it had been consumed—in something like one micro-microsecond of time." . . .

"Two cast-iron hemispheres, clamped over the orange segments of cadmium alloy. And the fuse . . . a tiny can of cadmium in a beryllium holder and a small explosive powerful enough to shatter the cadmium walls. Then— correct me if I'm wrong, will you?—the powdered uranium oxide runs together in the central cavity. The radium shoots neutrons into this mass—and the U-235 takes over from there."

"Um," Urey said. "There's more? And who's this author, Cleve Cartmill?"

"We're more interested in the editor of this *Astounding Science Fiction*. General Groves sent me to ask that someone who knows more about this work you're doing interview this"—he glanced at a card—"John W. Campbell."

"The technical details are quite wrong," Karl said, shaking his head, "and the method, 'radium shoots neutrons into this mass'—wrong too. Still, the scheme is pretty close."

Urey looked bemused. "Karl, you take care of this."

"Ah . . ." Karl suppressed his groan. "I'm not a literary type—"

"Do it."

Agent Riley took Karl to lunch the next day to get his opinion of the story. Riley paid; the security boys had good budgets. He got them a private room at the back of the Carnegie Deli to avoid being overheard and had Eric, Karl's constant guard, sit at the other end of the table.

"Cartmill's bomb would not have worked," Karl said as he munched through a pastrami sandwich. He even had a glass of beer. "We don't inject radium and so on. Still, he did stress that the key problem was separating nonfissionable isotopes from the crucial uranium 235, and that controlling the neutron emission rate was key."

"So how is it as a, well, a tale?"

"I prefer real science to fiction about it. And this—some evil alliance called the Axis—oops, no, the Sixa—who are prevented from dropping the A-bomb, while their opponents, the Allies—no, oops, that's the Seilla— refrain from using the weapon, fearing its implications. The story relates the experience of somebody with a prehensile tail—really!—named Ybor on the planet Cathor. Aliens. But they all talk like crew-cut, wisecracking, cigar-chewing, competent guys. Good grief."

Riley nodded with a sour smile. "You think it might be a leak?"

Karl smiled as he shook his head. He recalled Szilard's meeting about another story in this same magazine, in 1941, by Anson MacDonald, "Solution Unsatisfactory." "Death dust," that was it. Then a Pan Am Clipper had crashed with yellowcake . . . and FDR had denied the existence of any project to use uranium. He asked Riley about these connections.

"I saw something in the file. So what? No bomb in it."

Karl deployed his advantage. "I checked with others yesterday. Leo Szilard—you know of him?—he brought the attention of some of us to this story. My understanding is that Szilard's friend Eugene Wigner from Princeton did investigate the idea of death dust at the end of 1941, after reading that *Astounding* story. They concluded that fission products could make a large area uninhabitable, but they did not recommend the use in weapons of these particularly vicious radioactive poisons. In 1943 Fermi suggested that radioactive isotopes might be used to contaminate Germany's food supply. Teller then proposed strontium 90 as the most effective isotope. Oppenheimer out at Los Alamos rejected the proposal, saying, 'I think we should not attempt a plan unless we can poison food sufficient to kill half a million men.' Urey showed me the letter—classified, of course. Urey sees many interesting things."

"Wow! So that story had an impact on you guys?"

"Not me. I forgot about it." *Until that Pan Am crash . . .*

"I hope no Germans read that MacDonald story."

"I do too."

John W. Campbell

They went to Street & Smith Publications right away. Sitting at 79 Seventh Avenue was a brick facade mass with creaky elevators. The office door down a musty corridor said CAMPBELL on it, and inside was a woman named Kay Tarrant, who looked like an irritable schoolmarm. She peered at Karl and Riley as if they were prose that needed editing. Riley showed his ID and she nodded, with a face that said her long-held suspicions had finally come true. She led them into a messy office dominated by a broad desk. Tables of pulp magazines featuring garish colors, fresh from the printer, filled out the office.

John W. Campbell was a blond, six-foot-one man with hawklike features and a crew cut. Riley explained why they were there, identifying Karl with a nod, and plunged into an interrogation. Campbell watched Riley warily until the agent ran out of steam. He diligently never let his FDR-style holder go for more than a few seconds without a cigarette in it.

Campbell opened with gusto, the tone of a man who loved to launch into lecture. "Look, Cleve Cartmill proposed writing a story about a superbomb. I told him I had hardly any stories in inventory. Lost most of my best guys, went to the war effort." Campbell leaned back and talked around his cigarette. "Now, Cartmill is partly paralyzed, ineligible for military service, so I tried to egg him along. I needed stories. I sent him ideas about using atomic weapons in warfare, telling him it was fact, not theory, about fissionable U-235. I read about it in *Physical Review*."

Campbell turned his intent, challenging stare to Karl. "You know Urey?"

"Um, yes."

"Then you know more. I'd love to hear what you say about this."

"I know nothing, really," Karl lied. It was the easiest way to stay out of conversations that might wander into secret territory. He used it all the time.

Campbell brushed this aside with an airy wave of his cigarette hand. "Look, I figure they have quantities measured in pounds by now. I'll bet they have not brought the whole amount together, or any major portion of it. Because they are not at all sure that, once started, it would stop its reaction until all of it had been consumed. Bang!"

He slapped his desk, spilling cigarette ash onto it. "I bet they're afraid that that explosion would be so incomparably violent that surrounding matter would be set off—and that would be serious. That would blow an island, or hunk of a continent, right off the planet. It would shake the whole Earth, cause earthquakes of intensity sufficient to do damage on the other side of the planet, and utterly destroy everything within thousands of miles." Campbell's eyes were afire, jumping between the two men, as if he were interrogating them. "Right?"

Karl wondered if Campbell was drunk or something. Riley was unfazed. He said calmly, "Where were you educated?"

Campbell beamed. "Massachusetts Institute of Technology."

"So why are you editing a magazine?" Karl couldn't resist asking. This was his scientist's version, he realized, of a question old ladies sometimes asked him on the subway: *Young man, why aren't you in the service?*

"I care about big ideas. Science fiction, gentlemen, does not aspire to take over literature, but rather, reality."

"Where does Cartmill live?"

Campbell handed Riley one of his letters to Cartmill, from a file, and Riley said, "Cartmill's address—in Manhattan Beach, California?"

"Yeah." Campbell apparently did not catch any implication. "Needs money. His story was kinda marginal, but we'd gone through three drafts, so I used it. And"—a canny look—"why do you ask?"

Riley automatically said it was part of a background check. Karl asked,

"What about that 1941 story, 'Solution Unsatisfactory,' by MacDonald?"

Campbell beamed. "That's really Bob Heinlein. I bought so much of his stuff, he used pseudonyms to keep our table of contents from looking like a one-man show."

Karl said, "Do you really believe radioactive dust could be used well?"

Campbell puffed on his cigarette, and a wary look came into his eyes. The smoke was getting to Karl, who sneezed. "Maybe you boys know more about that?"

Riley gave Karl a sidelong glance. "Where's this Heinlein now?"

"Working at the Philadelphia Navy Yard. Something secret, I hear. Along with some of my best writers, de Camp and Asimov."

Riley took another magazine from his briefcase. "How about this? I got a librarian to check back on this Mr. Campbell, found it."

Riley spread the digest-size *Pic* magazine out on the desk. To Karl it looked to be a rather middle-brow publication about entertainment. But in the July 1941 issue, Campbell had authored an article, "Is Death Dust America's Secret Weapon?" with a sensational drawing, for some reason printed in dark blue.

"It's a story about radiological warfare, as you call it," Riley said. "One illustration has a caption, 'Even rats wouldn't survive the blue, luminescent radioactive dust. Vultures would be poisoned by their own appetites.' Did this idea come from the Heinlein story?"

Campbell smiled, eyes dancing. "Sure, Bob gave me the idea. I wrote that caption. Used to be a writer myself."

"You were publishing even before you flunked out of MIT in your sophomore year, 1931," Riley said with a thin smile.

Silence.

"I chose to leave due to financial difficulty." Campbell's voice was stiff, flat. "Plus, I failed German, so MIT dismissed me. The damned dean said German was the greatest scientific language, and no MIT grad should be without it. After this war, I predict the greatest scientific language will be—English!" He jabbed a finger at the ceiling. "After one year at Duke, I graduated with a bachelor of science in physics in 1932. You checked that?"

Riley ignored this. "I need addresses for Heinlein and those other writers at the Philadelphia Navy Yard."

"Ah . . . okay."

Campbell was subdued as he wrote out the addresses. He sat back, giving them a calculating look, and said, "Y'know, I keep track of our subscribers— over a hundred and fifty thousand of them. We've been getting a lot of changes of address these last few years—to Oak Ridge, Tennessee, and Santa Fe, New Mexico, plus Hanford, Washington."

Riley shot back, "Which means?"

"Most of our readers are scientists and engineers. They're going places I never heard of, lots of 'em."

For the first time Riley looked uncertain. "Means nothing to me."

"You sure, gentlemen?" Campbell peered at Karl, then Riley.

Under the piercing gaze, Riley said officiously, "I'd like that issue of your magazine to be removed from the newsstands. Now."

Campbell stood suddenly, military-straight, eyes narrowed. His challenging stare shifted to an amused scowl. "By removing the magazine, you guys will be advertising to everyone that such a project exists. And that it's aimed at developing A-bombs, ones that work like Cartmill said."

Riley stood too and shook his head, lips twitching. "You haven't heard the last of this." He and Karl left.

On the street outside, Riley said, "He knows something. That Cartmill story's theoretical use of boron indicates quite recent information."

Karl said, "We thought boron might be useful, sure, years ago. But it doesn't work."

"Manhattan Beach, California. The link to the Manhattan Project, Campbell's little poke about Oak Ridge, Los Alamos—too obvious to overlook."

"He was showing off. People with things to hide don't do that."

Riley was unsettled in his gray suit. "Look, we got the first lead on this from one of our agents. He overheard people at that Los Alamos place, talking about this Cartmill story."

Karl wondered how many scientists read this science fiction stuff. Maybe they couldn't get good books out in New Mexico? "So you think there's something suspicious?"

"Sure looks that way. I didn't quote a line from Campbell's piece in that *Pic* magazine—I should have. Look—"

Standing in the street, Karl read:

> For more than a year, there has been no news of the results attained in the most important scientific research in the world today—the research on Uranium 235. Behind this censorship of news that patriotic scientists have imposed upon themselves, there are moving events of immense importance—**for this war will be won or lost in the laboratory.**

Karl said, "In bold, too. He's overbearing even in print!"

Riley laughed. "Yeah, I nearly belted him."

Karl laughed too. "He likes to needle people. But really— If the war were truly to be won or lost in the laboratory, shouldn't he have had the patriotic sense to shut up?"

Three days later, right in the middle of a complex calculation, Karl got another visit from Riley, who didn't even sit down. "The Counter Intelligence Corps sent word to the California branch office of Intelligence. I had Cartmill placed under immediate surveillance. Plainly he knows too much. So who tipped him off? Campbell is being tailed too."

Karl shrugged. "I don't think there's anything there."

"Maybe." Riley paced impatiently. "We'll see. They're pressing Cartmill's letter carrier into service, see if he lets anything slip. The carrier said he's a science fiction fan and on good terms with Cartmill. But the real eye-opener is this—"

He tossed a list onto Karl's desk. "I went to Street and Smith, showed them ID, and they coughed up the *Astounding* mailing list in minutes."

Karl noted the circled entry: *W. von Braun, Deutsche Botschaft, 47 Stuckplat, Stockholm, Sweden.* "Um, so?"

"Deutsche Botschaft, that means German embassy. That von Braun— that's the name of the technical head of the German rocket program. I went through four layers of foreign intelligence people to track that down."

Karl frowned. "So this von Braun now knows about Cartmill's story. And the radioactive dust one too?"

"Damn right. I checked all the way back. This von Braun has had a subscription since 1933, just after the Nazis took over. He was in some kind of rocket society then, too. It went to his home when he was in school. Now he has the clout to get it sent through a diplomatic pouch from Stockholm. So von Braun knows. Dust, bomb—rocket."

Karl stared at the name for a long time.

6.

March 9, 1944

At Anton's good-bye party, people tried to discuss anything but the war. The Brits and Americans were slugging their way up the Italian boot. The Soviets had nearly pushed the Germans out of the Ukraine. The Japanese were getting hit on tiny islands hard to find on a map.

Karl made the rounds, refilling glasses, tending to his two girls, who had their own tiny table, passing canapés Marthe had deftly made from what was available in markets where ration books ruled. Even the Ureys, who had come to know and like Anton, turned and left any conversation that veered toward the incessant drum of war news.

So talk turned to the latest modern art openings at the Met. To Karl this was mostly abstract blob art or string-bean statues of people with big flashing teeth. None of such fads interested him. He liked the impressionist school, the pointillist techniques certainly, but if he wanted abstractions, he preferred mathematical models of physical processes, thank you.

One of Karl's cousins was painting on a bottle, one the man had earlier emptied before into himself, apparently as part of the creative act. Of the First World War (which his father tried to join by lying about his age), he said, "We went off to war and we didn't get anything. The Brits coulda given us Canada, at least. I think the motto after World War I should have been, 'How about Canada this time?'"

Some minutes later the same guy was pointing a finger at a woman friend of Anton's and saying, "Thing is, see, you're not entitled to your opinion. You are entitled to your informed opinion, sure. But nobody's entitled to be ignorant." *Well, at least I can agree with that,* Karl thought, and as a good host avoided the conversation.

Karl stood near Anton, letting other people wish him the best, and intently aware that this was the last time he would see Anton for, probably, years. He was to report at seven a.m. sharp tomorrow to the Navy Recruiting Office on Times Square. Anton had been rushed through his basic training at Newport, and now would ship out.

"They say will send me to Pacific, as I asked," Anton said. "I want to be deck gunner. Shoot down Japs!" His eyes danced at the idea, and he knocked back some Cabernet Sauvignon from Karl's dwindling stock.

Anton had invited not one but two girlfriends to the party. They were bright and chatted nonstop, and it took a while before Karl understood what was going on. "They're competing," Marthe pointed out, "for who gets to spend the last night with him."

"My . . . ," Karl said, genuinely at a loss for words. "He's not . . . engaged? To either of them?"

Marthe hid a small laugh. "The war has changed a lot of things."

Anton showed off Moe Berg to his girlfriends when the big man arrived, bearing a big smile and two chilled bottles of champagne. This provoked a ripple of chattering joy in the party, with Karl's mother, Rae, popping the cork with an expertise he didn't know she had. Anton's girls caught the foaming overflow in their wineglasses, laughing. Both eyed Moe with a certain appraising gaze.

Moe stood at a distance, enjoying it all, including the attention that followed him everywhere in the room he towered over. Rae asked him to dance to a waltz playing on the family phonograph. He moved with fluid ease as the whole room watched. Then Anton danced with one of his girlfriends, and the other chose Moe.

Karl and Marthe joined them. "This would never happen at a physics party," Marthe whispered to him. He nodded ruefully. The war had funneled men and women into familiar channels. Anton's girls were performing their impressions of what girls were supposed to be like. This was what men—people, everybody—seemed to think they should be: beautiful, treasured, spoiled, selfish, pea-brained. That was what a girl had to be, to be fallen in love with. Plus working in the war effort, of course. Then she'd become a mother and be all mushily devoted to her babies. Not selfish anymore, but just as pea-brained. Forever.

Well, maybe that can change, in time. . . .

Later Moe joined Karl in the cramped kitchen, sipping the Cabernet. Karl whispered, tipping his glass in a salute, "We just got word. Oak Ridge has just about enough of that, ah, tube alloy to make the right mass."

The big man beamed. "About time. Y'know," Moe said, nodding, "I calculated something from all my reading. Compiling all the foreign news, I'd say somebody's dying in this war every"—he tapped his watch—"five seconds."

This remark, framed by the swing-band trumpets now playing in the living room, seemed to Karl to frame the evening. Celebration against a grim, gray backdrop—which the party was trying to forget for a short while.

After the party, cleaning up, Karl mused on the family that had gathered here to wish Anton well. He would fight for a country he had first seen only a few years before.

And me? Karl asked himself. When his father had died in 1930, he could then see Joseph Cohen's life in full, from start to finish, and that carried a kind of godlike perspective Karl had never experienced before. It released him—free of his father's unrelenting pressure to become a medical doctor, at last.

Only by majoring in chemistry at Columbia had he escaped Joseph's skeptical frowns; after all, chemistry was a plausible way to prepare for medical school and show that Karl could handle difficult subjects. But now he could see his father's life as forever contained—made final, flattened as if within the pages of a diary, whose author did not know how it would end, but Karl now did. Joseph had died of Crohn's disease, and no one knew if it had a genetic source. Karl was seventeen when Joseph dwindled away, and somebody told him that was Hamlet's age when his father died too. Karl had felt bitter rage and disgust at the medical profession for failing his father. He would never join such a profession.

So he had gone on to get his PhD in chemistry with a dark cloud of uncertainty hanging over him. His father's life now seemed to him like a smaller, defined thing, a life that would be forgotten in a few generations.

Joseph had striven hard, tried to give his own life meaning—and now it was Karl's turn. Amid the biggest war in all history. Somehow.

A big meeting in New Jersey assembled again the small group that had begun the Manhattan Project in 1939, when it had no name: Fermi, Urey, Dunning, Teller, Szilard, the other big names—and Karl, the youngest of those who had started all this. Plus Groves, in uniform as always, sitting at the back and visibly working on papers while he monitored the technical talks. Plus several hundred engineers, officers, and assorted scientists.

Karl spoke first, on the purity of the centrifuge-made U-235, which he and others had monitored every week through over a year of Oak Ridge's steadily increasing production. "Easily pure enough to get a detonation of the, ah, gadget," he concluded, using the code term to avoid using "bomb" or any synonym, as practice had drilled into him.

Otto Frisch, leader of the Critical Assemblies group, reported on the combined theory/experiment team that had worked out the critical mass necessary. Though young like Karl, he had a certain authority because he and Lise Meitner had first fathomed that fission occurred in uranium. "When a pound—that is, 0.45 kilograms—of uranium 235 undergoes complete fission, the explosive yield is eight kilotons. To get a sixteen-kiloton yield of the gadget in our design, which we term 'Little Boy,' we must fission about two pounds—0.91 kilograms—of uranium 235, out of the hundred forty-one pounds—sixty-four kilograms—in the final assembly. The remaining hundred thirty-nine pounds—98.5 percent of the total—will contribute nothing to the energy yield. But the reaction will not happen unless we have that hundred thirty-nine pounds. Most of the mass is like a catalyst."

Murmurs of dismay from the audience of about a hundred men and Maria Goeppert Mayer. She nodded thoughtfully. Her work had helped Karl a lot, but she never liked the spotlight. Karl, on the other hand, had learned something of body language and positioning. He sat in the front row.

Groves sprang to his feet and strode to center stage. "Listen, we knew the shotgun design wasn't the best. Point is, we can't get the timing sharp enough to do an implosion gadget."

A voice from the back called out, "So we delay until we can do better!"

Karl saw Oppenheimer rise nearby. The willowy man blew out a blue column of pipe smoke and said, "We're making plutonium now in the reactor out in Washington. I think our Los Alamos group can figure out how to make it implode enough." Oppenheimer's baritone firmed. "And my team calculates we'll only need maybe twenty pounds of it."

A pause as eyes remained on Oppenheimer. Karl rose. He made his voice loud, not his usual habit, and roughened it. "This war is costing plenty every day—and people are dying faster every damn day of it. The issue here is speed, not cost or pounds."

Murmuring, uncertain glances among the audience. Karl and Oppenheimer eyed each other.

"The best is the enemy of the good!" Groves barked. "Enough debate. We go with *this* bomb. I've talked to Eisenhower on this, and he agrees."

Karl smiled; Groves phrased it as though Eisenhower were forced to agree with Groves. Words tumbled out in the discussion. Go for a target, maybe Berlin? Smash it, and not invade France—not just yet, anyway. Groves went on to tell about an idea, a "one-two" punch of the gadget, then the invasion.

Karl made a point of remaining standing and never taking his gaze away from Oppenheimer. The audience listened to Groves but watched the two men giving each other hard stares. To Karl it seemed to go on forever. Then at last Oppenheimer sat.

Karl did too. He felt a flush of embarrassment. *Like schoolboys challenging each other on a playground.* But . . . it had worked.

Teller spoke next, outlining how driving together two uranium 235 masses would work. They had to smash hard and fast. The total U-235 had to be bigger than the minimum to get a runaway explosion going—the critical mass. One of the two pieces was hollow, the other a bullet. It was tricky, but Teller's team was sure this would work—without testing.

Groves beamed. Karl could feel a decompression in the room, a rustling sigh. Karl felt a brimming joy. This was what it was to see a moment when history pivots.

Harold Urey sat next to Karl in the front row. He whispered, "Y'know, at first, way back then, I thought we'd have to implode the whole thing from pieces that were lots smaller than a critical mass."

Karl nodded and Urey grinned. "Wonderful, when one's ideas prove wrong. Disconcerting, sure, but ultimately liberating. Preconceptions are dull gatekeepers, yes? Only a fool resists the delight of contradiction by nature."

Karl thought ahead to the battles to come. "The universe bats last."

The major meeting about the "gadget" assembly made him think, as he played a piano piece that evening. The keys rippled beneath his fingers, light and quick. Marthe was filling their apartment with aromas that quickened his appetite. Elisabeth was big enough now to totter around the living room, tapping everything curiously with a red wooden building block. She listened to the sound, head cocked in wonder. With the block she picked up his rhythm. Then she tapped each object she came to, sofa to chair to rug to window, listening to the impact. *A scientist*, he thought. *She may become one of us. . . .*

The first time he had heard Bach in a live chamber performance he had realized that the instruments, cello and violin and harpsichord, were chambers that resonated from plucked or stroked strings. So they were chambers vibrating within a larger chamber, the room that contained him as well.

At the "gadget" meeting he had been one of many who made the strange music of nuclear physics sing a new song, creating a chamber for "tube alloy" that would make the first such explosion this world had ever seen. Chambers within chambers.

Chamber music worked through coupled vibrations, since the sound vibrations were comparable in size, in wavelengths, to the human body itself. Bach had somehow drawn forth great sonorous songs from embedded chambers, and so reached into the final chamber of the human heart.

What the gadget would do to human hearts remained to be seen.

Leo Szilard came into Urey's office, where he and Karl were working on a calculation, with a paper in his hand. "I have a petition for you to sign," Szilard said. "We must, right away."

Karl and Urey read it in silence.

A PETITION TO THE PRESIDENT OF THE UNITED STATES

Discoveries of which the people of the United States are not aware may affect the welfare of this nation in the near future. The liberation of atomic power which has been achieved places atomic bombs in the hands of the Army. It places in your hands, as Commander-in-Chief, the fateful decision whether or not to sanction the use of such bombs in the present phase of the war against Germany and Japan.

We, the undersigned scientists, have been working in the field of atomic power for a number of years. Until recently we have had to reckon with the possibility that the United States might be attacked by atomic bombs during this war and that her only defense might lie in a counterattack by the same means. Today, with this danger apparently averted—though we cannot be sure—we feel impelled to say what follows:

We believe that the United States ought not to resort to the use of atomic bombs in the present phase of the war, at least not unless the terms which will be imposed upon Germany and Japan after the war are publicly announced and subsequently both nations are given an opportunity to surrender.

If such public announcement gave assurance to the Germans and Japanese that they could look forward to a life devoted to peaceful pursuits in their homeland, and if Japan and Germany still refused to surrender, our nation would then be faced with a situation which might require a reexamination of her position with respect to the use of atomic bombs in the war.

Atomic bombs are primarily a means for the ruthless annihilation of cities. Once they were introduced as an instrument of war it would be difficult to resist for long the temptation of putting them to such use.

The last few years show a marked tendency toward increasing ruthlessness. At present our air forces, striking at the German and Japanese cities, are using the same methods of warfare which were condemned by American public opinion only a few years ago, when applied by the Germans to the cities of England. Our use of atomic bombs in this war would carry the world a long way further on this path of ruthlessness.

Atomic power will provide the nations with new means of destruction. The atomic bombs at our disposal represent only the first step in this direction, and there is almost no limit to the destructive power which will become available in the course of this development. Thus a nation which sets the precedent of using these newly liberated forces of nature for purposes of destruction may have to bear the responsibility of opening the door to an era of devastation on an unimaginable scale.

In view of the foregoing, we, the undersigned, respectfully petition that you exercise your power as Commander-in-Chief to rule that the United States shall not, in the present phase of the war, resort to the use of atomic bombs.

— **Leo Szilard and 58 cosigners**

Karl knew from rumors that as the war continued, Szilard had become increasingly dismayed that scientists were losing control over their research to the military. He had clashed many times with Groves, who had ordered his secretaries not to let Szilard in to see him, ever.

Urey whispered, "Good lord, Wigner signed!" A frown, twist of mouth. "I thought he was sensible. . . ."

Szilard stood against the blackboard as though he was addressing a large audience. "I'll say this: almost without exception, all the creative physicists have misgivings about the use of the bomb. I would not say the same about the chemists. The biologists felt very much as the physicists did."

"Use of the gadget is above our pay grade," Karl said.

"We must warn Roosevelt that the use of the bomb against cities will start an atomic-arms race with Russia."

"Not our job, Leo," Urey said mildly.

Szilard shook his head. "Suppose Germany had developed two bombs first. They dropped one bomb, say, on Rochester and the other on Buffalo. Then, having run out of bombs, she loses the war. Can anyone doubt that we would then have defined the dropping of atomic bombs on cities as a war crime, and that we would have hanged them?"

Urey flinched at this. "You think we're immoral?"

Szilard nodded. "We must use a moral calculus. Some think our possessing the bomb will render the Russians more manageable in Europe. I fail to see how sitting on a stockpile of bombs, which in the circumstances we could not possibly use, would have this effect. I think it even conceivable that it will have just the opposite effect."

Urey shook his head, clearly still getting used to the idea of himself as a war criminal. "Look, I agree about bombing civilians. It's reprehensible. Everybody's doing it now. But do you think the mere threat of this weapon will make Hitler stand down?"

Szilard stood stiffly erect in his three-piece suit. "I think, just detonate one in view of them, to frighten into surrender."

"We've only got one," Karl said. "Let's hope it works right."

"Only one?"

"Then another in three months."

"This bomb could kill a hundred thousand Berliners, say, perhaps more," Szilard said.

"Twice that number die every week, around the world," Karl said, keeping his tone steady and even, his eyes intent.

Szilard blinked, pursed his mouth. "Then you will not sign?"

"No," Karl and Urey said together.

"Then I will not trouble you further. I hope you, and we, do not regret your opinion." He sniffed, as if disbelieving their reception to his petition.

When he was gone, Urey and Karl looked at each other. Both shrugged; both then gave a rueful chuckle. But Urey kept frowning.

PART VI

SCIENTISTS
ON TAP

A pessimist sees the difficulty in every opportunity; an optimist sees the opportunity in every difficulty.
—Sir Winston Churchill

1.

April 3, 1944

"See what you think of *that*." Groves tossed a file across his desk. Karl snagged it before it slid off.

The cover said *Franck Report, TOP SECRET*, with many chapters and subsections he had no time to read:

> I. Preamble
> II. Prospectives of a Postwar Armaments Race
> III. Prospectives of Agreement on a Ban

A line from it caught his eye: "From this point of view a demonstration of the new weapon may best be made before the eyes of representatives of all United Nations, on the desert or a barren island."

> IV. Methods of International Control
> V. Summary

Karl read aloud, "To sum up, we urge that the use of nuclear bombs in this war be considered as a problem of long-range national policy rather than military expediency, and that this policy be directed primarily to the achievement of an agreement permitting an effective international control of the means of nuclear warfare."

Karl looked up, mouth tight. "Szilard is behind this."

"Sure." Groves leaned back in his chair. "He's on the committee that wrote that. This guy Franck is director of the Chemistry Division over in Jersey. Focused"—he read from a memo—"primarily on characterization of more than two hundred fifty radioactive isotopes that are created by the fission of uranium and the development of a process for chemical isolation of pluto-nium.' Um. Has a Nobel, too."

Karl had wondered why Groves was so focused on Nobel Prizes. Did he think he might win one? For developing a weapon? Not the Peace Prize, at least—though bringing peace early seemed to Karl a quite rational goal. He doubted the Swedes would see it that way; they were sitting out this war, making a handsome profit by selling goods and weapons to both sides.

"Szilard's been circulating his petition," Groves said. "I ignored it. This new report's just part of the story. So I wrote to Frederick Lindemann—that's Lord Cherwell—who's Winston Churchill's science adviser. Asked about Szilard. I found out he knew of Szilard's ideas on nuclear chain reactions long before the discovery of fission. He was head of Oxford's Clarendon Laboratory, so he was Szilard's employer from 1935 to 1938."

"So he'd back him up?" Karl asked to speed this along.

"My intel people told me about a meeting Szilard requested with Linde-mann when he visited Washington, DC, in 1943. I figured, if Szilard had mentioned secret information to Lindemann during this meeting, I could charge Szilard with violating the Espionage Act.

"Here's Lindemann's reply, and his attached account of the meeting."

Another folder slid across to Karl.

SECRET
TOP SECRET
PAYMASTER GENERAL
GREAT GEORGE STREET,
S.W.1
CONVERSATION WITH DR. SZILARD, MAY
1943, WASHINGTON, D.C.

When I spoke to Szilard in Washington in 1943, he was, so far as I can remember, mainly concerned with a topic which has inflamed so many scientists' minds, namely what sort of arrangements could be made to prevent an arms race with all the disastrous consequences to which this would lead. I do not recall that he offered any solution, although when we had discussed the same matter in Oxford before the war he had advocated some agreement between scientists not to lend themselves to any application of nuclear chain reactions to lethal purposes.

My impression is that his security was good to the point of brusqueness. He did, I believe, complain that compartmentalism was carried to undue lengths in America, but on the other hand, when I asked him about some point—I forget what—deriving from our work in Oxford, he replied that he was not at liberty to discuss it as he had passed into the employment of the American Government. We did not, so far as I can recollect, have any further conversation on technical processes, but he kept on harking back to his general anxiety about the future of the world.

Cherwell

Karl said, "I heard that Churchill said once, 'Scientists should be on tap, not on top.'"

Groves laughed. "Good one! Quite right, too. You agree?"

"Pretty much. The politicians get paid to make the big calls, not us."

"They only think they make the big calls. In war, it's us." Groves pointed to himself.

"What are you going to do about Szilard?"

"I polled the Oak Ridge and 'tube alloy' scientists—had 'em fill out a little form, check boxes. Only fifteen percent wanted the bomb used 'in the most effective military manner.' That's a quote—I said it to them that way. About forty-six percent voted for a military demonstration, to be followed by a new opportunity for surrender before full use of the weapon."

Karl blinked. "That's more than I'd have guessed."

"Me too. They're all pretty left-wing, I gather."

Karl shook his head. "I don't see anything left- or right-wing about this. The point is, end the war. Avoid this landing in France everybody's talking about."

"You think we could avoid the invasion?" Groves gave him a skeptical turn of mouth.

"If we try, yes. Use the bomb first."

"What's our U-235 production rate now?"

"In a few more months, more spinners, we'll be making enough for a new bomb every three or four months."

Groves slammed a fist onto his desk. "Damn good!"

"What'll you do about Szilard?" Karl repeated.

"After this letter?" He grimaced. "Wish Lord Cherwell had given me some ammo to use against him! I'm gonna sit on Szilard's petition, this damned report—*and* my poll—until we get into action. No reason to bother the president."

Karl got up to leave with a sigh of relief. Physics was easier than people.

Marthe said, smiling, "You are nearing success?"

Karl nodded. This was as far as Marthe ever went in discussing his work. She knew it was top secret and had worked out from small clues more or less what was up. She never tried to coax more from him. Yet when he came home after a long day of endless detail, he needed to talk. "I think we will know soon."

"This . . . does not involve you then, anymore?"

"You mean, can I get a professorship somewhere, after the war? Or even before that?"

She waved a hand. "Would perhaps be easier . . ."

The children were playing quietly together on the rug, and in the after-dinner calm Karl savored the idea of a life not concentrated on killing people. Just research, no real deadlines, orderly lectures, grad students to do the dull stuff . . .

"This last part coming up may be the hardest," he said obliquely.

"Involving you? But then it is a military matter only, *oui?*"

"It's more like a scientific experiment. Nobody's done this before. We want to learn as much from it as possible."

"But you are not military!"

"I don't think that's a firm distinction anymore." To erase the frown that deepened in her startled face, he leaned over and kissed her.

Harold Urey sat back and put his feet up on his desk, his favorite position for thinking. "Um. Not surprised to hear that Groves wants to block Szilard. He's always disliked the man. They could barely stand to be in the same room together. Tried to have Szilard held as an enemy alien in 1942, suspecting him of leaking secrets."

"Really?" Karl kept having these surprises.

Urey shrugged. "I dissuaded him. I suspect the Szilard petitions and dissent over the bomb's use carry the taste of revenge on Groves."

"Is that why Szilard burrowed into the reactor work with Fermi, rather than working on bomb design?"

Urey grinned. "Yep! Kept him out of my hair too."

"Groves said he felt that dissent alone meant nobody should pay attention to Szilard's views—even though he started it all, with the Einstein letter."

Urey nodded. "Once you start a boulder rolling downhill, pointless to run out front, try to stop it."

Karl felt tensions rising as they got closer to having a bomb. The saint of quantum mechanics was just down the hall, so he went to see Niels Bohr, whom he had not seen much in the constant travel and commotion of the project. Bohr's office was right by the SUBSTITUTE ALLOYS MANUFACTURING sign in the basement, the dodge name used after the Uranium Committee one.

Karl's main purpose was to ask about the bomb design, to see if Bohr had any new insights. The critical mass of U-235 seemed to imply that the available output from Oak Ridge was barely enough. Bohr was interested, somewhat bemused at how his field had exploded into what he called "a King Kong of science projects." When Karl asked about Heisenberg's giving Bohr a sketch years before, apparently showing a crude reactor, Bohr just shrugged. "Perhaps."

Karl was amazed to find over Bohr's desk a horseshoe nailed to the wall, with the open end up. When he asked about it, Bohr said, "Old European folktale. It is in the approved manner, to catch the good luck and not let it spill out."

Karl laughed. "Surely you don't believe the horseshoe will bring you good luck, do you?"

Bohr chuckled. "I believe no such thing. Not at all. However, I am told that a horseshoe will bring you good luck whether you believe in it or not."

Karl got right into it, detailing the varying estimates of the needed critical mass. "You think we'll have good luck, going with the minimum mass?"

"I would hedge a bit. Perhaps another five or ten kilograms."

"So you don't think our calculations are that good?"

"Perhaps. Truth and clarity are complementary. Never express yourself more clearly than you are able to think. Or calculate."

"We've only got the one shot."

A sunny smile. "If it is a fizzle, at least it will contaminate the target quite a bit."

Karl frowned. "You heard about that story in the magazine? Radioactive dust as a weapon."

"Yes, heard. It will not be as stunning, but will still disturb."

"I hope the Germans didn't get the idea. The rocket guy, von Braun, he gets the magazine. If he told them, maybe the Germans will use their stock of uranium that way, even if they can't get a bomb built."

"Yes, odd, isn't it?" Bohr pursed his lips and glanced at the horseshoe. "In the land of ideas, you are always renting."

Szilard, ever the intellectual bumblebee, had Einstein write another letter to FDR, urging a meeting with Szilard. No response. Karl guessed that Groves had put the kibosh on that, but said nothing. Szilard tried to talk to the State Department, which had better things to do. Further, he discounted with a wave of the hand the fears that the Germans were still ahead of the Allies on building a bomb.

Discussing this with Urey, Karl said, "I hear the army thinks that Congress will inevitably inquire why a billion dollars were spent on a weapon that killed none of our enemies." Urey nodded vigorously.

All this boiled around the edges of the rush to get a bomb assembled.

Before a critical meeting, Groves took Karl aside. "Look, I've started organizing a bigger effort at Los Alamos. Oppenheimer thinks a plutonium bomb may be more effective. Once we get a lot of reactors going, we can breed lots of plutonium."

Karl frowned. "How much plutonium does Los Alamos have now?"

"Uh, none. But it'll come."

"We're nearly ready to drop ours. We can have another one in three to four months. Game's over."

"I'm thinking longer term here. We can make maybe four bombs a year—that's pretty slow."

Karl bit his lip. *One or two might do it.* He wanted to blurt out a laugh at Groves's thinking but realized the man was under pressure from all quarters. "Let's stay focused. Meeting's starting."

The agenda was:

    A. Height of Detonation
    B. Report on Weather and Operations; following airplanes
    C. Gadget Jettisoning and Landing if needed
    D. Status of Targets
    E. Psychological Factors in Target Selection
    F. Use Against Military Objectives
    G. Radiological Effects
    H. Coordinated Air Operations
    I. Rehearsals
    J. Operating Requirements for Safety of Airplanes

There was a thick sheaf of reports for everyone at the table. Karl was no longer the youngest guy in the room. Luis Alvarez from Berkeley was about Karl's age and had a boyish manner common to physicists that stood out from the somber advisers. Alvarez reported on a flight he had built the detectors for, that flew over Germany. It looked for xenon 133, a waste signature of a nuclear reactor that could be seen clearly. But there was none. Groves frowned at this and moved on to the bomb problems.

The tech guys and then Groves had spoken for some time when Karl raised his hand. "What's the target?"

"We're charged with making a list. The president and Churchill and the Combined Chiefs will make the final choice together."

"Isn't it obvious? Berlin."

"That's for a higher—"

"Cut the head off the dragon."

Groves frowned. The lines in his face were deeper now, Karl saw under the harsh spotlight-style lights in their bleached white meeting room. "Look, we have to synchronize with the invasion of France. Hitting a tactical target might give us the biggest leverage."

"Kill Hitler and his gang, that'll end this war."

"Karl, we have to go by procedure."

"There's no precedent, so there can't be some procedure."

"So we should consider targets first." Groves smiled. "I like that."

Nods all around. Karl saw pure, delighted ambition spread on Groves's joyful face. He was a brigadier general, but there were slots above, too. He could bring to the table the physicists' expertise, estimates, probabilities, all about a superweapon that had never been used. He might get a bigger place at that table.

Karl took refuge from the press of work with his family. He delighted in simply going for Sunday walks, when the city opened itself to the bright promise of spring. Flowers sprang forth with sweet aromas and bright flourishes of color. Birds sang salutes to the spring day and cooed songs to one another as the sun fell. His daughters danced in the park, their tinkling laughter bringing smiles from the faces of strangers passing. Marthe walked with him and the children arm in arm, as though their family was a military brigade. Perhaps, in a way, it was, as a defense against the war itself.

Rumors rained down. Not content with the sensationalistic newspapers, people made their own truths and spread them.

Even within the secrecy community, tales slid like snakes, with a venom of their own. Szilard was still talking to people in Washington, DC, about demonstrating the bomb rather than using it on a military or political target. This bothered many at Columbia. From Urey came firm arguments he tried on Karl and Fermi and others. So armed, he took a train to Washington, DC, to counter Szilard.

In his staccato style, Urey rapped out his points. The bomb was not certain to work. A demonstration would alert German defenses. Maybe they would move prisoners of war into likely target zones, especially Berlin. No conceivable way of showing off the bomb could be as dramatic as real use against a big concentration of, say, German armaments, or a city.

When Urey returned, everyone gathered around him in the big basement lab and listened to him tell his stories. He read aloud a letter of Teller to General Marshall, quoting: "'Our only hope is in getting the facts of our results before the people. This might help convince everybody that the next war would be fatal. For this purpose actual combat-use might even be the best thing.'"

"Will this be enough?" Karl asked.

"I think it's pretty clear that FDR feels as we do," Urey said with a smile.

Carefully, Karl read the letter Groves had just handed him.

FEDERAL BUREAU OF INVESTIGATION
April 7, 1944
To: WHITE HOUSE

Recently, in connection with the operation of a radio station of a German agent under control of the Federal Bureau of Investigation but which station the Germans believe to be a free station, an inquiry was received from Germany containing the following questions regarding the status of atomic explosive experimentation in the United States:

First, where is heavy water being produced? In what quantities? What method? Who are users?

Second, in what Laboratories is work being carried on with large quantities of uranium? Did accidents happen there? What does the shielding protection against Neutronic hazards consist of in these Laboratories? What is the material and the strength of coating?

Third, is anything known concerning the production of bodies or molecules out of metallic uranium rods, tubes, plates? Are these bodies provided with coverings for protection? Of what do these coverings consist?

We have already advised the appropriate authorities in the War Department concerning these German inquiries.

I thought the foregoing would be of considerable interest to the President.

With best wishes and kind regards,

Sincerely yours,

J. Edgar Hoover

Groves took back the copied letter from Karl and Moe and put it into a thick HIGHEST SECURITY folder. "Seems like I hear more bad news all the time," he said gruffly. "This one's the worst."

"At least Hoover found it," Moe said. "I didn't know we still had counter-intelligence radio stations running."

Groves glowered. "You'd be shocked at how many agents the Krauts had through that German-American Bund of theirs. We got a bunch in '41, but FBI and OSS got the Krauts to believe there were more who had gone underground and—get this!—had shortwave radios. We've been feeding them fake data, and they come back with more questions. This one's the first from Germany about atomic stuff."

Karl got up and looked out the window of Groves's New York office at the usual traffic jam. No enlightenment there. "So what'll you do?"

Groves beamed. "I did this."

WAR DEPARTMENT
Office of the Chief of Engineers
Washington
22 March 1944
MEMORANDUM TO THE CHIEF OF STAFF

Radioactive materials are extremely effective contaminating agents; are known to the Germans; can be produced by them and could be employed as a military weapon. These materials could be used without prior warning in combating an Allied invasion of the Western European Coast.

It is the opinion of those most familiar with the potentialities of these materials that they are not apt to be used, but a serious situation would occur should any units of an invading Army be subjected to the terrifying effects of radioactive materials.

It is recommended that a letter similar to the draft enclosed be dispatched to General Eisenhower.

L.R. Groves
Major General, C.E.
Incl: Draft

22 March 1944

General Dwight D. Eisenhower

Dear General Eisenhower:

In order that your headquarters may be fully advised of certain materials which might be used against your Armies in a landing operation, I have directed Major A. V. Peterson, who will be in England on temporary duty in the near future, to report to your office and to acquaint you, or such officers of your staff that you may designate, with the problems involved. The matter is of the highest order of secrecy.

Faithfully yours,

Chief of Staff

Groves said after they had read both letters, "I appointed a committee—Conant and two Nobel guys, Urey, Compton—to study the 'death dust' idea. They think it's probable. We know the Germans got tons of uranium out of Czechoslovakia. They could spread it from the air, contaminate a whole damn landing area. General Marshall agrees, it's a threat."

Moe Berg said quietly, "There's no defense, yes?"

Groves gave them abrupt, impatient nods. "I've had the Victoreen Instrument Company built rugged Geiger counters for teams to carry ashore. They can carry sheathed packets of photographic film too, to expose and see if they get fogged from local radiation."

"GHQ UK knows this?" Moe Berg said casually, crossing his legs.

"They're on it, sure. I sent memos to the chief surgeon to look for radioactive exposure symptoms."

Karl said, "So you think a sea invasion, as planned?"

Groves sat on his desk, legs dangling, an unusual position for him. "Look, you guys I can talk to straight. Rest of the day, I gotta keep up the whole general thing." He took out a chocolate, popped it in his mouth as Karl and Moe stayed quiet. Groves was clearly exhausted and frustrated, off his game. "Yeah, that committee in DC—they report right to the president—they think so too. But there are plenty of unknowns."

"I don't see my role in this," Moe Berg said.

"You're a fine intelligence guy, Moe," Groves said. "We'll need you in the days leading up, and probably after. We know Heisenberg's key to this, but we don't even know where he is."

"Neither do I."

"But we know he's scheduled to give a talk in Switzerland in a few months. Some physicists, like that guy Wigner, suggested we assassinate him."

"*What?*" Karl blurted this out without thinking. *Killing scientists because of what they knew?*

Groves gave him a weary look. "It's a military decision, not for the scientists, Karl."

Moe said with a light air, as though this was just a new social engagement, "This means we're moving?"

Groves grinned. "Right. I've got to send a team to do preliminary work on getting the bomb set up, ready to deliver. Pretty big crew. I need guys I can trust to report back the straight scoop, what's really happening. You can't believe how many dull reports I read! Fat 'Top Secret' documents that take forever to get to the point. Not you guys—you're straight."

Karl blinked, uncertain. "This is far from my qualifications—"

"You're a physicist or something, right?" Groves browbeat him. "You'll fly in the following plane, measure the blast. But first you've got to work with the deployment team."

A silence. Moe Berg said carefully, "I see no role for me in—"

"You're a great spy, and I need one who'll do what I want. Not go through OSS—though you'll get paid by them. Just for me."

"I still don't—"

Groves chuckled, a deep bass growl. "You don't get it. You're going along to guard Karl, Moe. He's a classified asset."

"So's Moe," Karl shot back.

"Yeah, right. So Moe, if it looks like the Krauts could grab Karl, shoot him." Groves laughed, but no one else did.

PART VII

SIGHTING
THE SHORE

You can never cross the ocean until you have the courage to lose sight of the shore.
—Columbus

1.

April 2, 1944

When Karl awoke, Marthe's arms were draped across him. A last grab to keep him here.

When he had to tell her, a week after Groves delivered his bombshell, she had burst into tears. To his astonishment, he had too. All his suppressed fears came out. This war was a meat grinder, worse than any in history, and he had been ordered into its maw.

She had argued the obvious—that he had two children, was too old, thirty-one. But guys that age were getting drafted every day, he argued. And anyway, he had been ordered. "But you're not in the army!" she had shrieked.

True, and he stumbled through rehearsed phrases about his obligation to this, this thing, this weapon that could end it all. The most disturbing, embarrassing moment of his life. He had prepared for it more than he had for his thesis examination, and his logic came apart in seconds.

She fell into a deep silence then, not talking at all. Martine and Elisabeth noticed this and came to him, worried at the mysterious silence. He had waited until after they were asleep to deliver the news, and the silence descended the next day, so they had no clue. He said their mother was suffering from a touch of bronchitis, "a no-talk sickness," he added. They weren't fooled.

Both girls frowned and fidgeted, and he took them out on Sunday for a walk in a park that luckily had a Ferris wheel. The heights and views and clanking machinery struck them with wonder. Then they lunched in a shop featuring ice cream, and he introduced them to a banana split, another wonder. It worked. Spring had brightened the world, and blossoms every-where made the distant dying that wrapped around the planet seem like a bad dream, gone. By the time they got back to the apartment, Marthe had lost her stony face and greeted them with glad cries. But her eyes were red, and she avoided looking at him.

So now the day had come, and he lay beside her in the gray dawn. Pinned, savoring the swoosh of her lovely breath. In a moment he would have to awaken her and get his clothes on, seal his bags, snatch some coffee and eggs, and be gone.

He clung to the last moment with her. Soon he would have to hold the worried daughters in his arms and assure them that he would be back, all right, pretty soon, really. He had traveled a lot to Oak Ridge and lately to Los Alamos, working with the bomb builders, so the girls were used to trips of a week or more. Still, they sensed something.

That would be the hardest moment. They would believe him, and his betrayal would become obvious only weeks later, when he did not appear. Months, more probably. This war was a persistent horror, now in its fifth year.

He did not let himself think that it could be even more years. The bombs were coming. He felt in himself a cold resolve that he would gladly work toward slamming more and more bombs into the Reich. Szilard and the oth-ers who wanted a nice demonstration did not feel the slow-burning anger he did, at things they could not see, far over the horizon. That every few seconds, someone died in this damned war. That it must be over. Not someday. Now.

In the gray Manhattan light, the cool stone buildings rose like giant grave markers. There had been an odd cold snap. Walking along with his luggage, he heard tree branches cracking as they warmed, sharp reports like distant pistol shots.

The good-byes had been a bit hasty and he played it as nothing unusual to the sleepy girls. Kisses, hugs, a longer one at the door with Marthe, then he was out into the city, lurching along with two suitcases.

He walked alone. Going with Moe meant he lost his escort, Eric Thomp-son. Eric had been occasionally useful, escorting him and Marthe when they went out evenings. She sent him on errands when Karl was just staying home to calculate, too. It would be a relief to be rid of him; Moe was more fun.

Near Times Square he met the ordinary rattling green bus that took him out to a military air base, one he hadn't even known existed, in New Jersey. It began raining as they pulled out, setting his mood. He stared out the window at dreary streets. As he got off the bus crowded with men in uniform, he looked around the wet landing field. Moe Berg was there, sporting two stylish leather bags and a waterproof fedora. Karl realized he had forgotten to bring an umbrella.

The airplane was a fat Douglas with big engines. Amid the damp and roar of bustling groups, everything had to be shouted. The other men—all men, no women—were engineers he vaguely knew and some physicists from the new Los Alamos place, probably specialists in the design of the bomb everybody was calling Little Boy as though it were some toy. There were a few officers in uniform, too, in case anyone had forgotten that this was after all a war.

He had tried to steel himself for this whole "adventure," as he had once, stupidly, called it to Marthe. She refused to go with him when, thinking of it as training, he went back to the Newsreel Theater.

There he saw the reality of this warscape world in sharp images: infantrymen running, doubled over; mortars bursting like dirty flowers across a mud landscape; airplanes spiraling down, smoke tracing their dying curve; chaplains kneeling for last rites beside wounded; seas in flames; troops crouched beside shattered bridges; pillars of dirty orange fire coiling up from oil fields; stretchers with torsos like sacks of something, scarcely like men at all; marines raising their rifles above the surf as they waded ashore, eyes anxious. Misery without end. The real world outside his own serene research bubble, where clear, clean calculations dwelled.

It had not helped settle his mind. Neither did the flights.

The seats were sack buckets, really. You could snuggle down in them, but it was a strain on the back. The reading lamps were dim, the air smelled of hot metal, the food was K rations. The food was crammed into a tan-colored card-stock box with black lettering. The feast was canned meat in a sausage, an apple, biscuits, a commercial sweet Hershey's chocolate bar, toilet tissues, a four-pack of Camels, and chewing gum. Everybody smoked the cigarettes; Karl gave his away.

He had read that the war had made millions into smokers, and now he saw why. The tobacco companies were getting the military to do their recruiting. A private handed out more small packs of cigarettes, this time Lucky Strikes. Everyone puffed on them eagerly. Some of these men were no doubt headed for battle, Karl thought, so why not indulge a few bad habits? No alcohol, of course. In all, not much worse than the few flights he had taken with Groves to cut the commute time to Oak Ridge.

They hopped up to Botwood, Newfoundland, then to Greenland, on to Scotland, all to refuel. Top speed seemed to be around 125 miles an hour. This would take a full day, with the refuelings. Then they headed at last for London. They were on the great circle route Charles Lindbergh had pioneered. The airplane was reliable, but its drone drove him to stuff cotton into his ears. The cotton was in a cardboard box as they came onto the airplane. When he went to the restroom and peered down into the toilet, he saw whitecaps not far below.

Still, the worst part of it all was the breaks when they landed. They got out, joints popping and muscles yearning to get stretched, and milled rather than marched into a canteen. The refueling and checking for failures in engines, lines, wheels, and other gear took hours. These airplanes had been built fast and sturdy, but punishing use had brought them low. Their flight had some priority, which meant safety was number one. "We're more valuable," Moe said. "Our whole team is dispersed among flights. If we lose some, not so bad."

Karl sat with Moe and Alvarez—"Call me Louie," he said the second time Karl respectfully addressed him by his last name. An experimental physicist with some flying experience. In the canteen they talked amid the dense raw smoke, prickly smells of frying meat, acrid coffee, junky big-band music on tinny speakers, and incessant calls for numbered flights to get back onboard.

Worse, the talk surrounding them was eternal gossip about the war. Everyone knew this was the biggest event in world history and they were part of it and it was all up for grabs, so whaddya think?

Compared with the distant perspectives of the physicists, who at least knew geography and so maybe a bit more about military possibilities, the war chatter was just noise.

Plus fistfights. A big man in a navy uniform dragged a private out of his chair and started pounding him, shouting, "Think so? Think so?" as he slammed big, meaty hands into the man. Some MPs rushed in and dragged them off. Applause all round. Everybody lit up fresh cigarettes, mostly Lucky Strikes, and the jabber ran on. They were all in this together and sure it was dangerous, but jeez, this was some damn war, wasn't it?

They were all worn out by the time the Douglas droned toward London. Karl arranged to sit next to Luis and engaged the lanky, casual man in muted talk about the problems with Little Boy, the gadget's code name. It had to be shipped in separate flights, to be assembled in England. The army sent three complete assemblies, in case some flights didn't make it. German air interceptions were rare now, but still the gadget guys took the longer route through Greenland to avoid the risk. Karl's major job was figuring out whether the "gun team" had done their job right. They had been assigned to make sure the whole shebang slammed together at the speed of a rifle bullet, but weighing fifty thousand times more.

Luis Alvarez leaned back, stretching, and said, "Any successful team needs one rational guy who thinks this thing is sure as hell not gonna work. I guess that's you, Karl." Luis gave him a raised eyebrow.

Karl grinned at this insight. He did indeed think of himself as Groves's tame skeptic. Karl had pushed for this outcome with a fervor that often got him into arguments. His skepticism came from his sense of urgency. He nodded. "Somebody's got to ask questions, is the way I see it. Lift the hood, watch it run. Plus, I've got to be sure it doesn't run up costs, either. This whole damn war has been done on a budget."

Moe Berg said easily, "Congress can only print so much money."

"Time's money in a war," Luis said.

Karl had kept costs down in running the centrifuge program out of his stingy instincts. When he had gotten his PhD done, Columbia required seventy-five copies of his thesis. That would mean three hundred dollars for printing, so he delayed filing for his degree. When the paper based on it got published, he bought copies from the publisher at a quarter apiece and bound them up as the thesis.

Karl considered the two men on either side of him. "I feel promoted beyond my abilities, guys. Just six years ago I was grateful to just get a job with Urey, after coming back from marrying in Paris. Now . . ."

Luis yawned and said, "I'm a few years older than you Karl, I'd judge—and I feel the same way. This is a major transition in human history. We're harnessing an energy that drives stars—nuclear. A long way from burning wood and coal."

Karl recalled what Harold Urey said when they made their good-byes. "Not surprised he picked you to go. You know why Groves likes you, and not me? Because you're rock-solid certain. Me, I have doubts. The difference between 'Do it!' and 'Maybe this will work' is huge for Groves."

Maybe that was it. He still felt like an imposter, though, a midget on this immense stage.

London swam out from beneath cotton-ball clouds. They droned down onto a vast system of runways, bounced on landing, and stiffly worked the kinks out of their legs as they gathered up their bags.

Across the landing field, in midday sun, they passed through a murmuring military sorting hall. There were issues of *Stars and Stripes* with a Bill Mauldin cartoon of a beat-up GI sitting with his bare feet in his helmet, which was filled with water. He was saying to another soldier, *Tell th' ol' man I'm sittin' up wi' two sick friends.* Among photos and vague articles about pounding the Germans in Italy was a quotation from Eleanor Roosevelt framed in a border: *Yesterday is history, tomorrow is a mystery, today is a gift, that's why they call it the present.* True enough, Karl supposed. As he looked out the window at army trucks and muddy fields, he wished he could find a *New York Times*.

They took a bus into a forlorn London. There were grimy machine sheds and block-wide warehouses and smoky chimneys. Above these he saw a wan yellow break in the grim clouds. Trucks filled with sitting US soldiers rumbled along, and airplanes glinted in the sky. Their bus crossed a bridge, and he saw men fishing in a river beside a boat club that seemed to be made of random boards nailed together. The stained roads had the rank oil smell he recalled from his time here with Marthe. That had been 1937, and they had nipped off for a weekend in the heady days of first love, when their world was bright and brimming.

Streets here now buzzed with life, but whole blocks were smashed to rubble. Men in overalls worked in yards, many women wore trousers, and crowds pressed through the streets in shabby clothes. The women were shopping, holding wicker baskets and standing in lines they called queues outside the few shops that were open. The men were thin, grizzled, smoking cigarettes. Everywhere faces were lined, somber. He rolled down a window and breathed in damp air carrying gasoline fumes and smoke that made his nose itch. On a passing field he saw GIs playing softball. Somehow he had expected cricket.

Gray barrage balloons hung above on thousand-foot cables. They were supposed to snag bombers. Karl estimated the typical German bomber wingspan and the number of balloons per square mile, did the calculation. Given a random walk by an adroit pilot, an enemy had maybe a 50 percent chance of crossing London below a thousand feet. If that pilot flew above the balloons, the radar-controlled antiaircraft guns—a collaboration of the Brits and the USA, he had heard—had a damn good chance of shooting him down, because the guns could track and aim fast enough. The Battle of Britain was over, but the Germans kept up some pressure.

Their bus chugged through thick traffic of trucks and buses, then finally hauled up into a big courtyard. They filed into a tall, barnlike place full of cots separated by hung sheets, as though on clotheslines. Someone handed him an assignment slip. Karl found his bunk and stuffed his luggage under it. He was suddenly very tired and had trouble finding the "john," as somebody called it, which had on its door a mysterious WC. A shower helped, but the soap was rough and raw, smelling like floor cleaner. He came out of the steam with a towel around his waist and peered around in the dim glow of lamps in the high ceiling. The big room full of cots smelled of damp clothing. Snores echoed like angry birds. He did not look for Moe or Luis. He sat on his cot and slowly let himself collapse onto it, pulling up the sheets that smelled of some harsh detergent. Without a moment's thought, he fell into fitful dreams.

Freeman Dyson

2.

The next morning Karl came up from sleep as though drugged. He had gotten no instructions on what to do once here, so he lounged a bit, listening to a chorus of coughs and murmurs. When he finally lurched up, he found that Moe Berg had gone somewhere already. Fair enough; Moe had slept easily on the flights. Luis Alvarez was gone too. Karl had barely pulled on clothes and combed his hair when an orderly handed him a note to appear at the entrance *to meet escort*. The escort was a short, sinewy man with strawlike filaments of excitable hair that made him resemble an upside-down broom. His attire was frowzy, worn pants and tweed jacket with a dull school tie. "Hello," he said as they shook hands. "I'm Freeman Dyson, to brief you. Might I ask if you have had breakfast?"

He and Karl found the officers' mess and got in the cafeteria line. "This is better fare than we get in Bomber Command," Freeman said, helping himself to scrambled eggs and pancakes and syrup. "I'm in the ORS, Operational Research Section. You lot have handed us quite a problem."

Karl had the pancakes too. They were only a distant dull echo of Marthe's light, fluffy confections. Smothering them in maple syrup seemed a just execution. The scrambled eggs came from powder shipped from the USA, brought to zombie life with water and milk. "Problem?" *More like a solution.*

Freeman looked around. "Quite a problem, delivering your, um, package."

"Got to assemble it first." Karl bit into a brown sausage that squirted hot fat into his mouth, and made a face. Freeman told him they were by law at least half meat. Judging by texture and taste, Karl took the other half to be sawdust. The toast had already long cooled off too. And the coffee seemed to have mistakenly included machine oil.

"Bomber Command is quite busy. We're redirected from Germany to the German defenses in France. They sent me, a quite junior figure"—Freeman bowed his head in a humble nod—"to get some idea of what to expect. And in reverse, to tell you of the delivery problems."

"Um." Freeman was not quite what Karl had expected, not a rock-jawed military type at all. "As far as I know, no target selected yet."

"Indeed. I rather feel that the obvious is not necessarily wrong."

"Go for the amateur painter?" Karl was careful not to say anything that could be picked up as information to prying ears.

"Exactly." Freeman's smile was the real window into him, a delighted beam that appeared to float free from his face, strangely dynamic with its electric ears and perky nose.

As they walked toward a nondescript brown concrete building nearby, there came a loud rumbling. "Buzz bomb," Freeman said, and there it was flying overhead, zooming away from them. Sirens wailed. "Launched from sites along the French and Dutch coasts." Winged death stood out black against an eggshell-blue sky, marred by smokestack coal plumes. They stood by a flattened area of rubble and listened for the abrupt silence when the engine stopped. Sudden quiet. It was still in view when the slender tube with stubby wings began its exhausted fall. Karl spent anxious seconds waiting—then a muffled bang came. A silence. Then everyone around them moved on. Quite plausibly, someone had died. For the first time he felt that he was *in* the war.

"Simple pilotless airplanes," Freeman said. "Ingenious. More effective than bombers because they're much cheaper. Our pilots can tumble them by flying alongside and flipping their wings a bit—destabilizes their gyros."

"I heard something about the German who runs their rocket program," Karl said.

"Von Braun. He's behind these buzzing devils, yes. I hear that Bomber Command surveys show some bigger rocket being tested too."

Karl decided to go no further. He recalled the eccentric, blustery Campbell at that science fiction magazine saying that von Braun was a subscriber. So if von Braun had noticed that old Anson MacDonald story about death dust, could he send it up the Nazi pyramid to get the attention of people in their bomb program? Best to keep such speculations down, he judged. Meanwhile he let himself savor the range of accents and voices in this city so plainly under pressure. Voices were louder, speech faster, eyes dancing.

They went into the brown concrete blockhouse that Freeman said was the Admiralty Citadel, a bomb-proof operations center for the Admiralty and RAF. To Karl its brutal functionality was a rude sore thumb amid the centuries-old brick and stone of old London. Freeman said it had a very practical purpose. "In the event of a German invasion, this building would become a fortress, with loopholed firing positions provided to fend off attackers."

Down they went, staircase after staircase smelling of damp plaster, deep into the bowels of a bombproof citadel with foundations thirty feet deep and a concrete-steel shell twenty feet thick. Broad tunnels ran radially away on each floor, to government buildings in Whitehall. On one stairwell landing a German propeller was mounted on the wall. It was twisted and blackened, a victory badge.

Freeman said, "Churchill doesn't like this place, prefers the Cabinet War Rooms. He calls it"—here Freeman lowered his voice into a bulldog bass—"a vast monstrosity which weighs upon the Horse Guards Parade." Karl chuckled.

Uniformed Brits and Americans moved everywhere, intent, eyes hollow. Freeman had a cramped office. He offered tea brewed on a hot pad, but Karl waved it aside and said, "You're pretty young."

"I'm twenty. Plenty of those I went to school with are serving. Some are already dead. The government asked me to join the group studying bombing strategy. I felt I should come. We're civilians, employed by the Ministry of Aircraft Production and not by the air force. I'm straight out of Cambridge, fresh from an abbreviated two years as a student."

By now Karl had learned that the best way to get cooperation from people was to share some history, become something like a friend. "Why Bomber Command?"

"At Cambridge I attended all the advanced mathematics lectures. It was a wonderland of beautiful thought. I climbed roofs at night during blackouts to glimpse the flashes of bombing toward London. I can remember so vividly lying in bed at age fifteen, the start of the Blitz. I enjoyed hearing the bombs go off with a wonderful crunching noise. I thought it was the sound of the British Empire crumbling. I thought it exciting, new. Much has changed. Perhaps I can do a bit to prevent that crumbling."

"Ah. What're you doing now?"

"Finding how to murder most economically another hundred thousand people," Freeman said with a sad, wry smile of resignation.

"We have a better way, I hope."

"I know what you've done, from Rudolf Peierls. Good show, your team stuck with centrifugal. Rudolf now admits that in the gaseous diffusion method, they still haven't found the membrane to separate out the, ah, tube alloy. I gather you sprinted ahead."

"More like a steady walk. It took some doing."

"Bomber Harris gathered our team together and set us to thinking how to use your, ah, gadget."

Karl's forehead wrinkled. "Bomber . . . ?"

"Sir Arthur Harris, usually seen by us mortals in his air force limousine, passing us on our bikes. Our mammoth force of heavy bombers, which he commands, was planned in 1936 as our primary instrument for defeating Hitler, without repeating the trench warfare horrors of World War I. Bomber Command, by itself, absorbs about one-quarter of our entire war effort."

"This new, uh, gadget of ours will be enormously different."

Freeman nodded. "So I gather from the reports. Wizard, absolutely wizard. But . . ." A long pause, eyes distant. "Allow me to tell you a bit of history. My first day of work was a day after one of our most successful operations, a full-force night attack on Hamburg. For the first time, the bombers had used the decoy system, what you Americans called chaff. That's still classified, I think—packets of paper strips coated with aluminum paint. One crew member in each bomber was responsible for throwing packets of it down a chute, at a rate of one packet per minute, while flying over Germany. The paper strips floated slowly down through the stream of bombers, each strip a resonant antenna tuned to the frequency of the German radar. The purpose was to confuse the radar so it could not track individual bombers in the clutter of echoes from the chaff."

Karl realized there was much he did not know about how to deliver the gadget. "So you think . . . ?"

"That day, the people at the ORS were joyful. I never saw them as joyful again. It had worked! The bomber losses the night before were only twelve out of seven hundred ninety-one, or 1.5 percent. Far fewer than would have been expected for a major operation in July 1942, when the skies in northern Europe are never really dark. Losses were usually about five percent and were mostly due to German night fighters, guided to the bombers by radars on the ground. Chaff cut the expected losses by two-thirds. Each bomber carried a crew of seven, so chaff that night had saved the lives of about a hundred eighty of our boys."

"Ah, you think using it can shield a single bomber too?"

"Yes. Hamburg was a lesson that might apply here also, to your gadget. There was a firestorm. People were asphyxiated or roasted inside their shelters, terrible deaths. The number killed was more than ten times greater than similar raids. After that, every time Bomber Command attacked a city, we were trying to raise a firestorm. We never did."

Despite the deluge of war news, this he had never heard. "So it was harder than they thought?"

"I think I've learned why we so seldom succeeded. Probably a firestorm can happen only when three things occur together: first, a high concentration of old buildings at the target site; second, an attack with a high density of incendiary bombs in the target's central area; and third, an ability to create an atmospheric instability."

"So it takes all three at once? A tall order." Karl grimaced at thinking of mass murder as a technical problem. "Well, let's see. Our gadget gets number two. Berlin certainly fits for number one. Atmospheric instability means what?"

Freeman shrugged. "No swift wind, mostly. Certainly lack of rain. With all three requirements, we may ignite a firestorm larger than Hamburg. In the capital city that runs this war."

"So . . . it might be *too* effective?"

"There must be someone left with the authority to surrender."

"The generals will be out in the field. The amateur painter will be . . ." Karl stopped, realizing that he had assumed Hitler would rule from Berlin, but that could easily be wrong.

Freeman nodded sympathetically, his eyes clear and caring. "My point is that we don't know."

Freeman went on with more examples. The early Berlin air raids failed. Sir Arthur ordered fifteen more heavy attacks, expecting to destroy that city as thoroughly as he had destroyed Hamburg. All through the winter of 1943–44, the bombers hammered away at Berlin. The weather that winter was worse than usual, covering the city with cloud for weeks on end. Photo reconnaissance planes could bring back no pictures to show how poorly the bombers were doing. As the attacks went on, the German defenses grew stronger, British losses heavier, fighters got more deadly, and the scatter of the bombs worse. Finally, losses per raid rose to nine percent. Sir Arthur admitted defeat. The battle over Berlin had cost 492 bombers with more than three thousand aircrew.

Dyson concluded, "For all that, industrial production in Berlin continued to increase, and the operations of government were never seriously disrupted."

"I had no idea." Karl felt whatever assurance he had evaporate before Freeman's calm, measured reciting of facts.

"All I've told you is classified, top secret."

"Because . . . ?"

"Morale. We're beaten down over here."

"I can see it in people's faces."

"That, plus apprehension about the invasion about to start."

"I saw a joke repeated in the *New York Times*. That the English are saying the trouble with Americans is that they're overpaid, oversexed, and over here."

Freeman reacted with a laugh so hearty it shook him. This softened his formality, making him into a sage and friendly elf. "I hadn't heard that one. At my part of Bomber Command we have no American contacts."

"So the failure of your bombing campaign is secret, to keep up public support?"

"Afraid so."

"And now we plan to change that with one bomb."

"If possible. There were two main reasons why Germany won the battle over Berlin. First, the city is more modern and less dense than Hamburg, spread out over an area as large as London with only half of London's population; so it did not burn well. Second, the repeated attacks along the same routes allowed the German fighters to find the bomber stream earlier and kill bombers more efficiently."

"So if we deliver one big slam, what happens?"

"We have been wondering that. Of course, the higher-ups"—Freeman raised his expressive eyebrows sardonically—"will decide the target."

"But you think . . . ?"

"Cut the head off, yes."

"But with ten percent or so shot down—"

"We must be careful. This is a wholly new thing. A Lancaster bomber can barely carry it."

"Give the plane a big escort."

"That might just attract attention."

"So how do we get the gadget there safely?" Karl realized that using "safely" in the same sentence with the gadget was an odd irony.

"I'm unsure. We all are." Freeman gave him another arched eyebrow and a wry smile. "The way I see it, since we have got ourselves into the business of bombing cities, we might as well do the job competently and get it over with."

In the RAF

✦ ✦ ✦

After a dinner of decent beef and a crusty Yorkshire pudding with cardboard peas, "courtesy of the Yanks, oddly" as one officer remarked, Karl walked through the London night with Freeman in tow. For a major city it was eerie to see the swath of stars silhouetting the steepled buildings. Occasional German bombers still got through the English air defenses and struck, so the blackout held. In small pubs they passed, he could see, through the occasional opened doorway, dimly lit crowds lifting glasses and talking nonstop. Tension was gathering as the invasion of France neared.

He wondered if this war would bring fundamental changes in the Europe he so much enjoyed, especially Paris. He was starting to like London a great deal, hearing its many accents and oddities. There would always, he supposed, be men with pencil-thin mustaches whiling away rainy afternoons, smoking odd cigarettes and talking about the war that had dwarfed all others before. Or could there be another cataclysm up ahead, after this one? For him to talk over, maybe in some European bar, when he was old?

He had already been in several meetings throughout the afternoon, and noticed the difference in tone. The English had personal experience with injury and death, coming from the sky and in the news, every day. He and the others Stateside had worked with the best equipment they had ever seen, doing the sort of things they had always wanted to do—science, technology, enticing problems. His war had been far away, a "nice" war. It was embarrassing to recall that only a week or so ago he had gone to see newsreels to prepare. The people around him now had been in those films and needed no pep talks. No. Just results.

Freeman spoke softly as they strolled along the Thames in mild spring air. Looming out of the mist that shrouded the sleepy old streets were the hazy towers of St. Paul's Cathedral. "Let's go in," Freeman said.

Once inside, the dark clasped him in its moist fist, yielding gradually to the faint light through the tall side windows. Looking up, he saw the immense columns leading his eye up to the arches. The corbelled roof supported effortlessly the enormous weight of the nave, all shrouded in gauzy gray light. Stone pillars rounded with age led his eye to turrets, gargoyles, statues and ornaments to the otherwise clean lines of architectural grace. Then a defense spotlight suddenly streamed in through the stained glass, spattering everything with rose and blues and subtle purples, all in watery flickers.

He and Marthe had gone to Chartres, which matched this ethereal majesty. He had been to London, too, whose thronged streets already churned beneath the 1937 threat of war. Now he wondered how much of Europe's soaring splendors would survive this war.

Freeman said nothing and together, with one nodding agreement, they mounted the stairs to the very roof of all this stack of majestic stone. Karl felt eager, not even puffing as he climbed up into a suffused sprinkling of city light. Freeman said, "The continuing survival of St. Paul's means everything for morale." He pointed to an array of heavy wooden beams bracing an outer wall. A thin smile. "Parts have to be propped up by scaffolding—for renovation, officially. Wouldn't do to admit that it had suffered any damage from near hits, you know."

Abruptly the great bells sounded. He felt the notes peal through him, in wavelengths comparable to his body size—a sensation of immanent meaning, if only he could fathom it. The bells rang solemnly, mournfully, bringing crows cawing into the air, wheeling black against a gray moonlit cloud. A gargoyle leered nearby, tongue hanging down toward the hunched, huddled houses far below. *Out of the squalor and filth of the Middle Ages*, he thought, *the brute labor behind wooden ploughs, the black plagues, all came still this. The religious impulse endured. Even Dark Ages can yield some light.*

And these were dark times indeed. He wondered if the gadget would make their century even darker up ahead, in the decades beyond the most terrible war that had ever been.

3.

April 30, 1944 MEMO
SECRET
Use of Radioactive Material as a Military Weapon
From Drs. Conant, Compton, Urey
To Brigadier General L. R. Groves, Manhattan District,
Oak Ridge, Tennessee

Our key points are:

1. As a gas warfare instrument, the radioactive material would be most dangerous when inhaled by personnel. The amount necessary to cause death to a person inhaling the material is extremely small. We have estimated that one millionth of a gram accumulating in a person's body would be fatal.

2. There are no known methods of treatment for such a casualty. It cannot be detected by the senses. It can be distributed in a dust or smoke form so finely powdered that it will permeate a standard gas mask filter in quantities large enough to be extremely damaging.

3. Radioactive warfare can be used to make evacuated areas uninhabitable; to contaminate small critical areas such as railroad yards and airports; as a radioactive poison gas to create casualties among troops; against large cities, to promote panic, and to create casualties among civilian populations.

4. Areas so contaminated by radioactive dusts and smokes would be dangerous as long as a high enough concentration of material could be maintained. They can be stirred up as a fine dust from the terrain by winds, movement of vehicles or troops, etc., and would remain a potential hazard for a long time.

5. These materials may also be so disposed as to be taken into the body by ingestion instead of inhalation. Reservoirs or wells would be contaminated or food poisoned with an effect similar to that resulting from inhalation of dust or smoke. Four days production could contaminate a million gallons of water to an extent that a quart drunk in one day would probably result in complete incapacitation or death in about a month's time.

6. Note that some feel this weapon would violate international treaties on chemical weapons, though the dust effect is nuclear, not chemical.

Luis Alvarez tapped on the memo and said to Karl and Moe, "What's this got to do with our work, huh?"

They were in a cramped office inside the Admiralty Citadel, with the door propped open for ventilation, despite security regulations. Passing British officers occasionally eyed them with polite curiosity.

Moe Berg gave Luis a thin smile. "General Groves sent it in a high security pouch for us to read. He also cabled Eisenhower's office, saying this memo is based on animal exposure studies done Stateside. We just get the summary conclusions. We're his boys over here, with time to look into it more."

Luis shook his head. "I'm busy with assembling the gadget. Plenty of work. The Royal Air Force guys are working with our boys to get a Lancaster into shape for delivering it. I'm assembling the diagnostic packages to drop near the target. We've got plenty to do!"

Moe nodded sympathetically and sipped at his tea. They were in a secure building with office space and even a driver assigned. Karl had been reviewing the gadget assembly too, looking into details. This meeting had come as a surprise. "Groves sent over a guy named Sam Goudsmit to look into all the

Brit intelligence on the German radioactives program. He's sifted it through and thinks they have a lot of uranium from Czechoslovakia. If they haven't got a bomb, maybe they'll use the uranium for dust."

Karl said, "We should talk to Goudsmit."

"Huh!" Luis snorted. "I don't like to get deflected away from the main job."

Moe shrugged. "Nobody does. But Groves also ordered us to double up on tasks. He thinks you professional smart guys could screw up, if you're left to do things alone."

Karl disliked all the jockeying around of jobs. He liked to concentrate on a linear path and get things nailed. "We're shorthanded here," he said.

"There are supposed to be more guys coming in soon," Moe said.

Karl said, "Oak Ridge barely gave us enough to be sure the gadget will work."

"The invasion pressed the schedule forward," Moe said.

Luis gazed skeptically at Moe. "Seems like you're Groves's mouthpiece."

"Seems to be," Moe said with an ironic lift of eyebrows.

Sam Goudsmit

Sam Goudsmit was a short, stocky man who radiated intensity. He wore civilian clothes but had a military bearing, jaw jutting just a bit. His office was one floor above Karl's, and Goudsmit offered Karl and Freeman tea, the ritual everyone picked up here. None of them smoked, and his office was free of the pervasive cigarette stink that irritated Karl's nose nearly everywhere he went. Sam was careful to shut the transom above his door, to avoid being overheard. Maybe to keep out the smoke, too.

Karl and Freeman introduced themselves, and they spent some moments kicking around connections with friends. Goudsmit was Dutch born with parents now in a concentration camp, but his English had a clipped American tone. In London, accents told you a lot. Karl always thought of this acoustic signature as like animals sniffing each other out. Every technical person knew of Bohr and Fermi and the pressing job to be done. Sam got down to work right away. "Y'know, Groves left it to me to pick a meaningless name for our group, so I made it 'Alsos'—which means 'groves' in Greek." Sam chuckled at this small deception.

Plainly he felt the same as Karl did about the blustery military miasma. "We're to look into the German bomb, if there is one, and this 'death dust' thing too." Sam said this with deepening disdain. "Imaginary, I'd say—dust as weapon! Absurd."

"You've read the latest Groves memo on it?" Freeman said politely.

"I'm more a bomb guy. Worked on some of that at MIT, about assembly. That must've been due to you guys, right?" He peered at Karl. "Bombs are sure a much better weapon for a concentrated enemy."

Karl said, "You know we're about to have one. The 'gadget' is nearly assembled."

"Yeah, I know. Can't come too soon, for me. I'm from the Netherlands. I've got parents somewhere in the Hague, hiding from the Krauts. I want this war *over*."

Goudsmit's face compressed and his voice thinned with bitter passion. Karl thought of his own relatives in the Ukraine and Poland, from whom no one had heard in years. Millions like them were in eastern Europe, vast bloodlands now locked in a battle to the death between Germany and the USSR. He knew little of the damage rolling through those dark territories, but everyone knew the vast armies struggling there, bringing ruin by the day. Every day.

"We all agree," Freeman said quietly.

Goudsmit gave them a dire look and said, "Look, I've gone over all the intel on the German program we have, gotten from all around Europe. By the time Szilard got to Einstein, who got to Roosevelt, the Germans did have a fission project going—heavy water moderation."

Karl said, "Heavy water to slow down the neutrons in a reactor that uses U-235. That's what Moe parachuted into Norway to find. The RAF blew up that plant."

Goudsmit nodded. "I think they're still trying for a reactor, though. We have spotty intel saying so."

Freeman asked, "What are the chances they've worked forward enough to have a bomb?"

Goudsmit shook his head. "Not good. The German style for this sort of thing is to set up a lot of separate projects doing different things, which all compete for resources. Not our style."

Karl thought of his battles with Dunning and the English, who wanted to roll the dice on the diffusion method, despite not knowing how to do it. "We've had our problems, sure. We're building reactors now to get plutonium, but Oppenheimer and company out in Los Alamos don't know how to build a bomb with it either."

Goudsmit gave Karl a look of respect. "I hear you're the guy who kept pushing for the spinner method?"

Karl nodded, not letting his smile quite show how pleased he was, and Goudsmit went on. "So while there were other projects in the US, my impression is that you got it together in one big effort, run by this general. Must've been fun."

Karl allowed his smile to convey a lofting, sardonic humor. "*Fun*," *sure* . . .

While Freeman brought Goudsmit up to speed, Karl reflected on how word must have spread here about the American program, despite all the security rules. Physicists loved the new, the brilliant, and could not keep quiet about it. They would invent perfectly plausible reasons to tell others, and find ways to work in the field, if at all possible.

Now Dunning was working on one of the reactor teams under Fermi. Reports said he was doing a very good job. Dunning liked working with Fermi, who many thought was the world's best all-round physicist. Karl knew he had beaten Dunning by getting enough private money to tinker with the spinners. A sidestep that had gained advantage. Now time and hard work had delivered the right results.

Dunning was quite right, too, to work with Fermi. The man was an inspiration, smarter even than Teller. Fermi had gently suggested to Karl that he help lure Dunning away from Columbia in 1942—and "lure" was the word he used, too. Karl had instantly known this was the smart way to go around the whole Brit faction that favored gaseous diffusion of U-235. He still remembered the moment. Fermi had leaned against a blackboard, ignoring the white chalk swaths on his shirt and pants, and said, "He will not stop pushing his ideas, you know."

Karl had nodded—this was a swerve in the conversation, which until that moment was mostly Fermi outlining a calculation Karl could barely follow. He had been too embarrassed to take proper notes, even if he could have—Fermi wrote fast and talked faster, once he had the idea in place. "I know," Karl had said. Fermi gave him a significant, savvy glance, and they had gone on with the calculation.

And Fermi had then orchestrated Dunning's move away into reactor work. Only later did Karl realize that the delicate tipping point of influence had turned on that pivotal moment.

Karl shook his head, banishing the memory. People were talking loudly and he had lost track. . . .

Goudsmit spoke forcefully, looking at the faces around the table. "So they've got a lot of uranium from Czechoslovakia. What're they doing? Going for a reactor?"

No one knew, of course. Goudsmit leaned over the table, finger stabbing the air. "The Brits got intel in 1943 that the Kaiser Wilhelm Institute people were building a reactor. The real brains of the German 'uranium project' is Werner Heisenberg. Plenty of data on that. Heisenberg was a professor at the Kaiser Wilhelm, with von Weizsäcker and Hahn himself, who started it all back in 1938. That Berlin group was only one of several that began working on the nuclear program. Hamburg's got one. Plus Munich, Heidelberg, Kiel, Vienna. All of them small, it seems."

"Heisenberg is young," Karl said. "Can he run a program like that?"

Goudsmit gave Karl a steady look. "Hey, he's older than you, right?

Midforties. He's an odd guy. I've met him, back in prewar days when he came to the USA. Smart! That Nobel and all kinda puffed him up, though. Keeps up on the all rest of physics. He goes now and then to Switzerland to give talks. That's the only other country the Nazis let scientists go to, since it's neutral. I'll bet he'll come down sometime this year for some R and R on the lakes. Every time he's there, he's talked about quantum theory, no nuclear stuff at all."

"Which is suspicious," Moe said.

Goudsmit snapped his fingers with delight. "Right! Look, I *know* he's heading up their nuclear work. We checked it in a funny way—or mostly, the Brits did. They guessed, or I suppose maybe 'concluded'"—he raised his eyebrows—"from limited intelligence that there was no bomb crash program in Germany. They got that pretty clear, when Professor Peierls was pushing that gaseous diffusion thing—you know him, right, Karl?"

Karl sat up to get some height and project his voice more, a cue he had learned the hard way in many committee meetings. Very carefully he kept his face blank. "We fought Peierls for two years, against that"—he could feel his throat tightening, voice hardening, but couldn't stop—"damned, no-show, gaseous diffusion idea. Peierls pushed that along with Dunning, and they lost. Look, sure, he's a good physicist, but wrong. We're all wrong sometimes, right?"

He looked around the room and knew his face was no longer stiff and blank, but he did not know what it looked like now, and something told him not to try to find out.

Goudsmit visibly decided to let that pass, shaking his head slightly as if to clear it. "This guy Professor Peierls, he told me that he was convinced the Krauts didn't have a big, coherent program. See, he got hold of catalogs of courses in German universities. He compared them with those from past years, hunting them up in the Cambridge University library. He saw that the usual people were teaching the usual physics courses. So no big central project to take them away, use up their time."

Nods greeted this around the room. Moe gently nudged, "Back to Heisenberg?"

Goudsmit blinked. "Oh yeah. Reports say he's never referred to the nuclear program, in all his Swiss talks. Not even in casual after-dinner discussions. We know, 'cause we double-checked it with some of the Swiss who were there."

Moe leaned forward, tenting his fingers. "This is more my line of work. When he's in Switzerland, that'll be the time to get to him—to see if he's really running a big program."

Karl felt he had to say, "We're assuming that the war won't be over soon, after the gadget goes off."

Freeman said quietly, "One might quibble over the definition of soon." The pealing laughter that followed revealed the unspoken tension in the cramped office.

When Dyson told him that the two of them had to go to a high-level meeting, Karl tried to get out of it. He had plenty to do.

"Nobody will pay any attention to what we say."

Freeman nodded. "Undoubtedly. We will be there to answer questions on bombing and your 'gadget' device." He liked the term, always gave a little smile as he used it.

"We have reports, calculations—"

"They want to get it from us. Most of your team is out at the airfield, doing their flight training and miscellaneous. Same on my side—I analyze data, I don't have a hand in mission planning, really. Not much beyond simply saying some things we know about what works in bomber groups."

Karl shook his head. "I know nothing about that."

"I handle that, if anyone cares what analysis says."

Karl frowned skeptically. "So I discuss . . . what?"

"The physics and engineering details, your judgment of them."

"I don't know much. I've been running around for years now—getting spinners to work, mostly. Then Groves asked me to look at the bomb designs. Plus take part in figuring how to be sure they work."

"Very good. You know the estimated extent of damage?"

Karl knew what various people thought, which varied by factors of two or three. "Some. I can relate our ideas. Not like we're going to test them. Not with three or so months to get another warhead."

"Quite so." Freeman sighed. "We are less useful to our groups for now, so we go. Efficient, you see."

Karl thought Freeman was the sort who proved quietly useful, and he recalled Luis Alvarez's comment—*Any successful team needs one rational guy who thinks this thing is sure as hell not gonna work.* "Not willingly."

Freeman smiled wistfully. "Will does not come into it at all."

The White Hart pub was jammed, of course. Yanks and Free French, Aussies, Brits of several persuasions—all thronged the noisy, smoky rooms and spilled into the street. A woman stood with her hip cocked against a windowsill and said with a leer, "On the stroll?"

Karl stopped, not getting the meaning. She wore a tight skirt and sweater with a silver cross pointing the way to her breasts, in case he had somehow missed them. He edged away from her broad smile and stood outside to peer through the open windows. The pubs had just opened and the bar was a froth of shouted orders. Not his kind of spot, no.

He did enjoy overhearing English terms like "codswallop" for "nonsense" and "tosser" for "idiot" while he waited. Then he saw Anton waving a hand and pointing to two beers he had already scored, sitting on a table. By the time Karl wedged himself into Anton's vicinity, all possible chairs had been kidnapped. They pounded each other's backs and Karl called, "Outside!"

At last able to breathe, they leaned against the brick wall. Anton had hitchhiked up from a southern port in England to meet Karl. It was sheer luck they were in the same corner of the war at the same time. Now foot traffic brought more eager-eyed soldiers and the occasional woman in uniform toward the pub. The military owned these streets by sheer numbers.

"How's the navy treating you?" Karl asked, sipping his stout. It was the closest one could get to a real drink, in his opinion, given the horrible wine the locals called "plonk."

"Is fine! I sail on freighters. Plenty work, but no subs now."

Someone bumped Anton and some beer spattered on the pavement. "We seem to have sunk most of their navy."

"Yes! But am promise will get to Pacific once this invasion over." Anton grinned with raised eyebrows at the prospect.

"The invasion is the salad, not the dessert." *And wait until you see the appetizer we're giving them. . . .*

Anton laughed heartily. "Always with food, you are. I applied for combat duty and was approved. No navy combat left, much, here."

"Maybe we should take a walk. . . ." So many of the pub crowd filled the street now; he looked around. To move quickly was to make enemies. Karl got pushed back. Jostling. Then an elbow jarred him. A fist flew by. Shouts rose. The anger came from nearby but had nothing to do with them.

That did not matter now. A strange guttural rage rippled outward. He realized they were in a vicious free-for-all for which Karl's advanced degrees were no good. He ducked and dodged in Anton's wake. Anton had a way of slipping punches and pushes so that he always moved toward the street. This proved to be not the optimal path. The fight spilled into traffic. Somebody clipped him lightly on the jaw. Karl emerged from a section of the fight with no more damage than could be racked up to shaving. Anton ran ahead and Karl followed, straight into another crowd. It took a moment of wary dodging to discover that this was a ring of spectators.

A shrill whistle sounded.

"MPs!" Anton shouted.

They slipped between the hub and the bub and down a side street.

They trotted away until Karl leaned against the half-collapsed wall of a bomb site, panting. *I really must get more exercise. . . .*

"Well," he said in a thin voice, "you wanted to see combat."

Anton's eyes were bright. "Yeah, was fun!"

"Not my idea of it."

"Didn't you fight when young?"

"Once, with an Italian kid in a school yard."

"How'd you do?"

"Guess."

PART VIII

GROUND POUNDER

Richard Feynman

Nothing is worse than war? Dishonor is worse than war. Slavery is worse than war.
—Winston Churchill

1.

May 2, 1944

"Popcorn, that's the model," Richard Feynman said with a lopsided grin.

This brought doubtful frowns. Feynman shrugged. "Say you pop a handful of kernels. Out comes a thimbleful of nice white corn to eat. Yum! The rest is some sizzled kernels, but not popped. Useless. That's what this bomb will be like. A bang, sure—but you get maybe a few percent of what's there, waiting in the uranium. So the rest is kernels."

"What efficiency?" Karl asked, sitting back from the old wooden conference table. Feynman's Bronx accent was so thick, Karl wondered if he was putting it on. *Talks like a bum!*

Feynman gave an eloquent shrug again. "One, two percent. Tops."

The trio of men fresh off the airplane from Los Alamos were a bit groggy but had wanted to deliver their estimates. Another one, Fred Reines, added, "We did a big critical mass calculation, months back. Said you could get by with maybe thirty kilograms, but didn't recommend it."

Karl nodded. "Read your memo. We figured that too." He nodded toward Luis Alvarez, who had served as checker on the calculation. "So this bomb is coming in at around a hundred kilograms."

Reines sat back and gave an evil chuckle. "*That* will work for damn sure. Ha!"

Karl caught a tone that made him suspect Reines was a Jew. The man had a certain ironic delight. Karl had been thrown off when, coming into the big Admiralty Citadel plaza, Reines had burst into a Gilbert and Sullivan song in a big, booming voice. His first time in London, and he knew entire long verses. The tall man drew startled glances as he sang with a musical joy far from the severe, eastern European classical culture Karl knew.

Karl stood, energy boiling up. "We just got in the last shipment of U-235 from Oak Ridge, all machined out. Ninety-four percent pure. In time for Luis here to add it into the cylinder target and the disk bullet." Karl paused. "Have any idea how dangerous it is to machine metal U-235? The guys had shifts, to lower the risk. They wore suits that wrapped them in. Plus oxygen fed into masks. They had to melt the damn stuff, shape it in molds accurate to a fraction of a millimeter, then machine it down to smooth it. Down to a tenth of a millimeter."

Karl stopped, feeling now that his voice had risen. "Everything's been faster than it should be. We said we'd have the gadget for the invasion. But Eisenhower won't wait for us, for a single bomb, no matter what. So we're putting it all together now, out at the field."

He sat back, feeling the release of saying things, letting the pressure vent. The Los Alamos guys, three of them, just looked at him. He wished Dyson was here; that would help. But there were still barriers, classification regimes, things the Los Alamos team was not to know. *God knows why*, he thought, and realized he was more tired than he ever had been. *Must be the pressure.*

Feynman said kindly, his grin now gone, "We came with some of the shotgun assembly in our plane, but there was a whole backup setup on another. Both came through. We call 'em 'pre-assemblies.' Means partly assembled bombs without the fissile components. We got your measurements on the two 235 cores, adjusted the high explosives."

"What's the gun like?" Karl looked at them, the guys who had actually built the final assembly, working with a naval gun team. Luis was rolling out and spreading the blueprints on the table, and the third Los Alamos guy, Bob Serber, helped weigh them down with staplers.

Feynman said, "Gotta get out to that airfield and put it all together—Little Boy."

Karl now thought that *Götterdämmerung* would be more appropriate.

Bob Serber's mouth slid into an amused smile. "At Los Alamos we had movies shown on weekends in a big tent. I figured somebody named it after a short character in *The Maltese Falcon* movie. Bogart pushes him around."

Karl chuckled. "And nobody's going to push this Little Boy around."

He went through it all with them—nitrocellulose propellant powder, the gun and breech made by the navy, the tail fairing and mounting brackets by the Expert Tool and Die Company, basic safety mechanisms, triggers. He showed a slide used in his innumerable talks to figures from the British government, their Royal Air Force, and various people he doubted had any idea what made the bomb work at all.

Feynman said, "Y'know, everybody started out thinking that firing a small, solid bullet into the center of a hollow cylinder was the way to go. Not so! We've got to keep both parts below critical mass, so we don't get a fizzle when they just touch. So we have to fire the cylinder onto the bullet. That hole in the center disperses the mass, increases the surface area, see? That lets more fission neutrons escape, preventing a premature chain reaction."

Karl knew this from the Columbia work, but it was good to hear that the Los Alamos guys had seen the basic physics, too. He handed over a printed illustration from an earlier Los Alamos report, signed by the Oppenheimer guy. "This cartoon, we got last year."

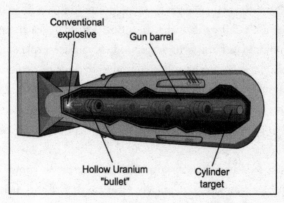

Little Boy

"Yeah, slam the cylinder into the plug," Feynman said. "Pretty, colors and all."

Luis Alvarez leaned forward on the table and said, "Guys, forget the mechanics. I want to know what it does to the target. I've got to calibrate the pressure meters we're going to drop on 'chutes to measure the shock wave."

Feynman shrugged. "We had a team—hey, Bob, your guys—look into bomb impact. Depends on where it goes off."

Karl looked around the table. "Let's say a ground impact."

Feynman screwed his mouth around skeptically. "I'd say the biggest effect will be from the flash of infrared. That'll set fire to everything wood within maybe three, four miles."

Karl somehow didn't think this young guy was taking the bomb seriously. He kept his tone light, casual. "There's not much wooden around the center of Berlin."

"How do you know the target's Berlin?" Reines asked in a resonant baritone voice.

Karl said carefully, "I think it should be. We want to get Hitler. He's underground all the time now, got to be—we bomb Berlin every night. I think we should go in at night. Catch the bastard in his bed." He had let a vicious note of grating contempt into his voice. Well, so be it.

Feynman brightened. "Now, this idea I like—a lot."

The man who had been silent, Bob Serber, said flatly, "I had time to think this through, on the planes coming over. A ground burst will be comparable to a Richter scale 5.0 earthquake. Big. But! Ordinary earthquakes occur scores or hundreds of miles underground. A surface explosion will have different seismic wavelengths and amplitudes. Periods of oscillation will be shorter, and the amplitudes will decay faster with distance from the site. The A-bomb target will suddenly become a superheated compressed gas, made from dirt and buildings. This gas expands, only to be slowed, stopped, and the expansion reversed."

Serber paused, as if he saw a movie running in his mind, a blossoming crimson blister on a dark city. "We estimate that twenty percent of the A-bomb energy will go into the ground wave. The rest goes into the air blast and cratering. The radiation in X-rays, gammas, and visible will convert into infrared and heat the surroundings. This will burn anything that can, within about two miles, instantly. The shock wave in ground and air will combine to flatten everything within at least two miles, probably more. It will yield 'ground roll' damage to any air-raid shelter or structures extending to at least several hundred yards underground. Steel-reinforced concrete will yield to the peak pressure. All deep structures will collapse within a second or two. I assumed the bomb will achieve an energy release equivalent to ten thousand tons of TNT. The more, the better."

"It'll be more, I hope," Karl said. "But we have to wait on our superiors, higher up, to decide if it's Berlin, and at night."

Feynman sat back and yawned, now looking tired. "Always respect your superiors, if you have any."

Marthe's letter paper was so thin he could nearly see through it.

> 510 W. 123rd Street
> April 21, 1944
> Tuesday evening
> My Dear Karl,
>
> I don't know when or where or how you'll get this letter, but I'm going to forge ahead anyway. New developments today—but not those we anticipated. First, the good news (?). Good thing I saved my $6 for a telegram; my fears of losing out on the new apartment dissipated this morning without a doubt: it's still available. However, I'll wait for you for the final decision.
>
> The other thing is less good. The bearer of bad news (Dr. Kugelmass) was right about Martine's intestinal condition. I had to telephone him tonight at Saranac Lake—much more difficult than how it sounds! The phone lines are so overloaded that it took about two hours of repeated attempts before I got through. He said that the same condition she had last year is back, and that the strict diet and unpleasant treatments would be the same. Poor Fou! Amazingly, she is as happy and active as ever, her appetite is good, and she's not suffering at all. It's going to be hard to get her to drink all that stuff tomorrow morning, including the paraffin oil. Dr. K returns to town Sunday, and we can discuss treatments

then. If you have a chance, buy her something interesting and new before you come home—she is interested in those little books again. Just seeing you again will give her great comfort.

Elisabeth is doing well. She laughs out loud when Martine jumps on the bed—the two girls are beginning to get along like a house on fire—to use one of your odd English expressions.

Anton is supposed to be posted to the Pacific somewhere, soon. He's in England now for a few days, I hear. He seemed happy about being in the thick of it, but I worry about him sometimes—so far from home.

The way the war is going enrages me. So slow!—when so many are dying. I particularly laughed at the American pounding of Kiska Island for two weeks, after the last Japanese had fled. Then there's France, where everyone is going to starve to death, and there won't be two sticks standing, nor any soul surviving, at least in the towns, at the end of the day.

I'm going to stop now, without lapsing further into grouchiness. I live in a desert when you are away, with no beauty for my eyes to behold, and no prose from you. I guess time is short and paper even scarcer.

Good night,
Marthe

He could feel her in the words, hear the whisper of her voice. The little letter somehow filled him with a quiet joy. He knew he would sleep better now.

2.

May 4, 1944

One of the infrequent German air raids, with a chorus of screaming sirens, sent Karl down into a subway, the "tube" as Londoners called it. Quite a few American soldiers sat together, chattering with Midwest accents for a while, the unspoken tension about the coming invasion skating in the air. That faded. The gloom and silence that followed, waiting through the booms and crashes dimly echoing down the rail lines, struck him as like a church. Our Temple of Self-Preservation, perhaps. There was little light, just enough from a gas lamp to make a gold tooth sparkle, or a teardrop glisten. From Bob Serber's remarks, he saw that if the gadget were to explode on the cobblestone streets here, no one in the tube system would survive. The blast wave would slam through the tunnels for many kilometers.

The next day he gathered the Los Alamos guys and Freeman Dyson. In the short while since his meeting with Feynman's gang, as he thought of them, Freeman had exercised what the dapper man called his best talent: *Sitzfleisch*. Freeman had explained that this German word had no equivalent in English, and literally translated as "Sitflesh." It meant the ability to sit still and work quietly.

"I did all your calculations over," Freeman said mildly. "The critical mass problem as the uranium bullet-cylinder approaches the target, the timing, the lot. It will work. I also think, from Karl's data on the 'tickling the dragon's tail' experiments you fellows carried out, that the yield will be about fifteen kilotons of TNT."

Freeman sat back and watched Feynman grin. "We can expect a probability of success quite high, then?"

Feynman never let go of the grin. "I sure believe so—"

The door opened and General Leslie Groves came in, with staff officers trailing. He was in full dress, not just field cap and khakis. *Of course,* Karl saw in an instant. This was the big show. Dress up. "You guys got a report for me yet?"

"You're here," was all Karl could manage. *I thought you'd stay in the States....*

"Not gonna miss the first test, no sir. Best place for it too—in somebody else's country."

The others around the table just gaped. Karl realized they were all in their twenties, with himself in his early thirties. Groves was maybe in his late forties. *The Children's Nuclear Crusade,* he thought.

Groves towered over the committee table, grinning. "Marshall finally let me get over here. This is gonna be fun! Gentlemen, I expect your summary report tomorrow morning on my desk. Funnel individual reports through Karl here, who will put it all together for me. In print, and in person."

After some handshakes and pleasantries, Groves was gone. None of his staff had even spoken. Without him the room seemed somehow smaller. The Los Alamos people and Freeman looked at Karl expectantly. They were waiting for some orders.

"We have to assemble this gadget—hell, this bomb!—in a few days," Karl said. "The Brits will carry it, but I know what Groves wants by being here—"

"We take the credit," Feynman said.

"Or the blame," Reines added.

3.

May 7, 1944

Bomber Harris was overweight and tired. His eyes drooped, and out of his ears grew hair long enough to catch a moth.

Karl sat with Freeman Dyson at the back of the small auditorium, whispering as high-ranking figures filled in the front. To get in, the two of them had to go through three security checkpoints and show that their briefcases held nothing questionable, like a recorder. Once in, they got thoroughly ignored. Karl said, "Good to be in the back. I'm far out of my depth here."

Freeman gave a wry smile. "I, more so. All the planning is going into Overlord—that's the supposedly secret name for the French landings—and Bomber Command has kept our little gadget away from anyone but the highest officers. Harris met with Eisenhower, Churchill, the rest. Now we get their decision, I suspect."

"I hope they looked at everything," Karl said. "I doubt any use against, say, tank divisions would have a big effect—they don't bunch up all that much."

Dyson said, "And a tank is a good bunker against the shock wave. Aha . . . Note how the birds flock together." The US Army and Army Air Forces wore khaki in various shades of brown, greenish, and tan: handsome jackets, creased pants, medals polished, shined black shoes, all very trim. They were few and sitting together, while the smart blue uniforms of the Royal Air Force surrounded them. "Nearly no civilians, just us."

Karl eyed the audience. There had been incessant talk about how to use the gadget, throughout the team of a few hundred Americans gathered around London. Karl had met with committees, argued in offices, learned to hold his peace in pubs and restaurants. Most of his work here was with the others from Los Alamos, some Columbia people, and Freeman. He eyed Harris and wondered what had come of the weeks of frenetic talk, up at the levels of the English Foreign Office and the American State Department, all under the distant brooding eyes of Roosevelt and Churchill and maybe Stalin. He had not heard that the Soviets knew anything about Little Boy. He doubted that the Allies told them something extra was going to arrive in the French invasion that the world had expected for years. He sighed and shrugged. "I think the right blow, a Berlin bomb and invasion of France at once, could knock the Germans out."

Freeman looked skeptical. "All the authorities say otherwise. Or so I gather."

"They're wrong."

"They've all been knighted."

"Then it's official."

This brought an outright laugh from Freeman. The lean, open face grew a thin smile, and there came a tip of the head in acknowledgment.

Harris rapped his knuckles on the microphone before him, silencing the room. He said, "I thought it useful to assemble all working on this mission, this bombing, which I have named Operation Goal, in the same room. I will now announce the decisions I have made, in counsel with the proper authorities."

An expectant rustle. "Operation Goal will occur exactly at the same time as the first invasion phase, the establishment of a secure beachhead, code-named Neptune." Harris paused, looking around the room, clearly relishing the moment. "Goal will target . . . Berlin."

A gasp from the audience. Harris added, "Operation Overlord, the landing of troops, will occur just after we drop it."

A thin, tall Royal Air Force officer stood in the front row. "Sir! I should think destroying the political heads of the German state will make it difficult to find anyone to bring about a surrender." He sat.

Harris nodded. His gravelly voice rang out, threaded with notes of strain. "I argued so too. But this is a political decision, after all. Winston and Roosevelt believe that as long as Hitler commands them, the government will never give up. I must say they could be right. Brilliant German military figures like Erwin Rommel, Heinz Guderian, or Erich von Manstein are in the field, fighting—

not in Berlin. They could come to the fore, if the Nazi politicians are dead. Rommel is the most popular general they have. We do know, also, that their General Staff has long felt hamstrung by Hitler's constant meddling. Add that to Der Führer's rigid insistence on outright victory or total defeat." He sighed heavily. "We are counting on the generals to be true patriots, I suppose."

The crowd rustled at the irony of this remark. Then the officer stood again. "But if we eliminate the government, sir—the Nazi Party officials, I mean—there may be a struggle for power, delaying any surrender."

Harris nodded to a lieutenant, who rolled down a map of Europe on a display. "They are holding the Soviets in eastern Poland. The Germans fear the Soviets far more than they fear us. Letting the Red Army into eastern Europe is their greatest fear—so I believe they will settle. So does Winston, I might add."

Over beers the day before, Freeman had explained to Karl that in the lead-up to the invasion, Harris had been ordered to switch targets for the French railway network. He protested loudly because he felt it compromised the continuing pressure on German industry. "They're using Bomber Command for a purpose it was not designed or suited for," Freeman quoted him. Harris tended to see the directives to bomb specific oil and munitions targets as a high-level command "panacea," his word, and a distraction from the real task of making the rubble bounce in every large German city.

"Berlin will be more than a bounce," Karl whispered to Freeman.

Harris looked out over the crowd, as though envisioning what was to come. "Our Lancaster bomber can carry the Grand Slam blockbuster. That's our biggest, twenty-two thousand pounds. Your 'gadget' bomb will be in that class. We will fly Lancaster escorts all around the central two, the drop plane and the measuring plane. No other operations will occur in that zone, all planes above their ack-ack fire."

"Our estimate is about ten thousand pounds, so okay," Karl whispered.

Harris went on about coordination details as Freeman listened intently. Then Freeman rose and held up a hand. Harris peered out at him, seeming to be startled to see a civilian in the auditorium. "Yes?"

"What altitude will the burst have?"

"I think we will go after the rat in his rat hole," Harris said. The applause was loud, startling, joyous.

4.

May 9, 1944

As Karl got off the grinding bus that chuffed out a tang of diesel, he saw the big planes nestled like awkward animals among English farms and villages. Here was the airfield where the gadget would get assembled and flown off to its target. Only two hours by train and bus ride from London, the countryside lush and sweet. He carried his suitcases beside Freeman as they walked among slow old men of the ground crew, doing cleanup and garbage disposal. Among their gray old heads, their hard and bone-bare domes, with liver-spotted ears, in shirts with collarless necks, he felt young and therefore vulnerable.

Freeman observed the buzzing landing strips with an expression of wonder. "I've been doing the maths for all this, yet never seen the real, working thing."

Except for the long ride across the Atlantic, Karl hadn't seen warplanes either. The Lancaster bombers seemed like immense, noisy birds, tended by insect-size crews attaching hoses, peering into the bellies with repair tools, guiding arrays of bombs out to the loading zones. They moved everywhere. From the flight line, engines purred as their props spun down. Others jockeyed for position as a formation buzzed into their places, shutting down with a flutter of coughs, then the crews getting out to smoke and jaw and move gear. This ferment stretched for a kilometer or more, a slow seethe dwindling away into the moist air, in air spiced with irritating fuel.

Freeman said with a reflective air, "I calculated that a crew member on a British bomber had a lower life expectancy than an infantryman in World War

I. For every bomber shot down, six crash in accidents. Usually the crew dies."

This bald fact made Karl look askance at the big war posters urging on the RAF. Obviously, these men needed morale boosters. In this war the flyboys were the most admired, even though it seemed to Karl the infantry fought in harder conditions.

For the Operation Goal staging, the Royal Air Force had decided to use an RAF base north of London. They reserved fenced-off space for Operation Goal, staked out an area for bomb assembly buildings, and dug the loading pits. There were wooden warehouses and administration buildings, all war-worn and shabby from constant use.

The Goal team each got what was, for the Royal Air Force, special treatment. Karl had a narrow room with a cot and wall pegs to hang clothes. A sergeant rounded up some clothes hangers, though. This was in a dull tin Quonset hut with a few rooms like his and the rest open cots in two rows. His room even had the luxury of a pine table smelling of turpentine and a bare bulb over it.

His carry bag had toothpaste and a towel. Experience in the open barracks in London had taught him to carry it close at hand. There was a latrine not far away, and the mess hall was half a mile along the edge of the flight zone. Windows were blacked out but easily raised during the day to save on electric power for lights. By the time he and Freeman got squared away, twilight had settled and they went outside, both interested in the buzzing bustle from the night-flight squadrons assembling. A silhouette loomed, an American Jeep grinding along with maybe a dozen people on it, some on the hood, with the view clear only for the driver.

"Going to the mess?" Karl called, and a voice answered, "Hop on."

They ran awkwardly along beside the slow Jeep, Karl not seeing how he could get on without knocking someone off. The Jeep stopped and an Irish accent said, "Come on now, you guys in those classified Quonsets. Green to our methods, I heard. Sit in the back, eh?"

The men who clambered out of the rear seats were young and swore in accents both Australian and Canadian. They found a few inches on the mud-guard, shoving, and the Jeep ground on. Karl felt odd to be privileged by these men who risked their lives every day, quite likely. They laughed merrily as the Jeep lumbered along the cinder path and planes taxied nearby, their choppy coughs seeming like mechanical laughter too.

They piled out and lined up for the cafeteria, which featured some mystery meat and mashed potatoes in cream. Karl took some of the buttered rutabaga and wrinkled his nose at it, wondering if the coffee here would help his digestion cut through the meat, showing thick veins of fat and reeking of fried oil. There were omelets of powdered eggs and bacon that was all rind and grease, for those crews just getting up. The "American Mess" for Yanks had real ground coffee in tins and tinned butter, while the English had "national butter" that was mostly margarine. So Karl kept quiet.

Still, by the time he and Freeman got to a table where a hand waved above the bobbing heads, he was hungry. Luis Alvarez was there with Feynman and Reines. Luis had a shiny brown quilted flight suit with him, slung across his lap in a jaunty way as he grinned. As Karl sipped the metallic coffee, Luis told them the latest hearsay about the invasion. It seemed Churchill wanted to go ashore in person, as soon as a few kilometers of perimeter were stable. Feynman said, "Dumb! The Germans will concentrate over the beach and hit anything coming ashore that's escorted."

Reines said, "Brilliant, then. We send nothing like that and the light bombers keep their bombs ready, while we get to shoot at them at short range. Our ack-acks and .30 calibers can hammer them while they're searching for a Churchill who isn't there."

This was like much of the incessant gossip currents swirling around the invasion, possible and maybe real, but with no plausible way to tell. The scientists and engineers Karl worked with had no particular expertise, and of course speculated endlessly, but he soon realized it was much like the sports talk he had always ignored. None of them actually played the game, did they? They weren't strategists. But here, that wasn't quite true. Pilots and flight engineers knew the war firsthand. Maybe that gave them some insights, maybe not.

The physicists and engineers didn't have any special knowledge, though. Best to stick to what he knew—a narrow alleyway, but perhaps, if they played this right, decisive.

5.

May 13, 1944

Feynman wasn't in charge of the bomb assembly crew, Karl was—but he asked the right questions. "This is a huge cylinder. Big, ungainly thing. Falls from four miles up, say. How good are the bomb avionics? Accurate to what radius?"

"Good question." Karl rose to answer this. In any tech meeting, he now knew he would take some peppered questions from the Los Alamos guys, and he was ready for them, with slides and documents he had gathered through the last weeks before coming here. Dealing with these guys was like a PhD exam every hour, and he felt like the student. Maybe not now, though; he knew the subject well.

In March, which seemed a long time past, Groves had brought him into the very end of the twenty-month-long testing about bomb dynamics. "I need one of my own guys to look over their work," Groves explained in New York, before sending him all the way to the West Coast on an army Douglas airplane, filled with officers sporting lots of brass, clearly wondering why Karl was among them.

All the bomb-drop work had been utterly unknown to the nuclear people. The classification bulwarks had kept parts of the Manhattan Project isolated, creating delays and errors. Avionics was another province of engineering no one he knew had even a nodding acquaintance with.

When Groves gave his gruff orders, Karl had been quick to correct that. He used the methods he had learned since those distant days when he worked for Urey and was shy about even speaking to the Nobel winners.

Now he knew that it was far better to find a savvy someone and ask them questions. That worked faster than plowing through the thick, already a bit moldy mimeographed reports that stood feet deep, when he asked a classification librarian for some basic background. When at first Urey had told him to check a number or detail from those mimeoed masses, he would look at them, and a particular drawing would bring memory flooding back. It was like a madeleine from that Proust novel he had tried to read, to go along with Marthe's urging that he strengthen his French—and kept falling asleep over. The memos had a similar effect.

The Army Air Forces had been testing proxies for the bomb for many months, dropping them onto Muroc Dry Lake in California. Karl passed around photos of big bombs buried in sand. "We checked the fusing gear, stability, ballistic characteristics." Then he went to the blackboard and started drawing, talking, calculating. Feynman sat back and yawned. Freeman was next to him and stared attentively at Karl's sketches.

Karl decided not to tell them of the myriad troubles the Muroc team had. At first they used the aiming mechanism of a machine gun to track the falling bomb. It fell hundreds of yards from the bull's-eye. Once the truck carrying the camera mount got stuck in sand near the middle of the target range. The driver decided to let the drop go on anyway, figuring that they had never gotten close. He was right, but not by more than a hundred yards. Those photos, sighting straight up, showed that the tail fins crumpled under the slipstream pressure, so bombs tumbled.

"Ah, so that's how you Americans discovered the cause of our inaccuracies," Freeman said. "I heard of this, but not the source. Brilliant."

Karl was grateful for any positive comments. "The Muroc guys did test drops every day for months. The target area was extra hard, to avoid having to dig the concrete-filled dummies from many feet belowground. It was a major engineering job, with earth movers to get them out. We needed to know the true air speed and time of fall. They measured rotation, yaw, striking velocity. All this was to judge how accurately we could hit from twenty thousand feet. Also, to tell us how much time the Lancaster would have to make its escape."

"How's it go off?" Feynman asked in his Brooklyn accent.

"The fuse was—and will be—a radar-prompter. It closes a relay at the most destructive height."

Feynman leaned back and put his feet up on the battered oak table they clustered around. "This guy I worked for, Oppenheimer, he has a team that worked out the optimum. Their calculation says the most destructive altitude is five hundred eighty meters, about nineteen hundred feet."

Freeman turned politely. "Are they with you? If I could speak with—"

"Nah, they're in Los Alamos. Now they're trying to figure out how to make a plutonium bomb." Feynman sniffed skeptically. "They haven't got more than a gram or two of plutonium so far, made in our reactors out in Washington. In a year or two they might have something that works."

Karl shook his head. "They must have assumed buildings of wood. There aren't many in central Berlin."

"So a high air blast isn't the best?" Reines looked surprised.

"Not if the guy you want is under twenty meters of dirt, steel, and concrete," Karl said.

General Groves said, "You guys get the benefit of having me make your case. I've been keeping this little army of prima donnas working harmoniously together for years. Now I can pitch for you. You did it! We've got Little Boy. Now you get to deliver the goods."

Karl did not like the idea of "delivering" anything himself, but it was impossible not to get swept forward by the tsunami of the French invasion. Back to the heart of Europe!—in a landing the Soviets had wanted since 1941. He could feel it in the airmen around them, a surging sense that this was the end of a terrible long suffering.

There were just a few men in the room to hear Groves, who liked to keep things simple. He could control small meetings easier. Freeman opened mildly with his quite English, even-toned, polite phrasing. "I am given to understand that you have arranged a solution to the escort issue—"

"Right!" Groves snapped out. "It's the P-51 Mustang, a great long-range fighter. An American body and a British Rolls-Royce engine, all souped up even further now, by our teams. It'll fly fast as a bat outta hell, get there to clear the sky ahead of you. Help out the Brit Lancasters, who'll confuse the Kraut fighters too."

Groves loved to lecture, giving orders in short jabs. An American, Captain Paul Tibbets, would fly the bomb plane, with some Royal Air Force crew included. Usually the United States flew day raids and the British night raids, so this would be a mostly Brit crew, with the American Bill Parsons arming the bomb once they were on the approach. "You scientist guys, you'll handle the dangerous or complicated tasks. "We can't risk having Little Boy totally in the hands of the Brits, y'know." A wink.

"Our air force team shipped multiple parts for the gun assembly on different flights, so we have backups. The U-235 came separately too, on several flights. On my orders, all crates carried the code name Silverplate, which commands instant cooperation from all military personnel. You get trouble from any Brits, you tell 'em Silverplate, that's the code."

Feynman leaned forward in his seat. "How're we gonna deal with the radioactive fallout from this ground pounder?"

Groves blinked. "I saw a report on that—"

"It'll shoot out a lot of fast decay isotopes, made from the dirt by the warhead itself. I've got a list. Where it goes depends on the wind."

Groves smiled. "You're Los Alamos, right? You guys keep track for me."

Feynman nodded. "I have a memory like an elephant. In fact, elephants often consult me."

Even Groves laughed at this, though it took a visible effort. "Okay, we'll look at where the dirty fallout lands."

May 17, 1944

Karl learned that the Brits termed the rushed, hot-eyed fervor of these days a "ratfuck"—which meant a rat race, all bollixed up.

The airfield sent squadrons of bombers out around the clock, hammering the Germans in France. This might help draw their fighters into the French coast and away from Berlin, but nobody knew the German mind-set on this.

He walked out with Luis Alvarez on the next of the test flights of the following plane, which would drop the shock detectors by parachutes and take the photos. Luis wore a flying suit over GI pants, a tatty brown sweater, and his leather combat jacket. Karl took his picture for, as Luis said, "History, my parents, and my girlfriend back home."

The Lancaster took off on an easy glide. Groves insisted on some trial drops from the actual airplane, not the B-17s used Stateside that Karl had watched. The Little Boy pre-assemblies were designated L-1, L-2, and so on. They had big guidance fins, getting laughs from the Brit loading crews. "What, you want these to fly?" one of them yelled. No Americans answered these jests, because that would lead to talk about what was so special about this bomb.

Most of his time got eaten up with details. The Los Alamos team was carefully assembling Little Boy, meticulous work, with Parsons in charge. The machined U-235 parts had to be fitted into the assembly, then the shaped charge explosives packed firmly into a frame. Checked and rechecked, then the whole thing had to be made rock solid, so vibrations and the buffeting during the fall would not misalign the firing.

Through several days he had seen Luis take off to test-drop L-3, L-4, L-5, getting the guidance right. These fell into open pastures. Nobody in the RAF had ever done many test drops, and certainly not from nearly thirty thousand feet, which no bomber could reach until recently. The results now were better, with the newest, larger avionic fins; the crew Luis went with could hit the bull's-eye within a hundred meters. "Good enough to blow old Adolf to atoms," Luis said. "That's why we should keep the A-bomb name."

"Atom bomb?" Karl asked.

"Adolf bomb."

The drop sequence was in good shape, so Luis could turn to getting the shockwave detectors launched from the following airplane, and the auto-cameras. Karl saw right away that the man was a quick problem solver, catching snags and hitches nobody had thought of. The Brit and American techs held him in awe.

Luis had worked on the "drop diagnostics" back at Los Alamos with some air force engineers. He had packed the boxy detectors in a frame that dropped them on parachutes, out the bomb bay. He even arranged to drop a small bomb below the test rig, to register a shock on the oscilloscopes back onboard, sent by small radio transmitters. Nobody had even done this sort of engineering before, since nobody cared what a bomb did far below; they couldn't detect it.

Then, on a run to checked the designed system, the takeoff failed. It turned out later that some thick oil had gotten into the Lancaster's fuel lines, due to a mistake in the fueling routine. Karl was walking to the assembly bay to see how the Little Boy assembly tests were going, when in the distance the Lancaster took off. Its motors choked, stalled—and the plane nosed over. He watched it slam into the ground with a dull thump, about a mile or two out from the end of the runway. Everybody started running.

No fireball, at least, Karl thought as he rode on the ambulance that wailed out to the wreck. The Lancaster's entire nose was crumpled in, the wings snapped, the belly slit open as if by a knife. The pilot and navigator, both Brits, were dead. The medics got to them first, but Karl leaped off the rear bumper of the ambulance and ran to the midsection. The bomb bay was splayed out across a cow pasture like broken metal teeth. He got in through the busted loader. Inside was a mash of broken struts and gear. He found Luis unconscious on the deck. Shallow breaths whooshed in and out of his mouth, and his heartbeat was firm, but Karl could not get any other sign of life from him.

It took him time to get out and find a medic among those dealing with the forward crew—who were dead too. Karl got one to come back in with him. The medic waved Karl away. "No bad bleeding. Knocked out. Looks like his leg's messed up."

Karl helped get the limp body out and down. Then the stretcher guys carried Luis away, and Karl watched the ambulance drive off, five corpses on the roof. There were no other survivors.

By then lots of people were around the site. The Brit damage team already had the problem isolated. "Damn crappy petrol!" one of them said, followed by some curses Karl had never heard before, and some he could not even understand. Obviously, he was not as sophisticated as he thought.

The next day Karl got in to see Luis, who was sipping some of the watery "orange juice" the RAF had in their mess. He was bitching about his broken ankle, and also the food, but that was nothing new.

Karl told him a joke going around, supposedly from a German prisoner. *Wehrmacht* soldiers said, "If the plane in the sky is silver, it's American; if it's blue, it's British; if it's invisible, it's ours!"

Luis laughed. "Hell of it is, I'm out of the action. No time to get this busted ankle to heal."

"Yeah, tough luck," Karl said, not really thinking that at all.

6

Freeman stood at the blackboard, his first time speaking to both American and Brit brass about his own expertise. The Los Alamos guys were there, including Luis on crutches, fulfilling the role Groves had assigned them: sitting in skeptical judgment on every aspect of Operation Goal, the Berlin bombing.

The larger crowd was the true audience, hearing the mission plan in detail. Freeman looked calm and even graciously nodded to the RAF generals and particularly to General Groves, sitting in the back of the briefing room, as always. "I have all the Bomber Command statistics, gentlemen. I found that we could substantially reduce losses by ripping out two gun turrets, with all their associated hardware, from each bomber. That reduces each crew from seven to five. The gun turrets were costly in aerodynamic drag, as well as in weight. The turretless bombers will fly fifty miles an hour faster, the aircraft johnnies say. So—we do that, the Lancasters will spend much less time over Germany. Particularly, over Berlin."

An RAF general sniffed through a thick mustache. "What about defense? You'll have none."

"I confess I had this idea several months ago, when I heard of the Yank 'gadget.' So I prevailed upon General Harris to try an experiment—a squadron of bombers with no turrets. The evidence of that experience was clear. That the squadron did not show more losses confirmed that the turrets were useless."

The RAF general said loudly, "You're giving them no hope of getting those damn fighters off them!"

Freeman nodded sympathetically and said softly, "The turrets did not save bombers, because the gunners rarely saw the fighters that killed them."

The RAF general said in a bark, "So our boys should go to Berlin, with this supposedly big bomb, unable to defend themselves?"

Freeman drew himself up. "I realize this goes against the official mythology of the gallant gunners defending their crewmates. But the better answer is to strip the turrets from the delivery plane and its following plane, the diagnostic one. Send the slower planes ahead, and the true bomber then catches up at higher speed."

From the back Groves rose and said, "As commander of this bomb-building campaign, which has lasted years now, I support this idea. The less time over the target, the safer they are."

As he spoke, Groves strode to the front, beside Freeman. He scowled, sweeping the room with his steady gaze. "I'll dismiss my men now, so we can talk war without the civilians."

Karl left with the others, oddly elated. He wasn't going on the mission, so perhaps Groves would be agreeable to his returning to New York, out of all this. The landing in France was now a matter of weather, and certain to come within a week. Little Boy would neatly shut down the Germans. He could be home for summer. To see his girls.

He went into Groves's office after the big meeting, to report on details of the Little Boy assembly. The general waved him into a chair. "Nearly done getting it together, right?"

"Yes, a few more—"

"Great work, ahead of schedule even. But sit down, got a problem."

Something about Groves's voice he didn't like.

Groves got up with a sigh. "It's Luis."

Groves came around his battered oak desk, leaned back against it, folded his arms. Karl recognized this posture, from seeing Groves use it along with his commanding voice. "I want you to take over for him."

"*Huh?* That's a combat job. I don't—"

"Look, it's a physics job. Something goes wrong, you'll be there to fix it. No GI can do that."

"There's no time to train, no—"

"Same time as anybody would have. You know this gear as well as anybody we got. The shock-wave recorders, the photo rig to measure the light from the fireball."

"It was a stretch for me to even supervise the Los Alamos team, assembling Little Boy. You can't—"

"But I can, Karl. Think! This is *our* bomb, but we're flying it in a Brit plane, from England. I want the core crew, like Tibbets, to be ours."

"I don't have any exper—"

"I want it so the whole damn *world* is gonna know it's our bomb, our guys were in at the delivery, and it won the war. See?"

Karl opened his mouth and then saw there was no way out of this. So he shut it.

He wondered for two days how he would tell Marthe about this. Venturing into actual combat, in a bomber, had never been on the agenda. She worried, naturally, about him even being in a war zone. Then the obvious dawned: he couldn't tell her about it. Their letters were intercepted, so no hint of real war news could go through. It was a relief.

The training was not hard, really. The Lancaster was fairly roomy, with its rectangular fuselage, and its mid-set wing and twin tail fins and rudders had a jaunty air. So did the ground crews. Karl liked working with men who used their hands and knew that this was even more important than the other bomber flights roaring off this field. The Germans had slammed them hard for five years now, and payback was a taste they liked to savor.

He liked the blunt way they spoke, too. A squat, broad-shouldered pilot took an order, nodded, and later observed, "Yeah, royal cock-up, innit." And when Karl discussed their fighter escorts, the pilot said, "The Heinie fighters stay down, thin on petrol they are—unless there're good pickings, lower than we'll be going. Those wankers get stroppy if ordered to go high, where it's hard to see at night. The tossers will have to find us in the dark at more than four miles up, with not much city glow these days, on blackout. We'll be chuffed to deliver the good news to Adolf, awright."

He let himself be lured out to a pub, to relieve the pressure mounting as the invasion approached. It felt odd to sit sipping lukewarm, tasty beer—a vast improvement on the bland, carbonated American product—and realize that those speculating on the coming brawl on the continent had no idea it was a one-two punch. The most apt statement he heard was, "Just because the newspapers say so, doesn't mean it's not true."

The tiny language differences—like Luis using "smart" to mean intelligent, when to Freeman "smart" meant well dressed—caused amusing confusions, when well lubricated with beer. Pub music was less pleasant. He mildly enjoyed "Take the A Train" and hated "Praise the Lord and Pass the Ammunition"—both of which seemed to blare from every radio he passed.

But one night, in the mess hall after a trial run of the diagnostic gear, a pilot next to Karl said casually, "We're nutters to do this, y'know. You're here one minute, then it's a dirt bath the next." Karl wondered if he was right.

Little Boy

Groves held a little ceremony when the bomb was fully done, tested, ready in a loading pit. After he got through with a speech, Feynman said, "Gotta wonder how we did it, don'tcha? In three years, too." He gave a lighthearted sigh. "Work is much more fun than so-called fun."

Groves even had champagne for the occasion. The scientists and flight crews crowded around the tables for a glass or two; it ran out fast. Freeman was in the small group, just in from London. He had been working with Bomber Command to coordinate the drop. It had to occur hours before the invasion, when the Mustang fighter planes were most needed over the beaches.

"The Mustang groups will go in well before the strike bombers," Freeman said, "in a fighter sweep—what we call an early supremacy action. We'll nail them before they get their damned *Gefechtsverband* battle formations set up. I had to look that one up—means 'task force.'"

The Mustangs were American, more of Groves putting a firm American stamp on the operation. They would make systematic strafing attacks, using "Clobber College" graduates fresh in from the States and the new 150 octane fuel.

At times it seemed there was too much coming at Karl now, quicker than he could handle.

Karl noticed that these days Groves wore his full dress uniform, with all medals showing. The general came around his desk, shook hands. "I hear you're all trained on the detection flight. Good. Now read this."

It was a photocopy of a letter from Teller to Szilard.

> I have spoken to Oppenheimer here at Los Alamos—all letters are read, of course, and he got yours before I did. . . . I am not really convinced of your objections. I do not feel that there is any chance to outlaw any one weapon. If we have a slim chance of survival, it lies in the possibility to get rid of wars. The more decisive a weapon is the more surely it will be used in any real conflict and no agreements will help.
>
> Once again, our only hope is in getting the facts of our results before the people.

Karl nodded. "More hand-wringing. Heard it before. So what?"

"This, too." Another sheet.

Recommendations on the Immediate Use of Nuclear Weapons
Scientific Panel of the Interim Committee

"Here's the main part of their report. General Marshall sent it."

You have asked us to comment on the initial use of the new weapon. This use, in our opinion, should be such as to promote a satisfactory adjustment of our international relations. At the same time, we recognize our obligation to our nation to use the weapons to help save American lives.

(1) To accomplish these ends we recommend that before the weapons are used not only Britain, but also Russia, France, and China be advised that we have made considerable progress in our work on atomic weapons that these may be ready to use during the present war, and that we would welcome suggestions as to how we can cooperate in making this development contribute to improved international relations.

(2) The opinions of our scientific colleagues on the initial use of these weapons are not unanimous: they range from the proposal of a purely technical demonstration to that of the military application best designed to induce surrender. Those who advocate a purely technical demonstration would wish to outlaw the use of atomic weapons, and have feared that if we use the weapons now our position in future negotiations will be prejudiced. Others emphasize the opportunity of saving American lives by immediate military use, and believe that such use will improve the international prospects, in that they are more concerned with the prevention of war than with the elimination of this specific weapon. We find ourselves closer to these latter views; we can propose no technical demonstration likely to bring an end to the war; we see no acceptable alternative to direct military use.

(3) With regard to these general aspects of the use of atomic energy, it is clear that we, as scientific men, have no proprietary rights. It is true that we are among the few citizens who have had occasion to give thoughtful consideration to these problems during the past few years. We have, however,

no claim to special competence in solving the political, social, and military problems which are presented by the advent of atomic power.

Karl said, "Good grief—'no claim to special competence' for sure! This is for politicians."

Groves shrugged. "And generals. Point is, this could be political trouble, if it gets out."

"Who would let it out?"

"I dunno. These are your friends. Think they might leak?"

"No. They wouldn't."

"I don't like this sort of idea getting out while we're trying to win a war."

For the first time, Karl perceived pressures he had not sensed operating on Groves. The general tossed the papers on a desk already covered with them and pressed a button. "Got something else up my sleeve here."

With a knock, a slim army lieutenant came in, introduced himself as James Benford, and handed Groves a briefing summary folder. "You have to approve these, sir."

Karl saw the heading:

OPERATION PEPPERMINT
European Theater of Operations United States Army (ETOUSA)
Portable Geiger radiation detection devices suitable for field use
Provides for:
• Centralization of all detection equipment and knowledge of its operation under ETOUSA;
• Establishment of a means of detecting the use of radioactive substances; and
• Channels for the reporting of such incidents to G-3 ETOUSA for immediate action.

"I have one with me," Benford said, bringing from a case a detector similar to those they used in the Manhattan Project, but more rugged. "We have a

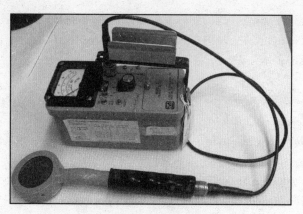

Geiger counter

hundred Geigers and fifteen hundred packets of film that will be fogged by radiation."

"How about the exercises?" Groves asked.

Benford was tall and lean and spoke with a soft drawl, his angular face betraying no emotion. "That report says full-scale rehearsals of Operation Peppermint were carried out to test the plan and the equipment. Ground and aerial surveys detected radioactive substances in trial concentration areas too."

"You're"—Groves glanced at the man's shoulder patches—"field artillery. Why're you in this?"

"The Geigers go in with the forward observers, sir. I'm one, going onto the beaches right after the infantry. To call in fire where needed. We're close to the front lines and mobile."

"Ah, smart. Very well, Lieutenant, I'll look over this report. That Geiger looks a lot like the ones we developed—right, Karl?"

Karl had been checking the meter and switches. "Looks like a copy. So you really think that idea from the magazine, that 'death dust,' is a real threat?"

Groves smiled. "I'd do it. Even if I had a bomb nearly done—which they might!—I'd be ready to salt our troops with the uranium we had. Oh—Benford, meet one of the men who got this ball rolling—Karl Cohen." Karl shook the offered firm grip and said, "Staying overnight?"

"Yes, sir—ah, I have to take back a written okay, General."

"You'll get it in the morning," Groves said, dismissing them both with a wave.

"Let's have a drink," Karl said to Benford. "We've both got a big day coming up."

The day before the big event, he was restless and had nothing to do. Realizing what might happen soon, he sat down and wrote to his mother, sister, friends, and lastly, ended his long letter to Marthe on onionskin paper with:

> I must reproach you (once again) for your manner of writing letters. You always fill up the space between your last factual sentence and the bottom of the last page with expressions of your undying love, devotion, etc. In mathematical terminology, the amount of your love is determined uniquely by that distance. This is how our lives are squeezed in this crazy war. If another event had occurred, such as the ceiling falling down in the kitchen, you would have one more factual sentence and you would love me one sentence less. Yet I know that cannot be.

In the long night after, he dreamed of her breathing softly in sleep on her bed, of how her warm breath would come from lips parted just a bit, and her hair spread over the pillow. Her aroma swarmed up into his nostrils. When he awoke suddenly and reached for her, he found only the empty air beside his cot.

PART IX

LITTLE BOY

June 5, 1944

Karl cut himself shaving, yawning after sleeping late into the day. In the mirror he was startled to see emerge from his wake-up fog a revelation: his similarity to his father. At a certain angle, a slanted cast of the dim light, the look of his mouth and jaw reminded him of a particular resolute manner, often seen as a boy—his father's stern face, more savage as his disease grew. Dead now of a disease later named for the doctor who described the symptoms, as usual— mild old Dr. Crohn, affable and distant, focused more on his clinical research than on his patients. *Dad's been gone fourteen years. I wonder what he would make of where I am now.*

Then the hooting squadron meeting call sounded, and he went to the war.

The landing fields buzzed at him as he made his way alongside them. The day before, a lesser aircraft had caught fire during takeoff, crashed, and exploded. Karl had seen the fireball while walking to a meeting. The pilot who survived had a concussion, a scalp wound, double vision, intermittent hearing in his left ear, a crushed vertebra, a ruptured liver, spleen, and kidney, and burns. The rest of the crew didn't make it.

Luis Alvarez had gotten off easy, then—just enough damage to keep him from today's flight. Karl thought of this as he sat through the mission briefing, the endless details of maps and timing, detailed on displays for the pilots and navigators.

Alvarez was there, standing outside on crutches, to see Karl off. They talked a bit about the parachuted detectors, how well they might work, the air cool and delicious as Karl savored it. Abruptly Luis said, "Afraid? I'd be."

Karl said, "Would it help if I were?"

Luis laughed, and so did he.

A private thrust a "bail-out kit" into his hands. Karl inspected it. On top were some five thousand dollars' worth of currencies. The private said it was the best counterfeit that could possibly be made, "standard issue"—Dutch guilders, French francs, Belgian francs, Reichsmarks. He found a packet containing fishhooks, razors, rubberized silk maps, a compass. Another packet held "high energy" wafers and halazone tablets for purifying water and Benzedrine to keep awake. He put it all aside.

He and the other scientists were aliens here, single-task people, on a one-shot mission. The real warriors ignored them. The scientists' cover story was simple: this was some kind of special bomb, nothing to really pay attention to, so just help out the specialists; these science guys wouldn't be around for long, anyway.

Then, after some coffee to sustain the crew through the night, he suited up. In field boots he walked toward his airplane, helping tug the gear on a weapons carrier. A silvery mist clung to the ground, ripe with woodland scents. He sucked the pleasant aromas in, thinking of his family and how alarmed they would be at what he was doing.

Amid the hubbub of preparations for this comparatively minor but enormously important mission, nobody paid him any attention. He felt like something of a fraud among airmen, even though he was dressed for the role: a black leather bomber jacket, courtesy of the US Army Air Forces, though this was not really their mission. It was an Anglo-Saxon mission, uniting both powers who had started the whole bomb program, giving what they could. His khaki trousers would be warm at the high altitudes, and he even had a white scarf, given to him at the briefing by a Scot pilot. Some of them did know what was to fall on Berlin tonight, and they all wanted it more than they could say.

The Lancaster bomber that loomed over him was the biggest working airplane ever. The USA had a bigger, newer Boeing B-29, but no one in England had even seen one. So it had to be the rugged Lancasters. In the months leading up to General Groves's order, that Karl come help with the bombing preparation, he had heard rumors. They described a high-level fight over which nation would carry this new weapon to its first use. One afternoon Groves had told him he wanted a B-29 sent to do the job, slamming his fist on a desk in frustration. By now Karl had learned to ignore most such displays and ride them out.

But the B-29 wasn't fully tested yet, and crews weren't familiar with it. So Groves bargained some US airmen onto both Lancasters that would make the run. Karl had spent a week of tedious training in how to release the pressure-gauge "bombs"—cylinders with noses and fins, which did indeed look like bombs, but just popped out parachuted instruments. They would fly with an outer screen of other Lancasters, a squadron to draw fighters, if any. The central two Lancasters were of Dyson's stripped-down model, so if they got attacked, the Little Boy carrier would streak ahead, and so would Karl's following plane.

The Mustang fighters who would clear the way over Berlin for them were leaving from another airfield. Here, the runway was oddly calm and the sunset fading into ruby splendor. He sniffed sweet spring in the mellow air and wondered if this would be the last time he ever did.

The Little Boy carrier, the "strike plane" as the flyboys called it, was named *Northampton*, just ahead. A team loaded Little Boy into a hydraulic lift and it whined up into the plane's bomb bay. Karl watched the tense airmen standing around, regarding the ominous bomb on heavy racks go up into the guts of the *Northampton*. "Looks like a long trash can with fins," someone muttered. It did, Karl realized. Over ten feet long, thirty inches wide, a tapered tail assembly that ended in a boxed frame of stabilizing baffle plates, weighing nearly ten thousand pounds—death in a box.

It took a long, suspenseful while. The team jacked Little Boy carefully between the yawning bomb bay doors. Not a lot of clearance, the shackle slipping around it to hold the array firm. A loud *clank* came from above, and everyone jumped. "Dropped a flange!" someone called. Uneasy laughter.

Now his turn. Amid the olive drab uniforms of the Americans and the stylish blues of the Brits, Karl got into the Lancaster trailing the *Northampton*. It was a long, black, four-engine murder machine named *Cumberland*. With its two big vertical stabilizers and huge bomb bay, the long, winged cylinder seemed to crouch down, ready to spring.

Bomber Harris called the Lancaster the RAF Bomber Command's "shining sword," but the aircrews called these particular ones dirty buggers, because they were painted black for night raids. Before they ever heard of the Manhattan Project, the Brits' thirty-two Lancasters had been adapted to take the new, bigger bombs, the superheavy Tallboy and Grand Slam. Uprated engines with paddle-blade propellers gave more power, with no gun turrets, to reduce weight and give smoother lines.

Dyson's impassioned speech in favor of ripping out the turrets had worked. The lead plane, *Northampton*, was ideal for the heavy gadget, Little Boy. Karl had let the Brits think the name was an obvious sardonic reference to the Brit Tallboy bomb. Few over here had read or seen *The Maltese Falcon*.

A ladder led to the *Cumberland*'s hatches through the forward landing gear, and Karl worked through the narrow, thirty-three-foot tunnel that connected pilot, bomb area, and radar bay. Some curious British way of speech made them call bombs "cookies." The weapons crew seats were steel, bolted to the deck, with a thin cushion. The steel was to cover their asses if flak came up through the floor.

He fiddled to get his headphones and mike to work, then listened on the intercom to the barking British voices. He recalled how different their offhand talk was in the face of so much war, five years of it now. He had heard that a famous bomber pilot had radioed back his problem with a nonchalant, "Our engine has packed up and we're going downstairs." No one came back.

Engines started, one by one, and the pulse of the propellers shook the plane's deck. Acceleration suddenly pressed him back in his seat. The rumbling, bouncy takeoff in such a big, lumbering airplane was now routine to him. He recalled that the Brits had started off the fission work, though they had pushed against using centrifuges. They were still trying to find some membrane to use in the gaseous diffusion method. Nothing much worked. And now it came to this—they got to fly the bomb against Hitler.

An airy, adrenaline lightness came to him as they lifted off. Landing gear thumped home and the pilot said over comm, "Berlin bastards, watch out!"

They flew fairly low to avoid high winds aloft. Karl knew the Little Boy weaponeer had been concerned about the possibility of an accidental detonation if the plane crashed at takeoff. So the weaponeer had decided not to load the four cordite powder bags into the gun breech until the aircraft was in flight. Fair enough. By now Little Boy was live though not armed, and would soon bring death.

He settled in and even napped. Somehow, when Carlos shook him awake with a cup of coffee, he felt refreshed. No nerves, even. He had devoted every effort for five years to this. It was time.

Idly he wondered what would happen if something went wrong and the bomb went off midflight, when they were following the lead plane. The fireball from the X-rays and gammas would be a hundred meters across at least. Anything near it—their Lancaster, its crew—would turn into not mere atoms. The heat would strip away all an atom's electrons and turn the plane, and him, into a plasma—a swarm of nuclei and electrons, erasing all of Karl Cohen in a microsecond. Such were the energies he had spent years calculating, but until now, never imagining.

The pilot took them up high as they entered German territory, and Karl watched their progress on radar. On went the oxygen masks, with their oily air. He checked the radio transmitters yet again and got reassuring signals on the oscilloscopes mounted on the rattling instrument racks. Karl had his own backup man named Carlos Amila, from New Mexico. He would take over if somehow Karl was disabled, most probably by some flak fire. He and the others were real aircrew with experience; Karl was useful American baggage, by order of General Groves. The drumming engine noise was not bad, because he wore earmuffs over his headphones. He asked Carlos to tell him if they got any talk from "up front," which meant the pilot.

The airplane had gotten cold, and he hugged into his flight jacket. Then he failed to sleep.

The engines' hard drone went on and his tension rose. *A snap job*, an airman had described it. Just let the 'chutes drop.

Karl had time to think of the sleeping people their small formation was passing over. Their world would end in a profound way when they awoke next morning. Carlos nudged him and shouted, "Flak suit!"

Karl got into his and located the polarized goggles everyone had gotten back in the flight briefing. They were to wear those while observing the blast. He watched Carlos struggle to put on a parachute, too.

"Aren't you going to?" Carlos pointed to the bulky parachute.

"If we're shot down, I don't want to be captured."

"Hey, if this works, the war's over, we go home soon."

"Not if you're a Jew and some farmer has a handy pitchfork."

Karl gestured to his flight suit, which wasn't a uniform but had stenciled above the breast pocket COHEN.

This made Carlos blink. He gazed off into the distance, thinking, and then tapped Karl's shoulder. "Put your phones on."

Karl did and heard the pilot say, "Approaching target zone."

Luis had prepared and tested the pressure gauges that the following plane would drop. They were bulky because of the parachutes, and he had to tumble them out in a brace, using a mechanical lever. He first rechecked the receiving antenna that would get the signals from the gauges. All normal. He watched the radar nearby intently as they approached Berlin from the north.

The pilot said, "No flak, no Kraut fighters. The Mustang boys did their job. Looks mostly clear over target."

There had been comm talk Karl had missed from the fighters, evidently. He felt even more the amateur.

In a chipper voice the pilot said, "Weather planes report some clouds. Nothing major. Partial visibility."

He and Carlos flipped the switches to open the small bomb bay. He could see a smattering of lights slipping by below patchy clouds. The moonlight helped him get a sense of perspective, and he tried to match that with the radar. He had memorized the flight path to the center of Berlin but could not make much of anything match up with his memory. No matter; his job was simple. Breaking the entire making and delivery of the gadget into compartments had a virtue: he could ignore the rest. He didn't need to check much now, just follow orders.

In *Northampton* just a few kilometers ahead, the bomb crew would be pulling the green battery plugs from the side of Little Boy, inserting the red ones to arm the detonator batteries. A last check of the release mechanism, just to be sure.

Then, he was sure, they would think about how split-second sure the firing fuses had to be in the gun at the center of the bomb. Those had never been checked in free fall.

He put aside such nervous anxiety. *Nothing to worry about now. It works or it doesn't.* At least with a ground-pounder hit, there was no altitude trigger running on a radar. Little Boy would blow on impact, to get the maximum shock wave into the soil, to collapse the maze of tunnels and bunkers they knew lay below central Berlin. The one that the intelligence guys thought housed Hitler was at ground zero, near the Reichstag.

Doubts lingered. After all, they'd never tested a real fission reaction in anything bigger than a speck of U-235. If somehow the uranium wasn't pure enough, or a hundred other things went wrong, Little Boy would be about as dangerous as dropping a boulder out of the sky.

"Armed and ready," the comm said with a bright British air of bonhomie.

They were about to obliterate a city. To build Little Boy, whole cities had been created, especially Oak Ridge. One city for another, then.

Their vector changed, a maneuver to take them away from the lead bomber. That gave the cameras, started already by the navigator, an angle to watch the drop. Their engines hammered hard.

The pilot said, "There will be a short intermission while we kill a monster." Carlos smiled. "And no flak," he added.

The pilot reminded everyone to don their goggles. Karl shook away the order. He wanted to see it all.

A chant came over the comm, radar course corrections. Now the bombardier would be flying the plane through his bombsight. Karl envisioned him turning the knobs beside the framing view, telling the automatic pilot about minor adjustments.

A loud *blip* on the radio told them all the drop was within two minutes.

They were very high. Clouds parted below as he checked the four pressure gauges yet again. A towering stack of cumulus clouds stood to their left, gray in the dim city lights. Above, a sky shot with stars. He could suddenly see scattered light in a pattern he knew from studying maps in preparation: the broad avenues leading to the Brandenburg Gate. He had played Bach's Brandenburg Concertos records many times, intricate magic alive in the air. The gate that led to the town of Brandenburg an der Havel. Their target was the Reichstag building, a single block away from the historic gate.

The keening tone signal sounded in his ears. *Time to let them go.* He gripped the controls tight and released the gauges.

Karl looked out the small window. A searchlight poked up feebly from the antiaircraft batteries below. No signs of flak bursts, which would be far below them. He peered carefully, hands tense. His chest was tight and he made himself breathe. The air seemed hot now.

In the dim searchlight beam he could see the *Northampton* jerk upward as the bomb fell. "Away!" came on his headphones. The radio tone stopped.

The Lancaster ahead dove away in a two-g turn. So did they.

Now the bomb was nosing down, inscribed with messages the Brits and Americans had enjoyed painting on it, most of them obscene. *Headed for the Nazi lair*, Karl thought with a sudden jolt of joy.

He held on hard as he saw the gauge parachutes open. Then he and Carlos slammed the bomb bay closed and turned, against the thrust of the plane's momentum, to the scopes. On the oscilloscopes the calibration signal popped up bright and clear. The gauges were reporting and would send their data.

"Our detector gear is working!" he called over the comm.

He held on as the seconds ticked in his mind. Forty-five seconds to fall the thirty thousand feet. They would be less than six miles away when it hit. If they had underestimated . . .

The Lancaster shook from the turn. Nothing came over the intercom. Rattles, pops, a slow, low groan of the airframe.

He flipped the switches on all the auto-cameras. They had different filters to step down the fireball flash. He suddenly wondered if the films would survive the burning flare, or burst into flames themselves. There had been no time to test that.

Below them, a basketball sphere like the core of the sun was being born.

His pulse thumped. Karl wondered how many were about to die.

A bright flash lit the compartment. Searing, brighter than the midday sun. From the angle of the beams coming through the narrow windows, he saw they were light reflected from the clouds in front of them and back through the tunnel connecting to the pilot compartment.

Karl triggered the movie cameras to capture the wave forms. On the oscilloscopes a pressure pulse registered an N-shaped wave. The parachutes were reporting in.

A second N came, a reflection of the shock wave from the hills framing the Berlin center. As expected, but—

The sharp shock slammed the plane. It wrenched Carlos out of his seat. He landed on his parachute and struggled up.

The entire airplane popped and cracked. Nobody said anything.

Karl got up carefully. He and Carlos stumbled to the small window and saw a cloud rising straight into the gray vastness. They gaped as the dirty finger pointing up began to mushroom. *Must be it hit the inversion layer below,* Karl thought. It was a sullen, angry cloud, roiling, rising, swelling. Lightning forked yellow around its flanks. Despite their engine throb, he could hear a strong, sustained roar.

He saw a small, secondary explosion in the mushroom column. A yellow sphere flared in orange and then smoke swamped it. It had to be chemical, but what— *Ah,* he thought. *All the iron in the buildings and soil has been thrown up in fine particles. Hot, too. It met the oxygen.*

"A rust bomb," he whispered. Weird, but probably right. And nobody had thought of it before.

Karl had never imagined what kind of cloud the blast would make. The pilot circled the mushroom cloud once as the cameras amidships rolled.

"Lookit that! Lookit that! Goddamn beautiful!" The voices piled on top of one another in his comm.

The white light had been, Karl thought, like the end of the world. Or the beginning of a new one.

They turned more and dived and the pilot angled them so they could see the dark cloud behind. It was a column of purple and gray now. Fires flickered along it. Some strange glow like moonlight glimmered on its flanks. Berlin was invisible beneath the spreading carpet of gloom below them. Carlos snapped pictures with his camera, as the manifest commanded. Karl had nothing to do but look at a world of somber clouds roiling beneath them like troubled lava, shot through with sullen red flaming tongues.

◆　◆　◆

Their pilot throttled back their engines once they were clear of German airspace. He wanted to let the *Northampton* come in first; it had less fuel and deserved the honor.

Karl leaned back into the humming aluminum at his back and let the vibration soothe him. He thought of nothing at all. Events were now rolling over him and he let them. Done and done.

He could not stop envisioning the effect of that vast fireball. He thought of those working in underground bunkers near the impact—engulfed in collapsing ceilings, choked and crushed under concrete, the lucky ones dying instantly, the rest gasping for air in final darkness. And those civilians a mile or two away, mashed in their homes, burned in the tongues of flames, lungs full of rasping smoke. Or those in the open at night, suddenly fried to a crisp by a flash of X-ray or infrared that swelled like a blister from the ground, searing everything that saw the swelling raw dome in their last instants, before the shock wave blew them into pieces.

All of it in part due to him. He stared at the humming dim compartment, lit by the oscilloscope bulbs, not thinking, just feeling.

Their *Cumberland* lumbered on and Carlos went forward, eyes bright, to talk to the others. They were a seasoned aircrew and Karl was not. The adrenaline surge he had felt ever since they flew into Germany trickled away. He sat and wrote a letter to Marthe, his fountain pen wobbly.

> This long, strange story of our mission will be known in its short version by the time you get this. But you and I know it started in 1938, when I got that lucky job with Urey. No newlyweds know what the future holds, but I think ours takes some sort of prize. In less than six years it's come to this!
>
> As I write this, only our plane crews and the unlucky residents of Berlin know the story. We and the British have run raids with three thousand tons of explosives, in the entire raid of hundreds of bombers. Tonight our lead plane gave the Germans a taste of maybe fifteen thousand tons, all in a single second's punch.
>
> So the days of big raids are over—forever. A single plane

disguised as a friendly transport can wipe out a city. That means to me that nations will have to get along together or suffer the consequences of sudden sneak attacks that can cripple them overnight.

And erase how many lives? We will know soon.

What regrets I have about being a party to killing and maiming thousands of Germans—just going about their lives, asleep tonight—are tempered. I hope this terrible weapon we have created may bring the countries of the world together and prevent further wars. Alfred Nobel thought that his invention of high explosives would do that, by making wars too terrible. Unfortunately, it had just the opposite reaction. Our new destructive force is so many thousands of times worse. It may realize Nobel's dream.

Love more than ever,

Karl

PART X

June 6, 1944

Success is going from failure to failure with enthusiasm.
—Winston Churchill

1.

It had been a rousing spectacle beyond anything he had ever known. Hundreds of shouting men streamed out onto the runway, where the Lancasters were turning into their parking position. Through the porthole he could see their shining faces, eyes wide. As he came down out of the airplane he was above their heads, so he could see a sea of cheering mouths.

The din drowned him. He got down onto the tarmac and somebody lifted him. In an instant four Brits in RAF blue were carrying him over an ever denser crowd. The dawn sky sent lances of yellow across cottony clouds, like an entry into paradise. He told them he wasn't in the bomber that actually dropped the gadget, just a following plane, but that didn't matter. That sent a thrill through him, and all the sweeter because he did not deserve it.

He supposed most men went through life feeling that they never got their due credit, but what delight it was to be cheered for something he had not done. Adulation swarmed all around him. This was what victory smelled like, with a sharp zinger of revenge.

The cheers still rolled on as he finally got his feet on the ground. A crowd filled the mess hall, and breakfast beer was everywhere. Karl took one and answered questions like "Whassat look like?" until Tibbets and his *Northampton* crew gathered with the *Cumberland* crew for photos.

Groves was in the mob, slapping everyone on the back, but Karl saw Moe Berg give a head nod to the side and followed him out, into a small room. Moe handed him a tulip glass and said, "The equation here is, pour one jigger absinthe into a champagne glass. Add iced champagne until it attains the proper opalescent milky look. Drink three to five of these slowly."

Karl had two and wandered off to sleep.

Dimly he stirred in rough wool blankets and recalled the warm, muzzy comfort of his mother, Rae, when she would read to him her favorite story, "The Piper at the Gates of Dawn." It was from *The Wind in the Willows*, and she read it to him again and again when he was ill or just needed comfort. And always, toward the end, he heard the catch in her voice and the long pause to find her handkerchief and blow her nose. Then the last words and he always fell asleep.

He rolled over and nuzzled his pillow as though it were Marthe, then fell back into an anxious sleep.

When he awoke he felt his body stretching like a continent on the bed. He was a king, vast, immune to life's abrasions, a survivor. *Man that is born of woman hath but a short time to live,* he had heard at an Episcopal funeral. *He cometh up, and is cut down, like a flower; he fleeth, as it were a shadow.* But not Karl, not today.

Karl studied the rough planking of the ceiling and thought.

Natural selection had spent over two hundred million years shaping mammalian tissues and nerves to the chemical swamp of Earth's surface. Those reactions depended on only electrons swirling around distant atomic nuclei, not on the protons and neutrons inside those nuclei. But then, for the first time, the effort that began in 1939 had unlocked that energy at the center of Berlin. For an instant the expanding energy ball had enclosed Hitler, stretching his tissues in opposite directions as it annihilated them. His brain had vaporized long before any sensations could stimulate his nerves and reach the three-pound boneless mass of wet tissue through its two sets of twelve cranial nerves.

The immense heat and pressure had reduced Hitler to a gas. He became a spray of light atoms. Those light atoms had five billion years ago been part of the vastly greater swirling spray of light and heavier elements that coalesced under their own gravity. Those atoms had formed the sun and the planets and much later the first simple life-forms. It was a superb way to die. Too good for him, really.

Karl sat up suddenly, the night falling away. He glanced out the window and saw midday sunlight. Breakfast!

Showering, he found a bruise in his side the color of an eggplant, the diameter of an orange, from when the shock slammed him into a strut. The bombing memory was already acquiring in his mind a certain polish, a fake gleam of glory. But he knew he was not bold and brilliant in action. He had just nodded when Groves had given a little speech, booming out, "We have spent a billion dollars on the greatest scientific gamble in history—and won."

Freeman joined him for eggs and ham. "We knew you had succeeded right away, at the Royal Society offices in London."

"How?" Karl could get only the one word out, around a slice of salty ham.

"Their seismograph. It was a Richter five signal, just as expected."

"Ingenious."

Groves appeared then in full uniform and took them all to his office. Walking there on the cinder paths, Karl felt airy, as if he had lost half his weight.

Groves handed them teletype messages.

GEN C LE MAY

REPORT OF CONCENTRATION RISING TO 40,000 FT ARRIVING FOUR HOURS LATER.

REPORTS SMOKE COLUMN STILL THERE HAVE OBLIQUE PICTURES BUT

DENSE WHITE SMOKE RISING TO ABOUT 30,000 FEET. MUSHROOM OF WHITE SMOKE OVER THAT. CITY COMPLETELY COVERED WITH GREY DUST LIKE SMOKE. TARGET AREA SHOWS FIRES. IMPOSSIBLE FOR THEM TO GET ANY DAMAGE ESTIMATE THROUGH SMOKE. PICTURES SOON.

THEY WERE BRIEFED NOT TO FLY IN CLOUD AND SMOKE OVER THE TARGET.

REPORTED THE COLUMN STILL THERE UPON THEIR ARRIVAL FOUR

HOURS AFTER BOMBS AWAY.

IS THIS THE INFORMATION YOU WANT?

"Sure is the info," Groves said. "You guys did it beautifully. Tibbets would be here, but he's not awake yet."

Karl let the conversation flow around him, still feeling a skating sense of unreality. Speculations ran on as others crowded into Groves's office. How long till the German generals surrendered? What would they ask for? Would we just let them go back to status quo ante as in the last war? Once we used the bomb on the Japs, this would be over—and what to call it? The Greater War? No, that one was now World War I; this would be II.

Then a master sergeant came elbowing in. He shouted for attention and put a radio on Groves's desk. After some static, the voice came in clearly, unmistakable now for years, the ranting harsh notes. They froze.

"Goddamn," Moe said. "We didn't get the bastard."

Within an hour Groves's teletype rattled out a translation.

> My fellow Germans! I live! Yet another of the countless atrocities that have befallen our lands has stricken Berlin— but not me.
>
> I am speaking to you so that you can hear my voice and know that I myself am not injured and well.
>
> The vast crime in Berlin has destroyed the entire center. But it cannot destroy the inevitable victory of the National Socialist Reich! My survival is a confirmation of the task imposed upon me by Providence—and that nothing is going to happen to me. The great cause which I serve will be brought through its present perils, and everything can be brought to a good end.
>
> For I can solemnly state in the presence of the entire nation that since the day I moved into the Wilhelmstraße, my sole thought has been to carry out my duty to the best of my ability. And from the time when I realized that the war was unavoidable and could no longer be delayed, I have known nothing but worry and hard work; and for countless days and sleepless nights have lived only for my people!

This evil attempt to wipe out virtually the entire staff of the German High Command has failed. We do have losses, but I have moved to restore order.

In order to restore complete order, I have appointed Minister of the Reich Bormann to be Commander of the Home Forces. I have drafted General Guderian into the General Staff and have appointed a second proven leader from the eastern front to be his aide.

In all the other agencies of government within the Reich, everything remains unchanged. Few people can begin to imagine the fate which would have overtaken Germany had this attempt at assassination by bombing succeeded. I myself thank Providence and my Creator not for preserving me—my life consists only of worry and work for my people. I thank him only for allowing me to continue to bear this burden of worry, and to carry on my work to the best of my ability.

"Nice touch," Moe said with a thin smile. "'Assassination by bombing'— that's right, and his including that phrase shows it."

"I wonder where Hitler is?" Groves asked. "You, Moe, look into that."

Karl recalled his dreamy fantasy just a short while before, of Hitler disintegrating in the crimson blister of the bomb. Wishful thinking. Vivid, but wrong. He thought but did not say, *The whole world is looking for him now.*

2.

At least there was some physics to do.

The film and shock-wave data allowed Karl and the Los Alamos team to calculate the yield, about thirteen kilotons of TNT. The film images in visible light and infrared showed that the fireball was about a hundred yards across.

Luis Alvarez, using a cane to walk now, said, "I wish I'd been there to see it." Karl nodded, speechless. *We killed so many. . . .*

Freeman Dyson sat quietly at the end of their worktable, calculating, and then, as they argued details of the shock-wave analysis, he said, "I have another way."

In a few quick, modest moments he sketched how he used the radius of the fireball in each frame of the film, with the time of the frame, to calculate the energy necessary to expand the fireball against atmospheric pressure. "So I calculate about fifteen kilotons," he concluded.

Feynman applauded. "Elegant!"

Fred Reines tossed on the table a teletype translation from the German radio broadcasts. "They're announcing state funerals. We got a lot of the party heads, not many military."

Karl had seen the same news. "Surprisingly few civilians dead, about eleven thousand. Lots of buildings down, including some museums. I hope they moved the great art away by now. The bust of Nefertiti was there; I saw it once."

Feynman eyed the teletype bundle as though it were a rattlesnake. "Until now, y'know, this was fun physics."

Nobody spoke for a long time.

✦ ✦ ✦

Karl noticed that at the entrance to the air base a big display showed high-level Nazis they had gotten with the bomb, as a kind of consolation.

Heinrich Himmler   *Hermann Göring*   *Joseph Goebbels*

He looked at the first three, whom he recognized, and thought of how many lives these men had already taken. Now they knew what was meant in a novel he had read called *The Big Sleep*. Something about how everyone sleeps the big sleep in the end; it didn't matter where you rested. Fair enough.

These men had been evil. Theirs was an evil existing for the sake of itself, for the pleasure of it. These were not the faces of men who sprang from a sad, limited, tormented, or unbalanced childhood and now acted out their angers on a larger stage, as some psychologists explained it. To Karl they came from a primordial blackness reaching up again through a dark and vulnerable soul, revealing all the horror that had always been within mankind, frustrating all rational analyses. Blackness for its own sake, without mercy or scruple.

He wondered if he felt any guilt over these men's deaths and realized that he could not. But the countless Berliners who had died along with these princes of evil, yes, he did regret. How many more would it take?

"How soon can we get another bomb?" Groves asked, frowning, pacing his office like a restless bear in clothes too tight. Moe sat in a chair, pretending not to read an issue of the *Times* of London.116

"Late August," Karl said. "I just got a teletype from Oak Ridge."

"No way any faster?"

"We used sixty-four kilograms—that's one hundred forty-one pounds of ninety percent or better U-235—on Berlin. We and the Los Alamos boys agree: better to overdo it and not risk a fizzle." Karl paused, not liking what he had to say. "Right now we have about thirty pounds at Oak Ridge."

"Damn!" Groves all but growled. "How low could we go, your theory guys say?"

"Maybe thirty kilograms—sixty-six pounds. But at that mass it has to work *exactly* right to work at all."

"Damn! So again—when can we get one just like the last?"

Karl knew how gradually more centrifuges were coming online at Oak Ridge. "September, to be safe."

3

Freeman said to Karl one morning, "Let's take the train to London."

"Well, I . . ."

"We both need a break from this gloom."

True enough. The Normandy campaign was inching inland, as Rommel slammed all the tank and infantry he could at the Allies. The carnage was steady, large, thousands dying every day. Karl read the newspapers after Moe was done with them, and mostly fretted.

So he went with Freeman on the long, rumbling London train ride, to have dinner with the Nobel laureate Paul Dirac. "His lectures were like exquisitely carved marble statues falling out of the sky, one after another. He seemed to be able to conjure laws of nature from pure thought." Even in lectures he spoke as little as possible. Dirac's colleagues jokingly defined a conversational unit of a dirac—one word per hour. "A student in class raised his hand and said, 'I don't understand the equation on the top right-hand corner of the blackboard.' Dirac said nothing. The class murmured nervously. After a long interval of uneasy silence, I asked Dirac if he would answer the question. Dirac laconically replied, 'That was not a question, it was a comment.' Then he left."

They met Dirac in a small, elegant, Regency-style restaurant in Soho. The district was famously swanky and vice-ridden, but Karl found it mostly, as the English would say, tatty. The war had worn London down.

The man who held a chair at Trinity College, which had produced Newton, Nehru, and Maxwell, was slim and dapper in a black suit, and greeted Karl with a nod. Over a rather thin meal with overboiled vegetables, Karl learned that Dirac had elegantly treated the centrifuge separation problem, when asked years ago by the English nuclear program. His work had never made it through the security barriers to the Manhattan Project.

"I wish I'd had your work to help," Karl said, and Dirac nodded. They laughed at Dirac's description of the poor writing he had to wade through to find out what was known by the engineers. Bad punctuation leaped out at him, sloppy grammar, misuse of "who" and "whom" and other crimes against the accusative.

It was a delight to speak of something other than the war, though Karl knew that couldn't last long. Freeman led them to a cocktail party at the substantial apartment of an Austrian chemist who had barely gotten his family out in 1938. It was somewhat merry, with crosscurrents of several languages through the crowded rooms. Everyone wanted to talk about the A-bomb, and Karl did not. In fact, he couldn't—it was still formally classified, though on every front page. Groves had given orders to drop no hints to anyone, especially about where the work was done and the attack staged; the Germans could still go after it.

He could hear the class system in rounded vowels that bespoke Eton and Oxford. By now he saw that status kept the wheels greased in the British military's endless protocols and musty hierarchies. He learned that "seasoned skiver" meant lazy scheming, a minimal effort to get by without getting caught. Dyson was a Cambridge man but spoke without class affectation. Still, in many ways, humorless martinets abounded.

So Karl listened, mostly. The invasion had somehow led to more news from the eastern front, and at this party, news of the siege of Leningrad was the latest revelation. People there had tried to get by on virtually inedible food substitutes: cottonseed cakes that were normally used as fuel in ship furnaces; sheep guts, together with calf skins from a tannery, which were turned into "meat jelly"; fermented birch sawdust that was turned into "yeast extract," which, dissolved in hot water, was considered "yeast soup." As the civilians grew more desperate, they scraped dry glue from the underside of wallpaper, or boiled leather shoes and belts, hoping in vain that they could be eaten or at least chewed. "Zoologists survived the siege: they knew how to catch rats and pigeons," a man from the Foreign Office said in rolling vowels. "Impractical mathematicians died."

As he ate beef stew, Karl recalled Marthe's joke about French slang—that a term for the English was *les rosbifs* because the French thought that was the only food worth eating here. He doubted anyone in the Leningrad famine made jokes about food.

The rooms got stifling, fed by substantial alcohol and general war jitters. Karl hung his jacket in the hall closet and got out onto a high balcony for air, with darkened London slumbering below. Dirac followed him. "That closet is the richest room in the city, I'll wager."

Dirac's opening a topic startled Karl more than the sentence. "Why?"

"Our host is a friend; I helped him ship his goods here from Austria. You noted the coat hangers?"

"Yes, heavy."

"They're platinum."

Karl smiled. "Platinum is silvery, so . . ."

"The Nazis forbade currency and property transfers, so he used his chemist credentials to buy a lot of platinum, then fashioned it into wires, shaped them into coat hangers, and painted them black. Nobody in customs spotted them. He's selling one at a time to support his family."

Karl laughed. Even war could be funny. Maybe especially so.

Groves looked sternly at Karl across his cluttered desk and said, "Why go home now? We're close to victory."

"There's nothing to do except wait for the next bomb, and . . . I want to see my family."

Groves shrugged. "Don't we all? Okay, Karl, write up what you think about using a smaller chunk of U-235 in the next bomb. Then we'll find a way back home for you."

Going out onto the airstrip, he felt as if he were lighter, the day brighter, life better.

✦ ✦ ✦

Feynman pushed teletype sheets across their worktable. "Get a load of what Oppenheimer sent. Calculations of how skimpy a critical mass we can get away with."

Karl said, "We agreed we'd each do our own estimate, then pool them. But we need to see the Los Alamos calculation, not just their result."

Feynman shrugged. "He's got some of it here, at least. But get this—he starts off with, 'I thought of a verse from the Hindu holy book the *Bhagavad Gita* (XI,12): 'If the radiance of a thousand suns were to burst at once into the sky, that would be like the splendor of the Mighty One.' Religion!"

Karl let that one go by. As soon as he corralled the estimates Groves wanted, he was flying home. "Okay, let's start—"

The door opened and Groves came in, face red. "Just got an intelligence report. A captured SS officer says there's a plan, proposed by the Luftwaffe and approved by Hitler. They'll set up special POW camps for captured British and American airmen, smack in the center of large German cities. So our guys would be human shields against A-bombs."

Fred Reines stood, shocked. "That would contravene the 1929 Geneva Convention!"

Groves smiled sardonically. "You think Hitler cares?"

Feynman grimaced and said, "Figure they'll do it?"

Groves grimaced and circled their table, emitting a low, frustrated growl. "If they do, we go after their tank divisions."

Three hours later, their estimates in order, Karl went to Groves's office to tell him, "I'll have the report written up in a day, General. Can you arrange my flights back home?"

Groves nodded over a stack of paperwork. "Hate to lose you, Karl. You stepped in when Luis went down, and I appreciate that." He sighed. "Now we're done, I don't know how much longer I'll be here either."

"They'd send you home?"

"Yeah, that's the hell of it. General Marshall let me come over because the bomb is my baby. You guys did the essential, and nobody over here knew diddly about it. So I got into a combat command!—what I always wanted. But now Oppie is running Los Alamos and Fermi is out in Washington State, getting those reactors started along the Columbia River, to make that plutonium—which we don't need now. I can't let that go for long without supervision."

"Good luck, sir." Karl left to find a typist. He might try dictating the report and filling in the numbers once he'd checked them again. That might save a day. It amused him that Groves wanted to stay here at all. Karl certainly did not. Not after Berlin.

He got it done by early evening. Karl was tired of the base, and the endless details of how to trim down the critical mass, all done amid the roars and rattles of planes landing and taking off, fleets of metal spanning the skies. He was far out of place here. An army sergeant under Groves, who managed moving gear around, took him aside and said, "Need a break? Step on out?"

"I miss my wife . . . sure."

The big problem was how to get free of the constant hum and hammer of the base. They were thoroughly encased, far from towns, and the security perimeter was three barbed-wire fences deep. So the sergeant improvised.

They got a Jeep. The tricky part was, drivers had to report in miles driven daily. So at night the sergeant tipped the Jeep onto its back and ran it in reverse. The wheels spun fast and sure in the air, and the simple mileage gauge ran backward. That way they quickly subtracted the forty miles needed to get into the nearest town with a working pub and back. Karl managed to wedge Feynman and Freeman into the back, and Feynman kept them laughing with jokes all the way. He proved to be a charmer in the pubs, too. Soon enough the Englishwomen had formed circles around him at the bar, and Karl got to sit with Freeman in a corner.

"I hear from a friend the Germans are working on some kind of advanced rocket," Freeman said. "Much bigger range than those little V-1s." *Ah*, Karl thought. *Maybe a bomb carrier that could reach . . . New York? With an A-bomb, if they're making one?* But he said nothing; it was never smart to talk about technical matters in a pub.

That night he felt light and happy, only a day or two from going home. The atmosphere of ordinary pubs now seemed warm, reassuring, and details like the long pull levers to summon a pint had a touch that he knew he would miss. The others in the chatty crowd were still coming down from the euphoria after Berlin, and he let their elation lift him into a kind of buoyant nostalgia for the present moment. Yet at the same time he knew he had gotten over the war and would not miss it.

He slept well but had dreams of wandering in a silent mansion, of opening doors down endless gray corridors, only to find behind each door a brick wall. Pretty obvious symbolism, yes, he realized. But no Freudian, he.

4.

The next morning he picked up the typed and copied report and marched right over to Groves's office, whistling. The Los Alamos guys and he were fairly sure a warhead needed close to the uranium mass Little Boy had carried, say within 80 percent. Using a bit less than the Berlin bomb could shave a week or two off the time to deliver the next bomb. The explosive yield would be lower, but time was more important, everyone said.

It was a fine summer day. Karl whistled as he strode along. He was going to ask Groves to fly him down to London, to an airstrip where he could get a flight to the USA. He knocked on the door and Groves barked something, but when he opened the door, the lanky army lieutenant, James Benford, was there. They were studying a map. Both turned and looked up at him with dismay.

"That damned Campbell guy was right," Groves said. "I guess the Krauts do read his magazine."

Benford showed Karl the main highway leading from the Normandy beaches toward the city of Angers. He pointed out details and said with a soft drawl, "The road's good and straight. Our armored came down it, some British, too. I was up on a hill to the southwest, calling down our battalion's fire on the German panzer division retreating back inland. I saw this gray airplane come down and fly along the highway, quicker'n you could follow it in field glasses. It dropped a long stream of dark dust on the highway, starting with the first of our tanks. Nobody could hit it, too fast."

"It's uranium, got to be," Karl said. "Probably both isotopes, not bothering to separate them—if they even know how. But the cleaned mixture is still pretty radioactive."

Benford's lean frame stiffened. "You got that right. I had the Operation Peppermint teams go down there, scoop up some of it. Their Geigers wailed like a stuck pig. Their films clouded up right away."

Groves asked Benford, "That valise you're carrying, what's in it?"

Benford picked it up, a worn leather case. "A sample of the dust. They told me to bring it here for you to see, since it's your area, General."

Groves stepped away from it. "Hell, is it shielded?"

"In a steel box," Benford said.

"If it's uranium, it'll be putting out alpha particles, which couldn't get through that leather anyway." Karl waved the issue away. "Normally I'd say take that sample to the chem guys in London, but look—let's have it. We can rig a little lab work to see if it's uranium. Oh yeah—any troops reporting sick?"

"Some, seem to be. A few said the dust made them sneeze. Then a while later they felt feverish."

Karl blinked. "Issue simple face masks, if you can find them. Mostly, just get away from that highway."

Groves picked up the map and taped it to his work board. Something about the man seemed not dismayed but elated.

"I see why they hit us there. It's the fast track toward Paris." He jabbed the map with his forefinger. "German commanders at all levels failed to react to the assault phase in a timely manner. Communications problems hindered their maneuvers, and Allied air and naval firepower knocked them down hard. Local commanders didn't mount an aggressive defense on the beach, as Rommel told them—I read the speech, we captured a copy of it on the first day."

Ah yes, Kart realized. Groves was their go-to general for things radioactive. Here was a brand-new war, and the major point for Groves was that *he was in it*.

Groves gestured in big sweeps around the map. "The Kraut High Command is fixated on the Calais area, Eisenhower says—I heard him just yesterday in London. So we're flanking around them. That's von Rundstedt's front, but Hitler won't let him commit the armored reserve—or so Military Intelligence says. They're got the terrain advantage, but we've got air power. So they use this goddamn dust to stop us. We've gotta—"

Karl held up his hand and Groves stopped. "They're telling us something."

"Huh?" Groves frowned.

"There must have been tons in that fast airplane. It flew low to drop the dust right on the highway."

Benford drawled, "I'd say it was no more than a hundred yards up, maybe less. Loud as hell. Screams. And *fast*."

Groves peered at Benford, puzzled. "I heard about that fast plane at a briefing just two days ago. They call it a 'jet.' Sucks in air, mixes fuel with it, ignites, heats the air, pushes it out the back. Same idea as that V-1 of theirs, but better managed."

"Fast and low, then gone. Best way to dump it on us, hard to shoot down," Karl said.

Groves spat out, "What'd you mean just now, tell us something?"

"They dropped tons on us. That means they have plenty of uranium. Guess why?"

5.

That evening Karl saw a London newspaper with a cartoon on the front page. Unnoticed in the blitz of news about the Normandy invasion plus the Berlin A-bomb, the Allies had taken Rome. Now they had moved up the coast, nearing Pisa. The simple line drawing showed the tower of Pisa, leaning over. In the next panel an airplane dropped a bomb in the sea beside it. Big blast. Next panel, the tower is upright. A neat, hopeful way to say something good could come of this war, he supposed. He wondered.

The war news was all about Normandy, otherwise. But not a whisper about the dust. That was classified. Nobody mentioned it in the mess hall, which meant that security was actually working.

Freeman had a simple cot in the Quonset next to Karl's. He was one of twenty in the long half cylinder of a room, not a private room. Karl found him lying on the cot, reading a book by some author named Lovecraft—which he assumed meant it was some kind of romance novel. Freeman looked up and grinned. "Karl, this author is American and plainly loves twisted language. Listen: 'The idiot god Azathoth, that last amorphous blight of nethermost confusion which blasphemes and bubbles at the center of all infinity.' Superb nonsense."

Karl snorted. "Why are you reading such stuff?"

"It's a novel of horror. Seems appropriate in a war, somehow."

Karl realized that he shared a language with the English but would never quite fathom them.

◆　◆　◆

The next morning his brief report on the dust weapon had a diagnosis, but no cure.

> Inhaling the dust brings uranium into direct contact with lungs. Dust on skin is also effective. The natural U-235 fission puts alpha particles—two neutrons, two protons, that rip through cells easily—into the bloodstream. The health effects of alpha particles depend heavily upon how exposure takes place. External exposure (external to the body) is of far less concern than internal exposure, because alpha particles lack the energy to penetrate the outer dead layer of skin.
>
> However, if alpha emitters have been inhaled, ingested (swallowed), or absorbed into the bloodstream, sensitive living tissue can be exposed to alpha radiation. The resulting biological damage increases the risk of cancer; in particular, alpha radiation is known to cause lung cancer in humans when alpha emitters are inhaled.
>
> Respirators with suitable air filters, or completely self-contained suits with their own air supply, can mitigate these dangers. Gas masks can keep dust from the lungs but cannot be worn for long periods; they annoy people.
>
> Washing is useful, of course. Evacuating the immediate contaminated area—which seems to be highways so far—is essential. Rain can bury the dust a bit and so limit the impact of the alpha radiation, which is short.
>
> Geiger counters cannot detect alpha radiation through even a thin layer of water, blood, dust, paper, or other material, because alpha radiation is not penetrating. Alpha radiation travels a very short distance through air. It is not able to penetrate gear, clothing, or a cover on a probe. Dry clothing can keep alpha emitters off the skin.
>
> The consequences of low-level radiation are often more psychological and radiological. Because damage from very low-level radiation cannot be detected, experience in laboratories in

the 1930s shows that people exposed to it are left in anguished uncertainty about what will happen to them. This is a terror weapon. Some may believe they have been fundamentally contaminated for life.

Aftermath of the Berlin Bomb

The bomb was already dirty because of its inefficient gun design (1.5 percent).

Very little of the uranium fissioned, so most of it dispersed as radioactive waste. That reduced the bomb's explosive yield but increased its long-term lethality and terror quotient. Little Boy's blast and fireball excavated many thousands of tons of soil. Radiation contaminated soil and dust and rock. Most of the contaminated soil rose up far into the sky and slowly returned as radioactive fallout, some as muddy black rain.

Groves slapped the report down on his desk. "So what do we do?"

"Don't drive on those roads. Tell troops to take baths. Get light dust filters—cloth will do—for them to wear in contaminated areas." It was easy to rattle off answers, but Karl knew doing it would be hard, in the middle of a war.

"Troops shouldn't have to worry about breathing, for Chrissake!"

"The Germans want to stop us using the roads to Paris, any way they can."

"You bet they do, and this is perfect for that. Your note about the Berlin bomb—you think the Germans got the idea from looking at fallout?"

"They have good physicists, like Heisenberg. He would get a Geiger counter to the site. Plus, check the fallout. Von Braun must've recalled that magazine story, way back in 1940."

Groves got up, paced. "You physicists can't find a fix for this?"

Karl shook his head. "Cat's out of the bag."

Groves consulted the maps of France on his wall. "You said 'guess why' the Germans have uranium to throw around. Meaning?"

"They have uranium, so they have a bomb program. That's for sure. So, two choices. Either they have a lot of it because they haven't gotten the iso-topes separated, or they have plenty to spare, or—"

"They're damned close to having enough U-235. The dust is a stall to keep us out of Germany, while they get their warhead together."

Karl didn't like the way this was going. "Um, maybe."

"Well, I need you to deal with this. And the Los Alamos guys, even that Dyson. The Krauts will use this damned dust a lot."

"Wait, I'm going home. Remember?"

"Not now you aren't. Sorry, Karl. This is a *war*."

And I've somehow become a soldier, Karl thought.

He recalled the dream of two nights before, of endless gray corridors he trudged down to pry open doors, finding only brick walls. It had been convincing, but only in the way that dreams are, as long as you are still asleep. Now it seemed like a prediction.

The death dust didn't stay secret for long, of course. The London *Times* proclaimed it in red ink: RADIOACTIVE POISON FROM THE SKY!

"That will make every trooper in France anxious," Luis said. "The psycho-logical impact will be bigger than the contamination."

Worse, Feynman came into their working offices with a report from a little chemical operation he and Luis had set up. "That dust, it's cleaned ura-nium, all right. We should get the London chem guys to use a mass spec on it. I'll bet it's just purified U-235 and U-238 in the same ratios as natural ore."

So it really was as everyone had guessed. Karl walked them through the options. If the Germans had enough uranium to throw it around, did a bomb look likely, soon?

"No way to tell," Luis said. "They could be just messing with our heads."

"They've got their backs to the wall," Feynman said, his voice carrying a touch of wonderment, as if part of his mind was figuring out how he could have gotten himself into this. "And now . . . so do we."

Luis looked puzzled. "How so?"

Feynman got up and paced, just as Groves had before. "If they have a lot of uranium, our ground attack stops. They have time to work on a bomb. They've no doubt sampled the fallout from Berlin and guessed what we put in it." He turned and jabbed a finger. "And *now* they know even a simple bomb works."

"So what can we do?" Karl asked them all around the table. Shrugs and embarrassed looks blossomed from them: Luis, Feynman, Serber, Freeman.

"All our bright minds," Feynman said sardonically, "and we can't figure how to stop the enemy from dumping dirt on us."

Freeman said with delicate precision, "We are hothouse flowers, really. Not made for the blunt edge of war."

Nods all around. Feynman sighed. "Right, Freeman. If I were a lizard, I'd be a belt by now."

"See what you think of this." Groves tossed a letter on his desk. "It's from Teller to Fermi."

> First, Szilard was right. As scientists who worked on producing the bomb, we bore a special responsibility. Second, Cohen was right. We did not know enough about the political situation to have a valid opinion. Third, what we scientists should have done but failed to do was to work out the technical changes required for demonstrating the bomb very high over German territory and submit that information to the president.

"So?" The rest was about physics gossip. Karl tossed it back. "Everybody's a Monday morning quarterback." He had learned this sports analogy just recently, since military men spoke that way constantly.

Groves toyed with a chocolate bar, as if tempting himself with it. "Security sent it to me; they read everything coming out of Los Alamos. But Teller's no kind of weak-kneed sort, y'know. If he says this, he's speaking for a big fraction of the scientists."

"I did say I don't think we know the political situation, so we should just shut up."

"Damn right! It's up to us, the commanders, to decide—"

"More like Roosevelt, I'd say."

Groves gave him a sliding, sideways look. "Well, yeah. I never thought the response to our bomb would get us in trouble. Long-noses in the papers are saying we shouldn't have introduced radioactives into weapons. Look at what little Adolf says—"

Another sheet, a translation:

> This abomination, this horrific bomb that blinds and maims and poisons our lands, is a violation of the Geneva Convention! The Reich shall not be restrained any longer by this Convention. In our reply to our enemies, we shall treat them as they treat us. Expect the apocalypse!

"Cheerful fellow." Karl was tempted to shred it but restrained himself. "Nonsense—the convention says nothing about radioactives, Freeman tells me."

"Right, but everybody's scared of radioactives. Most people don't read the fine print, y'know."

"We have to end this damned war. Hitler's slaughtering Jews every day."

Groves made a sour face and stood. "I see that in my classified briefings. Stories from people who got out of Europe. Trainloads of Jews, Gypsies, prisoners, all going to awful camps that even have incinerators. Plus, plenty of troops die on the eastern and western fronts."

Karl struggled to keep calm. He wanted to know more and yet he didn't. "Everywhere, the casualty count goes up constantly. The war's reached a meat-grinder phase."

A frustrated silence fell. A knock at the door. Luis Alvarez came in, using a cane. "Here's the telex on the Teller idea."

Groves took it, tossed it on a pile of similar sheets. "Y'know, Teller's working on another kind of bomb—uses hydrogen, fuses it together. Opposite of fission. Says it will be much better than our uranium ones." Groves beamed with pride. "So the project will continue on, after the war."

Luis chuckled. "Edward is full of enthusiasm about possibilities; this means they probably will fail."

Karl knew Teller's style. That led to a joke, well circulated, that a new unit of unfounded optimism was designated as the teller; one teller was so large that most events had to be measured in microtellers.

Karl saw it might be smart to ask when Groves was in a good mood. "General, I was wondering if I could again—"

"Nope, Karl. I need you here. Things are happening fast."

Though he spent time with army teams who wanted to talk about handling radioactivity, it all bored him. The Army Air Forces were making some dent in the German program, though. Vague stories appeared in the newspapers; Groves got the details.

The air force had kept close watch for dust-dropping planes. An American, Chuck Yeager of the 357th Fighter Group, shot down the jet Messerschmitt 262, which he caught during its landing approach. Karl had been learning German, for something to do, and he remarked to Feynman, "Appropriate. 'Yeager' is an English version of the German *Jäger*, which means 'hunter.'"

Other downed jets followed. But the Germans were turning out several a day, and "death dust" flights came whenever there were suitable roads or intersections to block with it.

Then came the V-2 rockets. They were ballistic missiles, nothing like the sputtering V-1 semi-jets that pilots could shoot down, or flip with their wings. They fell in July, straight down on London, from high altitudes. The first ones had high explosives and blew down houses, offices, in a fairly well-grouped distribution, charted by Freeman. "Half are within a five-mile circle," he said. "Remarkably good aiming, for a rocket that climbs to about fifty-five miles high—which we can see on radar."

Groves became more and more bad-tempered in their meetings. Karl could see the man was a sort of caged bear, wanting to have a greater role, now that he was in the fight. "We can't *do* anything about the damn dust, even though uranium is our, well, *our* weapon."

Then one V-2 burst about two hundred meters above central London into a dark plume—a "death dust" warhead. Wind blew it down a seven-mile streamer, driving tens of thousands from the streets into the countryside. Uranium was not a battlefield issue anymore, but a civilian one.

"I need you guys to find a way around this stuff," Groves told them. "I'm not a scientist, but there's got to be *something* we can do."

Feynman said forlornly, "I agree with the first part of that sentence, at least."

Groves sent Bob Serber to the city to retrieve samples of the dust, following a suggestion Karl and the others made: see if the U-235 content of the dust was rising, showing that the Germans had an isotope separation plant going.

Tests showed there was no enrichment. "They're just slinging purified uranium at us, straight from the mines," Bob said.

But the next week Bob fell ill. A red rash spread from his face all over his body. The bumps were as big as marbles and itched "like the bejesus," he said in a feverish daze. He died two days later of smallpox.

"So *this* is how the Nazis take the moral high ground?" Groves demanded.

Freeman said quietly, head bowed, "It has been argued that rational people would never use biological weapons offensively. Their point is that biological weapons cannot be controlled: the weapon could backfire and harm the army on the offensive, perhaps having even worse effects than on the target. Agents like smallpox and other airborne viruses would almost certainly spread widely, and ultimately infect the user's home country."

Groves wasn't interested in theory. "Just got a message from London. Another V-2, just across the river from the House of Commons. This one had no radioactives. But it did have anthrax."

Gasps.

"Exactly, gentlemen. I wonder if they have more tricks to come."

"How are the V-2s launched?" Feynman asked, leaning against the wall, since there were not enough seats in Groves's office. He managed to make his leisurely slouch seem like a sardonic signal.

Groves checked his stack of reports. "From portable carriers."

"Not a fixed launchpad, then," Feynman said. "Maybe the flyboys can hunt them down on the roads."

Groves nodded. "I'm sure they're doing that now—instead of supporting our troops."

Karl got up and tapped the map of France on the wall. "Which slows our advance, gives them more time to work on their bomb—if they have one."

Around the crowded room, faces displayed geometries of despair.

"Oh, by the way, Karl," Groves said with an offhand wave. "I got an order to send you into London to meet with Moe Berg. Dunno why."

6.

Claridge's Hotel in Mayfair was a bit pricey, even for Moe Berg. It turned out that he wasn't paying, though. This fact enhanced Moe's smoothness, for Karl.

"This is Brigadier General William Donovan," Moe said with a deft bow and hand salute. "Our host."

"I've heard so much about you Manhattan guys, good to meet one who was in at the beginning," Donovan said. Karl knew him as the head of the Office of Strategic Services, so his military posture fit. So did the smile, cut off and stored away as soon as it had done its job.

They ordered dinner in the hotel restaurant, all three getting roast beef and Yorkshire pudding. As the waiter departed, Donovan said, "We've got a job for you. Moe recommended you as a good expert on this atomic business, with experience traveling in Europe."

Karl started to object, but a glance from Moe told him not to. Smoothly Moe said, "I got sent to Italy, Karl, to find out what they were doing in rockets. We managed to get some of their experts out to the USA. Pretty tough, but damn good food. Now I'm going back to see what's up with atomic stuff."

"Italy?" Karl knew the Allies were slugging their way up toward the Alps.

"No," Donovan said. "Switzerland. To judge some physics."

"Or physicists," Moe added.

"Look, I'm an expert only in the sense that I've made all the mistakes that can be made in a very narrow field."

Karl noticed that the waiters did not sit anyone within hearing range.

Donovan was not bothered about being overheard when he leaned forward. "The Brits got intel in 1943 that the Kaiser Wilhelm people were building a reactor. We know they imported tons of uranium ore from the Czechs, the stuff they're dropping on us now. This guy, Werner Heisenberg, has moved from the Kaiser Wilhelm Institute with Carl Friedrich von Weizsäcker. Plus Otto Hahn himself, the guy who found fission. There's a program at Hamburg under Harteck, some other places too."

Donovan was now a humorless man who scowled at nearly everything, and he detailed names and movements. Karl avoided Donovan's merciless, flinty glare and classic, aggressive harrumph. He had heard that many in-between people—the intelligence people whom Dyson said seldom displayed that virtue—carefully buffered "Wild Bill," as they called him, kept him from going too far.

"This is beyond my competence," Karl said.

"You want to end this war or not?" Donovan said, eyebrows raised.

"Uh, I—" He thought of Marthe and all the years he had been away from home, when he wanted to be with his family. "Yes. Soon."

"Heisenberg will be within reach, so you two can figure out if he is head of a real bomb project. Glad to have you, Karl."

With that, the issue went away. Donovan gave more of the carefully measured smile, and their beef arrived.

He and Moe were taking their leave when Donovan came back to the point. "Heisenberg goes to Switzerland regularly to discuss physics, a kind of vacation. He's going soon, this summer. If he talks like he knows enough nuclear physics, drops some technical comments, pointing plausibly to a bomb project, you're to render him *hors de combat*."

Moe seemed puzzled, but Karl knew this meant "outside the fight." Donovan said flatly, "Moe, go in with a pistol in your pocket."

Karl was startled when a Military Police major appeared with a slim suitcase. "Here's your background reading," Donovan said to Moe. There were German agents around, he said, and somehow they might go after the case. The major handcuffed Moe to the attaché case with a nickel-plated bracelet.

Walking to the train station, Karl said, "I don't follow this cloak-and-swagger world of yours."

"It's a lot like the blind men and the elephant. Donovan figures it means you just get a lot more men and fill in the elephant. Sometimes you lose one or two."

"How comforting. Any German agents could just kill you and cut off your arm."

Moe laughed. "'An inconvenience is only an adventure wrongly considered.'"

Until they got word on Heisenberg, Karl continued working with the Los Alamos guys, who were in close contact with others back in New Mexico. The better they compacted and trimmed down the U-235 needed for the next bomb, the sooner they could go after a good target.

But what target could that be? There was no obvious, essential asset, after Berlin's center was gone. They didn't know where Hitler was, or even the German bomb project—if there even was a central place for the bomb assembly. So Karl stayed in London and at the airfield, through July.

At times he allowed himself to think of what he should be doing in a rational world, in summer's warm miasma. Back in New York, Martine was four and Elisabeth just one, and he could see them in his mind's eye, scampering around amid wood smoke and ravenous, buzzing bugs. They would be filthy and delighted, trying to catch perch in a tinkling stream, using little lines baited with canned corn nibs. Marthe's aroma would carry hints of calamine lotion and simmering skin beneath a spotlight sun. At twilight the girls would madly chase the Morse code of fireflies amid the sizzle of hamburgers, their laughter ringing like tiny bells.

He sighed, opened her most recent letter beside a dim lamp, and made out the words with relish. Their favorite names for the girls, Mots for Elisabeth and La Fou for Martine, jumped out at him.

> June 29, 1944
> My Dear Karl,
> I read your telegram eagerly. I hope the difficulties of the trip, the crowding, and the rations have not yet overwhelmed your zeal for this mission. Yesterday I saw the first newsreels of

the Normandy invasion—pretty grim. Everyone in France must be huddled around radios and holding their collective breath and praying it will succeed. The pictures from Berlin are terrifying. Indescribable damage. Thousands of casualties. The newspapers here said a single uranium bomb did it all! I'm saving the newspapers for you, with details about de Gaulle, too. Also an important series of articles by Willkie, who looks like a candidate to run against Roosevelt, in the *Herald-Tribune*.

I took La Fou to the Automat on Broadway for lunch. She was overjoyed, as you can imagine, especially now that her intestinal problem has subsided. She is now in the five-year-old group at school, though she is still four. Mots is always the same inimitable Mots. She is beginning to walk (without knowing it) by pushing a chair from one side of the kitchen to the other. Also, she says, "Hi ho . . . bang-bang." Only "Silver" is missing.

I hope you like this elegant (sic!) paper—the latest gross product from our fantastic industry. Shortages and rationing get tiring, not to mention time-consuming standing in line. The cheap, pulpy paper just reminds one of them.

So far, funds are not lacking. But if you have to stay away until, say, the fall of Vitebsk*, it will be necessary for you to send me a check (but not a Czech, because what would I do with him?).

I dearly hope to see you soon. Hugs and kisses from the whole family.

Marthe

*can find on map?

He looked up Vitebsk, which seemed like a misspelling but was a city under Nazi Germany occupation, just liberated. Much of the old city had been destroyed in the battles between the Germans and the Red Army, and most of the local Jews perished in a ghetto massacre.

The military types all around him thought of war as about strategy and tactics, but to Karl it was about death. Thinking of his home, he recalled how Martine had asked him not long before he left them, "What happens when we die?" All he could think to say was, "We go back to where we were before we were born," which was at least in a way true. "Oh, okay," and she had skipped away

In childhood we all live in the bright light of immortality, he thought.

He had hoped she didn't note the glistening in his eye, the burr in his throat as he spoke. A diffuse longing rose in him in a smooth wave, a longing like nostalgia for the child present right now, and who would soon be gone down the well of time, when he returned—to be replaced by another lovely child, larger and more sunk into the wondrous, deadly world.

Time waxed on into August. Karl got restless. He played poker with British and American fliers. They were savvy about bluffs and little unconscious signs, so they did pretty well. He studied them and picked up a few tricks himself. Mostly he found a book on poker probabilities in London and studied it. He memorized the cards shown and kept a running calculation. Betting the odds on each hand, never going big unless the calculations said he had a huge chance, his winnings gradually grew. He cultivated a reputation as a cautious, polite player. As his opponents drank more through the long evenings, his "luck" improved. He sent a weekly check to Marthe. The girls appreciated the gifts she bought for them. He even got photographs of them holding the dolls and toys. At nighttime the photos made him weep.

Then Donovan sent a telex through Groves's office marked *TOP SECRET*. Heisenberg would be in Lucerne somewhere around the second half of August. Groves frowned at this and said, "I told them I needed you here, Karl."

"You don't really. When a second bomb gets here, Luis can—"

"You've already done the following-plane job. Luis and the others—except for that Feynman, who's always off calculating something he says will be useful, someday, somehow—have better diagnostics worked out. Faster cameras—"

"Then let him fly the following mission."

Groves opened his mouth, closed it. "I like to keep my team together."

"Goudsmit thinks Heisenberg's crucial. Moe's uncertain he can follow Heisenberg's talk in German, about physics he only understands superficially. He—"

"Okay, I've approved your going." He sighed, and Karl saw the man was both frustrated and tired. Berlin had been a big event, but the war had passed him by, into territory no one understood. "I couldn't block the brass upstairs, anyway."

"General, to me you *are* the brass upstairs."

Groves sat back and laughed. "Good to hear it. Get going."

PART XI

GROUND TRUTH

It was at Waterloo that General Cambronne, when called on to surrender, was supposed to have said, "The Old Guard dies but never surrenders!" What Cambronne actually said was, "Merde!" which the French, when they do not wish to pronounce it, still refer to as, "the word of Cambronne." It corresponds to our four-letter word for manure. All the difference between the noble and the earthy accounts of war is contained in the variance between these two quotations.
—Ernest Hemingway, *Men at War*

1.

August 17, 1944

Karl and Moe sat in the wardroom of a tubby landing craft, rocking with the sway as the engine throbbed a few feet away. The diesel coughed an acrid tang into the salty air. Their craft was bobbing on the waves of a dishwater sea with a lead-colored sky above. In the acronym-rich army, this was an LCIL, for Landing Craft Infantry Large. The wardroom was seven feet square and had bunks and a table with four places. Earlier they had managed to wedge eight men in there for a poker game, a nickel to ante—a high price for them, some of whom might not see tomorrow.

Karl studied the faces around them. Few spoke, and not all the sweating was from the weather.

He was a long way from partial differential equations, diapers and kindergarten, dental bills, gas ration cards, whirring centrifuges. There had been times—quite a few, after leaving New York—when Karl wondered what the hell he was doing in such unlikely events. Neither of the career choices he had faced just a bit over a decade ago—chemistry versus concert piano—had ever seemed remotely likely to lead to . . . *this*.

Moe, as usual, was reading three newspapers he had somehow found back in Corsica, plus a *Stars and Stripes*. In the two days' voyage here, he had also consumed three armed-services editions of novels, shutting out the jammed quarters and seldom even looking up. Plus, he had total memory. Especially, he knew plenty of details about the rising tide of casualties around the world—a huge cost, but some victories. Karl mostly tried to forget such numbers.

Nearby, the French cruiser *Montcalm* was banging out salvos. Each boom rocked their craft in a side-wash. She was firing at a German pocket of resistance miles from the shoreline. Their engine rumbled as they sped past. The watch officer turned on the small speakers around the craft, and here came the suave voice of a BBC announcer. "The Allies are now in a position to say the joint American-French landings came off with surprising ease. The air force and the big guns of the navy smashed coastal defenses, and the army occupied them."

A lieutenant and the engineering officer both began to laugh. The lieutenant said in a plummy English accent, close to the BBC one, "There is nothing like a broadcasting studio in London to give a chap perspective, y'know."

Karl was nervous and not afraid to show it. But it was hard to just sit. He and Moe had done a lot of that on the flight to Corsica. He went up on the observing deck to watch the French shoreline drawing nearer. Their craft had a rectangular superstructure and a narrow strip of open deck on each side. "These things move pretty fast, and they make a fairly small target, bows-on," Moe had explained before they got aboard on Corsica. Painted on one side of the superstructure Karl noted a neat Italian flag, with the legend ITALY underneath so that there would be no mistake, and beside the flag a blue shield with white vertical stripes and the word SICILY.

There was also a swastika and the outline of an airplane, which could only mean that the ship had shot down a German plane in a landing either in Sicily or Italy. How? They must have carried at least machine guns. He noticed a metal stand that must have been used to hold a high-caliber weapon. Apparently this time the military expected less opposition, so they didn't arm the ship as heavily. The constant buzzing of fighters overhead supported this theory. Karl watched a Mustang come zooming along the rocky beach, on a patrol of some sort. Somehow he did not find the sight reassuring.

The armada on view was called Operation Dragoon, a second invasion of France, with Allied ships and troops on hundreds of gray vessels flying various flags. Reports said the Italians who had been defending this coast had gone home, leaving thin, stripped-down German divisions. Their briefing said the German troops were only second and third grade, even Volksdeutsch leftovers from Poland and Czechoslovakia. But there were plenty of targets, to judge from the naval guns' relentless barrage. British and South African troops had just taken Florence, backed by US heavy weaponry. The navy had taken Guam and Tinian, an island Karl had to look up to see its importance; it was within striking range of Japan, using the new huge B-29 bombers. That could come in handy when there were more A-bombs, he realized. Which should be just a week or two.

But the Warsaw Uprising against the Germans, valiant at first, had come on hard and finally failed. The approaching Soviet Union armies just stood off and let the slaughter go on. The Germans proclaimed they had wiped out all the Jews Warsaw held. They might be right, given the savagery of the war in the east. Every day brought more brutality.

The unsuccessful bomb conspirators against Hitler in July were shot immediately or hanged with piano wire, and then their bodies hung on meat hooks. Reprisals against their families continued, proudly announced by German radio. Karl wondered if this rising against Hitler, after the Berlin bomb didn't get him, was in some distant way his fault. Berlin as a target had seemed obvious. Now nothing was.

Meanwhile, the Allies had failed to close entirely the Falaise Pocket that led to eastern France. That left a gap that the Germans, fleeing east to escape the Allied pincer movement, filled quickly. The bomb had not turned out to be the war-ender they had all hoped it would be, and now the dust seemed to be equally useful.

Between the hammering of the big naval guns, Karl could hear faint explosions from the western side of the shore. The landing craft's hull was a lurching box for carrying men, no more. It pitched and rolled, and Karl was glad he had earned his sea legs on his Atlantic crossings in the 1930s. Some of the troops nearby were still vomiting over the side. This brought amused smiles to the officers, who sometimes referred to their calling as an "ambiguous farce."

Several groups on deck were rubbing "impregnating grease" into shoes to make them impervious to mustard gas. There had been a great last-minute furor about the possibility that the Germans might use gas against the invasion, and everybody had been fitted with impregnated gear and two kinds of protective ointment. The ship's rails were topped with rows of crusty, drying boots.

"This is the first time I ever tried to get a pair of boots pregnant," a private called out sociably nearby.

"You tried it on about everything else, I guess," another yelled as he worked on his own boots.

Nobody said anything about "death dust." Karl supposed they were taking their dangers one at a time. Maybe combat training made you do that. Now that the dust was in play, why use mustard gas, a trickier weapon overall?

Voices pealed in tones of rickety bravado. Seaweed flavored the air and gulls cawed. He felt utterly out of place as they came into shore. The craft had a stern anchor, which it dropped with a splash just before going aground. Two forward ramps whined and ran out as she touched bottom. Moe came up, and they waited as troops in drab-green field jackets walked quickly down the ramps and formed up into ranks on the pebbled beach. They carried mortar and machine gun parts on their backs, in addition to a full pack. Some carried carbines, and most had M-1 rifles packed in oilskin cases. Two had pickaxes and blocks of TNT, for pillboxes. "Me, I like a BAR," one of them had said to Karl, explaining, "Means Browning automatic rifle. You can punch a lot of tickets with one of these babies."

The ship naturally lightened as men left and they stepped onto dry, crunching stones, within view of the Marseille dockyards. The troops marched away toward the rich green hills. Moe and Karl stood out in their street clothes.

Moe gestured toward town. The landing craft lieutenant had thought they could not set foot on the beach except in the company of a commissioned officer, but Moe had a letter that shut him up. Karl had read it, brisk and firm and signed by Eisenhower.

Now they were on their own. "We can move faster that way," Moe had said. "My preferred mode."

The warm, comfortable air and humming traffic made this not seem at all like the jumping-off place for an invasion. "No mines and underwater obstacles," Moe said approvingly. "They're already cleared. It was a different story when I went into Italy near Rome, to talk to the physicists there."

A corporal arrived with a Jeep for them, and they headed toward the city. "We're going first class," Moe said wryly.

The general invasion plan had been for planes and big guns of the fleet to put on an intensive bombardment before the landing. That seemed to have worked. Shattered pillboxes and bunkers still smoked beside the road. At the Marseille dock, traffic murmured amid a chemical stink. The harbor surged, a lake of ripples with an oily sheen. Troops went ashore on a wooden plank, chuffing compressors and whining turbines adding their music. In the damp heat a cat lay on a tarp on the busy quay, asleep with four legs in the air. Khaki was everywhere, distant booms rolled in, and troops marched off big gray ships and into armored personnel carriers with .60 caliber machine guns on their decks.

Ten minutes later they were purring along a beautiful broad avenue beside crisp, sandy beaches. Cannes was a bit east of them. A few burned German tanks dotted the sunny shore. They were the big Panzer IVs, Karl noted, already towed off the road where they'd met their end.

Karl turned toward the light blue sea and watched the brown girls lying on towels only a few meters away. The exotic contrast of a luxuriant holiday spot and the sprawl of discarded military gear somehow made him think of Marthe. She was far away and he was here, in her homeland.

"Our best way to get up north and into Switzerland," Moe said, "is along the Route Napoléon, to Grenoble."

"So we can only go as fast as the army pushes the Germans back."

"Right. You said something about having family near here?"

Karl had waited until he saw the situation here before making his idea clear. "If we aren't going anywhere for a day or two," he said, "I'll look up my in-laws."

Moe beamed. "Fine with me. I'd like to see some countryside."

Karl chuckled. "Ah yes, you're my bodyguard." Moe just nodded. A day in the rich green country would do them both some good, after months in cities or the rattling metal boxes of transports.

Marthe's parents, Eugene and Madeleine Malartre, had gotten back to France in June 1942. Eugene was a lieutenant colonel in the French army, who refused to leave his wife to fight with the Free French. This did not sit well with de Gaulle, so they had holed up at a farm inland from the French Riviera not far away. Madeleine, Marthe's mother, had developed enteritis from the rough food. Mostly, they farmed vegetables and bought what else they could. Marthe had managed to get letters to her parents in Grasse, a small town now about ten kilometers away.

Long lines of soldiers marched through the narrow streets, headed for the battle. There was little road traffic. The Germans had taken all the gasoline, leaving the locals with horses, bicycles, and odd *vélo-taxis* made by cutting a motorcar in half and pulling the passenger end with a bicycle. Karl thought they looked like part of a circus act.

A skittish energy layered the soft summer air. Children down alleys played hopscotch and sang "La Marseillaise" and laughed a lot. People smiled at the passing troops.

A woman on a street corner lounged against a brick wall and gave Karl a flat, challenging stare. She had long blonde hair, black at the roots, and maybe a quarter pound of makeup that looked like pasty flour. He realized he was not just another American, not a uniform or an obvious logistics guy. His clothes were not worn or ragged, and he was well fed. A clear step up as a customer, then. With a thin smile she swayed her hips, her eyes never leaving his. He looked away, thinking sad, bad thoughts.

They got to a hotel that Moe somehow already knew, and there was a room for them—bare but livable. "Rest up," Moe said. "We can't move until the Route Napoléon is open, which could take days."

There were American officers in the hotel, but he and Moe ignored them, and they did likewise. Obvious OSS agents ducked in and out, probably making contacts with locals. Karl sat in the garden below and had a glass of local wine. The savor of France settled over him. *War with style.*

Troops assembled and a chaplain came to conduct services. He was a captain attached to the amphibious engineers, a husky man who had been throwing a football around a half hour before. Karl did not want to go up to his stuffy room, so he stayed, having never heard a Christian service before. The captain took his text from Romans: "If God be for us, who can be against us?" He didn't seem to want the men to get the idea that the cause was depending entirely on faith, however. "Give us that dynamic, that drive, which, coupled with our matchless supermodern weapons, will ensure victory," he prayed.

Karl found all this talk makeshift. So many seemed to believe people were each God-made, one-of-a-kind, with an immortal soul breathed in. Plus, some God or other—there were many brands—listened to prayers and might do some good for you. This view of the world—people as vehicles of grace, battlefields of good and evil, soldiers as even apprentice angels—seemed so far from the reality that smacked you in the face, cold and hard, that he could barely suppress his skeptical smile until the mercifully short service was over.

His father had once said to him, after perhaps one glass of a decent red wine too many, that Jesus had been an addled though talented fraud, the afterlife was a sham, God a sadistic madman, and Christianity "bad, bloody, merciless, moneygrubbing, and predatory." Karl felt much the same but had the sense not to say so within earshot here, or even very much to Marthe. Yet he was a Jew of sorts, a cultural Jew. He felt it from his family ties, not in some airy theology of chants and ceremony and odd dietary rules.

Finally he had enough and got up, fetched Moe, and went for a walk. He strolled restlessly, feeling useless. Crowds were everywhere, noisy and smiling. For the moment, the French had lost the ironic nihilism they had flirted with at the best of times.

Some units, mostly artillery, had leave to come into town. They carried five-franc notes printed in America and issued to the troops for use after they got ashore. It was the first time Karl had seen these, reminding him of old-time cigar-store coupons. There was nothing on them to indicate who authorized them or would pay off on them—just *Emis en France* on one side and on the other side the tricolor and *Liberté, Egalité, Fraternité*.

An angry crowd was yelling and tearing down a billboard. Karl supposed the Germans had erected it when they fully occupied this region in January, making it officially held, subject to German law. They had known some kind of invasion was coming from the south. Now they apparently thought that the radioactive dust could hold their western front firm.

JETZT GEHT'S UMS GANZE—WIR SCHAFFEN ES DOCH!

"'Now it's all or nothing!—but we'll make it!'" Moe translated. He had brushed up on his German on their flight here, and Karl was impressed at how quickly he acquired vocabulary.

"Pretty desperate," Karl said. The crowd yelled and smashed the wooden sign into chunks they could carry away. "At least they're getting firewood out of it."

Then he saw a small French sign slapped up beside the German one: ECRASEZ L'INFÂME! "That one says, 'Stamp out the abomination!'"

Moe chuckled.

They spent the evening eating, after preparing a meal of rations and some delicacies Moe had brought. Karl did not reveal the food he had brought ashore, thinking it better for later.

The aromas and sounds of France clasped him in memories. His New York self had never consciously thought about doing anything other than mastering the piano, becoming a professional performer, or advancing into the thick swamp of theoretical chemistry. His father had wanted him to become "a doctor," which meant a practicing physician, certainly not a PhD. Through early adolescence he had suffered from his father's increasing references to how useful chemistry would be when Karl was practicing, or would help him understand the new disease treatments that were coming along, or how good grades in chemistry and mathematics would help in getting into the very best medical schools, maybe Harvard even.

He had grown up in a close clutch of family and friends who all thought, quite properly in his view, that a man did serious work and brought home the money, so that a family could blossom from his labor, and from his love for a woman with whom he would spend his entire life. That was how the world worked. Karl had never been the kind of guy who felt bare female toes creeping up under his pants leg at a dinner party. He knew he would have to seek out and court a woman he wanted, that it might be a struggle to find her and win her, and then he could build the kind of life a man needed, the one he had seen working well enough in the families all around him in Brooklyn.

Then France changed him in 1936. He met Marthe, and somehow their courting came as though in a warm, comfortable dream, all in the wonderland of Paris, where the next move forward was a slow glide through days of quick, bright moments between them, all effortless and deftly natural. All this had surprised him. Of course there had been dodgy moments of timidity, of awkward humility across the gulf of languages they both fumbled through, and even of alarm when Marthe misunderstood him, or he her. But those were mere bumps in the glide. Against the lumbering political dramas raging all around them in those years of 1936 to 1938, their gathering romance and then kindled passion was a small thing, of course, but everything to him— and then, blessedly, to her.

The coastal towns around him now were harder than he remembered France being, and rougher. As soon as the Americans arrived, crowds cheering in the streets turned to mob some women who had been mistresses of Germans, mostly of officers. The mob shaved their heads but left the prostitutes alone, by common consent. "A prostitute is who she is by nature. So are Germans, it is their nature," a French gendarme, who had stood aside as all this happened, explained to Karl, with a resigned sigh and a shrug.

2.

The next morning, trying to find "Eugene Malartre" without mentioning that he was a French army officer, in hiding, was difficult. Artillery boomed in the distance, but they heard no small-arms fire. The Germans, they heard, were falling back along the roads to the west. "As expected," Moe said, and no more.

Moe got a corporal to drive them to the town of Grasse, where Marthe sent her letters to a hotel, to be held for her parents. He found the Hôtel L'Oasis easily; not many hotels were open anymore. The desk clerk was surprised to see Americans. He told them excitedly that the Germans had just been driven out a few hours before. Karl could hear machine-gun bursts toward the north. No artillery landed in the town, and troop trucks were grinding through the main street, just outside the hotel.

The clerk pretended to know nothing about any people named Malartre. Moe leaned across the desk and towered over the man. Karl told the clerk that Moe was authorized to use force to find the valuable Colonel Malartre. This had some small effect, and Moe made moves to go around the desk. Tense seconds passed.

"Okay, how's this?" Karl said as he fished out a pack of Lucky Strikes from his backpack. He explained about being a relative of the colonel, while the clerk's eyes never left the Luckies. Soon enough the clerk allowed that perhaps in this exceptional case he could reveal the approximate location.

The Jeep had gone, but Moe was sure he could get another from the troops moving along the main drag of Grasse, which was the Route Napoléon itself, when they needed it. They discussed directions to hike out of town to find the Malartre refuge. It was rumpled-looking country in the foothills of the Alps. The clerk had lit up his cigarette before they went out the front door.

In the damp afternoon heat they sweated their way downhill, across a ravine ripe with smells, then uphill across a pasture and into the side yard of a farm. Sweaty work for Karl, easy for Moe. The moist aromas swarmed in the air as they approached the farmhouse from the side without windows. Birds sang their chorus among the fragrant, leafy trees. The long gables of the house bespoke several centuries of hard use, seldom repaired. It was thirty-five degrees Centigrade, and the damp air swarmed with happy insects and rich scents from the fields.

They were walking uphill into an ample barnyard when a barking shot came, a *splatt*. A man in overalls toppled over, fifty meters away. The shot came from uphill, in the forest beyond a stone wall to their right.

They were caught in the open. Karl and Moe sprinted forward and hid behind an outhouse. The smell was rank, disgusting. Karl darted his head around the corner to get a look. The sun was in his eyes, but scanning the trees, he glimpsed a bit of gray, moving uphill from them.

Moe was watching around the other corner. He leaned back and said, "That farmer's wife is dragging him off. The sniper seems to be holding fire for her to do it."

"Looks like a German uniform up there," Karl said as he heard a woman's voice, high-pitched, frantic.

"Probably separated from his unit. Doesn't know what to do."

"Stupid to shoot a farmer. What's that lying beside him on the ground?"

Moe said, "A pitchfork. The Kraut must've thought the farmer spotted him and would attack, or summon help. We can't leave that German there."

"Why can't we just go around him?"

"He's shooting civilians. Dunno why, maybe he's crazy. And he can maneuver, so we won't know where he is." Moe eyed the nearby trees.

Karl did not like the way this was going. "So what can we do?"

"I'll go around him. You stay here. Do nothing."

With that he was off, sprinting back across the barnyard about forty meters to reach a stand of trees. Moe was startlingly fast, showing his pro baseball years. Karl watched him turn left and run with high, long strides beyond view. He supposed Moe would run uphill for about a hundred meters, turn to his left, and come in behind the German.

This was crazy indeed, crazy on stilts. They were supposed to stay out of the invasion chaos and keep moving. He sweated in the heat. Seconds trudged on. He heard the wife still calling frantically in high-pitched screams to someone from beyond the barn up ahead. In the strange stillness, he listened carefully. A distant *crump* came from back toward the west. He could not distinguish between bombs and artillery rounds coming in, but there came the rising burr of airplane engines, so he supposed it was bombing. An insect flitted around his face and he felt exposed here, hiding behind an outhouse and inhaling the shit odors that were always worse in the summer. *The hardest thing to do is nothing*, he thought.

A rocky rattle came from toward the wall. It sounded like the stones of the fence banging together. Karl darted his head around the corner. Running toward him was a German in a light gray field uniform. He carried a nasty-looking rifle with a big clip. His head was turned to look at the barn, so he did not see Karl. But he was fifty meters away and headed this way.

Karl drew back, knowing he had only seconds. He listened and heard now the man's panting, then the pounding of his boots on the dried mud. *The sun is behind him. . . .*

He crouched just behind the corner. A shadow fell into view. *What—?*

Karl turned and thrust out his left leg, keeping low. The German's right leg caught on Karl's calf and the man toppled forward. He slammed into the dirt headfirst. His right arm jerked out with the rifle in it, and Karl snatched it up. The German rolled away, looking up in surprise. Karl juggled with the rifle and got the butt around in time to smash it into the man's face.

"Ahhh!" The German's arms flailed.

Karl stepped back. For good measure he kicked the man in the skull, a solid *crunch*. The body rolled away, stopped, didn't move. He held the rifle gingerly and pointed it at the man.

What next? Of course the German might not be alone. But there was no sign of any others in the trees, and an odd, pregnant silence fell across the barnyard.

He felt every second passing. He moved to put his back to the outhouse, held the rifle, surveyed the yard, and the day ticked on. Then, faintly, came the sound of feet pounding, and coming from the trees was Moe. "Ah! You got him."

Moe was sweating and disheveled as he crouched beside the German. Blood ran from the man's nose and across his cheek into the dirt. "You fetched him a good one, all right. Unconscious, breathing, nasty bang."

"He deserved it," Karl said woodenly, the words hard to get out.

"Agreed. I got around behind him, but he must've heard me. He ran downhill and climbed over that wall. Dunno where he thought he was going."

"Let's tie him up."

"Yeah. Don't let that wife get at him, though."

Karl turned. The wife was running toward them with a butcher knife in her hand, eyes wild.

Without thinking, he raised the rifle and said, "*Arrêtez!*" The woman stopped, blinking. Startled, she looked at the knife in her hand.

In French she said she was happy for their "assistance" in getting the German, and could she please kill him? Karl said no, and where was her husband? She pointed to the house. A *pockety-pock* sound of an engine running badly came, and around the far edge of the house a decrepit, rattling small truck rolled.

Moe went to help the fallen farmer. Karl was jumpy with adrenaline and in quick order a short, alarmed farmer from next door arrived, saying he had heard the shot. There were rumors of German stragglers nearby, and he was proud to see someone had bagged one. The farmer's name was Giles, and he had a medical kit in his truck. In short order Giles got a pressure wrap around the farmer's wound. It was in his side, bloody but not to any vital part. The wife breathed a happy sigh and kissed Moe, who had just finished tying the German's hands behind his back. She ended with a frustrated laugh and cried, "*Impossible!*"

Karl had to agree. The whole incident was a soup of happenstance and happy accident, and he felt fully alive, skin prickly and eyes dancing. Moe patted him on the back, and Karl embraced him.

They even got an early supper invitation. The farmwife offered bread and jam and a glass of milk. They ate some quickly as Karl asked for directions to the "place where the Malartres live," and the wife nodded. "What do you want with them?"

"I am their son-in-law."

Her mouth twisted in disbelief. "You are a relative? But you are American!"

He took out his pocket photo of Marthe with her parents. The wife insisted they take some bread, which they refused. She waved her hands, describing directions to the "tiny plot" where "the officer in hiding" dwelled.

Karl and Moe searched the German, still unconscious. Folded up in his backpack was a single sheet of stiff cardboard. Moe spread it on a table.

IM NAMEN
DES DEUTSCHEN VOLKES
VERLEIHE ICH
DEM
KRIEGSVERDIENSTKREUZ
2. KLASSE
BERLIN

DER FÜHRER

"So this guy got a combat decoration that meant a railway pass. 'In the name of the German people.' Stamp-signed by Hitler, too." Moe chuckled at the scrawl above *Der Führer*. "But you decked him without a weapon."

Giles rattled off in the truck with the farmer beside him and the German lying in the truck bed. Moe had dumped him in, still unconscious. As he turned away said, "You want odds he survives the trip?" with a twinkle in his eye.

Payback time, maybe, Karl thought. He recalled how he had dealt with bullies in his Brooklyn grade school—by walking backward, watching them, so they couldn't attack from behind. He had done it by instinct and was deeply surprised when it worked; they didn't expect it. His instant decision to trip this soldier had been instinctive too. A fluke, but no reason not to beam with pride. He was actually *fighting in the war.*

The Malartre hideaway was just a kilometer away along a steep, tree-lined dirt road. Magpies thronged the trees, with a curious loud trilling call, as though they had a kettle whistle stuck in their throats. A low wall of chisel-cut rectangular stones framed the farm, but the home needed a paint job. A man and woman came out of their small cottage surrounded by rich fields of vegetables—spinach, onions, lettuce, artichokes, green beans, raspberries, carrots, more. The couple stood beside the stone wall, eyeing him and Moe suspiciously as they came up the pathway.

He had never met Marthe's father, who had thick, coarse white hair that fell over his forehead. His skin was leathery and yellowish-white, like an old wrinkled-up kid glove. His long face was dignified and melancholy. He had something of the beauty of an elderly eagle, powerful though discouraged.

"Madame Malartre, Colonel," Karl said, bowing a little and nodding.

She suddenly recognized Karl, eyes wide. "Ah!" She gave him a broad smile in her tanned, triangular face. "Please call me Madeleine." When they had met in Paris in that hurried autumn of 1938, his mother-in-law's formality had mellowed as they all conspired on how to get them quickly married and out of France. Now she wore rough cotton shorts and a bandanna around her hair, a lean farm woman.

He turned to the muscular, broad-shouldered man in pants and a sweat-stained shirt. A bow and nod again. "Colonel."

"Dr. Cohen." A stiff handshake, spine ramrod straight.

"Please, call me Karl." A curt nod in reply.

He introduced Moe, and Madeleine said brightly, "Tea?"

It seemed appropriate to begin with an eating ritual. Inside the living room, which held a dining table, Karl swung his backpack off and unveiled his gifts: coffee, chocolate bars, some stale and hardened K rations, pipe tobacco, sugar, honey, dry finger sausage, gingerbread, cookies, a whole salami veined with pearly fat. As they surveyed the gastronomic wealth, he showed the topper—photos of Marthe and the girls. These lightened the mood and sent gleeful cries in a room with worn pine boards covered by a wrinkled red carpet. Moe seemed unsurprised by this suddenly appearing food. Smiling, he stumbled through some simple French as Karl went to the bathroom. The floor creaked, and when he flushed the toilet, the refilling tank on the wall gave a baritone siren scream. He used the sliver of soap and realized he should have thought to bring some.

In halting French, Moe had brought them up to date on the incident with the German soldier. The colonel wanted to know details. Karl downplayed his role, but Moe did the opposite, and the colonel laughed about the tripping. "The soldiers left behind in the retreat, they hide," the colonel said.

"Afraid of us?" Moe asked.

"No!" the colonel said firmly. "The swine are afraid of what we French will do to them."

Their hosts offered some of the honey, dry sausage, and gingerbread Karl had brought, and he and Moe declined while the couple happily dug in. They were frightfully thin and worn, though sturdy. They described how once the Germans had moved in, declaring this region occupied like the Vichy zone, the bread ration had been cut to a few ounces a day. The whole countryside lived by farming and bartering. The Malartres ate the rabbits they raised but could not get enough corn for chickens.

The colonel had not joined the Maquis, civilians who resisted the Germans. He had left the army but not joined de Gaulle's Free French, either. "I wanted to help my wife survive the occupation, not run a camp for repatriated Algerians, as I was asked, nor fight in North Africa," he said. A resigned shrug. "Family versus France."

Madeleine said fiercely, "Now the *Boches* occupy us, they take, take." A wave of hands, wide eyes. It emerged that other farmers who'd had the luxury of trucks or cars lost them, requisitioned away, along with canned goods and even shovels.

To break the mood, Karl launched into details of their daughter, the girls, how they fared in New York and his rise at Columbia University. "We'd like you to come visit as soon as possible. At our expense, all."

Madeleine perked up. "Marthe is enjoying herself?"

"We have dinner with the professors there. She dazzles everyone with her French cuisine, even under rationing."

Madeleine and the colonel beamed. Karl imagined life here, crouched beside an old radio and listening to the war news since 1940. He hesitated, then plunged ahead. "I have been working with Albert Einstein, too."

This startled them. Probably Einstein was the only scientist they had ever heard of, and now their son-in-law knew him! The colonel stood, patted Karl on the back, and went to a cabinet, returning with a bottle of Margaux, a dark, musty 1928. He insisted on gingerly pouring them all a glass of what was obviously his prize vintage. They all stood, and the colonel gave a toast to "Peace, prosperity, Karl and Marthe."

They sat and had some cheese, the only food apparently not in short supply here. "This war will be over soon?" Madeleine asked pensively.

Karl could not tell her what he was doing, of course, so he resorted to generalities about working on the war effort. "Then why are you here?" Madeleine asked.

"Ah, I can perhaps help with the American army's understanding of such technical issues. Moe is my assistant."

They seemed to think this was reasonable. A scientist traveling right behind the army, in a war that was more and more about technology. But the colonel studied Karl closely as he asked, "What does this new bomb mean in the *longue durée*?"

"Too early to tell about the long run," Moe said.

Madeleine frowned. "And this deadly dust?"

Carefully Karl said, "The Germans will do anything, no matter how foul, as you know better than I."

"Might they use it again?"

"Quite possibly." He decided not to mention the possibility of dust use to block the invasion only a few kilometers away.

"Tell me more about the children," Madeleine insisted, and they were back to safe territory. Moe used his schoolboy French to talk to the colonel, and Karl relaxed.

Before he knew it, the Margaux was gone and shadows stretched long across the vegetable garden. He hated to leave. Moe suggested they find a room at the Hôtel L'Oasis. He invited his in-laws to dine with them. Karl doubted that they could get a room.

Moe gave him a small smile and said in acceptable French, "I believe that clerk can quite possibly be persuaded."

As it turned out, he was right.

4.

The Route Napoléon was the mountain valley winding way Napoléon had taken when he came back from the island of Elba, on his way to the Hundred Days before the allies broke him at Waterloo. It went around the main ground battle to the west, the farming plains and rivers where the American divisions and some Free French were pushing the Germans hard. Karl and Moe enjoyed a respite. The Germans had decided not to hold the Route Napoléon. Moe used the time to procure an army Jeep, rejecting an offer of a driver.

They had gotten on the Route Napoléon at Grasse and made some progress in a day. They took turns driving through the long jams of trucks and troops and tanks. At a jam the next day they climbed a hill and could hear the muffled, rolling barrages as Allied artillery slammed into the retreating German units. Fighters dogged the German columns on a distant highway. Moe had somehow gotten a pair of field binoculars, and they watched the tiny gray dots that were German tanks. The shelling threw smoke into the air. "Burning gasoline," Moe said, and as if in answer, a fireball blossomed into the clear skies among the German column. Troops unseen were hitting them with accurate fire.

It was three hundred kilometers to Grenoble, where they could cut over to Switzerland. Going through Grenoble was a fragrant parade, La Jasminade, a tribute to the flower with young women in skimpy costumes on board flatbed trucks, throwing flowers into the crowd to celebrate their liberation. Karl and Moe grinned and bore through the crowds, honking and dodging people who wanted to throw garlands over their necks. "Damn early to celebrate," Moe said.

"The next bomb will be ready in a week or so," Karl said, though he wasn't supposed to talk about that.

"What's the target?"

"That's the question. Maybe we can answer it up ahead."

They bounced along nearly a hundred kilometers among military traffic. Distant booms of artillery came up to the road from a battle to the east. Moe managed to drive fast enough to fend off the mosquitoes, slipping through openings Karl would never have tried. The soft summer air bore the tang of sweat and the sharp bite of gasoline.

GIs were walking alongside the road, weighed down by guns and fatigue. Karl could see it in the sagging bodies, burdened down by machine gun barrels, steel tripods, and leaden boxes of ammunition. These weights on backs and shoulders made them seem to sink into the mud as they slogged on fifty feet apart, dispersed in case they hit an ambush. They did not slouch but stepped with deliberate care. Their faces, flashing by the Jeep as he and Moe took turns driving, were dirty, with beards many days old. They were young, but the grime and whiskers and exhaustion stole years from them. Yet they kept on steadily, advancing against an enemy that might steal all the rest of their lives away. The antlike lines of GIs went on and on and never ended. Karl felt somehow ashamed to look at them.

"They're fighting, we're not," he said to Moe.

"Sure we are. You more effectively than me."

"What?"

"Without you guys, Berlin would still be there."

Karl blinked at this and said sharply, "Stop."

"What?"

"Stop."

Before the Jeep pulled up, he was out and turned downhill. The man who had caught his eye was approaching—KIRS, his stenciled name badge said. Karl went to him and said, "You're limping."

"Busted my damn knee back there a ways." A deep, sliding southern accent. Maybe from near Oak Ridge?

"Get in the Jeep."

"I can't—"

"Get in."

Moe raised eyebrows in silence as Karl helped the private carrying a BAR into a narrow wedge of space behind their seats. The BAR rested on the private's knees, weighing him in. Moe started up and their motor ground up the hill until Karl saw a sergeant marching along with a backpack. He gestured to Moe to stop.

Karl got out and said to the sergeant, reading his name badge, "Sergeant Macaffrey, this man shouldn't be marching. That busted knee will just get worse, put him out of action. I'm taking him up to the nearest aid station."

Macaffrey frowned and widened his eyes, encountering a puzzle. Karl looked stern and knew what Macaffrey was thinking. Who was this civilian, driven around by a big well-dressed guy? Macaffrey could go with the standard army response and shake this civilian off, but what was up with this? Macaffrey was even more tired than his men, and Karl watched his face change from surprise to calculation to . . . relax.

"I, I guess okay. Aid station's supposed to be maybe ten klicks ahead. Six miles or so."

"Thanks, we'll get him there. You'll have him back in time for action."

Back in the Jeep, Moe roared off before Macaffrey could change his mind. Karl leaned back and said, "You need a day off your feet."

Kirs said, "Don't we all."

They made surprisingly good time. The US command had taken all lanes, so there were no civilians. There was some room to pass on the road, which was usually just two lanes. Moe drove intently and with skill. He avoided troops or other Jeeps that blundered out of line. "You trained at this, too?" Karl asked.

Moe grinned. "My position with the Office of Strategic Services Special Operations Branch pays four thousand a year, and in return I had to let them teach me to drive again."

"Wow, that's more than I earn."

"And you're the one who decked that rifleman."

Karl enjoyed that remark, but he also felt it was phony to be proud of a chance lucky stroke. They sped along the mountain roads, until at a broad patch a big sign displayed a red cross.

Karl found the aid station unsettling. There were wounded waiting for treatment, men with bloody uniforms and big bandages. Their faces were drained, gray, and dejected, their eyes fixed in the far distance. He helped Kirs into the admissions tent and got him an orderly, who took over. "I'll be back with my buddies by the time they march on up here," Kirs said, smiling. The orderly shooed Moe and Karl away, quite properly.

"Where's the action up ahead?" Karl asked a supervising lieutenant.

"What're you, some reporter?" the man shot back.

Moe took care of that with another letter, this time from the man's division commander. He had a deft way of silently handing the envelope to the officer, waiting with downcast eyes, then taking it back and folding it into the envelope while the lieutenant studied him and Karl, clearly wanting to know what was up with these two civilians. Moe just shook his head and the lieutenant showed them on an army map where the few German units were operating. "Looks like they've given up on this road. They've retreated up the Rhône valley to our west."

Moe nodded, compared the army map with theirs. Then they got back into the Jeep and moved off. Karl thought, *In war, you do what you can. Step aside from your mission, do what needs doing right now.*

They came down to run along the Durance River, where no boats were visible. The quick German vanishing act had left the way clear into the pleasant town of Digne-les-Bains. They stopped there beside the beautiful lake, again with few people in view and no craft on the water. The French had learned to keep their heads down, after four years of bombers and Gestapo. They ate some tired C rations, improved with two baguettes bought from a bakery whose warm, bready aromas sent Karl's memories back to his first time in France in 1936, and the enchantment of those delicious days. They started out of town and Moe pulled over to a view site, looking due west into the lower green fields of the Rhône Valley.

The view was captivating. Karl said, "I'll bet we can find a good Côtes du Rhône this evening to go with the C rations. The vintage comes from down there."

Moe flourished a thick roll of the American-printed five-franc notes issued to the troops. "Might at that."

"How'd you get so many?"

"I used my letters."

"What else have you got?"

Moe flashed his enigmatic smile. "You'd be surprised."

"I don't like surprises, not in a war."

"I think we're about to get another." Moe pointed.

Karl had not been watching the sky. Motes danced and zoomed far away. But one was much faster than the others. "Our flyboys are trying to gang up on a Messerschmitt Me 410, I'd say," Moe observed, and produced a big pair of binoculars. "They developed this *Schnellbomber* for jobs like this. A jet plane. Works by heating air and pushing it out the back. Far beyond anything of ours. So I gather from the briefings I've had."

Jets were not news to Karl, but this one seemed magically swift. He watched the bee swarm of silvery American Mosquito fighters he had learned to recognize back at their air base. They buzzed across the sky but could not get near the gray Messerschmitt, which swooped and turned with effortless grace. It made a hollow noise that reminded Karl of a dentist drill, much different from the angry buzz of the Mosquitoes. The German led the Americans across a clear blue vastness, headed nearer to where they stood. Once the Americans were nearly to the mountains nearby, the Messerschmitt dodged away in a breathtaking turn. It zipped off, diving toward the west.

"The Rhône is in the distance, see?" Karl said. "It's headed—"

"For the major highway," Moe said, voice calm. He handed the binoculars to Karl. "The one our main advance goes up."

In the hazy distance, Karl studied the Messerschmitt. He had heard about it, first seen in June over France. The Germans were unveiling new technologies as their troops withdrew, hammering home weapons coming from years of preparation—just like the Manhattan Project. V-1s and V-2s, the death dust, now this.

Moe casually added details. The jets were so fast German pilots needed new tactics to attack bombers. In a head-on attack, the closing speed was too high for accurate shooting. Even from astern, the closing speed was too great to use the short-range thirty-millimeter cannon to maximum effect. "So they use a roller-coaster method, coasting along above, then a quick dive to aim and fire. This guy is doing something else, though."

As Karl watched, the Messerschmitt banked and turned parallel to the distant Rhône River. It zipped north, over the highway. A gray cloud burst from it, trailing like smoke—but darker, falling.

"Death dust," he said. "They're dropping it on our guys going up the valley."

"Damn." Moe took the binoculars back and studied the distant motes.

"Pitchblende, judging from the dark color," Karl said. "We had some come in big tubs in the early days, crude ore, to separate out the uranium and work it chemically. Y'know, before all this, potters used it for coloring." That seemed a long time ago.

The Messerschmitt made another run along the Rhône, a swift arrow dropping more, then darted across the sky and was gone.

"Let's step on it," Moe said.

They were crossing a narrow valley beneath a high ridgeline when Karl saw the Messerschmitt jet coming toward them. It flitted out of a cottony cloud and then through another, turning toward them in a steep bank. Over the Jeep's steady hum he heard a thin, hollow *skreee*. This Schnellbomber was a dull gray dot as it dove straight at them in a long, straight descent parallel to the road ahead.

"Damn!" Moe said. It came at them fast, and Karl thought Moe would pull over or turn onto a side road. But instead he sped up, the Jeep rattling as it covered ground. They had just passed a half-ton truck convoy a few kilometers back, and Karl said nothing. Now the airplane was maybe a kilometer above them and still coming down, but flying nearly flat. A thin blue-black plume began to purl from it, as if it was spraying the pitchblende in a solution. The cloud fell toward them, aligned along the straight road. No traffic ahead. The swirling mass swarmed down the road at them, and only then did Karl realize he could button the doors all the way up. They had kept a vent on each side open for air in the mild heat here, and he got the thick snap clasps closed on his side just as the uranium hit them. He reached over and snapped secure those behind Moe.

His nostrils caught a sharp metallic scent. "Don't breathe."

They were doing maybe sixty now and he saw a farm truck pulled off, the driver getting out of the cab to look. They flashed by it and Karl saw the uranium was indeed in glittering black droplets, spilling down the air. Eddies churned and dampened the road ahead. The sky lightened.

"Good, got through it," Moe said. He kept their speed high.

"I'll open the vent full. See if we can blow out anything that got in."

"Great. How much of a dose do you think—"

"Can't be much." He coughed, and so did Moe. "Get it out, right."

"They mixed it with water, I bet." Karl looked back through the smudged plastic back window. The plane was out of sight and the cloud wafted around the road, settling in after the exhaust of the jet stopped roiling it. "To keep it from blowing away, drop it right on the road. As soon as the drops evap away, it's free to get in our lungs."

"Using it on each highway. They've got a lot of it."

Karl nodded, inhaling the moist, crisp air of late summer in the Alps. "I wonder why."

5.

They reached the town of Gap late in a damp night. Troops were few, having already pushed beyond, to Grenoble. Moe did his trick of finding a decent hotel, and they stayed away from the GIs who wandered the streets, looking for booze. But they did find a little restaurant with a classic zinc bar. Karl flashed some of the USA-made francs and talked the owner into a bottle of Côtes du Rhône. Once the other patrons saw they were Americans but not soldiers, smiles blossomed. Karl's rusty French helped. Halfway through the bottle a pianist came in and banged out songs on a dilapidated stand-up piano that needed tuning. The pianist even played some jazz, shouting, *"Laissez les bons temps rouler!"*

Karl whispered, "Let the good times roll," and Moe nodded. Somehow, without Karl even noticing, Moe had talked a lovely girl into bringing them hot crepes. The world had improved, for the moment.

Still, Karl didn't sleep well. They got a coffee-and-baguette breakfast and Moe went in search of refueling. Karl followed, walking to stretch his legs, to an army depot that was really just a co-opted gas station. They were still getting more petrol from a cylindrical truck, just filling the underground tanks. Moe's letters cleared all obstacles. Men moved quickly but there was a line of trucks, so they joined it. A sergeant took the wheel, waiting in line for them, obviously impressed with Moe's letters.

They strolled along a small stream and abruptly came upon a surprise. Some American soldiers were burying the bodies of many Germans they had killed the day before, in a last-stand shootout to protect the gas station.

Karl stared at the sprawled bodies, riddled by mortars, machine-gun fire, and grenades. Whole lives, traded for a bit of ground and gasoline.

One of the Germans had lost his head. A GI kicked it like a soccer ball. Then another guy. They started laughing maniacally. A sergeant said, "Fer Chrissake, yer animals." That made things even funnier to them until the sergeant ordered them back to their work. Moe discussed the event as really an extended aesthetic problem, rather than a moral problem. The German was dead and the GIs under pressure. Maybe a buddy had been killed here in the attack. "But denying the veneer of civilization is what helps you do inhumane things," Moe said, "so the sergeant is right."

The Germans had plainly not counted on the Americans having mortar teams that hammered relentlessly, pouring in dozens of rounds to simply demolish their defenses. The bodies had rotted a bit until the GIs had time to finish their battles and pull out the corpses. "They thought we'd try to rush 'em," a rail-thin Southerner said with a chuckle. "They're always amazed we have so much ammo."

Wait till you see what's coming next, Karl thought with relish, but said nothing. The next A-bomb—the term invented by Wells had caught on, despite its error—would be ready within a week Where to use it was a frequent topic back at the base in England; Karl had no opinion.

The burial teams wore thin cloth strips that hung little bags of camphor under their noses. Once Karl got a whiff of the bodies he knew why. Moe's only comment was, "The surest way to become a pacifist is to join the infantry."

While they waited back near the fuel depot, some GIs coaxed Moe into a baseball game they had set up on a soccer field. Once Moe threw the ball, the guys knew they had someone different in the game. He snapped it around in arrow-straight volleys. To Karl's eye, his throwing motion was a kind of muscular drawl. Nobody had gloves, but Moe easily snagged balls out of the air. If GIs snagged Moe's throws, they yowled and dropped the ball. When he came to bat, which they made him do right away, he knocked the scruffy ball into the distant woods. Someone called out, "You're that catcher!" and they crowded around. Moe's casual, pleasant manner as he dealt with them reminded Karl of the man's fundamental talent: people liked him. By that time the gas station was ready, so Karl got their Jeep cleaned up and Moe came ambling back, grinning.

"Feel good to play again?"

Moe laughed. "It's always good."

As they drove north, Moe said, "My high school English teacher pointed out that baseball is a mythic game. She was having an affair with my baseball coach, the PE head, so the topic came up. You start at home, see, but you want to leave home. To do that you must face a challenge. If you face that ordeal and are successful, you may go out into the world and travel—three destinations, each well defined and defended. But even as you go, your goal is to return to the happiness and safety of home."

"Wow, baseball as a myth?" It felt good to talk, talk about anything; much better than pointless thinking.

"I think baseball is fundamental to Americans because it's a character-versus-character sport. Pitcher versus batter, batter versus fielder. Two characters contesting. Not like soccer, the big European sport. That's all teams passing the ball, footwork, and only a final two-person contest with the goalie. Different cultures entirely. Makes Americans more than imitation Euros."

Karl laughed. "So you're a catcher, a spy, and a philosopher, too."

"In this game you gotta be."

It took a full day to reach Grenoble. Here, too, an odd serenity prevailed. The Germans made no effort to defend all of France now. People sought bargains in shops with mostly bare shelves. Years of constrained trade had made scarcity the norm.

Karl helped find their way to a small army detachment trying to get oriented. He helped a cliché Brooklyn sergeant negotiate in French with the locals. They left off the Jeep with a master sergeant who had too much to do. "This is a good break," Moe said. "We can just take a train to Zurich."

"I wonder if Heisenberg will even come to give his speech."

Moe nodded, lifting his hat in ironic salute. "Me too. That's how this game goes, mostly. But he likes to travel, and Switzerland is the only place his keepers will let him go."

"Fair enough." Newspapers said the Allies had been halted in the Rhône

Valley by the death dust. Troops who would bravely face heavy fire balked at breathing in poisons. The same stalemate prevailed at the "western wall," where the German tank divisions were holding firm.

Karl wanted to get back to his family and out of this war. Maybe this one more thing would do it? He got on the wheezing train with more fear than hope.

PART XII

STALKING
WITH EINSTEIN

Chance is a nickname for Providence.
—Nicolas Chamfort

1.

August 20, 1944

It felt odd to sit comfortably in the first-class section of the rumbling train, watching the gray mountain passes and lovely sky-blue lakes at the peak of summer, and read of many bloody deaths, only a few hundred kilometers away.

Moe had gotten the tickets without trouble, because the price was exorbitant. Also, first class were the only seats still open. People were fleeing from the battle area into Switzerland. Many carried stuffed suitcases and even canvas bags.

Karl had talked to a portly gentleman about this while he waited in the Grenoble station. The man had a W. C. Fields nose, a red-veined bulb. It sat below watery blue eyes behind rimless glasses, eyes wary and wise. "My wife and I, we will maintain to the Swiss border guards that we are merely vacationing for a week or so. The Swiss, they look the other way. Let the Geneva authorities worry about an excess of 'tourists'!" His cheeks bulged merrily at the thought. "After all, we bring money. The Swiss have profited well from this war."

Karl nodded. He had said nearly nothing in the last few hours, not to draw attention to his American-accented French. Moe sat silently reading his six newspapers. Karl read a *London Times* report on the fight in Normandy. The death dust had stopped Patton's flanking movement, but the Germans fleeing east had run into a pincer flanking attack.

> The pocket area is full of the remains of battle. Villages destroyed and derelict equipment make some roads impassable. Corpses of soldiers and civilians litter the area.

Thousands of dead cattle and horses lie on recent fields of fire. In this hot August, maggots crawl over the bodies, hordes of flies descend. Pilots report being able to smell the stench of the battlefield hundreds of feet above it.

Even Eisenhower issued a statement.

The battlefield at Falaise was unquestionably one of the greatest "killing fields" of any of the war areas. Forty-eight hours after the closing of the gap I was conducted through it on foot, to encounter scenes that could be described only by Dante. It was literally possible to walk for hundreds of yards at a time, stepping on nothing but dead and decaying flesh. Many swollen bodies had to be shot to expunge gasses within them before they could be burnt and bulldozers were used to clear the area of dead animals.

Karl knew now far more about what it meant to be a soldier here. The death dust dominated the news, though it was too soon to see mentioned the dust drop they had seen the day before.

Men who reported "rad sick" showed nausea and vomiting, and predispositions to infection and bleeding. The only response has been for units to flee the dust area.

Swiss guards boarded at the station just before the border crossing. Karl and Moe sat beside each other silently, handing over their counterfeit French passports. The guards' questions they managed to answer with only "*Oui.*" The W. C. Fields guy had been right.

They pulled into Geneva and quickly changed trains for Lausanne. Moe managed to snag two more newspapers in Italian and German. They pulled out of the station and coasted along the serene blue of the big lake as Moe restlessly sorted through the papers. "Nothing much new here," he said scornfully. "Mostly German propaganda about how they're inflicting huge casualties and holding their ground. Nothing much about the dust."

"Usually these days they brag about their new technologies," Karl said, musing as he gazed out the window at placid, beautiful mountains.

"Oh, there's plenty on V-1s and V-2s. But the dust, no. Probably since it's a war crime under the Geneva Protocol, I'd guess."

War crime . . . , Karl thought. He took the German *Zeitung* from Moe and sure enough, they were full of stories about the victims of the Berlin bomb. Plenty of pictures with vivid captions. On walls, "flash-burned" shadows of people vaporized. People dissolved into gas and desiccated carbon statues. An old man seemingly tap-dancing, trying to walk on legs with gnarled feet. Children with their skin pulled away by searing winds. His work.

He sat back and let go of the moment. He had to focus here. This whole attempt to get to Heisenberg was spying, and he had no idea how to do it. He had simply gone along with Groves and the others, hoping that Moe would actually do the skullduggery or whatever, leading to the interrogation of Heisenberg—somehow.

The scenery rolled by without his seeing it. After a while he turned to Moe, getting up his courage, opened his mouth—and saw Moe had tossed aside the newspapers and was reading a small hardcover book, *The Mask of Dimitrios* by Eric Ambler. "Uh, isn't that . . . ?"

"A spy novel? Sort of. Really enjoying it."

"Doesn't that give away . . ."

"What we're doing?" Moe chuckled. "Look, ordinary people read such novels too. I do. Maybe I'll pick up something useful."

"But I thought those sort of books were just—"

"The seductress in black velvet, the British secret-service numbskull hero, the omnipotent spymaster, ominous villains with trick knives in umbrellas?"

"Well, yes. Useless to us."

"There's plenty of that junk. But this Ambler knows some clever things."

"You've got your experience to rely on. I've got none. You dropped into eastern Europe, Norway, got—"

"Good judgment comes from experience, sure. Experience comes from bad judgment."

"You didn't get caught."

"To be ignored, look confident, or even bored. Don't look around much."

"That won't be easy, with Heisenberg. He must know a lot about their uranium, at least."

"Right. They're using his uranium as dust. Whether he's running a bomb program may be secondary now."

Karl shrugged. "Too many maybes in this war. When do we meet Heisenberg?"

"My contact at the Eidgenössische Technische Hochschule is Paul Scherrer. He says the main reason the Germans come there now is to enjoy the schnapps, cheese, and chocolates that they can't get at home. Heisenberg speaks tomorrow."

"How do we approach him?"

"Scherrer will introduce us. Well, maybe just me."

By now Karl knew Moe enough to know the man would reveal information only when it was useful in the events drawing near. That way, if questioned, Karl had little to reveal. So he sat silently until Moe added, "Because I might have to shoot Heisenberg."

Karl decided to downplay what was coming. "Ironic—this Hochschule is where Einstein got his first degree, yes? Then he couldn't get a real physics job, so he took a post as a patent examiner in the Bern office."

"Ah yeah, I met him once when I was at Princeton. I stopped him on the street—everybody recognized him—and he said, 'Pardon me, sorry! Always I am mistaken for Professor Einstein' and brushed me off. But I knew the truth. Princeton's a small burg."

Karl recalled the somber Einstein he had met, to get the letter to Roosevelt worked out and signed. What would have happened if Einstein hadn't been persuaded by Szilard? The Manhattan Project would've started much later. He would not be here now, in far over his head, rushing downstream over the foaming white rapids of history, rocks all around, in a tiny little boat. . . .

"So we just show up for the Heisenberg talk? And I signal you if I think Heisenberg's shown any sign of a bomb program?"

"Some scouting first, but yeah—just go in cold."

This didn't seem to bother Moe, but it certainly unnerved Karl.

"The food's good around here, so it won't be a complete waste," Moe said contentedly.

2.

August 21, 1944

Karl would not have chosen the fine old Zurich hotel along the lake, but Moe brushed aside objections that they should maintain a low profile. They had breakfast on the veranda, Moe with his newspapers and Karl savoring the best coffee he had found in years. The hotel manager had even placed a small chocolate beside his cup, a hint that they mixed well—which was true. Karl felt an odd guilt at enjoying the serene peace and pleasures of a nation not at war.

"I'm unsure who to be at this event," Moe said, putting down his issue of *Le Monde*.

"I think I'll stick with my French passport, since it's all I'm carrying."

"I've used three identities in Europe, passports to match—a Swiss physics student, an Arab businessman from Algeria, a French businessman from Dijon. If Heisenberg's tenders ask, I can show one of those."

"You're a bit old to be a student."

"Fair enough. All right, I'm a professor from . . . ah, I see your point. Anyone at the Eidgenössische Technische Hochschule is bound to know the Swiss physicists."

Moe's dark complexion made the conclusion clear. "Make it an Arab studying here," Karl said. "That explains your inept French accent. Maybe slur it a little too."

"Good! I had the manager ring the Hochschule, too. Heisenberg speaks at four p.m. Reception after, I'll bet. They make a big show of him when he visits. Even the manager knew he was in town. He says all the bourgeoisie are agog to have the great man among them."

Moe's French accent was lapsing amid the German speakers of Zurich, so his own East Coast vowels came out as *boojwazzee* with hints of Jersey. "We should clam up this afternoon," Karl said. "You're going as an Arab, I'm supposedly French, but face it—to the Germans we'll sound funny."

"Right. We'll sit up front, and you'll pick up on Heisenberg's technical stuff. We need a code phrase that tips me off to whether he's got a bomb program going."

"I'll say, uh, 'necessary and sufficient.'"

"Make it just 'sufficient,' okay? Then get up and leave. I'll give you five minutes to get to the train station."

"Why?"

"Because then I'm going to shoot him."

They walked through Zurich to get a feel for the city. It felt relaxed and softly welcoming, compared with wartime London. All the streets curved, following old cow paths. Karl realized that he had lived most of his life among straight streets, and to him their right angles said City, like New York and London. Zurich was busy saying Country, so the boulevards looped and swooped about gracefully like noodles.

Karl memorized the route from the Hochschule to the Bahnhofplatz and saw he could walk there to a train within ten minutes. It felt odd to make such a calculation. If he needed to use this route, he would be on the run, and so should bring his baggage to the Hochschule as well. He saw an older, majestic building from the Austro-Hungarian Empire days, whose pinnacle had the color of old copper pots left in the sun. Taxis waited at its broad entrance. Take a taxi there, then, for the Bahnhofplatz. Leave the luggage. But after that, what?

Moe spoke casually in French as they walked along the lake, both of them figuring that they needed the practice. Moe had learned to round his vowels from Marthe, and it helped Karl as well. French had its sublime facets, and Karl remembered fondly those "training" dinner parties, with their daughters staring in wonder, trying to grasp why their parents and this big stranger were saying things they could echo but not grasp.

"I got a lot of intel from that Goudsmit guy. Seems that in August 1939 our Heisenberg was a member of an Alpine reserve unit. Something he did to get along with the party, I suppose, in a minor way. He's in his forties, not a likely conscript. But because of that, Goudsmit says, he was called up and assigned to work on the German bomb program."

Karl stopped to view the majestic granite mountains across the lake as a cool breeze swept down from them, caressing his cheeks. A sweet tang of coming autumn wafted on the wind. "I doubt even the Nazis would 'assign' a Nobel winner, just like that."

"Yeah, does make you wonder. I think our Goudsmit has a chip on his shoulder about Heisenberg. He met him, says his English is pretty good. He'd have been brought into the Uranverein, but respectfully."

Karl noted that Moe got the German accent right in rendering the "Uranium Club" and hoped he would be able to follow Heisenberg's lecture. Karl's German was weak as well.

Moe brooded, eyes down. "It seems Heisenberg functioned as a kind of roving ambassador for German science, starting in 1941. The government gave him that freedom and funding, so why not? He visited several cultural institutes—the Hochschule here was his favorite."

"This canton favors the Reich. Heisenberg must feel at home here. But he shows different cards at different times too. In his visit in 1943 to Holland he explained—according to an eyewitness, an agent who reported to OSS—how history had legitimated Germany to rule both Europe and the world."

This shocked Karl. "He went along with the party."

"Sounds like he had to deliver a script," Moe said this flatly, like a disinterested prosecutor talking his way toward a death sentence.

Karl tried to retrieve his memories of his time traveling across Germany in 1936, just a few days. "I heard about some trouble Heisenberg got into, back when the Nazis started casting out 'Jewish physics'—the *Deutsche Physik* movement. It was in the papers. Heisenberg had been lecturing to his students about relativity, invented by that notorious Jewish scientist. In an editorial, Himmler, the Nazi propaganda guy, called Heisenberg a 'White Jew,' whatever that is. Said he should be made to 'disappear'—sent to a camp, I guess."

To Karl's surprise, Moe took up the story with assurance. "Right, so

Heisenberg's mother visited Himmler's mother to help bring a resolution to the affair. Turned out they were old friends."

"Your newspaper reading—you recall a lot, don't you?"

"Part of my job. Always liked it."

"So how do we approach Heisenberg, if he gives nothing away in his talk?"

Moe leaned forward intently. "Then I don't shoot. No grounds to. Can you ask a solid physics question after he's done? To break the ice?"

"I can try," Karl said uncertainly. "Then what?"

"We go to the reception after."

"You can get us into that?"

Moe's eyes twinkled with mirth. "I have a few tricks."

"I did some background reading in London on our Werner. He got some money from the Reich Ministry for Armaments and Ammunition—Goudsmit showed me the OSS report. For what, we don't know. And I checked the German journals. In 1943 he published papers on his S-matrix quantum method in *Zeitschrift für Physik*. That's the method he got his Nobel for, really—it's a calculation that describes only observables, the before and after of quantum events. No talk about wave functions or anything—a 'just the facts, ma'am' kind of thinking."

Moe furrowed his brow, not following. "So now he's spending his time on abstractions?"

"Some, at least. But that could be a cover."

"Maybe he's just a true patriot. Goudsmit invited him to visit in 1936 and he came. He refused an invitation to emigrate to the United States, went back home."

Moe stood. "Y'know, I don't want to hang around here all day. Let's—what do they say in gangster movies?—case the joint."

3.

The notice outside the Eidgenössische Technische Hochschule said that Heisenberg was visiting since yesterday. So the man and his escorts were here somewhere. The entrance was formidable, and along the grand corridors Moe knew how to find his contact's office.

Walking there, Karl's eyes flicked over every face, trying to guess if they were German agents, even Gestapo.

Einstein had trod these corridors, he realized, half a century before. Einstein had walked, where they now stalked.

In 1900 Einstein had gotten a mere teaching diploma, not a research degree. Then he spent seven frustrating years as a patent inspector in Bern, but managed to publish the "miracle year" papers in 1905. Finally he used one of those papers to present his thesis and get his research PhD in late 1905, from the University of Zurich nearby. Despite having published brilliant papers in quantum mechanics and inventing relativity theory, he had been stuck at the patent office. He could not get a teaching position until 1908, and then in Bern, not Zurich.

Paul Scherrer had an anvil jaw and the sage, weathered look of a well-dressed gentleman in his fifties. A plaque said he was principal of the Physical Institute, and his ample office even had a coffee setup. Karl let Moe do the introductions and explanations, to which Scherrer simply nodded. His English was excellent, and he nodded at each of Moe's questions. Yes, Heisenberg was not here, but would be at his talk. The Gestapo escort kept close to Heisenberg, but Scherrer would see about getting them into the reception.

Scherrer glanced at Karl, obviously puzzled about this silent stranger—but said nothing.

They were out in less than two minutes. Scherrer did not want to be closely identified with them. Rightly so, Karl thought, if Moe had to kill Heisenberg.

They decided to make lunch substantial. They might be on the run or worse later, and calories were scarce, even here. People were starving in much of Europe, and Karl knew it; but they were here, in a peaceful island. Moe was a fount of never-ending cash, especially a wad of Swiss francs.

So Karl ordered at their hotel a tangy roast pork with sauerkraut and caraway seeds, plus smoked goose breast with plum sauce. He had a charming local red wine with it while Moe, with a pheasant, gave a real-life illustration of a term Karl had heard of in novels.

Moe *discussed* his bird, as gourmets used to say of people eating lamb chops. He was quite absorbed in dissecting the bird for every morsel as he said, in answer to Karl's questions, "When the Office of Special Services hired me, I learned safecracking, bridge blowing, lock picking, codes and ciphers, hand-to-hand combat—that was all delightful! And I ran through the OSS fun house with its narrow halls, sudden drops, traps, bangs, and shrieks. They gave us a surprise meeting with a Hitler picture too. We were to shoot him in the head on sight."

Moe sat back and admired the view from the veranda. "Hope I get the chance to do the real thing!"

Karl said, "Maybe this next 'gadget' will do the job."

"If we can find him, yes. It's like chess now, with Hitler the most valuable piece, the king."

"You play?"

"My older sister taught me. After a while, I spotted her pieces. Then I began playing myself—Berg versus Berg. Mostly I won," he said with no trace of humor. "But to get Hitler, we have to know what square he's on."

Karl took a last look at the lake and mountains. The placid waters fed by great rushing waterfalls, meadows sloping in green majesty, the endless fragrant pine forests with their tang of turpentine—here was where nature and myth fused to shape the Germanic soul. That had led to such wonders in music, science, philosophy . . . and now to horror. He breathed in the silky air and despaired.

In their room, he watched Moe Berg eject the magazine from his pistol. To Karl, having never handled one, a gun was just a gun. Moe held the pistol down between his legs and thumbed ten brass rounds from the magazine. He inspected each one, saying, "Looking for rust. Salt air gets to these." Looking down the sight, he snapped the action and trigger several times. He studied the ejector and firing pin and then slid the rounds back into the magazine and slipped it into the pistol butt. "All ready. Only get one shot, probably, better make it good." He oiled the mechanism and carefully put the pistol into his leather briefcase.

Karl said, "I think I should sit a few chairs away from you."

"Fine. I may act freely, then." Moe paid careful attention to his suit and tie as they got dressed. Karl wore a jacket and tie with a gray fedora. He was supposed to be a fellow scientist, with little German—which was true. "Surprise is everything. In training, I heard stories about real gunfights in the Old West. An ancient survivor of seven barroom shootouts described how he'd done it. He had a holster—many didn't—and when he saw that shooting was about to start, he'd reach down and pull the trigger. The bullet would go into the floor, of course, but the main point was the noise. While his opponent tried to figure out whether he'd just been killed, this guy would in leisurely fashion draw his revolver and shoot him dead."

"Your first shot will be into Heisenberg."

"Yeah, and the Gestapo guys, they'll go for me. Get away then."

"But—"

Moe waved away further talk. "Before I went into a ball game, I always took five minutes to focus. Let's walk slowly."

Werner Heisenberg (left) and Niels Bohr

4.

In the lecture hall, the tall-backed benches for students were as dignified as church pews. A hushed murmur stirred, and they surveyed the room. "No Heisenberg yet," Moe whispered. "Those three down in front look like classic Gestapo. One's got Obergruppenführer insignia, so it's a high-level escort."

The three were in stiff suits with bulging vests, plainly armed. They were hatchet-faced, wary, eyes turned to the gathering crowd. The Swiss didn't allow German military to parade around in their garb, but Nazi Party uniforms seemed allowed. The Obergruppenführer's flinty gaze was unmistakable.

Moe and Karl went in separately, down to the first row. They sat three chairs away, not looking at each other. Karl thought, *I might never walk out of this room.*

Moe settled in with his small briefcase and took out a notebook, looking as scholarly as he could. In the briefcase was the pistol and what Moe called an "L"—a lethal cyanide capsule. He would take it as a distraction while Karl escaped in the chaos—if it happened. Moe would be dead inside a minute.

Karl tried to carefully pay no attention to anyone, on Moe's advice. But one fellow caught his eye, in a formal suit and constant stare forward, his eyes sunk into dark sockets. He had a jerky tension in him, as if anticipating something, or maybe everything, that was coming. Karl recognized him from Goudsmit's photo gallery of scientists at the Kaiser Wilhelm. This was Carl Friedrich von Weizsäcker, a firm Nazi and high-level physicist. The big gang was here, all right. For what?

A moment later Heisenberg came in through a side door, unheralded. Karl felt a bit of a shock, as though a deadly contest had started. The audience applauded and the great physicist nodded with a thin smile. Compared to his photos, the man was frail, five foot six, thin in a worn, dark three-button suit. Food was scarce in Germany. He was just forty-two, but wrinkles crowded his eyes as he started setting up a blackboard, with Paul Scherrer's help. With a quizzical smile, he dutifully awaited Scherrer's introduction and began speaking in a whispery voice. He paced, his right hand in his coat pocket, his heavy eyebrows shadowing the bony cast of his face.

Moe was deftly taking notes and even sketching Heisenberg with a Parker pen. This caught Heisenberg's attention, a move Moe had told Karl to anticipate. Where Heisenberg looked, the Gestapo would too.

Karl was focused on Heisenberg's quick German, sifting through terms from quantum mechanics, searching for telltale words for neutrons or isotopes or fission. None. Heisenberg dashed down equations on the blackboard, his chalk clacking. They were transition probabilities, Karl saw, which might apply to anything, including fission. But then the quick hands drew matrices in rectangular frames, and Heisenberg was off into arcane details of how to calculate quantum rates. Had he described fission in terms of his own formulation of quantum mechanics? Karl felt a tremor of alarm. Heisenberg's rapid German might blow right by him and conceal vital clues.

He had arranged with Moe to indicate a clear nuclear sign by placing his gray fedora on the chair next to him, in case there wasn't a chance to use the word "sufficient." He held the fedora in his lap and didn't pretend to take notes at all. His heart thumped and concentrating was hard.

Karl followed Heisenberg's pacing, and out of the corner of his eye saw movement. The three Gestapo men had moved into the row of seats behind him. Firm faces, eyes intent. They didn't pretend to follow the discussion, just sat and watched him and Moe. If Karl gave his signal, he would leave his seat after a coughing fit, get well away, before Moe acted.

So went the plan. Moments ticked by. Karl felt his chest tighten.

Heisenberg's notations crowded across the blackboard. He stopped to erase them, talking rapidly. Karl could catch maybe half the content, at best.

Heisenberg's chatter swelled as he got to his main points, animated, shooting forth clipped German words like darts.

Karl felt his hands tremble and thrust them together in front of him. He was breathing too fast, wind wheezing through his nostrils. Never before had he felt this tension squeezing his chest, bringing a metallic taste in his mouth. The room seemed now to be hot, the chalk smell choking, a prickly scent of leather from the Gestapo, so near.

He made himself follow the darting, rasping German words. *Partikel . . . wissen . . . Ansatz . . . wir haben . . . multiplicitiv . . .*

An urge to get up and leave came over him. He fought it down, though his feet were now itching on their own, twisting in his shoes. *Flight or fight?* He wanted neither.

Heisenberg turned and looked directly at Karl, still talking but eyes curious. Did the man suspect?

Karl's made himself think carefully, clearly. The quick, rough German words did not come from nuclear theory. He could barely make sense of the elaborate equations and soon lost the flow, just listening for telltale words. *Rank . . . Hierarchie . . . Kollision . . . Querschnitt . . .* Heisenberg started describing how a hierarchy of particles came out of his analysis. *Lösung . . .*

Suddenly Karl knew the man wasn't leading up to some original nuclear ideas at all. The thrust of it was a new theory of mesons, particles of baffling complexity.

He sat back, breathed deeply. His hands stopped their jitter, feet went still. With a sigh he turned so Moe could see him give a broad smile. Heisenberg caught this and crinkled his brow, puzzled. Karl didn't care.

The rest of the talk was a relief. Karl sighed and felt a weight pass from him. They had come all this way for nothing. Now they could get out of here and he could get the hell out of this war.

5.

It was not quite a mansion and yet not quite anything else. This was what polite pretension looked like. A pricey private home, site of the reception.

An early-evening moon stood sentinel over them, lucid in a sky rich in stars. Karl thought about the immensity hanging above them. They were small things crawling here beneath the silvery starlight, clashing in a war that was microscopic on the scale of stars. Some of the twinklings he saw across the raw abyss had been launched long before humans even evolved. They shone by nuclear processes and cast silver light into the solemn black universe around them. The banks of the lake were silent and slumbering, the fields of some mere planet. A low waft of fragrant pollen rose in the night air. But instead of pondering immensities, he was struggling in a mad battle.

Karl and Moe approached the swanky private residence with Paul Scherrer at their side. Moe had seized the chance to talk to Scherrer after Heisenberg's talk, which had apparently meant as little to the audience as it had to Karl.

"Werner told me much more than he ever has. It's all going to pieces, so he talks—at last," Scherrer said with an urgency Karl could hear in his short, sharp gasps for breath as they both kept up with Moe's long strides. "Werner's moved his family, and the program he's running, to a small Bavarian town outside Munich."

"And his program?" Moe shot back. "The one he didn't talk about today?"

Scherrer shook his head in dismissal. "It's not much, he says. They've brought it from the Kaiser Wilhelm—got out before the Berlin bomb.

They've got that nuclear work around Hechingen, the town his family's in."

Moe said, "We need to talk to him privately."

Scherrer's English was far better than the rickety German of Karl and Moe. He said carefully, "You have seen his guards. I need to work within that constraint. I wish for you to hold your tongues until I can get a small chat with him tonight."

Karl remembered his great truth, learned in the project: *Never pass by a chance to shut up.* Yes.

"He says he's working on his matrix theory and cosmic rays," Scherrer said in his brisk clip. "A bit on nuclear work, but the program is in the hands of the experimenters. They're trying to build an *Uranmaschine*, he described it as. I do not know quite what that means."

"We do," Moe said. "But not a bomb?"

"He said nothing of bombs, except that is why he moved the program, and his family."

"What's the setup for this dinner party?" Moe asked mildly. He still had the briefcase with him.

"We have a reception, then the buffet. People mingle. Later Werner will perhaps make a little speech."

"And the Gestapo?"

"They are nominally escorts for Werner and that von Weizsäcker, his experimental head. So they take part, mingling with the Lausanne notables and other guests."

"I hope you have a good bar," Moe said jovially.

"Ah, alas, this war imposes some hardships. The Hochschule provides a punch bowl, in fact several. The supper is light as well."

"That's fine," Karl said. He was still full from the fine lunch. "We're here to talk."

"So I gather," Scherrer said significantly, with a sideways glance. Moe had used his ingratiating talents well.

Moe nodded. "Remember, we're Frenchmen—and me an Arab—with weak German skills."

"Weak French, too," Karl said.

"As I can tell," Scherrer said wryly. "Never mind. These are mostly academics and political figures. They all like to talk far more than to listen."

Karl gave him a chuckle at that. They entered the grand portico, nodded to the Swiss guards beside the wide doorway.

A Gestapo officer stood ramrod straight just inside, giving them the classic slit-eyed glare. Moe gave the man not a glance, just ambled in with his long strides. Karl followed, and they made their way without any fanfare. Nobody noticed them. The crowd murmur was already well lubricated by the three prominent punch bowls, arrayed along a very long table that also held the buffet.

A high gallery ran across the broad length of the room. A vast cowled fireplace stood empty, and people used its mantelpiece to rest their glasses of amber fluids while they gestured. Their animated hands flew as they talked with the cheery gaiety parties have when they are young. Karl pretended to inspect the inlaid paneling with ivory fittings as he eyed the crowd. The atmosphere was relaxed, moneyed.

Heisenberg stood at the focus of well-dressed Swiss, chatting amiably. Not far away were four obvious Gestapo types, this time in dark suits appropriate for the evening. The Obergruppenführer wore a severe black suit and a swastika emblem tie, red on black. He whispered orders to the others in officer-in-charge fashion. He was speaking to the nearest agent, who was an obvious cliché—big, ruddy, blond hair showing brown at the roots, teeth capped white, a smile both broad and mean. Karl tried to watch them sideways, and each time one of the Gestapo seemed to be looking back.

At least the Gestapo were off to one end of the room, easy to avoid. But near Heisenberg as well. "I doubt we can get Heisenberg alone," Karl said.

"Circulate, listen, don't talk," Moe said. "Everybody likes a nodder who listens. Leave the Gestapo to me."

Karl recalled Moe's OSS training and decided to follow orders. He could make out that most of the chat was about the war raging at the western foot of the Alps. Some thick-necked Swiss Army officers spoke with brass on their shoulders and lead in their voices. They had access to news Karl had not heard. The Germans had used even more death dust. The Americans and Brits were flanking around it, in both southern France and the north. So the Germans were using their new jet planes and older fighter-bombers to step up the dust campaign. That meant forcing the Allies into fighting in hilly battlefields, slowing the advance. What about this new bomb the Americans have used—just once? Were there any more?

Karl said nothing. The onrushing new weapons at the climax of this war—V-1s and V-2s, the A-bomb, dust, jet planes—made everyone uncertain, shocked.

He saw von Weizsäcker jesting with some ladies, looking carefree for a man whose country was on the verge of disaster. He decided to avoid the man and went to try the finger food. At a punch bowl, Moe brushed by him and said in a flat tone, "Lay off it. Stay sharp."

Back to the knots of German speakers, then. He was there only a few moments, listening to tut-tuts about a war that was mostly distant, though exciting, scenery to these people. Karl did see Paul Scherrer amble into the crowd around Heisenberg, then walk off. In a few moments more, Heisenberg made his way out of the crowd and joined Scherrer. They both went over to the Gestapo officer and talked. Then Heisenberg left by a side door, into the back garden on the lake.

The Gestapo watched all this, too. They all held glasses from the punch bowl, plus some of the delicacies from the handsome buffet. As he watched, three of them went back for more punch. Food was in short supply in *Deutschland*, and this was their holiday.

Moe again swept by, this time with a gesture to Karl to follow, but whispered, "In a minute."

Karl waited, ignoring the Gestapo, but noticed that Moe took the side door into the garden. He stalled a bit and saw another door, farther away. Once through it, into a vacant sitting room, some glass French doors gave onto the garden. He found Moe admiring the lake view with Heisenberg. Scherrer was not there.

As he walked toward them, Karl could see through the windows the Gestapo smoking, talking, not looking at the garden. Scherrer spoke loudly and seemed to be regaling them with a story. Karl's nerves were strumming, skin prickly, heart thumping, an odd stinging in his nostrils. *I'm way out of my league here.*

Heisenberg turned, nodded to Karl, and in accented English said, "I have been waiting for you to appear."

Karl blinked. "What?!"

"Scherrer told me of you; he is a friend. But I already expected some contact, somehow."

Moe said sternly, "Does the Gestapo know who we are? Or might be?"

"They suspect everyone. But gentlemen—events nuclear now dominate this dreadful war," Heisenberg said mildly, his eyes veiled. "We have studied the nuclear debris at the Berlin crater. Uranium, as we expected. I must compliment you gentlemen on completely outdistancing us."

Moe said, "Your program is not advanced?"

Heisenberg shrugged. "Why conceal it now? After my 1942 conference with Albert Speer, who by then was minister of armaments and war production, he gave us some money. We are building a reactor, a peaceful use."

"Not separating the 235 from the 238?" Karl asked.

"Separation, we calculated, was too difficult. I and the others, we felt from 1940 onward that any bomb was unlikely before 1942, when army said the war would be over. So Speer concluded that reactor research should proceed."

Karl said, "What irony! It was fear of a German bomb that led to the invention of our bomb."

Heisenberg raised an eyebrow. "When the Reich began losing the war, they believed, also around 1942, that these weapons could not be made quickly enough to change the outcome."

Moe was wary, watching the garden, the party inside. Karl felt an anger building. "Our whole goddamned raison d'être was your lead in nuclear physics!"

"I dismissed from the outset the possibility of producing pure U-235 in significant quantities," Heisenberg said mildly. "The engineering was beyond us. Also, not until Stalingrad did the Reich use centralized planning and control. So there was little coherence in the nuclear program. It was dispersed among many laboratories, with funding provided by three separate government agencies. An enormous task. How did you do it?"

"Centrifuges," Karl said. "Plenty of them."

"Ah! We did not think they could be so effective."

"It took a lot of work."

"So we gathered. However . . ." Heisenberg looked canny, eyes narrowed. "We embarked in 1942, to produce a reactor capable of going into a condition we called 'fast critical.' I calculated that a chain reaction would build in a few thousandths of a second."

Karl shook his head. He could hear the tinny, distant party chatter and wondered how long they had out here. "That could work, give you an explosion of sorts. But it would have been far too heavy, far too feeble, to make a practical weapon. You'd need a compact assembly of pure fissionable isotopes—"

"Move it along," Moe said.

"Okay, we know the main answer, you have no bombs—but why do you have enough to drop dust?"

"We kept the mines in Czechoslovakia working. Our reactor, partly built, the army took. Now they hold the pitchblende for the Luftwaffe. The radio-actives are not near our reactor effort, I can assure you. We had already cleaned the pitchblende of oxides and lead, so it was ready to use for the dust. That fellow of the rockets, von something—"

"Von Braun," Moe supplied, eyes on the windows.

"Yes, he pushed this dust idea, after Berlin. Speer liked it. As did Hitler."

"You worked on the dust?"

Heisenberg shook his head. "I had no expertise. In this war, I work through quiet interventions within the bureaucracy, rather than overt public protest. Even that is highly dangerous now. I had hoped that the regime's most extreme manifestations would not last long. I had hoped that they would make possible a Germany, which could lead Europe to a more orderly future."

"Wrong about that," Moe said stiffly.

"Like many comrades in the *Jugendbewegung*—ah, the Youth Movement of the Weimar era—I was beguiled by romantic nationalism and our supreme German culture. We are the answer to such horrors as the Soviets." Heisenberg said this earnestly, searching Karl's face, almost beseeching him.

Karl said, "Look, we want this war over—soon."

"As do I. Your attempt on Hitler would have done it, I think. It has blown a large hole in the Nazi Party people. Plus the Wehrmacht General Staff."

Moe brightened at this, glancing at them, then back at the windows. People were moving quickly around in the party; something was happening, but Karl let Moe tend to that.

Karl said carefully, "We have more bombs. We can try again."

"Three months now and no more bombs. So I do not believe you."

"You will soon."

Heisenberg frowned skeptically at this. "Perhaps you have no more."

"Don't bet on it."

Heisenberg said warily, slowly, "Do you know of the *Wolfsschanze?*"

"No," Moe said. "I do recall that 'Wolf' is a self-adopted nickname of Hitler."

"There are *Führerhauptquartiere*—places where he lives. They are heavily guarded by *Reichssicherheitsdienst*, a special corps of Reich security service. The 'Wolf's Lair' as you would say, it is in the woods about eight kilometers from the small East Prussian town of Rastenburg. He uses it to direct the eastern front. The Soviets are pushing us hard there now. Savage people."

Moe turned to confront Heisenberg, Karl saw, using his body to intimidate the much smaller man. "What's it like?"

"A well-concealed bunker, deep. As you have guessed, I was called in to consult on the dust. We flew in at night, to avoid the danger of your air force. A big discussion, it was. Von Braun was there, von Weizsäcker, myself. Hitler was dancing with joy at the idea von Braun brought forward—gotten, they say, from a fiction piece, by an American. I suspect von Braun made it up himself, and the fiction story is a ruse."

"He didn't fake that," Karl said. This Heisenberg seemed smug, and Karl could not resist adding, "We have a reactor too."

"What?" This brought eye-widening skepticism. "Both a bomb and—"

"Turns out, reactors helped us along some. Fermi built the first one for us."

Heisenberg's mouth pinched. "Our bomb work did not have the top priority." He said this slowly, looking into the distance, not at the house. "I estimated we would need a ton of refined, separated U-235 to make one bomb, perhaps. Apparently I was wrong. Yours must have been smaller than that, to fly it at all." Another pause. Silence. Karl waited. "So with lesser funds, many of the young scientists von Weizsäcker needed got drafted. This was after Stalingrad. They were sent to the front. Many of them died."

This digression made Moe's face tighten. "How is this 'Wolf's Lair' defended?"

Heisenberg hesitated, his puzzlement showing how hard he was barraged by all this news. "I was there just once. It has heavy, colossal structures. Reinforced concrete as defense. Hitler much fears air attack."

"We can deal with that," Karl said dryly.

Heisenberg fished in his jacket pocket. "I want you to take back to your superiors my assurance that a surrendered Germany will cooperate to keep the Soviets out of our lands. And also, since you verify that fact, just now— that we in the nuclear program did not invent this dust idea. It was *yours*."

"Yeah, we get that," Moe said sardonically.

"*Jawohl. Also, das.*" Heisenberg handed Karl a slip of paper, as if shaking hands.

Moe's eyes widened as he watched the party within. Karl glanced over. People were milling around, flustered. No sign of the Gestapo.

Moe smiled. "Time for us to leave. Please, Herr Doktor Heisenberg, we may need your help to say our good-byes to the hosts."

As they came into the large party, Karl saw shifting eyes, puzzlement, amid short, rough German sentences he could not follow. Nobody paid them much attention as they worked their way toward the front doorway.

Suddenly the Obergruppenführer came angling in from their left, face flushed, hair mussed up. He spat out some fast German to a woman. It had the tone of something's-happening-but-I-don't-know-what. Moe kept walking calmly away, his gait smooth and easy. Karl was glad to follow, trying to look casual. His heart was hammering.

Out the door. No Gestapo guarding it. With that they picked up the pace, moving swiftly through a side garden, around the large house, and out to the dark street.

"What was going on in there?" Karl asked.

"A bit of diarrhea for the Gestapo."

"Uh, how did—"

"I noticed that they were drinking from one punch bowl near them and got a cup, while adding a touch of my own. The OSS developed it for us."

"So they're—"

"Shitting their guts out, for several more hours."

Karl could not suppress his laugh. Only when they were blocks away, under a streetlight, did Karl open the paper. It read:

54.079344°N 21.493544°E

6.

August 22, 1944

The next morning they rose early and before breakfast went for a bracing walk through the town. Their train was not until ten o'clock and the view was stunning, making Karl regret that they had to leave, to go back into wartime France and out through Marseille. They passed a *Konditorei* and the cloud of luscious smells from it, and on impulse went in. They ordered confections and coffee in the nearly deserted shop and dug into the warm cream cakes. Moe went through his quickly, got more, and with a big gulp of the aromatic coffee, said, "Nobody has money, so these places just barely survive. Y'know, the profession *Konditor* developed from bakers, meaning "confectioners," once the medieval bakers, around the fifteenth century, figured out bread. So some started to rarefy the dough with honey, dried fruit, and spices."

"Lebküchler," Moe said, pointing to the establishment sign. "Experts at adding good things to light breads." This arcane knowledge was usual with Moe, bits of lore picked up in his constant reading.

They walked to enjoy the aromas of shops and stalls until Moe whispered, "I was rather concerned last night, the way that obvious SS team were looking at us, asking questions."

"Me too. I hope our accents held up."

Moe scowled. "They asked me some nuclear stuff, and I played dumb. Then they switched to S-matrix theory. Baiting me, plainly. I gave some garbled version of Heisenberg's remarks and broke it off."

"Well, you *did* sit in the front row."

"Yeah, maybe a mistake. Let's get back. I'm packed."

"Me too," Karl said. They hastened along, and when they entered the hotel, the manager came over with anxious eyes.

"Men were here just now, asking for you. German."

"*Polizei?* Gestapo?" Karl asked.

"They wore suits, but yes, seemed to be, from what they said. Wanted to know when your train was."

Moe rumbled, "You told them?"

The manager, a slight man, blinked. "I—I thought I had to—"

"You have a car?" Moe asked.

"Well, yes, but the Bahnhofplatz is only a few hundred meters—"

"They'll cover the Bahnhofplatz. Here—" Moe handed the man a roll of bills. "Your car— We want to rent it for a few hours."

Dancing eyes as the manager counted the bills and bit his lip. "I don't know, I—"

Moe loomed over the manager. "Where is it—and the keys?"

"Down that way—"

Inside five minutes they had their bags in the car. Karl slammed the passenger door and Moe backed them out of the tiny garage. "We don't dare use the train, right?"

"They probably didn't want to arrest us at the dinner. This is easier, grab us at the train station, nobody in the physics community knows."

Traffic slowed them and Moe turned onto a side road, out into the countryside. "We can pick up the big highway once we're over the hills and down the valley," Karl said, consulting a map from the glove compartment. His heart thumped as scenery flashed by.

They were only a few kilometers out of town when Moe said, after a glance in the rearview mirror, "Somebody following us. There must've been a lookout at the hotel."

He floored the little car's accelerator, but as Karl watched, going along a narrow valley road, the big black car behind kept getting nearer, emerging from each curve a bit closer.

"This road straightens out soon," Moe said.

The black Mercedes loomed behind but did not smack into their rear bumper. "They'll wait for the straight, then come alongside us," Moe said, "and force us off the road."

As soon as a stretch opened up, the Mercedes came alongside. Moe sped up. They fell behind a car length.

Karl gripped the armrest. "It's two of those Gestapo guys," he said over the engine roar. The car smelled hot, metallic. "The big blond one is grinning at us."

"I don't like it when they're happy," Moe said. "Hold on."

They were approaching a rising curve to the left. They shot over the peak and started down. The moment the big car behind them edged over, Moe hit the brakes hard. He swerved left, into the opposing lane.

The Mercedes shot past them. He saw startled faces in the windows that flicked by.

The braking howl filled the air and drove Karl forward. He caught himself on the dashboard. *There should be seat belts in these—*

Moe slammed harder on the brakes as the Gestapo sped ahead. They were braking now.

When the car came to a screeching stop, Moe gunned it in reverse. Karl hung on. They skidded backward. Moving fast, Moe turned the wheel a hard right. They went into a slide. Shrieking tires. The front end slid around with eerie grace. They went up on two wheels. Hovered, leaning. Karl braced himself and they slammed down hard, pointed back the way they had come. Moe rammed the gear into forward and they took off. Away from the Gestapo, who had overshot them.

The engine roared. They hit high speed and then slowed, Karl looking back. "Can't see them."

"Take this, keep it close." Moe produced the pistol from his jacket. Karl took the gun and, to keep it secure, put it between his legs. Freud would have loved that, he thought.

They fled. The engine whined in protest. A kilometer flew by.

Moe slowed, took them into a dirt road to the right. A hundred meters in he found a place to turn around and went back. He edged the car into a side slot where they were out of sight of the main road but could see anything that went by. Minutes ticked on, nobody speaking. The engine swarmed with heat, making the air wobble over the hood. A farm wagon came by, drawn by a tiny truck away from Zurich. Its tinny engine sounded like a joke to Karl in the warm, mellow air. He wondered what could happen next. More minutes.

"No following car. Good! Let's go see." Moe's tone was steady, calm.

Karl realized his hands were still clenched around the seat mounts and his muscles ached with tension. He eased up, sighing. "Shouldn't we just head for the border, some side road?"

"I don't like having them behind us. We have to know where they are."

Moe took his pistol back and snapped its action, feeding a round into the chamber. Then he set the hammer carefully down and put on the safety. "Here." He handed it to Karl. "Have it ready for me."

They turned out onto the paved road. All quiet. Moe drove carefully away from Zurich as they came back along the road and approached a rising curve. When they came over the crest, they saw first the wagon drawn by the small truck, and beyond it the Mercedes, upside down, about seventy meters beyond the truck. They hadn't hit the truck, which was slowing.

"They must've gotten mad," Moe said, stopping to appraise the view. "Easy to make errors of judgment that way."

They slowed, crawled forward. Karl asked, "How can you tell?"

"Tire marks, see? Driver tried to make a U-turn halfway down the slope. On a flat road, that'd be no problem. On the gradient, the inside wheels are higher, so look at those black tire tracks. See, about two-thirds of the way through, they roll it."

Karl estimated. "It went over fifty meters. See the torn grass? Top is caved in. Nobody moving in there."

The farmer was already at the wreck, walking around the car, looking in. He tried the door, couldn't open it.

Moe snorted. "Job done, I'd say. Those boys just got a little overexcited."

They had to go off the road to inch by the Mercedes. The farmer waved at them and said in German, "Can I get help?"

"*Ja.*" Karl gestured, as if horrified. "*Schnell.*"

Through the smashed windshield he saw two bodies heaped up like a collection of parts, not men. Blood spattered the side windows, bright red turning brown at the edges. One head was all blood. The Mercedes had held up pretty well, but not its contents.

"Let's go," Karl said. "Nothing can help those guys anymore."

7.

They reached Geneva on the main road by midafternoon. Moe brought them into a small parking lot a few hundred meters from the train station. It was a pleasant day and everyone was smiling, but Moe said, "Stay sharp. The Gestapo has plenty of agents in Geneva. We know that quite well. A few of our OSS guys died finding that out."

Karl's job was to call the hotel manager in Zurich. Moe stayed out of sight, saying, "I'm conspicuous." A station clerk let Karl make the call, charging a hefty fee. Karl mangled his French and German to tell the man to take the train and pick up his car. "Your keys we'll leave with the station master. Tell him your name. There will be more money in the envelope. Sorry we had to do this."

"I think I know your reasons," the man said. *"Amerikaner, ja?"*

"Uh, ja."

"Good luck to you both. May all this be over soon."

Not quite soon, Karl thought. *If we survive today, that is.*

He went out into the main hall of the train station and out toward the tracks. There were long lines stretching from the ticket booths, and Karl wondered about getting back to the French coast. The dust drops were picking up, a newspaper headline he had glimpsed said in big red type. He ambled back toward the car and Moe appeared, out of nowhere. "Off to the right," Moe said. "In the Opel."

Karl knew enough now to just fake a move upward, then glance—and there they were. Three faces, surveying the crowds, trying to look inconspicuous. He turned to remark to Moe that they were obvious Gestapo types, but Moe was gone.

Karl walked on, wondering what to do. No doubt there were other Gestapo, or simply spotters, around the train station. Maybe he had been targeted already? He moved into the thick of the crowd, and then, when a truck blocked the view from behind him, ducked into a narrow alley. As he walked to the end of it, Moe appeared suddenly from a narrow side alley. "Good dodge," he said. "Now we need a cab."

"Why?"

"They can't easily follow us in this traffic. Anyway, we're headed for the airport."

"Why?"

Moe shook off the question. "Go out and hail a cab. Now. Bring it around back here, near the tracks. I'll come out fast."

Karl did this, scrupulously not looking for Gestapo. He snagged the cab and directed the cabbie with finger pointing and stuttering German. Moe appeared out of nowhere, got in, and Karl said, "*Flughafen, bitte.*"

They got there swiftly, with Moe hushing him when he tried to ask what was up. The Swiss airport was small and modest, three boxy buildings. Once out, their bags in hand, Moe directed Karl to a sign saying GEFREITE. Karl vaguely knew this meant "military." A small man rose from behind a desk, asking, "*Darf ich Ihnen helfen?*"

"*Wir möchten ein Flugzeug chartern, bitte.*"

"*Das ist sehr teuer,*" the man said. A personal plane would be expensive, indeed. Karl asked if they would they take the Allied-made francs. A skeptical scowl.

"Tell him we have real cash." Moe opened a wallet Karl had not seen him use, full of bills. "*Wir sind Amerikaner.*" Moe turned to Karl and said, "That about uses up my words."

The man gaped as Moe laid out crisp American bills, all hundreds. It took eight before the man nodded. "*Wohin wollen Sie?*"

"Rome," Moe said. "*Schnell, bitte.*"

The plane had to be sorted out, but their bags got tagged and tickets punched. They sat in a deserted private lounge of old brown sofas, waiting. It smelled of cigarettes; people were still nervous about flying, and they medicated themselves before it. Karl wondered if there was a bar in this place. "That guy overcharged us," he said.

"Sure. You want quick service, you pay. A universal language."

"You're always one step ahead of me."

"This isn't your area. I needed you to do the physics talk in the garden."

"He was trying to give away just enough. Otherwise, he stayed clear."

"I liked how you handled Heisenberg. He figured right away you were a Jew. That helped. He knows what's going on in Germany, everywhere they occupy."

"This late, he must."

"I figure he sees the whole Reich is facing the breaking point. If we get Hitler, finally, the only power base left, aside from the domestic police, is the field marshals out fighting us and the Soviets. Heisenberg prob'ly thinks the marshals are still real patriots. Not Nazis."

"Hope so."

"Those guys at the station, that the Gestapo sent after us—it means they want to know what we learned. God help Heisenberg, though."

"I think a Nobel keeps him safe, for a while."

Moe shrugged. "Maybe. Heisenberg's some sort of moral weasel, to me. A klutz when it came to bomb physics, as you teased out of him. But still devoted to *Deutschland über Alles*. He's just doing the smart thing, for the circumstances."

A ground crew was working on a nearby small passenger plane, two props. Moe pointed. "Good. I told one of those mechanics I don't want to go over the Alps with one engine."

Karl said nothing. Moe was relaxing, stretching his long legs as they watched the airplane get fueled. "As for us, I figure it's easier to get to Rome fast than into France slow. Especially now, with that damn dust everywhere."

Karl let moments pass. "Y'know, I was scared through all this. Especially today."

Moe nodded. "Aristotle once remarked that to know courage you must also first know fear."

Karl tried to make himself feel elated, and failed. "I'm not cut out for this."

"Maybe the baseball helps me. I'm used to watching the players, to pick off a base stealer or a guy who takes too big a lead from the bag. Seeing the big picture."

"You're a philosophical ballplayer, for sure."

Moe sat back, basking a bit. "I took philosophy at Yale. I liked what Kant says, how's he put it? 'Out of the crooked timber of humanity, no straight thing was ever made.' Heisenberg the genius proves that."

Admiral Wilhelm Canaris

8.

Their airplane taxied into place outside, with ground crews attending. Karl picked up his suitcase, eager to go. *Private plane. Now, this is the way to travel. . . .*

He barely noticed a soft sound from behind, a whisk of air. Karl turned. At the back of their waiting room a door swung open and a phalanx of German officers entered, stepping together as if on parade. Karl saw them first. His jaw dropped. Moe had been studying their airplane. He turned, saw them too, and casually glanced back at the airplane, plainly estimating the distance.

"We can't make it," he whispered. "Those officers are carrying sidearms too."

Karl tried to look uninteresting, head ducked down, fidgeting with his luggage. But with stiff steps the lead German officer came right up to them and stopped, scowling. Another officer beside him said in clear though accented English, "We have come to talk."

Moe looked them over thoroughly before replying, "We are diplomatic personnel. You have no cause—"

"We know who you are," the lead officer said in a more clipped, efficient English.

He was graying and sober, with a long face creased by care. Karl thought the accent was Prussian. The guy certainly had an air of being in charge, but Karl did not know the complicated German rank insignia. A slow cold formed in him. Here was the true enemy. One he had helped kill many thousands of, and would again if he had the slightest chance.

The officer drew himself up, and the others around him followed suit. "We wish to speak, that is all."

Karl could not let that go. "Who do you think we are?"

A confident, sliding smile. "You were sent here to interrogate Heisenberg. The Gestapo missed you at first, but you dealt with them when they finally understood."

Moe shrugged. "We exchanged pleasantries with Professor—"

"For espionage." Still the smile.

By this time the officers and guards had spread out into a semicircle. Their faces were intent, guarded, bodies stiff, tense.

Karl thought, *We were so close!* and said, "I am a physicist and was interested in Professor Heisenberg's new field theory." This at least was somewhat true, but he doubted that would matter.

"Do not fear for your safety. I should introduce myself." He waved a hand and two officers nodded, left the room. "I am Admiral Canaris, commander of the Abwehr."

Instantly Moe said, "I gather you are of an anti-Hitler faction in the Abwehr? Are there many such in your Military Intelligence agency?"

"You presume correctly. You have studied us, I see." Another stiff bow. "I was alerted to your presence by our embassy here. We have agents there."

"How'd you find us?"

"Originally, an observation by our trade mission. You, Mr. Berg, we have quite a file on."

"I'll bet. You know I'm a civilian—"

"Ballplayer of some kind, yes. You have other roles as well, we know. You may know something of our Abwehr. Among our *Kriegsorganisationen*, ah, war organizations, I have formed a circle of like-minded Wehrmacht officers. We wish an end to this war."

Karl was unsure what this parrying meant, but said, "Does treatment of Jews come under your Abwehr?"

A frown, a dismissive wave. "We have nothing to do with the persecution of Jews. It is horrible, yes—but no concern of ours. We in the Abwehr hold ourselves aloof from it. I protested the rounding up of Jews in our Polish invasion."

Several new officers came in, nodded. Canaris swept a hand toward the door in invitation. "Please join us for refreshments before your flight. I have told the airport officials to await you."

"Suppose we want to leave now?" Karl asked as they were ushered down a side corridor lined with more German officers, into a room with chairs and a buffet table. Someone had hastily arranged an odd social event. There were even German soldiers serving as waiters, awkwardly dealing with a coffee machine and pastries. A sense of unreality crept over Karl, making him even more edgy. He wondered if they knew he was a Jew. Almost certainly, though he had pointedly not given his name. Moe didn't either; they knew him.

"My name is Smith," Karl said.

"Ah, yes, perhaps," Canaris said mildly. "Mr. Smith, were you to leave now, would be bad. You would be neglecting your duty to do so, in fact." A thin smile. "We wish you to carry back more information than you have already gathered."

"*Sie haben sehr gutes Englisch,*" Karl said to stall. He watched several more officers quietly enter and stand by the walls.

"Thank you." A Prussian nod. "I studied it. I have learned to trust the truthfulness of British intelligence, and now perhaps the Americans."

Canaris gestured with authority, seating them at a round table with five chairs. The German uniformed waiters rushed to place before them dainty fresh pastries, which Canaris identified, pointing and rolling out their complicated names. "Bienenstich, Gugelhupf, Käsekuchen, Kirschtorte—Bitte, essen Sie!" With a flourish from the waiters, the coffee arrived in hearty, steaming mugs. Karl felt a dizzying sensation of unreality. He was afraid yet able to keep his eyes from darting among the gray uniforms that embodied all he hated.

Canaris bit into a *Kirschtorte* and nodded with satisfaction. "Our most famous—ein Schwarzwälder. Cannot get these in *Deutschland* any longer. So I looked forward to this little expedition, for feasting reasons. Heisenberg had same motive, I believe."

"He said as much," Moe remarked, plainly moving the conversation along.

But Canaris was not to be rushed. "I was in contact with British intelligence during the Polish invasion. Then, during our conquest of the Soviets, we received a detailed report of all the enemy positions, matters known only to the British." A lifted eyebrow.

After this swerve in topic, Canaris offered Karl another pastry. *Let him ramble*, Karl thought, and after a sip of the strong coffee, he took the light, airy confection. The cadre of officers had retreated to the other side of the room, beyond easy hearing. Canaris wanted to talk a bit, soften them up, and seemed more a diplomat than the stiff Prussian manner implied. He even smiled convincingly.

Moe slid in a mild, slow sentence. "Then you are speaking to them, the British, again?"

Canaris sighed. "No, alas. We in a certain faction of the General Staff High Command have tried. Carefully, of course. Detection would mean execution. Several signals to London went unanswered. We suspect someone is blocking these signals of compromise."

"Compromise? You mean . . ." Karl let the sentence dangle.

"A negotiated cease-fire on our western front," Canaris said with a steady gaze, poised as he delivered the words. Karl realized the man had rehearsed.

Suddenly it all seemed clear. The Abwehr had used Heisenberg as a stalking horse. Once they had spotted Moe and Karl from a distance, and the Gestapo had departed with Heisenberg, there was time to make contact. But the Gestapo were watching the hotel. So Abwehr held off, probably confused. The Gestapo were deadly, and yet this morning was the very last minute to make contact. Moe got them away so fast only the Gestapo could manage to follow. Then Moe's deft chipping off the Gestapo pursuit had no doubt tangled up matters more. It also gave Canaris time. Maybe enough to fly here from Zurich? Then German army efficiency had sliced through the thicket, saving the Abwehr agenda at the last minute. As the German army now wanted to do with the whole war. At least, in the west.

Moe said casually, "You were behind Operation Pastorius in 1942, I believe."

Canaris blinked and Karl suppressed a smile. "*Ja*, that failure led Hitler to rebuke me. I began to look for a way out of this war."

Karl had heard of this attempt by eight Nazi agents, sent into the United States to sabotage generating plants supplying electrical power. Groves had been sure their targets were the laboratories in Oak Ridge, but apparently the agents didn't know what the power plants were feeding into. Suspicious local police nailed them pretty quick. Five of them were executed.

"And your comrades?" Moe swept a hand to suggest the others in uniform, neatly lined in an arc. The officers eyed the discussion carefully but said nothing.

"They came to realize the Hitler madness in their own time." Canaris gritted his teeth. "For some, it was when Hitler commanded our Security Headquarters, our Reichssicherheitshauptamt, to retaliate against the Italians for Mussolini's arrest by the kidnapping or murder of Pius XII and King Victor Emmanuel of Italy." Canaris said this mildly, a simple matter of fact.

Moe let a bit of surprise show in his widened eyes. "I never heard of that."

"It was a secret, since I and others blocked the attempt. The Gestapo concealed it with a cover story. It worked. When there are no facts to support lies, facts must be made."

Karl leaned forward. "So all those here with you want Hitler gone, and a separate peace?" He knew he had to get specifics, to make a report on this strange incident credible. If they ever got to report it, of course, which seemed unlikely. The gray uniforms were not reassuring.

"We saw things differently. After the 1942 Soviet campaign failed, I told General Fromm there was no way Germany could win the war. Continuing it was stupidity and tragedy. Just like the first war! In 1943 I visited Spain, I made contact with British agents from Gibraltar. We were active around the British naval base of Gibraltar, watching with cameras and radar to track Allied supply ships in the western Mediterranean. It was a useful way to send messages to London about our anti-Hitler faction in the General Staff. I helped form a circle of like-minded Wehrmacht officers. We are of the Prussian tradition, not the National Socialist elements that party forced into the military profession in the 1930s. Our circle knew we could not in safety oppose the party outright."

Moe said, "We had heard rumors of this, but no hard details."

"We are united. Walter Model, an old friend, known in the General Staff as the Führer's Fireman—even he has joined us now. We lost some when you annihilated our offices in Berlin with that terror bomb."

"We were aiming for Hitler," Karl said stiffly.

"Of course. We wish you had caught him. We have spoken much of this, since that bomb. We have been careful, and this chance visit of Heisenberg suddenly opened an opportunity. Our very lives were in peril to even discuss such treason. But we tried before, to let the British know. In 1943, in occupied France, I was conducted blindfolded in Paris to the local head of the British Intelligence Service. Their agents took me to the Convent of the Nuns of the Passion of Our Blessed Lord, 127 Rue de la Santé."

"I know where that is," Karl said. "But you could get in touch with the Brits in Paris? Unbelievable."

Canaris gave them a sad, wise smile. There was a forlorn elegance about him. "Intelligence services find it useful to retain connections, even perhaps, in time, friendships. I met a man, code name Jade Amicol. By my own efforts I found later he is in reality Colonel Claude Olivier. You may check that datum with your own sources."

"We will." Moe leaned forward. "What was the point of this Paris meeting?"

Canaris nodded. "I wanted to know the terms for peace, if Germany got rid of Hitler. Just as I do now."

Karl asked, "You heard back?"

"Churchill's reply came two weeks later. It was simple: unconditional surrender."

Moe said, "Why should it be different now?"

"This war has become even more terrible." The words carried a weary husk.

Karl kept most of a snarl out of his voice. "Mostly due to your side."

Canaris sighed ruefully. "You are correct. I wish to stop this insanity, prevent the Soviets from reaching my country, stop the huge losses."

"A bit late for that," Karl shot back.

"I knew we were led by a madman in 1942. After the staff review of the eastern front, with you Americans in the war due to the stupid Japanese, Hitler seized me by the lapels, demanding to know whether I was insinuating that Germany would lose the war. No one pulled him off me. I said no, of course." A long, weary smile creased his face.

Karl noticed some movement among the other officers, and pure fear spiked in him. The creepy unease he had felt now became impossible to suppress. He stood up, looked for a way to leave, run, escape—

"I believe your airplane is ready," Canaris said, standing. "Please, take some of these delights with you. And—" A flourish of a manila envelope, delivered by an assistant. "I have written in my own hand our proposal. Please take this to those who need it."

Karl said, "Who do you represent?"

"Many. Perhaps the most important to you, von Rundstedt and Rommel. They are of our *armée centrale*."

Karl blinked; these two were commanders in France.

"They want to parley?" Moe asked.

"A cease-fire, to allow some moments for thought."

"In the west alone?"

Canaris sighed. "We have no avenues to speak to the Soviets, who are at the edge of Poland. So much happens now, *so schnell*—so fast. My old friend von Rundstedt, he feels that had he been able to move the armored divisions he had behind the coast—countermanded by that amateur Hitler—your invasion would not have succeeded."

"Von Rundstedt is your commander in the west," Moe said, disbelief plain in the skeptical tilt of his mouth. "You're sure he backs you?"

"He is frustrated by continued interference from higher levels, especially with the disposition of his inadequate forces."

"And Rommel?"

"He is our most popular general, by far—and a complex case. Rommel opposes assassinating Hitler. He believes an assassination attempt would spark civil war in Germany and Austria, making Hitler a martyr for a cause that would then outlast him. Instead Rommel insists that Hitler be arrested and brought to trial for his crimes. He feels we of the older army, the Prussians, must come to the rescue of Germany, as he puts it."

Karl could not restrain himself, though he knew he should let Moe carry this. "And our atomic bombing Berlin—how did that change things?"

Canaris allowed himself a thin smile. "We realized that hope of a stalemate, as your armies approached, was now impossible. It broke the morale of much of our populace—which the earlier bombing had not. The drama was immediate."

Moe said, "You Prussians, why do you turn against the rest of the army?"

"There was always opposition to Hitler in conservative circles. Remember, his National Socialist Workers' Party, as the name suggests, came from the left. Their principal opponents in the 1920s were the Communists. He beat them in the streets, wiped them from the country. Hitler's dazzling successes in 1938 to 1941 stifled army opposition. After the Soviet campaign failed, we start to whisper among ourselves. Now we are desperate—but the Nazis control much of the army through their SS units. Hitler imposed *his* views on the military chain of command—disaster! We despair always of the Nazi incompetence and crimes. In 1943 we planned a coup against the entire Nazi regime. Many Nazi officials we would accuse for known crimes. Hitler would be arrested as an insane person. We would base this diagnosis in high court on his exposure to mustard gas in the first war. We carefully, quietly assembled a secret dossier detailing many of the crimes committed in eastern Europe by the Nazis: the Zossen documents." Canaris brightened, eyebrows raised, voice lofting from its stern drone to a cheerful note. "But then your Berlin bomb came to our aid. You can now find Hitler and . . ." He smiled, eyes narrowed.

A long silence.

Moe nodded. "I will convey your message."

Everyone stood, and Canaris made a ritual of shaking hands with Moe and Karl. All officers were at rigid attention.

Moe looked Canaris in the eye. "Can I trust what you're not saying?"

A brisk nod. "Every word."

PART XIII

GÖTTERDÄMMERUNG

It is not because things are difficult that we dare not venture. It is because we dare not venture that they are difficult.
—Seneca

1.

September 16, 1944

It took many days to process what had happened.

Somehow, during their fast trip back, Karl thought not of the war raging beneath the wings of the light bomber, but of the sole performance he had heard of Wagner's opera *Götterdämmerung*. That was what this war had become now.

When traveling across Germany in 1936, he had avoided the overt signs of the Nazis, who were pervading the culture more and more. There was much to admire in German society, particularly the science, and he visited Berlin and Heidelberg with joy in his step. Conversations in his halting German with physicists and chemists were stimulating. He had bought tickets to the Ring Cycle at the Bayreuth Festspielhaus and sat through the Wagnerian version of an Old Norse term, Ragnarok. The legend was about a gigantic war among various beings and gods that ultimately led to the burning, drowning, and renewal of the world.

Now, eight years later, a grand and terrible opera like that played out with real deaths, far below them as they flew. Moe had somehow fetched by radio a light bomber, that met them immediately after their landing in Rome. They were the sole passengers as the airplane skirted around the French war zone and landed at the very airfield where the A-bomb team worked. No big reception this time, because nobody in England knew what Moe was carrying in a plain manila folder.

Within two hours of landing, they were in central London, deep within the Admiralty Citadel. The brutally functional operations center for the

Admiralty and RAF now had jammed corridors, constant talk barking down the halls, an air of incessant tension. From offhand remarks, Karl gathered that apparently the French campaign was not going well against the continual death-dust raids. Details were secret. Speculation ran amok.

Yet as he and Moe entered an inconspicuous, medium-size conference room, quiet prevailed. They were in their seats against the wall, facing the long table, when suddenly there came one of those double-take moments. Karl saw General Eisenhower at the table. His uniform jacket was hooked on his chair back and his shirt showed sweat crescents at the armpits, wrinkles, even a coffee stain. Eisenhower frowned, conferring with other officers both British and American. They were murmuring as they read, together, the manuscript from the manila folder. Their presence and concentration were a shock, even for the ever-prepared Moe, who for the first time ever seemed nervous. "Wow," was all he said.

Eisenhower the man looked much as Karl recalled from newsreels. But today his face seemed lined, compared to the confident, smiling general who'd talked in those newsreels to the troops in full battle gear, the day before Normandy. His eyes were heavy-lidded and his smile was gone. Karl had gathered some news about the slowing of the Allied advance in France. Apparently the tactical battle plan was not working in the face of the death dust. As the meeting assembled, Eisenhower frowned deeper. "This is the high brass, all right," Moe whispered. "I recognize maybe ten. Don't know why we're here."

The answer came soon. Eisenhower glanced at a page and said, "The agent concerned, the courier . . . Moe Berg? The baseball player?" He raised skeptical eyebrows and glanced around the room, puzzled, as Moe rose. "Sit here." Eisenhower gestured to an empty seat at the table.

As Moe sat at the center table, Eisenhower said in clipped tones, "I want to hear straight from you what happened with Canaris." Eisenhower's piercing eyes silenced every murmur in the room.

Moe went through the entire incident in meticulous detail. He brought up observations Karl had not even noticed, such as the decorations General Wilhelm Canaris wore, an Iron Cross and the German Cross in silver. Moe went through the Canaris revelations in a steady, studious way, often using

Canaris's exact phrasing. Karl knew he could not have done anything like it. Moe had perfect recall, apparently without effort. *No wonder he was so good in Norway, eastern Europe, the rest of his rumored exploits.* The examination took over half an hour, and then Eisenhower pointed at the manuscript. Karl could see it was handwritten.

"You read this?"

"No, sir."

"Excellent. Without going into details, I can inform everyone here that it proposes a 'separate agreement' between us and the German General Staff. This will come, Canaris assumes, after Hitler is dead."

"As accomplished by us, yes." Moe kept his face without any hint of emotion. Karl realized that he could not have done that, either.

Eisenhower twisted his mouth into a suspicious grimace. "And you gave us the coordinates of his Wolf's Lair hideout in East Prussia? Got them from this Heisenberg guy?"

"Yes, sir. He just handed them to us at the very end of our talk in Lausanne."

"Why did he do it?"

"I think he wants Hitler out and the war over. He also told my colleague, Karl Cohen, several details about their atomic bomb program."

"Cohen?" Eisenhower looked around the room. Karl felt a dash of panic, opened his mouth, then stood. "Ah, you. What did you deduce from that talk?"

Karl opened his mouth, but words did not come out. He swallowed, mouth suddenly dry. "Ah . . . ah . . . I think he was saying, though indirectly, that they do not have a bomb program. They have started building a reactor, but haven't gotten far."

A quizzical look. "We've done that? Some kind of reactor?" Clearly Eisenhower knew little about what came before the bomb. Maybe he didn't need to.

"We successfully took our reactor in Chicago to criticality in December of 1942."

Eisenhower studied Karl intently. "And we took another year and a half to get a bomb."

"Right. The reactor was useful, sure. Taught us a lot. But getting the right kind of uranium, called U-235, separated out . . . That took time. And a lot of people, building centrifuges—"

"So the Germans aren't close to a bomb at all. Great! Groves—" Eisenhower turned, lifting his eyebrows. Karl saw he had completely missed recognizing Leslie Groves, somehow less visible here among all the brass, sitting halfway down the table, facing Eisenhower's side and so away from Karl. "Groves, looks like your worries were wrong. Good!" He turned to Karl. "This dust they're using is from that program, though?"

Groves said carefully, "It must be. They're throwing it away to stop us on the ground in France." He was in his usual bulging uniform, but now with what was called an Eisenhower jacket, deftly tailored to his body in olive drab, brass highly polished.

Eisenhower looked pensively around the silent room. "If we were in the jam they are, we might do the same."

"I don't think so," Karl said. He knew it would be smart to hold his tongue, but here was the only chance he would get. "We're already hearing the Germans say we're using terror against them—obliterating cities with one bomb. I don't think we'd use that dust as they do. It comes damned close to the Geneva Protocol's prohibition of gas warfare, doesn't it?"

Dead quiet. Eisenhower stared at him and then stood, replaced his chair, paced a bit. A good way to dominate a room, Karl thought, instead of just sitting. The general said, very slowly in his flat, Midwestern accent, "This is all a new kind of warfare. We haven't thought about it much. The bomb, the V-2s, the dust, those jets— The lawyers yak it up a lot, but we don't need them to tell us our business. Not now. Not when we've got men dying by the hundreds, the thousands, every damn day."

Through the men grouped around the table and in the wall seats an odd ripple ran, a discomfort without a voice, not a murmur but a slow rustling as bodies shifted uneasily in hard seats. They had gotten the drift without reading any documents.

Eisenhower studied the handwritten sheets in silence. Others at the table were reading copiesthem as well. After some whispered consultations, two aides left the room. Eisenhower looked at Moe again.

Eisenhower riveted Moe with a hard stare. "There are records here, in your summary, of German messages sent through to British intelligence over the last few years. I'm pretty sure they never made it. What more did you gather of what Canaris knew?"

Moe said, "He thought the British gave the German staff locations of Soviet bases and units in 1939. You see—"

As Moe explained further, Karl saw a British colonel nod. Eisenhower noticed that. "Plus," Moe continued, "Canaris said explicitly that his faction sent word through British agents in France, to Churchill."

Eisenhower raised his eyebrows. "I heard of this. Some funny kind of contact, Churchill was amused. Someone called it the Hail Mary pass."

Karl was still standing. He said, "Canaris met the English agent at the Convent of the Nuns of the Passion of Our Blessed Lord, 127 Rue de la Santé."

Eisenhower blinked, perhaps at the detail. "It's our policy to keep a united front. Churchill said so, in reply to that overture. That's getting harder to do."

An officer nearby asked, "Why, sir?"

"The French"—he nodded to a French officer at the end of the table— "are irritated at the dust pollution of their prime farmland, highways, some towns. Nobody knows how long that radioactive stuff will take to go away, not be harmful. That strikes a chord."

Eisenhower chewed at his lip. Among his aides, whispers flew. "Then there's this other matter," he said carefully. "The coordinates for this Lair. Tell us about that in detail, Berg."

Moe rendered a flawless account, ending with Heisenberg pressing the map location of the Wolf's Lair into Karl's hand.

Eisenhower's gaze swept to Karl. "Have you looked where that is on the map?"

Karl stood. "No. I had no maps."

Groves said quickly, "We can't be sure that's the exact hiding place, sir. This was a physicist, after all, called in by Hitler himself to report on this radioactive tonnage the Germans have. Heisenberg's an amateur hiker, no better than that. He probably got a glance at a navigation map, made a guess."

Eisenhower frowned. "So?"

Groves voice thickened to a growl. "We should *plaster* the area. I've got the next A-bomb damn near ready to go. Assembling. Two more days, maximum."

Karl could not stop himself from saying, "Heisenberg is a precise man. He gave the coordinates in detail." Immediately he thought, *Am I just standing up for my profession?*

Groves gave a stiff smile, but his face was red and his eyes narrowed to slits. "He got a Nobel Prize for analyzing uncertainty, right? He says there's no such thing as an exact measurement."

Karl kept his face blank. "That's quantum mechanics. It doesn't apply to bombing mechanics."

Eisenhower gave a quick, small smile but looked puzzled. He conferred with his aides in murmurs, looked up. "So, Groves, you think we should use our second bomb on that area? To be sure we get Hitler?"

"Damn right, sir."

"How long until we'll have a third?"

"Three months, maybe a week or two less. Same as last time. They're spinning those centrifuges at Oak Ridge hard as they can."

"I see."

Silence. Into it Groves ventured, "If we miss him again, there'll be hell to pay."

Eisenhower frowned, said nothing. Karl was standing uneasily, sensing that the tension in the room was at a tipping point. Groves was going to get his way. But . . .

He opened his mouth, licked dry lips, and said, "General Eisenhower, I think Heisenberg gave exact map positions because he knew them that precisely. He wants Hitler gone. And I might point out that it is conspicuously easy to take out the Lair with a conventional daylight bomb raid. Use those penetrating bombs we have, the ones I heard about a few months ago."

Groves barked, "Cohen, shut up! I'm sorry, General, this man is just an atomics guy—"

"Never mind that," Eisenhower said with a wave of his hand. "It's a good point. We've got many reports from follow-up teams. They say that the fallout from Berlin made people sick many hundreds of miles away. German radio is playing it up big, accusing us of violating the gas warfare provisions of the Geneva Protocol I hear about this from General Marshall, the president, even congressmen."

Groves's mouth twitched. "Politicians can't—"

"That Wolf's Lair is in East Prussia, legally an ally of ours. Its fallout could blow over onto the Soviets, and into the rest of eastern Europe." Eisenhower looked around at several nodding heads.

"This is *Hitler*, sir!" Groves stood up suddenly, voice booming. "We have a chance to end this war with one bomb. I say—"

"Sit down, General," Eisenhower said sternly. He had the look of a very old and wise cat contemplating a young and inexperienced mouse.

Silence. Eisenhower let it grow, studying the faces around the room. *He knows how to command a room by doing nothing,* Karl thought. He noticed he was still standing and sat.

"I have to meet with Churchill," Eisenhower said. "Be ready to convene again."

People rose and murmured, tension releasing in rising noise. Scraping chairs, worried grumbles. And something else he could not name.

Karl and Moe maneuvered to stay away from Groves. By chance Karl was near the rear door when Eisenhower passed by, flanked by staff, not noticing Karl at all, eyes troubled. The general muttered to an aide as he passed, "That Groves is as bad as Patton. Keep him away from me."

2.

September 24, 1944

Marthe's long letter was full of homey details, evoking memories that seemed so far away now.

> I felt lonely so invited the Ureys and Fermis over for dinner. They were full of questions about you and the work—so is the entire world since Berlin! I knew nothing useful, of course, and plied them with food! I made one of my favorite recipes, a wonderful chicken *en croute*—you remember? It's a five-star creation since it's hearty enough to fill up the men, fancy enough to impress the daylights out of the women, and can readily be prepared ahead of time—terrific for the hostess! Martine did her best as hostess too. Elisabeth looked at it all with big round eyes.
>
> Enrico said he has a job for you in the Fermi Lab (that's what the Ureys called it—big laugh from Enrico) when you get back. He wonders if you're still interested in his using the uranium reactor for electrical power, now that you've had a huge success with the bomb. A fine evening! I think perhaps Urey might have a job for you at Columbia, too.
>
> Our youngest is growing nicely and has not yet quite

learned to cry havoc. Elisabeth walks to catch up to her sister.

They miss you, Martine especially—where's Daddy, she cries.

So do I.

The girls had head colds, Marthe went on, which she, still new to English, struggled to find a word for, inventing "stuffedupedness" instead.

Karl sat back on his bunk and thought. The walls were so thin he could hear someone who reliably snored like a train and another who played a leitmotif of nasal mutter. Marthe's cuisine had always been fine, after some rookie meals in their first year of marriage, and he thought about the chicken *en croute*. A far cry indeed from the mess hall, or what he could find in most of London—greasy fish and chips or cardboard-like pub grub.

Marthe had added a postscript on the back of the last piece of onionskin paper, and enclosed some photos.

> Anton writes he is on an aircraft carrier in the Pacific, no more details (security). He says it is big enough to be a city and yet tilts in high seas. He wants to see action, "get in the game," he calls it.

Get in the game, indeed. But this wasn't like soccer—the one athletic event Anton had talked Karl into, with disastrous, humiliating results. After that, Karl had contented himself with taking Anton to a baseball game—where they had seen Moe Berg play. The world was connected in odd ways.

He studied the photos. One immediately made him embarrassed at his irritation only moments before, about his sleeping conditions.

Anton beamed forth from the center of it, hands clasped almost as if in restrained joy. Karl's face burned. These men were facing true danger right now and looked as if they were off on a fun trip, no thought of their future.

The next underlined the point.

On the back of this one, Marthe's delicate blue ink penmanship read, *He's wearing a helmet with his back to us, at the firing position of the big gun. This is a big ship, to use such guns!*

Karl judged, from the flat deck to the right, that this was an aircraft carrier.

405

The long, thin barrel pointed up must be antiaircraft. He recalled the futile bursts of antiaircraft below the bomber he'd flown in to Berlin. Here was Anton, manning antiaircraft on a ship, against Japanese attacks. *We're in the same line of business, really . . . killing the enemy.*

The enlisted's bunks

Naval gun

He had largely ignored the Pacific campaign, but did know that rumors were running that the next big battle was to liberate the Philippines. Another arm of the war reached north toward Japan, with the goal of getting within bomber range of the island. There, commentators thought the next targets were a place called Iwo Jima and, beyond that, Okinawa—the first of the Japanese home islands, a formidable bulwark with a heavily defended mountain. Pundits said the Japanese would fiercely defend both, but Okinawa was their homeland,

and for the invading navy and marines would be a huge maelstrom of suicide attacks in brutal conditions. He hoped Anton wasn't headed for any of these places. But the look on Anton's face told him that the men actually facing such catastrophes didn't seem deterred. They brimmed with confident joy.

He listened to snoring and bombers taking off in the dead of night and thought the long, slow thoughts that came up from his unconscious when he was tired yet somehow alert.

The world is full of odd people trying to get even. . . . Who had said that? Certainly this war was getting odder by the day. The events in France and Switzerland had altered him in ways he could not say. Everything before this war—and they were already starting to give it capitals when they spoke, the War—seemed now to have the rusty patina of ancient history. Even dinners with the Ureys and Fermis were memories wreathed in nostalgia for him, from a world without German corpses and veils of death dust. He was thinking of this when he finally fell asleep.

3.

September 25, 1944

Richard Feynman leaned back with a grin, feet on his desk, hands behind his neck, chair tilted at a jaunty thirty-degree angle. "Y'know, I feel the same way about Groves as Ike does."

Karl had just finished telling Feynman, Freeman Dyson, and Luis Alvarez about the meeting with Eisenhower. No one had told him not to, after all. Moe would have disapproved, but he wasn't here, in the physicists' office at the air base, just next to the building where the second A-bomb was nearly done.

"I wish Groves would go away and stop trying to run everything," Luis added. "We know how to do this without him looking over our shoulders."

Karl considered the exchange with Eisenhower, which he had not related in any detail, just some veiled hints. "He wants a hand in deciding how to use the bomb. Probably thinks he made it happen—sort of. But he's not really a combat officer. Army engineers aren't, unless they're at the front. So he frets and takes it out on you."

Freeman stirred his tea and said with soft deliberation, "I like my tea strong enough for the spoon to stand up in it. This war ration stuff is pitiful."

They looked at one another blankly, talk exhausted. Freeman said, "Let's get out, go for a walk, enjoy the weather." Karl got his point: Less chance of being overheard, too.

Alvarez nodded, and Feynman said, "Sure. I like long walks, especially when they are taken by people who annoy me. Like Groves. But without me along."

Getting into the fresh autumn air of England was a breath of life for Karl, after so many days in rooms. The British aircrews had spread out into the distant fields to eat lunch, far from the constant buzzing of taxiing bombers. Karl noticed a man lolling on a grassy bank eating a lunch, in a pose reminiscent of Michelangelo's Adam in the Sistine Chapel, but reaching for another sandwich rather than the hand of his Creator. Not, of course, that Karl believed in a Creator at all.

There were American fliers in among the rolling fields too, a change since Karl had been sent to France. He asked about it.

"Some ground crews came in yesterday," Freeman said, "specialists in this new bomber of yours—the B-29. I was sent out here as well, though I cannot fathom why. The order did not say."

Luis sat on a stump and unwrapped some indigestible-looking glop he had sneaked away from the mess hall. Karl shook his head when Freeman offered some melted chocolate. "I don't want to lose the memory of those pastries in Switzerland." Though the best were from the Germans, he thought guiltily. He was still processing that sudden, startling meeting. Thank God—the one he didn't believe in—he had then the sense to remain nearly silent. *Never pass by a chance to shut up.* Maybe he should now—secrets were secrets—but now he needed to talk.

He thought about Marthe's letter, the offer from Fermi, and maybe even a faculty position, from Urey's hint. He didn't want to take more academic work. He wanted to *do* things. Nuclear power reactors were a grand prospect. Yes—he wanted that, as soon as this horrible war was done. Not weapons. Never.

He turned to Freeman, who was conspicuously straying away from the guys in the A-bomb assembly group, eyeing the trees for birds. "Look, I found out some things—"

"Hey!" a soldier called, running out to them. "Groves has come in, wants to see you all."

Karl sighed. Once again, at the beck and call of big shots in uniform. Yellowing leaves of an early autumn muttered softly in an easy wind, and he wanted to stay outside. He was not made for war.

Trudging back to the base, where machines labored into the fragrant air,

he thought of the war and how a fancy-pants knowledge of nuclear physics had gotten him into it. Something ironic there, for sure. He knew now
that after seeing the bombers in their arc over the countryside, with all that
implied, he would not be able to think or feel the warm English certitudes:
slow, rhythmic cricket matches on the summer green, the clink of teacups at
polite garden parties in the vicarage, the sweet smell of grass after a fresh rain
on a July morning. Instead his world would be raw and strange now.

Groves said, "We've just won a battle."

"I take it that's a metaphor," Karl said guardedly.

"Moe and me"—Groves slapped Moe on the back, startling the big man—
"we held our own in a meeting about who goes after the Wolf's Lair. It's now
a joint Brit-American operation."

"Great," Karl said, though he didn't really see how this mattered.

"I need to go into a meeting right now with you guys." He nodded at Karl,
Freeman, and Feynman. "I want a show of force, bringing in the people who
found out where it is."

Freeman blinked doubtfully. "I did nothing at all—"

"You're to show I got Brits on my side of the argument too," Groves said
gruffly. His practiced glower focused on Freeman, who averted his eyes and
quite pointedly said nothing.

They marched—no other word for it—to three wooden buildings over
near the end of the landing strip. EXEC OFFICER a sign said, leading to an
ordinary war-issue room with wooden chairs and a long table, maps laid out
on it. Karl saw the map was of Poland, with a crosshair on a position that
had to be the Lair.

Various British officers stood oddly at attention with USAF men, and
Groves went through some military rituals Karl had seen and still didn't
understand. They reminded him of the stiff manners imposed on boys and
girls attending their first formal dance, girls in dresses like flowers, boys
in uncomfortable suits and ties for the first time, just as Karl had been—
nervous nods and invitations, swanky swing music, false anxious smiles, awkward missteps. . . .

But he had launched into memories, a symptom of the homesickness that beset him now. He snapped himself back into the moment.

Once seated, Groves said, "I *and* General Eisenhower want an American component to this assault."

A Royal Air Force officer whose breast pocket ID read ALDISS said mildly, "Understood. The prime minister has been on the line about you. I am forced to agree."

A meaningful pause, nothing said but glances around the table. Aldiss continued, "As deputy air marshal, I have assigned the Lancasters to the first run. They are more used to daylight raids. A morning hit."

Groves scowled. "We get the night?"

"No sir, you have later in the same day, using your B-29s."

"I think we should go in first—"

"I understand we will follow a two-shot strategy, as approved by our superiors." Aldiss raised an eyebrow.

Karl admired how Aldiss glided smoothly in with his approved accent, as if explaining arithmetic to a slow child. "Our Lancasters hit them hard. Give the Germans time to think the raid is over, have them come out. If Hitler is still alive, he would emerge and get away as fast as he can."

Groves frowned. "B-29s are high-altitude fliers, damn it. I like having them out of antiaircraft range."

Aldiss nodded, pointing to some air recon photos on the table. "But they carry heavy tonnage. And we will deal with the ack-ack first, as is standard. Hitler would escape most probably by air. Perhaps to reach his Bavarian redoubt, the Eagle's Nest. But we can pin him to his Wolf's Lair by making this nearby airfield"—he held up several close-ups—"a pincushion in our Lancaster squadron raid. No one can take off from it after we've put a hundred or two craters in it."

Groves consulted a USAF officer next to him. Karl had not even noticed that guy before. Things were moving faster than he could process. Not his game, no. "Granted," Groves said. "I want an American wing to go in on the second raid. Say, an hour after the first."

"Accepted. The PM made that clear. This would be a low-altitude run, necessarily. We will put spotter craft ahead of your formation to suggest where to pinpoint."

"I'd say so. Colonel Baxter"—turning to the USAF officer—"who do we have to command that squadron?"

Baxter looked unsettled but managed a steady tone. "In my judgment, we have several men who could lead that. They have experience going after close-in targets—trains, convoys, ships in canals or at harbor. They're training on B-29s right now."

Groves smiled slightly. Karl could see he was glad to be somewhat in control of the conversation. "Who are those?"

Baxter considered, said forthrightly, "There's Cogburn, who is as fine a target man as we have. He is scrupulous about not hitting civilians and will pull out if he has any doubt about the target being German military. A religious man about that too."

Groves drilled in. "How many missions?"

"Over twenty-five. I should think he is the best choice for you."

"Who else?"

"There's a Dobson fellow, not my favorite, but with a good hitting record. Twenty-something missions. We have fighters assess the damage after a fighter-bomber raid, and they say Dobson hits targets, sure—but also, everything nearby. Kinda sloppy. He seems to think that anything next to, say, a tank formation is likely to be infantry or support troops. In a fraction of a second, you sometimes have to make that call. I think he goes over the line on that, but he is accomplished."

Groves smiled. "Where do we find this Dobson?"

4.

September 26, 1944

The Lancasters took off in regular, teeth-rattling rumbles. Karl watched them beside Groves, who was nervous. From an anxious orderly the general took coffee by the fresh cup every few minutes in the foggy, predawn chill.

"Great airplanes," Groves said. "Not as good as our B-29s, but good."

Karl ventured, "I never thought you'd want to see me again, after that meeting with Eisenhower."

Groves turned to him and gave a rueful, high-eyebrow frown. "Gotta admit, I felt that way for a while. But then one of Ike's staff said to me that they liked how I let my people say their piece. You and Moe, they meant."

"We were just reporting—"

"That's the point. You guys *met* with Canaris. You got the real deal, stuff that's not in the documents—plus Moe's a genius at remembering details."

"A lot better than I am. Heisenberg's hard to convey—"

"Point is, Heisenberg was a lure. A stalking horse. Canaris at Abwehr must've gotten the scoop from the Gestapo goons, maybe with intercepts. So they knew the Gestapo smelled something, which was you. They let all that happen, you got in and out of Zurich—pretty damn good, that, after Moe killed those two thugs in the car. So I guess, then Abwehr came in at the last minute. Pretty sharp, knowing you'd go for the train, then back off, go for air. Made the Gestapo look like fools."

"We had no idea."

"That's the point. The bait never knows."

"All to get the word to Churchill."

"Yep! Moe's memory is so good, the Brit MI5—that's intelligence—was able to track down who blocked the signals Canaris sent. Churchill's guys sniffed around, found evidence of smothered messages, pointing to someone in British intelligence. Laid a trap, don't know the details. They found a guy named Kim Philby, a Cambridge guy no less. Soviet agent, turns out. He took some persuading. Might have gotten a bruise or two. These guys are softies. He gave up some others in MI5. Churchill said to work him over a little more, he'd crack like an egg. Philby did, pretty quick, too. So now they've got a whole viper's nest of them locked up. Call 'em the Cambridge Five."

All Karl could think to say was, "Wow." *A smidgen of information goes a long way. . . .*

Groves said, "Moe knows a lot too—a Princeton man and baseball player! He said to me after his debriefing that Napoléon believed one spy in the right place was worth twenty thousand men in the field."

Karl ventured, "We were lucky. I do think this attempt is the best. It's just conspicuously easier to take out the Lair with a conventional daylight bomb raid. Save the second bomb."

"Right. But this has to work, or else—well, I dunno. Hard to see what's the right target for the second." Groves bit his lip, thinking.

"The bomb's done been assembled, just yesterday. I saw Luis and Feynman paint a name on the side of it. *Here's Hopin'.*"

Groves chuckled and fetched a Hershey bar from his breast pocket. "Aren't we all?"

The Lancasters' roar was now routine, one heavily loaded bird lifting off behind another, laboring into the dawn air. The British were going after the Führer. Karl could see smiles and grim determination both, brimming in faces, in whole ranks of air ground crews gathered by the hundreds along the airstrips. Everybody knew this was different. Maybe more important than the Berlin raid, even.

Groves said with a twist of his mouth, "There they go. The next act is ours."

It was beyond dawn when the B-29s took off. The crews had a bangers-and-mash breakfast while the English had leftovers from last night, termed "bubble and squeak," which smelled like day-old chili. Again Groves stood with the covey of USAF and army officers, with Karl and Moe toward the back. The great silvery beasts took off like roaring, pregnant birds.

Karl asked Moe, "Think they'll get him?"

"Everybody's taking odds in betting pools. I put a hundred on us."

Karl blinked. A pool on death? He took a few breaths to process this. "Y'know, all this comes from a scrap of paper Heisenberg gave me. He didn't know anything about Hitler's schedule."

"Where's he going to go now? The Soviets are his biggest problem, coming into Poland. He's got us stalled in France, so a guy like that, he wants to be close to the action. Not stuck on a mountain peak in Bavaria. It's a good bet. Want to join?"

Karl felt a sudden elation, as if his body was lighter, the world brighter beneath the fresh sun. "I'll do a hundred, sure."

Everybody in the mess hall was grouped around radios. No word from the German radio stations. The day had waxed on, the Lancasters back first, looking battered from years of use. The raid had to use bombers rather than short-range fighters because the target was all the way over, deep into East Prussia. Not all made it back.

Karl watched the bomber command pilots and crews lining up after their return from the Wolf's Lair mission. The British called a squadron formation and sounded off during roll call. Some names went unanswered. Now the dead were the Not Present, voices stilled. The only witnesses they had, eventually, would be those who remembered their deeds, the yellowed newspaper reports, the fading echo of their funeral epitaphs. They were now the Absent, Forever.

Then the B-29s returned, sleek and glinting in the slanting autumn sunlight. They roared like lions on takeoff, a challenge to the sky itself. Miraculously, they all made it back. Apparently the German defenses were out of gasoline or ammo.

The Americans, always more noisy and boisterous, took over the mess hall. Karl worked his way to a table lined with airmen and spotted a lanky guy with DOBSON on his left breast. "Congratulations. Good run?"

Dobson gave a lopsided grin in a face that had a parabolic chin. "The best.

Only been flying those birds a few weeks, but they're beauties. Better navigation, handling, the works. We got in low, no Kraut flak, no fighters, either. I saw some trucks and staff cars, went after them. We swarmed around that place. The woods were blasted pretty good already. Went after anything that moved in among the trees."

The whole table listened to this, then clinked glasses. Karl realized that the water glasses were a suspicious tan color—they were toasting one another with beer. "Great," was all he could manage.

English fliers were chummy with the Americans, and Karl learned that "dog's bollocks" was a synonym for "awesome," and B-29s were "the bee's knees."

Suddenly a rumble of noise came from one of the groups around a radio. Cheers. Shouts.

A Royal Air Force officer sprang to his feet. "The Jerries say the Führer is dead—killed in action on the eastern front."

The cheering was bedlam for minutes. Karl struggled through the mob, nearly fell, and reached the Brit officer. "When?"

The man gave him a puzzled look, then understood. "Late morning. Looks like you Yanks got the bugger."

5.

September 26, 1944

Karl found that beer was a perfectly reasonable substitute for wine, after all. Though the headache was fearsomely worse.

He woke the next morning to a world without Hitler, ever again. That thought alone struck him. The Beast was gone.

Not that the war was over, no. Not until that afternoon, in an oddly mellow, flowing announcement from the BBC. In Oxbridge tones the formal Foreign Office notice was, "The German Provisional Government, headed by General Rommel, has announced a cease-fire on their western front. The Allied High Command immediately issued an order for a cease-fire of all troops, land and naval and air, on all European fronts. The Soviet Union has not spoken as yet."

"Churchill and Eisenhower move fast," Moe said.

Karl considered how the world had shifted. "Roosevelt, too."

The BBC announcement had been strangely calm. Yet it caused celebrations that made Karl and Moe and Freeman retreat to the fields beyond. There seemed an endless supply of apparently hoarded beer and whiskey. Speculations ran rife in the autumn air. Wars were the best rumor factories of all. There were suddenly plenty of what the US Army called "beer hall Bradleys" after Omar Bradley, said to be the most popular general of them all in this war. The loudmouths knew better. Unfortunately, so did many others, which did not bode well in a beer hall.

"The Germans don't want a peace, per se," Karl said. "Just a cease-fire,

Canaris said. For the new government, after Hitler, to form and unify and make a proposal to all sides of the Allies."

"How long?" Freeman mused.

"I think the German General Staff will move quickly to get some veil of civilian rule," Moe said. "We did them a big favor by eliminating most of the high Nazis in Berlin."

Freeman had field binoculars and was watching birds flit among the trees. Without taking his eyes from them, he said, "The Germans can switch their death dust to the Soviets, who're pouring toward Poland now on a few jammed roads."

Karl was amused. "So the dust will be in Soviet territory. . . ."

"Precisely so, I would expect," Freeman said mildly. "Now they can take all their super new weapons they've been using against us and throw them at the Soviets—the V-1s and V-2s, jets delivering dust, jets fighting off their bombers."

"Plus, we won't be bombing their factories or troops," Moe added. "And the Ploesti oil fields are still in German hands, so they'll have fuel."

Karl said, "We're sworn by treaty not to make a separate peace."

Moe raised an eyebrow. "In my debriefing I recalled your remark on the Convent of the Nuns of the Passion of Our Blessed Lord, at 127 Rue de la Santé. The MI5 used that location to find where the report to MI5 had gone, and then led to Philby. Churchill had undoubtedly heard of it—the biggest breach of British intelligence in memory."

"By the Soviets, no less," Freeman said as Karl absorbed this.

He doubted he could now recall that address, after all that had happened—but Moe did, and had. "So . . . the whole alliance falls apart. . . ."

"And the war ends, yes," Freeman said. "For us. A bargain, I would say." He took a drink.

An English officer came striding across the field quite deliberately. He stopped, saluted with a ramrod spine, and said, "Arthur Clarke. I gather you're the men who brought us those superbombs. I'd like to shake your hands."

Karl found him an agreeable fellow, a bit younger and brimming with ideas. He and Freeman were soon trading technical estimates of the German rockets that had been falling on London, killing dozens daily. The cease-fire was taking hold only slowly, as hard-line Nazi units fought with the regular German army units, and chaos prevailed.

Clarke said with a broad grin, "Yet this V-2 is the best thing we're getting out of this war."

"What? Why?" Karl asked.

"We can go to the moon in a rocket like that!"

Karl snorted. "Next thing, you'll tell us maybe we can use uranium to make a rocket go really fast."

"But of course! All right, that's *two* good things we're getting."

A cable envelope sat on his bunk when he managed to get back to his quarters. His heart thumped.

> WIRE FROM NAVY SAYS ANTON KILLED IN PHILIPPINES. SO SAD.
> MARTHE

Stunned, Karl peered around at the room, which now seemed Dickensian in its dinginess.

"Look, the European war's over," Karl said. "I'm no use here anymore. I want to go home."

General Groves gave him a sour shrug across the new desk in his new office, close to central London. "These things take time." He sat forward and laid the *Stars and Stripes* on his desk. Karl saw a big photo beneath the headline

JAP KAMIKAZE SINKS CARRIER *ST. LO* IN PHILIPPINES

Karl sat down heavily, feeling as if the wind was knocked out of him. "*St. Lo* . . ."

"Yeah, they named it after one of the spots where we had fierce fighting after the Normandy landing, since the carrier was being commissioned just then."

Karl made himself put the tide of emotion aside and focus. He stood.

"Okay, look—the Soviets aren't standing down, the Germans are pounding them from the air, using death dust, even—but that's got nothing to do with us." Karl hammered these words out, leaning over Groves's desk. He peered at the man with a ferocity he had never shown the Big General before.

USS ST. LO

Groves leaned back, hands behind his neck, thinking as he propped his feet on his large desk. On the wall now was a photo taken of the Berlin blast, the crimson blister rising from the ground amid total darkness, the few city lights invisible in the glare. The exposure was good enough to show small puckers and dull spots in the cherry-red dome. No doubt the physicists, particularly the ever-curious Feynman, were studying those now.

"Right. Y'know, Karl, I want a hand for us in the Pacific war."

"What target?"

Groves chuckled. "You're always thinking. I like that. You even get my jokes. Gonna miss my sense of humor if you ship Stateside?"

"Very much." *You have to lie sometimes.* . . . Groves was always telling underlings jokes he had heard, not realizing they were shopworn by the time they reached the brass.

"Y'know, the propaganda guys are way ahead of us—look."

Karl turned to see a new poster on a side wall.

"So we've got a bomb, Karl, with another in three months. Where can we use it to hammer the Japs? Make 'em stop?"

"I've heard of an island, Iwo Jima—"

"Not big enough. We have trouble reaching a Jap city, but with the B-29s, we could do it. Even Tokyo, maybe."

"How about a military target?"

"They've got army headquarters in some of their cities, like Hiroshima in the south, easier to reach. But this latest Philippines battle, where that carrier went down—their navy is never bunched up enough to get a lot of them. That *St. Lo* was ten miles from the nearest Jap battleship, giving them a pounding, when the kamikaze got 'em."

"Go for the homeland, then," Karl said, mentally reviewing the maps he had seen. Maybe something closer to the mid-Pacific? "Or . . . there's a big island, part of Imperial Japan, I think. Lots of army, I'd guess. Okinawa or some such name."

"I think something closer too. We'll see." Groves stood and offered a hand. "I want to thank you for what you've done, Karl. That was a brilliant piece of luck you and Moe brought off."

"An accident." *Sort of . . .*

"What's the saying? 'Fortune favors the prepared.' Well, you and all the other eggheads got us this bomb, and accident decided it was on our side. Thanks."

They shook in silence.

With a grin he could not suppress, Groves reached into a pile of paperwork on his desk and pulled out an envelope. "I got orders to the Pacific last night, by the way. I'm headed out. In the same packet came some other orders—for you. New York."

Karl let out a whoop that he was sure could be heard throughout the command staff building. "My . . . God."

"Thought you didn't believe in God." Groves was still grinning. Karl tore open the envelope, saw his departure time. One hour!

"I don't. Okay, maybe for this one time. Good-bye, General—and . . . think about Okinawa."

He stepped outside, and the waterfall of events struck him there. He wobbled over to a bench and sat.

Here, now, was where some scrap of faith would be . . . useful. He had been at a few Jewish mournings, sitting shivah. He knew that shivah meant "seven," signifying the seven days when mourners were supposed to sit low to the ground and say a Kaddish, a prayer. That was what an ancient uncle had called *Menschlichkeit*, what you did to be a man. Show solemn respect, display your emotion. All Karl had ever done, at occasional Old World family events, was echo a "Shabbat shalom" as he came and went. He usually replayed a Bach piece in his head, or else puzzled over some chemistry, while adults droned on.

Now he was without the comforts of belief, of any faint faith. Anton had yearned to get into the fight, and now it had gotten into him. Just at the moment when the Beast was blown, as Huck Finn would put it, into pure scatteration.

He felt something on his face, and his finger told him it was a tear. The watery view before him jostled with movement. Men whooping and running in both celebration and contest. Englishmen playing soccer on a bright green field in warm, buttery sunlight. Anton never to be among them. *The only game we played together . . .*

He sat and watched with acrid bile in his mouth and knew he would never be able to see that game in the same way again.

PART XIV

LOOKING
BACKWARD

We shape our tools and afterwards our tools shape us.
—Father John Culkin, SJ, on Marshall McLuhan

1.

September 20, 1963

The telephone jangled him up from a pleasant dream. Something about the war again, but soft and warm and . . . he could remember no more.

He sat up. Marthe was already in the bathroom, and the telephone's harsh clamor made him jerk it off the cradle. "Allo?"

"Dr. Cohen," a thick German accent said, "I am from the *Frankfurter Allgemeine Zeitung*, a newspaper in—"

"I know. I just woke up—"

"—and I have traveled here to perhaps interview you about your war experiences—"

"I have already said I won't do any more—"

"—now that today you are to be decorated for them in a ceremony of high—"

"It's for my nuclear power work!"

"Did you know that 'Who's Afraid of the Big Bad Wolf?' was Hitler's favorite song, Dr. Cohen?"

"Not Wagner?"

"No, the wolf song. Why, do you think?"

Karl blinked to clear his eyes and saw the steepled slate roofs of Paris shining in a golden sun. "Maybe he always saw himself as the wolf. His liking for his own Wolf's Lair in Poland then caused his death."

He knew this was a mistake, as soon as he said it.

"We Germans wish to hear more about your secret negotiations with the Abwehr, leading—"

Don't give them an opening, he reminded himself. The receiver rattled in its cradle. "Marthe!"

"Ummm . . . ," came from the bathroom, and her head appeared, her hand brushing her teeth. She put down the brush and said, "They will follow us everywhere today."

"We'll go out the back, then."

Before going down to breakfast, he arranged his notes on a quaint round coffee table with a leather center and a stout rim of oak, standing on carved oaken legs with large griffin feet. He had worked on a speech but still had only pieces. Maybe he would have to wing it, despite his habit in technical talks of meticulous detail, well-scrubbed.

He and Marthe worked their way through narrow corridors once meant for scurrying servants, now long vanished. Down they went to a daily breakfast buffet stocked with pastries, bread, fresh fruit, and lovely light croissants. Their three daughters were already digging into the Cayré Hotel's bounty, while he and Marthe each had a breakfast tray with the three Cs, coffee, chocolate, and croissant, *le complet.* The girls asked for hot cocoa in place of coffee, plus a *petit pain grillé* in decent French.

Beatrix was an blossoming fourteen now, their postwar child. Elisabeth a fully flowered twenty. Martine at twenty-three was now shacked up with some actor and had just arrived with a suitcase of dressy clothes. They exchanged cheery greetings and Karl thought how much easier this was, better than earlier trips, when the girls pinched, poked, and punched in the backseat of rented cars.

Now they had their newly bought, well-cushioned, and slope-snouted Citroën DS19. Paris was the end of a gyration that began in Rome, purred up to Germany for his nuclear reactor work in Karlsruhe, and now here. Early on a wise bellhop had intervened when Karl tried to cram the family in. This meant thirteen suitcases had to be jammed into the trunk. The bellhop had solved the geometric problem, and Karl had carefully drawn a 3-D diagram, so he could reconstitute the miracle later. While his girls were young, he was now fifty and needed to take notes.

Elisabeth leaped up with the vigor the young unconsciously enjoy and asked if he liked her dress, freshly bought for the occasion, a sophisticated two-piece silk knit. "*Ça, c'est jolie, n'est-ce pas?*"

"*Formidable!*" Karl sat and perked himself up with coffee. The bar and bistro within the hotel hosted breakfast too, stylish with modern furniture and a sleek all-wood bar, mounted with murmuring coffee and tea machines that lifted the burden of waiting on tables. Marthe's parents had termed the girls *jeunes filles bien élevées*, which he had rendered to Beatrix as "young girls well brought up." And indeed they were, thanks to Marthe far more than he.

Their chatter rang like birds in treetops, distant and eternally beautiful. If there was a meaning to existence, Karl felt, he was closest to it here. He recalled, as Marthe arranged their day of museums and mirth, the airplane that had delivered them to Rome in June.

On the flight over first he, then Marthe, had edged down the aisle to sit beside Elisabeth, each counseling her that if she wanted to marry her boyfriend from Guatemala or some other Central American swamp with too many vowels, most of them *a*, then it was perfectly all right with them. That the two parents each, without informing the other, took it as a delicate diplomatic task was soon a source of hilarity. Elisabeth responded with a laughing smile and "Nope, his daddy took his T-bird away," a reference to some pop song whose import Karl failed to grasp until Elisabeth mentioned the Beach Boys.

Marthe had reported back from her girl-girl talk that Elisabeth took quite calmly the immense fact that she was now venturing into the landscape where she could create another human being, a prospect that to Karl seemed more frightening than, say, getting a driver's license.

All this he felt as they finished breakfast, hustled into street garb, and turned left onto boulevard Raspail. The sisters still swam in the bottomless vortex of feminine hilarity, drawing fresh cause for mirth from every vagrant element that fell in. He realized that, striding along with the blooming girls and his wife, he was a *homme à femme*, a man who loved women, in all senses of the word. *And the world exists for young people.*

Elisabeth sidled alongside him as they neared the Louvre and said, "Father, you should write about your experiences in the war. Y'know, everyone has a book inside of them."

He grimaced. "Maybe, and inside is exactly where I think it should remain."

They passed a restaurant named Le Rivoli and memory came flooding back, from 1936. He and Marthe had finished dinner in exactly this spot, a good one-star Michelin restaurant. He had splurged on this third date, after two hiking outings with the International House gang. As he was paying, Marthe had asked over dessert, "Do you always wear your glasses?"

He had been distracted with the tip calculation in francs. "Yes, except in bed."

She quickly reached over and gently took off his glasses with one deft flick. Her game, expressed not in words but easily understood across the language barrier, was that he still had to walk to his tiny apartment, which he had been too embarrassed about to show her yet. He actually managed it fairly well, though there were few streetlights, and it was dim. It had been worth it.

With the girls in tow, he and Marthe dutifully visited with her ancient aunts, in their apartment high in the Marais. They sat on musty padded Empire furniture and whispered their life histories to him amid the dusty shelves of bric-a-brac of women living in past times, in a nest with no eggs. To them marriage and death were the only markers in life, like nineteenth-century novelists. They recalled the war as a series of privations and loud noises. Then they put on a new radio station that catered to pop music from America. Flat-accented voices came on with a song titled "I Would If I Could, But I Can't So I Won't" without getting into burdensome, hard-to-rhyme specifics. The aunts wanted explanations of the lyrics, and the girls shot them out with startling gusto. All this told Karl that the world he knew, the pre-Elvis, pre-pill, still-puritan America, was gone.

The girls found older art fussy, so they went to the modern art must-see, Galerie Avant-Scène. "Looks like an academy for secret policemen," Karl said, to which Marthe snickered and shot back, "More specifically, to see this in Paris, it is like a monstrous carbuncle on the face of a much-loved and elegant friend."

One of the main exhibits was "demonstration art," such as a glass of water on a glass shelf labeled *An Oak Tree*. Elisabeth asked, "Do the staff have to change the water from time to time because of the dust that collects on it? If so, is it then no longer the original work?"

Martine added, "Do the staff therefore have as much right to be called artists as the man who filled the glass and applied the label?"

Karl smiled. They had reared their daughters to question always, and so unlike many of the young, experimental modern art got no free pass with them. Elisabeth said wryly, "The whole point of experiments is that many fail. That's their point, really."

A large room devoted to "an internationally known junk sculptor" finally drove them out. For lunch they went back to Le Rivoli and had a fine bistro meal. After, he went to the *Hommes* room and was gratified to find it modern, freshly scented, with a gleaming, well-plumbed toilet. When he and Marthe had come here on that "date," which he preferred to call their courtship, it had been a filthy relic.

Back then the same space held what Parisians then termed a Turkish toilet, a tiled basin at one end, with markings for feet like parentheses. He had known those well throughout Europe in the 1930s, crowned by overhead tanks that once erupted into an impromptu shower on him. Now, instead of the bar of gray soap bolted to the wall, with a single dank towel hanging limply above a yellowing sink, there was a clean, modern porcelain set. Times had polished much, after the Big War. Parisian food was even better. And no *dame pipi* waited outside, expecting a tip.

Their leisurely stroll through Paris streets, in these easy last days of summer's obliging warmth, somehow made him recall his boyhood in Brooklyn, with its clanging trolley cars and bristling little factories, ripe cornfields and fragrant green trees beside wooden apartment houses, the autumn zest of leaf fires, the solemn quiet of fall's return, with jagged pumpkin smiles, like valentines now yellowed.

"I want to rest a bit before the festivities," Marthe said, and they duly underwent a random walk back to the Hotel Cayré. Among the bleats of taxis there came a passing mammoth roar—the SuperMach jet taking off, thundering batlike on its way supersonically to New York. Of course, there had to be stops to check out fashionable shop windows for the girls, who marveled at the soft autumn hues of new dresses, the slick slope of impossibly priced burnt-cherry shoes. Marthe cautioned them on the height of the high heels, the suppleness of certain leathers—expertise far from Karl's analytical realm. He inhaled the aroma of Paris, even liking the pigeons who waddled with their Chaplin-style walk, eyes beady for handouts.

As they entered the Cayré, Karl thought, *Wake, eat, walk, meet, talk, see, eat, walk, dine, sleep. So go the days of our grand tour. But now comes the crescendo to a sweet summer symphony.*

The girls peeled off to go back to the shops they liked, and Marthe took the tiny elevator to their room. Karl wanted to just sit with a relaxing cup of tea in the lounge, maybe look over his notes again, but as he entered, there was Moe Berg, lounging with his casual elegance, reading several newspapers.

"I thought I should pay my respects," Moe said, rising to shake hands. "To the camera-shy physicist."

"Ha! I'm a chemist in disguise, y'know. My God!" Karl clapped Moe on the back and hugged him in a burst of excitement. "You came all this way—?"

Moe smiled and returned the hug with one resembling being in an oversize overcoat. "Doing a bit of a job for State. Couldn't miss this."

"I haven't seen you since—"

"That dinner with your wife in October 1955. You had the veal." Moe signaled to the concierge with an arched eyebrow. "That bottle I mentioned?"

"It's a little early for me," Karl said. "I've got to give a speech—"

"It's for the other gentlemen."

Karl suddenly noticed two men at a far table. They were pretending to look out at the street scene, but he caught a too-casual glance by one of them—and felt a shock. "That's . . ."

"Canaris, yes."

"He's getting on." The lean man began to stand, moving slowly, the gray head watching his feet carefully.

"He's seventy-six. Survived by his wits after we saw him. Somehow managed to elude the Gestapo in Switzerland."

"The other guy, I recognize him from somewhere. . . ."

"That's Rommel."

Another shock. The men were formally dressed in old-fashioned double-breasted suits that accentuated their ramrod spines, shoulders firm in a military stance.

Rommel. Soldier turned chancellor, oddly prefiguring Eisenhower's later

Generals Karl Rudolf Von Rundstedt
and Johannes Erwin Eugen Rommel

arc to be president. The German surrender after the cease-fire on the western front had led quickly to the army taking over, with Rommel as head of state and von Rundstedt to head the army. Six years of war had made the generals the best-known figures in what was left of the German elite. Rommel now rose also from a leather chair, a bit more agile as the two came forward.

Karl got through the introductions by nodding and letting Moe carry the conversation. Canaris shook his hand with bony enthusiasm, his voice dry and thin. Rommel's English was rough. His craggy jaw jutted with the pride made famous after the war, when he stood for a Germany with minimal occupation by the victors. Especially, Karl recalled vaguely, Rommel had led and inspired the hard-bitten fight against the Soviets in Poland and Hungary, saving most of eastern Europe from occupation by the Red Army. Adroit use of the V-1s, V-2s, jet airplanes, and death dust, plus the divisions withdrawn from the west, had yielded a stalemate in the bitter, deeply cold winter of early 1945.

Rommel bowed and said formally, "I must admit, Dr. Cohen, that I conspired with our present Bundestag to be here. We wish to thank you and Mr. Berg for your help in ending the war. And also for bringing the nuclear power to us in *Deutschland*. We wish to negotiate with your General Electric."

This was obviously rehearsed. Moe and Karl simply accepted, nodding. Moe added, "Thus, State's business. I thought bringing you together would slay two birds with one deft stone."

"Which General Electric could feast upon," Karl said. *Of course, they needed today's ceremony as a cover story for why they're here.* "You would add your prestige, Herr General Rommel, with that of Herr Admiral Canaris, to a public campaign?"

Canaris said in his whispery way, "It is for the best, *nicht wahr?*"

Their wine arrived, so they sat and negotiated, with polite jockeying about how to bring more nuclear power to Germany, complete with late Marshall Plan loans. Talk rolled on in mixed German and English, with French tidbits as well. Karl let it flow, taking businesslike notes in his upper mind, letting the lower surf on the language alone. The Romance languages were rich in verbs, German in nouns—indeed, so in love with them that *Deutsch* capitalized them all, like facts looming over emotions—while English sat efficiently in between, useless articles like *der, die, das* shaved away.

German had a lumbering, bull-in-china-shop feel, yet their culture gave birth to essential words that told much of what lay within: *Schadenfreude, Angst, Weltschmerz*—joy at the misfortune of others, anguish, sorrow at the world— words revealing the yawning abyss in their souls? But then there was a fine word that sounded like what it meant, *Gemütlichkeit*.

Still, this culture had, in the summer of 1945, summoned the strength to suggest that they and the British collaborate in forming Israel, with Marshall Plan largesse. Rommel had done that, with Churchill buying in. Truman sent some Jewish military experts, and the Arabs folded.

Now a Jewish state sprawled from the Mediterranean to the Jordan River,

King Solomon's borders, with Palestine beyond to the east. Israel sported three nuclear reactors with matching desalination fountains, too, babbling brooks coursing through emerald farms bigger than its glinting, murmuring cities.

Karl registered that Canaris was presenting a book to him, and accepted with a murmur, reading its title: *Berichte aus der Parallelwelt.* "Reports from the parallel world?" The jacket showed a burning map of Germany. He put it gingerly on the table between them.

Canaris smiled, eyes animated, the transparent joy of a published author. "I have considered our fate, had we not met with you two gentlemen."

"An hour later," Moe said, "and we'd have escaped."

"Into a worse world," Rommel added with a grim scowl.

Canaris spat out quickly, "We could not bring in the others of our Junker culture—Halder, von Rundstedt, von Manstein, Guderian, von Kluge—if you did not take our message, and caught Schicklgruber in his cave."

Karl recalled that this had been Hitler's earlier name, from a father who was a bastard. Canaris had lifted his voice in shrill derision as he pronounced it.

Rommel leaned forward with a frown. "We did not expect so quick a response, since Churchill had rejected the 1943 Canaris overture"—a nod to the older man—"and yet the Allies ceased fire within days. *Wunderbar.*"

Moe stretched his legs, and eyes turned to him. "That's still a secret. An old one, though. I can say a bit, since I was sent on a mission to France—sorry, Karl, didn't tell you—to confirm the messages sent to MI5. A Soviet agent, Kim Philby, gave up the whole Soviet network that had been misleading Churchill in many ways. That was the last straw. The Soviets had betrayed the alliance, blocking vital information, even negotiations. They were determined to bull their way into Europe. Churchill saw that we could avoid a lot of deaths if you would stand down."

Canaris blinked. "You know this . . . how?"

Moe smiled, a slow, steady grin, remembering. "From our Office of Special Services. Quietly. We didn't want the Soviets to see we'd cracked their ring, and their codes."

"Which we got from you—and which let us tap into the Soviet communications. Ah, yes." Rommel grinned too. "I recall when we turned them back at Warsaw, at Budapest, and far from Prague. They were outraged! Tens of millions have not had to endure Soviet occupation."

Canaris tapped his book. "Ending the European war in January 1945 saved enormous numbers of soldiers on the eastern front. More millions who would have died in those Nazi death camps."

Karl and Moe glanced at each other, stayed silent. A gravitas hovered in the air, the background Paris sound seeming to fall away, the colors outside fading, in favor of the mists of memory.

Rommel said, "In 1939 we did not foresee the death trains, gas chambers, and crematoria. The National Socialists spoke of such, but we did not believe it would be, that people could . . ." His voice drained away and his face took on a gray, forlorn cast. "*Was muss sein, muss sein.*"

Karl knew this meant "What must be, must be" and saw these men, in their twilight, still struggling to make sense of their moment in the crucible of history, while ostensibly here to further nuclear development—nuclear, the new. But really paying tribute to their shared past, on the anvil of the war.

He said softly, "Hardship, war—extraordinary stresses lead us to do extraordinary things. Maybe that's what they're for."

Rommel nodded enthusiastically, eyes glinting, and Karl saw the fire that had led an army *Korps*. To be the first chancellor of the brand-new German Republic, yielding to Adenauer the same year Eisenhower became president—the greatest achievement by any German general, ever. "We have now lived nearly as long under the American nuclear umbrella, which keeps the major nations from war, as the gap between the world wars. The second one I call the Big War not just because of its size. It has given us an extraordinary thing—a fear so great of what happened then. To avoid repeating anything like that, we in the advanced world will not risk another big war."

Rommel gave a wan smile and sipped more wine. "So the horrors we fighters brought served to make the aftermath . . ."

"Better," Moe said. "Maybe better than we deserved."

More than once in his brush with real fighting troops in France, Karl had thought, *I must remember these men when I am safely in the future.* And now he was.

He felt in the silence that followed among the men a sense of something coming to completion within him. Unnoticed until now, he saw those Big War events through the precious wrong end of a mental telescope, sharp and toylike, as once he had seen the world of nuclear physics as grand and wonderful, with the telescope pointed the right way. Only now was the war finished, for him.

They talked awhile as Canaris described the parallel world he had imagined, one with Soviets ruling most of Europe, even China. H-bombs were common, and the arms race was to develop rockets to carry them. Europe was frozen into this locked, nose-to-nose future. Depressing.

"There is a word for such exercises we Germans do," Canaris said. "*Vergangenheitsbewältigung*—coming to terms with the past."

Karl rose. "I believe your culture will take a long while to do that. Now, I've got to prepare for the evening," he said, and left.

In the lobby a woman approached him with a broad smile and in a thick French accent said, "I made an appointment through your embassy, Dr. Cohen. I am to do a feature on your wartime experiences—"

"Nope."

"Means—no? But your embassy—"

"I don't work for them. I'm a nuclear power guy now."

"You don't want to disappoint the reporters from *Paris Match* and the like, do you?"

"I do."

"Maybe later, then?"

"Later. Much later."

After all, World War III might intervene, and he would be off the hook.

2.

Slender as a fish, Marthe flitted nude in the window's pale aquarium glow. His eternal femme fatale bride's tinkling laughter ended a short, eloquent lovemaking. They had learned to "squeeze in a squeeze" as she put it, and indeed it drained his building, vexing unease about the evening to come.

He let a trickle of contentment flow for just a moment more, from the reliable springs of their marriage, with its routine, its affection in long silences, its calming warmth: love's logistics. It seemed they had been married forever now. He was too young to feel old, a mere fifty, here to celebrate the War. People called it that now, as though there were no others. Nobody spoke much of the Great War, because there was a newer, bigger one, huge still in the world's mental rearview mirror, in many ways still here. People still spoke of the lesser wars since, but not much—and of the numbers of dead, called "tolls" as though they were payments to travel somewhere.

By the time he had on his tuxedo, Marthe was in her elegant silvery dress, dark hair elaborately done, her profile as cool as the head of a silver coin. He could stay in the background, cheerfully let her draw the eyes. His thin hair failed to conceal the sunburned skin of his domed head, a look he hoped implied cerebral energy, and no lasting interest. Maybe he should wear a hat?

This evening would be mostly about the war, not him. Scientists had limited appeal, even if their work had been decisive in the Big One. Years before, he'd given a talk at UC Berkeley on nuclear power when a dog somehow wandered across the stage behind him. The floppy-eared dog faced the audience and wagged its tail. The crowd clapped and shouted with greater enthusiasm than they did when he finished his speech.

In the hotel lobby stood the American Embassy's dutifully sent escort. He had a solid, square-shouldered voice from some rectangular Midwest state and eyed Moe Berg uneasily. The girls arrived and the family marched past the escort. They had decided to walk to the old France Academy of Sciences building rather than take the embassy's limousine, and Moe strode along as a shield between the family and traffic. Moe tucked a small book that Marthe recognized into his jacket pocket. "You are learning Arabic? I learned some when I was living in Lebanon."

Moe gave an elusive, sliding smile. "I gather it is the next theater of 'interest' in matters diplomatic." The quote marks came through clearly. He and Marthe exchanged some traditional greetings in Arabic, and Moe complimented her dress, using the traditional form, which first requests the husband's permission to even mention such a thing. This Marthe explained to a bewildered Karl as they passed through a throng of Chinese tourists. That the Chinese Republic was prosperous enough to export tourists was still a surprise to Karl, who recalled the ferocious fighting that had cast out the Communists there. In 1959 he had gone with Marthe to see the first Chinese nuclear reactor, built by General Electric outside Shanghai, and these tourists looked both happier and taller than the crowds he had seen then.

"What's up that you can talk about, Moe?" he asked to deflect conversation back into English.

Moe said, "Newspapers today detail the anti-Soviet riots in Latvia, Estonia, and eastern Poland. They're getting more ingenious at sabotaging the tanks. Sand is mysteriously showing up in the gasoline." His eyes twinkled. Karl knew that after the Wolf's Lair, Moe had done some fancy parachute work in the Balkans, at the very tag end of the European war, bringing Tito over to the Allied side just in time to block the Soviets there. That adventure had led to a full career in what was now the CIA, where Moe was some sort of director.

"Looking good," Moe allowed with a skeptical tilt of his head. "I am on such matters the agency's go-to goy. Though the Israelis are our principal source for hard data." He grinned. "Just the situation I like. Tension, apprehension, and dissension have begun."

At a traffic light Marthe's parents appeared, intersecting their route to the ceremony. Glad cries, with now-retired Colonel and Madame Malartre, he sporting a lush gray mustache that made him seem, in his striking old-style military uniform, a festooned gift from the nineteenth century. The still-sturdy couple now lived in Paris, and they greeted Moe with happy yelps. The colonel's broad white smile split the weathered face below eyes in sockets as wrinkled as walnuts. Karl heard Moe inquire into the fate of the German soldier they had captured, and the colonel twisted his mouth with sly disdain, saying, "Best not to dig up the past." Karl took this to mean the man had met a subterranean fate. He did not mention that for him, in the months after that, every dropped spoon or slammed door sounded like the German's shot.

Their company was now a gabby knot, moving slowly along a boulevard beneath clouds that leaned forward as if in a hurry, losing shreds of themselves to their haste. No need for humans to echo them; the reception came first. He wanted to simply take in the warm Paris ambience.

Change sprouted everywhere. Since his return in 1944, the America he knew had become one with commercialism as an outright ideology, plus an implausibly booming economy. Too many people were busy spending money they hadn't earned to buy things they didn't really want, to impress people they didn't like, Karl thought.

Music had charged off in new directions, so his daughters knew names like Buddy Holly, telling him excitedly that Holly currently had *two* great songs in the Top Ten, whatever that meant. Eastern Europe was partly small, eccentric countries and the rest gray, dull Commieland. His few visits there he recalled for the grim, gray scowls of the state chauffeurs in their clunky Zils and the cardboard food. Maybe consumerism wasn't so bad, in comparison.

The family had moved to California in the 1950s, where Karl managed the General Electric nuclear power plants in the west. He liked the mild climate, the Sierras making it something like Colorado with a seashore. It took him several years to overcome the natural though secret belief of true New Yorkers, that people living somewhere else had to be, in some sense, kidding. Now Americans, with their homes of untrammeled scale and long, lush lawns, were spilling out into the world, bringing nuclear power into the cramped landscapes of Europe, China, even Japan—who, despite the two warheads used on Okinawa and Hiroshima, embraced nuclear as an answer to the high oil prices the Arab cartel had enforced.

As he enjoyed Paris, he let his mind wander through the tributaries that had led to this parade of family and friends. Through all the nineteen years since the war, the larger world balanced the little known about his war work, a strength of sorts, by taking away a scientist's chief asset, his privacy and time to do more research. In a personal world sliced in thin sheets now, he contented himself with running General Electric's nuclear program, keeping to the physics, ignoring the swamps of cost-effective parts-sourcing.

His airy rise had been propelled by Admiral Rickover's knowing what he had done. Rickover had brought him in on the submarine nuclear reactor program, now powering nearly a hundred vessels. That the subs were mostly launchpads for missiles bearing fission bombs was a sign of the times. Once the Bomb had been extraordinary, *gee whiz*. Now it was a tool in preserving the peace and avoiding the far worse H-bomb.

"I say, Karl, this is your day," said a familiar voice, and he turned in surprise to greet Freeman Dyson, on another line converging on the Académie building. It now had a neighboring building, one so ugly it might have been designed by the Soviets, who were looking for foreign projects to get some western currency for their starving economy. "I had to see this."

Freeman looked eternally young, hair the usual random walk, and Marthe hugged him. "I take it this is not an official GE meeting?" she asked. Indeed, Karl realized, Freeman and others likely to be here today were on the General Electric Reactor Safeguards Board, of which Karl was chairman. Maybe he could get the company to pick up their travel expenses, retroactively? The girls were all smiles to see Freeman, and to Karl's surprise, Freeman clapped him on the back.

He recalled that when he'd left the air base, Freeman had done the same, also surprisingly, and had said, "Also, of course, this violates the famous British reserve, with our introverted love of privacy, which leads us to wall and fence our front gardens, curtain our windows, and sit next to complete strangers on public transport and tell them all about our extended families." He had laughed then and he did so now, too.

"Glad to see this, Karl. You're much whispered about. My principal claim in Princeton is that I worked with you."

"Not just a claim, Freeman—you did the data mining."

"Ah, I see your point. I did assist on the Okinawa drop, as the British representative. Quite simple, after we'd seen the Berlin effects. Another ground-pounder drop near the top of that mountain, killed the army inside, without too many of the villagers on the mountain's other side. Precision, rather."

Plus Hiroshima a few weeks later, Karl thought, *and so the war ended in crimson blisters.*

Their crowd grew. Karl saw parading at the head of a column of tourists a Bavarian girl in the traditional garb of apron and knee-length white socks. The Germans were anxiously amiable, voices ringing high in the sweet warm air. If they had been dogs, their tails would have constantly wagged. The swirl and charm of these streets still caught at his heart. *As good as it gets*, a phrase he had heard somewhere, rang in him. Yet he knew that beyond these blithe provinces the world called the West, the world's pain played out in the presence of God's unimpeachable policy of No Comment. *The silence of these skies . . .* , he thought, and wondered if maybe he needed a glass of something delicious and reassuring. Red, yes. Maybe a Burgundy.

The eighteenth-century facade of the Académie had a modern side addition, a rhomboid of the new steel-glass-cage fashion, apparently some sort of John D. Benefactor Memorial Bowl.

A shouting throng outside had the now-obligatory younger people in their thuggish denims, bristling beards, sandals, necks free of ties and even collars and, he suspected, a washcloth. The *avant* were here, best to be on *garde.*

A placard in red said NO MORE BOMBS and another, DISARM, with, illogically, a hammer and sickle. The knotted faces didn't seem to register who the Cohen mob might be, but Moe was hard to miss. A Frenchwoman in a beret challenged him, grabbing his arm. "You! *Americain!* You afraid of the Soviet truth?"

"If you don't like my peaches, don't shake my tree." Moe gave her a look that made her hand drop away.

As they pressed through the howling crowd, someone gave Moe a shove, apparently trying to get toward Karl. Moe turned the shove into a sprawl, headfirst, and the man lay still. "Still just apes beneath the velvet," Moe murmured, and ushered them forward. The angry shouts and sweaty bustle faded behind them. Karl recalled his moments with Moe and Heisenberg and thought, *Maybe this explains Berg's mysterious aura. He keeps prying eyes away, so they can't define his position and thus change his own momentum.*

Within, the reception had a receiving line for those to be honored. The leading figure was the French president, a man with hair as thin as Karl's, plus a gap-toothed grin like a pumpkin's riding below berry-bright eyes. Marthe's soft French deftly shoehorned them all through the receiving line of academy toffs. With his amateur French, he made his way through these Continental intellectuals, knowing that his crisp, short sentences would imply a lack of a certain sliding subtlety, of the qualities they liked: ironic, conflicted, without the steady footing that science could give. The men could arch a skeptical eyebrow the size of a rat.

But no matter; the Académie would today confer honor on a smattering of those who'd brought about the A-bomb's ending of the war, establishing something of a new tradition. In 1945 the Physics Nobel had gone to Hahn, Strassmann, and Lise Meitner, for discovering fission. Then the 1956 Peace Prize went to Eisenhower and Khrushchev for agreeing not to build the hydrogen bomb. That agreement was now also called the Szilard Treaty. Today the H-bomb was a threshold no one dared cross without exciting hostile moves by all other powers. That wall had been building since Eisenhower's Man of War, Man of Peace campaign in 1952.

Such views had accelerated after the grave gray giants of the world, such as Bertrand Russell and even Einstein himself, had pronounced profoundly in the mid-1950s that hydrogen-bomb war between the USA and USSR was inevitable unless some higher body held all such weapons. Russell had even predicted that the death of civilization, under a myriad of the H-bomb's crimson blisters, was inevitable and would happen before 1960.

An official host escorted them forward through a side entrance. The man was dressed rather like a butler and moved like a dancer in a Hollywood movie of the 1950s, in tie, creamy tails, and wing collar, all with matching toothy smile. He led Karl and Marthe, with his family all around, into a large, bowl-like room for the reception. Plenty of press people moved through the crowd, looking for prey.

The noise clasped them. A man presented to him with European formality a copy of *The Theory of Isotope Separation as Applied to the Large Scale Production of U235*, the McGraw first edition. Not exactly a title to see on drugstore racks and in airports, but Karl signed happily—perhaps the tenth time he had ever done so.

He caught sight of Leo Szilard, who was chatting happily with a crowd of press around him. *Good, they'll ignore me*, Karl thought. But Szilard caught sight of him and embraced Karl in the French manner, with flashbulbs popping.

Szilard had moved up in the world and sported today a dark blue blazer with a silk handkerchief tumbling from the breast pocket like a paisley orchid. "We are different ends of the spectrum," Szilard said. "He had his own way of ending the war." This got a puzzled laugh and more questions in French, which Szilard fielded, luckily.

"How do you feel about the continuing trade bans on the Soviets?" a reporter asked.

"It has been—what? Seven years now!" Szilard's broad smile gleamed; were those false teeth? "And we have done so much damage to the Soviet economy, they have learned what collective economic power can do. So keep it up."

"Do you trust them?" a *Los Angeles Times* reporter shot back. "They handed over their hydrogen warheads to be dismantled, but just one could—"

"Yes, yes, we, the British, French—all have fission warheads. We could do great damage to any Soviet attempt, if they used just a single hydrogen fusion warhead. So, no, not a true threat."

The *L.A. Times* man turned to Karl. "Did you support the Szilard Treaty? The USA has not built an H-bomb. Does that make us weaker?"

Karl kept his voice level, dispassionate. "No, stronger. We don't have to spend money on weapons we can't use."

"But we say we won't use fission, that is, A-bombs—"

"They're limited in yield, so a lot less scary than H-bombs—which can be a thousand times more powerful." Karl found himself slipping into the vice

Marthe had long warned him about, Lecture Mode. But the damned man had *asked*—so: "Next is to limit A-bomb numbers."

He had rehearsed that and stopped short of saying what the max A-bomb yield was, a heavily classified number. Instead he stepped back to let Szilard hold forth on the new nuclear rocket programs. It had taken him years to learn that trick, and Szilard loved the spotlight anyway, his smile creasing his cheeks, in danger of turning into a smirk.

Freeman murmured at his elbow, "Let him go. I'm working on an even bigger nuclear rocket, called Orion. We might take a cruise out to Saturn on it by the 1980s or so."

Karl blinked at this, said nothing. The future was coming at them like a freight train. Szilard had eventually gotten his limits on nuclear weapons use, all right, so there would be no world with hydrogen fusion threatening civilization. A-bombs were menace enough, the world had realized.

A *Paris Match* reporter interjected, "Do you feel the Einstein-Russell proclamation makes sense? To let only the United Nations hold all A-bombs?"

The question came to both of them, but Karl stepped forward, for once. "No, bad idea. The UN won't agree on when to act, and with A-bombs, you'd better be fast. And who's to stop the UN from using them against, say, us?"

A French reporter said, "We feel the same, but what do you—"

"I hope we can keep conflicts regional, like our quick blocking of the Soviets in Mongolia." Karl was learning to turn the question the way he wanted it. "Chinese Republic troops did that job, with just our airpower as backup. We've got the Soviets bottled up, and now they won't have H-bombs to shake at us."

Karl stepped back quickly. Shouts followed him, so drawing on his command of the French language, he said nothing.

He hadn't said anything that substantial in years in public—the real discussion, as always, was in private, secret meetings. But sometimes he couldn't resist. And anyway, further agreement might come from the meeting of Nixon and Khrushchev, here in Paris next month.

Szilard whispered to him, "They really want you to tell your war stories."

"Not gonna."

Joy sprang in Szilard's face. He turned with a broad smile to the press. All this time, and even with his fame, Szilard envied Karl; a minor scientist, after all, who had stumbled into chance roles—the Berlin bombing, Heisenberg, Canaris—events still only partially known to the public. *Sour grapes, the champagne of the intelligentsia.* Karl turned away and put it out of his mind.

"Karl!" And here was the general.

Groves had an arrest-photograph air about him—looking like someone who, with as much dignity as possible, had smoothed his hair and straightened his collar after knocking someone in the head. "Those Frenchies out there thought they could gang up on me. Ha!"

His rumbling, weathered voice now sounded like a grinding mixture of gravel and goo. Karl gave him a quizzical smile. "They're still railing on against the bombings?"

"Yeah, you'd think they'd shake my hand about Berlin. Or better"—he shook Karl's energetically—"yours."

Karl went through the reintroductions of Marthe and the girls, thinking that others, never to be here, had died before they got their deserved honors. Fermi, Oppenheimer, many who had worked on the centrifuges and reactors. He missed Fermi especially. A regrettable thing about death was the ceasing of a personal brand of magic, never to be regained.

"Damn good you're getting this," Groves said. Karl nodded, bad at taking compliments. "You should be on this government judges panel I'm on, giving out prizes for innovation."

Karl admitted, "I always duck that stuff."

"Me too, but Eisenhower made me." Groves scowled. He wore a sleek suit, now that he was in industry, but retained the brusque manner. "So who accepts? Midgets. So who do they choose for the prize? Another midget."

Karl suddenly felt an impulse and said, "Did you have any idea back then how this, the bomb and all, would work out?"

Groves shrugged. "Who could? Think—an ordinary Joe in 1900 might've predicted the rise of the automobile, say. Some smart guy could've seen the interstate highway coming, sure. A good scientist could've predicted the traffic jam. Only a genius could think of backseat sex at the drive-in movie while watching *King Kong*." Karl laughed.

He helped his family steer through the throng. Most here had the casual, lofty ease of those spending someone else's money. This was just another state ceremony. The air of business-as-always struck him still. His postwar experiences of Germany and Japan had differed from his visits to Britain and France. Germany and Japan had to start from scratch, thanks to the bombing's obliterations, but they had not suffered the long, horrible battles over their own lands. So they could grow faster than Britain and France after the war. Ironically, the Allies had won, so they had to labor on, encumbered by prewar institutions—and economic sclerosis. So now too, the eastern Europeans were outdistancing the former Allies, especially the senile Stalinist-style Soviets.

"Ah, monsieur," said another fellow in a set of formal tails. *"Apéritif? Monsieur, madame, mademoiselles?"*

The girls went first, Elisabeth with a Sancerre, Martine with cognac, and oddly, Beatrix eyes wide at the crowd, taking a Coke. He would have to teach her about alcohol, yes, in time. Marthe and he asked for a Bordeaux. He swirled his in its glass, reflecting on the equations that described its elliptical gyrations, and sipped. *To steady the nerves,* he thought, a phrase that seemed somehow British—so he clinked glasses with Freeman.

"The ceremony, it begins." A formal man beckoned, brisk and bossy.

"Not without us," Karl said. He nearly laughed as the man's mouth shrank like a sea anemone poked with a stick, and he slunk away. Seats in an auditorium, calls to order, hub and bub. The press hovered. Karl could feel the cameras licking up his image, his words, and flinging them at light speed around the gaping world, which would scratch its head and go on. He stopped sipping the wine; more of the glaze of alcohol would make him see the slow, stagy proceedings as if beyond a glass wall.

A host proclaimed the majesty of the moment with a flutelike flavoring in his speech, which only French could do. Yet he had careful, opaque gray eyes, perhaps wondering if there would be a political demonstration in the crammed bowl of hushed faces.

There was another American here, a woman novelist he had never heard of. She seemed to be receiving this prize because she had not published anything since the Truman administration and so had achieved the most meaningful silence. Some French seemed to prefer their Americans that way, especially Sartre, whom he saw in the distance standing and smoking, ignoring the ceremony, and arguing with a woman in black who cocked an eye at the line of Cohens in the front row as if they were vagrants out of place. Jews, yes, right up front.

In French so swift he could barely follow, the host said the American writer lady had brought forth like a dutiful waiter the rich tureen of thick soup, made from the tortoise upon whose back the universe rested, in legend. Karl frowned. The novelist herself appeared from a nearby seat, hunched and gray. Her face had been tugged into deep crevasses by the drawstrings of some older sorrows. Writing seemed like rugged work to Karl. Maybe easier than fission? Her sad eyes, the narrow, thin-lipped smile, seemed to say so.

Her voice was whispery and left no impression on him. More flowery French talk poured forth, gone the instant he heard it. Then he heard his name, and applause rose like a flutter of loud birds. He took the stage, stomach tightening.

He instantly recalled a similar feeling. He had been standing in a line of shivering wet children, inching up a ladder to the top of the great water slide at Coney Island—a shaky iron platform a vast height above turquoise depths that continued to churn after swallowing their last victim, a slim yellow-haired girl. The child behind him nudged the backs of his legs and he staggered forward slightly, off balance, while all Karl had wanted was to think about it a bit—and then he was off, head down, into the fray of frothy life.

So he went—striding forward to the podium, notes forgotten in his jacket pocket, into the wave of solid applause. Words echoed in the big bowl and he could not fasten on them, remember them for later. The host presented the sash, the square tribute award. Words flitted by him.

"—his tireless labors in the dark days of the early war—"

The official, formal award was written in rolling, flourished language on a framed document with a sateen finish and counterstamped embossing. The Order of the Légion d'Honneur was the highest decoration in France, with a Republican cross and a sash they made a fussy show of fitting on him.

He looked out at the expectant crowd. Europe had, until that greatest of wars, the ability to shrug away its history and remain whole in its angers and agonies, consigning them to flags and monuments, like flecks of pyrite weeping rusty tears down the face of a granite escarpment. But this occasion was different. The Big War, as some called it—though not him—could not be weathered away. The future would have to be different.

Légion d'Honneur

He had to make his speech now. He stepped forward, taking in the bowl of faces. Here was a heaven of sorts, more compact and less tragic than Moe Berg's Yankee Stadium, stretching for some eternity, defined by baubles and crimson cloth.

He began. "Peace . . . doesn't usually come from being peaceable." A worrying murmur rolled up from the faces. "The only future that can justify a Big War is one with a Big Peace. If that takes the raw fear of fission weapons, so be it. That tens of millions died means that more millions or billions should live better, now, from the same science that now makes electrical power. That lights our future, so people of all nations can see before them expanding horizons."

Silence. Maybe they were thinking it over. He wanted to speak to them of those war years, a landscape in a turbulent time, a timescape dangerous and now curiously haloed by triumph, its spectrum shifted through the years into a rainbow land it never was. They were all now living in a *Berichte aus der Parallelwelt*, a better world than perhaps they deserved.

He wanted to tell them something of that. "Remember, in an astonishingly short while, this will be a long time ago. We hear that struggle as World War Two. I think it should be World War Through. No large scale conventional war can occur again, because it can be trumped by the bomb, or the 'death dust.' World War is Through."

He gave them a little smile. Should that be his concluding line?

Suddenly out there in the bowl a face seemed to suddenly clear, to stand out from the crowd.

He was in the fifth row, and when he turned aside, as if listening intently, there was his look: something about the chin lifted up, expectant, a flinty certainty in the eyes, a tilt of his head in a hopeful slant . . . Anton.

Karl blinked and felt the tears running down his face, coming without warning, then his throat tightening as he tried to murmur, and failed. The man smiled and he saw it was not Anton, of course not, after nineteen years. The unknown young man's jut of chin called forth something that was still in this world, something elemental, a forward thrust undiminished by even death, that dwelled in the secret hearts of all now.

Biographies are but the clothes and buttons of the man.
—Mark Twain

In order to know the truth, it is necessary to imagine a thousand falsehoods.
—H. G. Wells to Oscar Wilde

History is not merely what happened. It is what happened in the context of what might have happened.
—Hugh Trevor-Roper, historian

I had the mistaken idea, based on what happened in World War I, that we would stay out of the war, and it is very unfortunate that I felt like that. If I had been more convinced, as Wigner and Szilard were, that we were going to get into the war, I would have pushed harder to begin making the bomb. I figured out that roughly half a million to a million people were being killed a month in the later stages of the war. Every month by which we could have shortened the war would have made a difference of a half million to a million lives, including the life of my own brother. If someone had pushed the project harder at the beginning, what a difference it would have made in the saving of lives.
—John Wheeler

AFTERWORD

Alternate history provides a way to think about the fragility of our past. Its fictional devices let us see what might later seem inevitable as the outcome of many unpredictable forces, and chance too—and so to learn from it.

World War II is the source that keeps on giving, for it touches on many problems we have today, especially the role of all-powerful weapons like nuclear, biological, and chemical ones.

Nearly everyone portrayed in this novel existed. Four of the named characters are still alive: Freeman Dyson, and the Cohen sisters, Beatrix, Elisabeth, and Martine. The only completely fictional major figure, standing for many, is Anton. This is an alternative history novel from a specific premise: that the errors in judgment at the beginning years of the Manhattan Project might well have gone differently, yielding a very different World War II.

Such a mixed nuclear and tactical war could lie in our future, so this thought experiment has implications for our real world in the twenty-first century. The next war that sees nuclear weapons used will probably also involve substantial ground forces. Think of Pakistan-India and the deep angers of the Middle East, where resorting to nuclear weapons seems inevitable among demons posing as religious purists.

Characters

Nearly all the people depicted here existed. Many I knew.

The invented refugee Anton is a composite of European Jews helped into the USA in the war's early years.

Rabbi Kornbluth is a fictitious investor-leader who supplies the funds needed in the crucial early years of centrifuge development. (Kornbluth is the name of a major early writer of alternative history stories.) This act gives the momentum needed to find the new engineering methods that solve the basic stress and mechanics issues that, once overcome, make the method superior to the gaseous diffusion method. Indeed, we knew by the early 1960s that the centrifugal method would have proved even better than the calutron machines that did supply the uranium for the Hiroshima bomb. Karl Cohen led the review that proved this.

In this novel, Rudolf Peierls and John Dunning failed to make gaseous diffusion prevail; in reality they won. Gaseous diffusion cost more money than any other separation process in the Manhattan Project, but had no major effect on the war. The story's swerve away from real history most obviously appears here, where the choice of separation method yields the different path the plot then follows.

Any portrayal of real people in fiction is an interpretation. I knew personally many figures in this novel: Harold Urey, who greeted me at the grad students reception at UCSD in 1963; Karl Cohen, my father-in-law; Edward Teller, my mentor as his postdoc at Livermore Lab; Maria Goeppert Mayer, for whom I graded the homework and exams in her graduate nuclear physics course at UCSD; Freeman Dyson, whom I met at the UCSD daily coffee in 1963; Leo Szilard, another coffee break savant; Luis Alvarez, whom I invited to give a colloquium at the University of California, Irvine, because I wanted to meet such a fabulous character, and whose account of the Hiroshima bombing I used here; Richard Feynman, an idol to all of us; Sam Goudsmit, raconteur extraordinaire; Paul A. M. Dirac; John W. Campbell, editor of *Astounding*; Fred Reines of UC Irvine; Arthur C. Clarke, who was a radar officer in the war and then a science fiction writer, and many others. I have tried to echo their manner of speaking and thinking. Indeed, I included my own father, James Benford, who went into Normandy on the fifth day of the invasion and fought across France, Luxembourg, Germany, and Austria.

Further, every document quoted here is authentic, though some have dates altered to conform to the plot.

The central idea for this novel came from the protagonist I chose to follow through it, Karl Cohen, who wrote this about the war:

> When Japan attacked Pearl Harbor, the effect on the US atomic program (Manhattan Project) was a one-year delay. The US Army was preoccupied with the new war in the Pacific; they failed to appoint a person to head the Manhattan Project with enough power. In 1941 the people in charge favored Urey's centrifuge approach to producing the fuel. By 1942, General Groves was in and Urey was out of favor. Building the gaseous diffusion plant took longer than expected, and the result was a one-year delay in the project. The delay meant that the target changed away from Germany. The object of dropping an A-bomb over Germany was to prevent an invasion.
>
> How many more concentration camp victims would have survived if the war had ended one year earlier? For one, Anne Frank. Most CC victims succumbed eventually to the rugged conditions. . . . The difference between 1944 and 1945 as the end of the war is probably quite significant in terms of lives.

So in Karl's thoughts the bomb might have removed the need for a D-Day. In this and many other ways I have necessarily given interior thoughts no one knows, but his views I have echoed.

Edward Teller I worked with and came to know. In his autobiography, *Memoirs*, he takes up the issue of this novel:

What if we had the atomic bomb a year sooner? The easiest and least expensive method of separating isotopes, a method used throughout the world today, is based on a centrifuge procedure that Harold Urey proposed in 1940. General Groves chose the diffusion method instead. Karl Cohen, Urey's able assistant during that period, believes that Groves's decision delayed the atomic bomb by a year.

If Dr. Cohen is right, atomic bombs of the simple gun design might have become available in the summer of 1944 and, in that case, would surely have been used against the Nazis. Atomic bombs in 1944 might have meant that millions of Jews would not have died, and that Eastern Europe would have been spared more than four decades of Soviet domination.

Teller goes on to argue that "those same bombs would have done irreparable harm to central Europe." But of course, no one would have targeted anything but Germany. This novel shows how widely read the fear of the bomb was, even when it beckoned as a solution to the growing savagery of the war.

His words made me think, because in the last year of war, whole societies collapsed. A million died each month, the Soviet Union captured many countries into subjugation, and the devastation of the Axis powers took decades to repair.

Anne Applebaum's *Iron Curtain: The Crushing of Eastern Europe, 1944–1956* (2012) details this. As she sums up in an interview:

> "The Soviet Union literally occupied, packed up, and shipped out of Eastern Germany, out of much of Hungary and indeed much of Poland, which was not well known at the time, factories, train tracks, horses, and cattle. All kinds of material goods were taken out of those countries and sent to the Soviet Union. . . . One of the reasons for the postwar success of the Soviet Union was that it occupied and took

over the industrial production of these countries. It itself was very weak and there were even famines in the Soviet Union after the war."

So keeping the Soviets out of eastern Europe, as depicted here, would have saved millions and shifted the balance of economic power considerably as well. The resulting world might well have meant one with more compromise between the West and the weak Soviets, and a better history all round. So the end of this novel argues.

Alternative histories are ways of thinking. The entire history of nuclear weapons is interlaced with scientists considering the future, using science fiction as a prompt. H. G. Wells's "atomic bombs" and the Robert Heinlein and Cleve Cartmill stories in *Astounding Science Fiction* were indeed broadly discussed at Los Alamos (as told to me by Edward Teller). The investigation into the *Astounding* stories now seems odd, because the writers had no classified information at all, just good guesses. Still, this possibility of a leak was viewed as very important by the security agencies, including the FBI. As Robert Silverberg has wryly remarked, "Turning war secrets into second-rate SF stories might seem, to the dispassionate eye, a very odd way indeed of betraying one's country." (See *Asimov's Magazine Reflections*, "The Cleve Cartmill Affair, Parts One and Two," September 2003, October/November 2003.)

Moe Berg

In our world, Moe Berg turned down the Presidential Medal of Freedom for his many espionage feats during his lifetime, including spotting the Norwegian heavy water factory and much else. The Medal of Freedom was awarded to him again after his death, with his sister accepting on his behalf, and now appears in the Baseball Hall of Fame.

In early 1945 Berg did go to Switzerland, as depicted here a bit earlier, to kill Heisenberg if necessary. Sitting in the front row of Heisenberg's seminar, he determined that the Germans were nowhere near their goal, so he complimented Heisenberg on his speech about field theory and walked him back to his hotel. Moe Berg's report was distributed to Britain's prime minister,

Winston Churchill, President Franklin D. Roosevelt, and key figures in the team developing the atomic bomb. Roosevelt responded: "Give my regards to the catcher."

Werner Heisenberg

The verdict of history is that Heisenberg, as opposed to people like Fermi, was simply not especially competent at engineering physics. The theory that he blocked the Nazis from acquiring an atomic bomb has lost credibility.

As depicted here, he could have had a radical change in attitude if Berlin had been A-bombed. His men had gathered over 120 tons of uranium from Czech mines. Sam Goudsmit's Alsos team snatched this up from what was to be Soviet territory in southern Germany at the very end of the war. This large stash could have been used for "death dust" warfare. Indeed, some Germans thought it should have been.

In our world the Allies held the major German physicists at Farm Hall in England after their capture. Intelligence agents eavesdropped on them and find out their true beliefs. A consistent theme in the Farm Hall transcripts and in Alsos investigations is that the Germans seem to have honestly thought that their work on the "uranium problem" was well beyond what anyone else might have been doing. They thought the Allies would be desperate to "buy" their reactor research in the postwar era. Apparently they were not moved to check to see whether this arrogance was founded, and the depression and desperation one hears them going through after Hiroshima and Nagasaki reveals their sudden irrelevance. As Otto Hahn chided them right after they learned of Hiroshima: "If the Americans have a uranium bomb, then you're all second-raters."

The night after Hiroshima, the German scientists in captivity at Farm Hall were astonished that their enemies had made a bomb. As two physicists put it:

> *Carl Friedrich von Weizsäcker:* If we had started this business soon enough we could have got somewhere. If they were able to complete it in the summer of 1945, we might have had the luck to complete it in the winter of 1944–45.

Karl Wirtz: The result would have been that we would have obliterated London but would still not have conquered the world, and then they would have dropped them on us.

Then they tried to imagine how they could've gotten enough uranium to build their bomb:

Weizsäcker: We would have had to equip long distance aircraft with uranium engines to carry out airborne landings in the Congo or Northwest Canada. We would have had to have held these areas by military force and produce the stuff from mines. That would have been impossible.

So they were not without imagination, at least. But it was hard for them to imagine that the Americans had bested them by a long margin. Then:

Heisenberg: Yes. (Pause) About a year ago I heard from … the Foreign Office that the Americans had threatened to drop a uranium bomb on Dresden if we didn't surrender soon. At that time I was asked whether I thought it was possible, and, with complete conviction, I replied: "No."
Wirtz: I think it characteristic that the Germans made the discovery and didn't use it, whereas the Americans have used it. I must say I didn't think the Americans would dare to use it.
A bit later *Hahn* said: Are you upset because we did not make the uranium bomb? I thank God on my bended knees that we did not make a uranium bomb. Or are you depressed because the Americans could do it better than we could?
Walther Gerlach: Yes.

Considerable irony abounds here. The "Americans" who made the bomb included refugees Enrico Fermi, Eugene Wigner, Hans Bethe, Rudolf Peierls, Niels Bohr, and Edward Teller, along with a small army of lesser-known refugees from Hitler's Europe. This fact never seemed to occur to any of the German physicists at Farm Hall.

In 1930 the Germans were the leading scientific nation, and knew it. The Allies agreed. Their fear of a German bomb led to American invention of the bomb. Such forces still work today.

Samuel Goudsmit

He was selected as the scientific leader of the Alsos mission in part because he did not know anything about our programs. He often said that if he had been captured by the Germans, he could not have told them anything. Since he did not know about our plutonium program, he did not look for the German program and made the erroneous assertion that there was none.

In fact, it took the resources of three countries to produce the bomb: the United States, Great Britain, and Canada. But there was more to it than that. In some sense it took some of the most valuable scientific talent of all Europe to do it. Consider this partial list: the Hungarians John von Neumann, Eugene Wigner, and Edward Teller; the Germans Hans Bethe and Rudolf Peierls; the Poles Stanislaw Ulam and Joseph Rotblat; the Austrians Victor Weisskopf and Otto Frisch; the Italians Enrico Fermi and Emilio Segrè; Felix Bloch from Switzerland; and, from Denmark, the Bohrs, Niels and his son Aage.

This talent, the B-29 heavy bomber program that could deliver the bombs, plus Manhattan Project efforts—all together cost more than fifty billion in today's dollars.

Wilhelm Canaris

This admiral heading the Abwehr was executed in the last days of the war by Hitler's SS. He stated at his hanging, "I die for my fatherland. I have a clear conscience. I only did my duty to my country when I tried to oppose the criminal folly of Hitler."

Indeed, he was the great protector of the German opposition and led several assassination plots against Hitler, starting in 1943. He persuaded Hitler not to invade Switzerland and make it part of the Reich's Greater Europe. Switzerland became a major site for his operations for German army intelligence. Canaris approached William Donovan of the Office of Special Services, the American intelligence operation, with an offer for a truce on Germany's western fronts. Roosevelt turned this down in 1943, saying he wouldn't negotiate with "these East German Junkers." Canaris also reached Churchill, in the manner I've described in 1943, who rejected such a deal.

Leo Szilard and Edward Teller

I knew Szilard while I was a graduate student at UCSD. We often talked about science fiction and Szilard's own stories, especially "The Voice of the Dolphins." His scholar's conscientiousness could not smother his novelist's wit and respect for the plain, bare facts of history. Introduced by Freeman Dyson, I discussed the bomb and the war years with him often. He encouraged me to write "fiction about scientific thinking" and I did so, selling my first story while there in 1964, leading to a successful sideline as I became a professor at UC Irvine. He and I had similar influences (physics, mathematics, fiction, philosophy), and his ideas are still afoot in our world.

Szilard encouraged me to apply for a postdoc position at the Lawrence Radiation Laboratory in Livermore, though he knew I might work on nuclear weapons eventually. My job interview with Teller was both stimulating and unnerving; at the end of it, I suspected Teller understood my thesis better than I did. It was also terrifying; I had no warning who would interview me. Teller thought well of Szilard and to my surprise hired me immediately. Many of the small nuggets of history in this novel I learned from him.

Many Manhattan Project scientists supported a nuclear weapons ban after the war: Oppenheimer, Szilard, even Teller. They were split during the war, and in my view, they assumed they had more power over the decision to use the bomb than they did. The decision was rightfully political. The scientists overestimated their influence and were ignored. Indeed, in retrospect, the prospect of a group of physicists determining the use of the bombs seems as likely as a unicorn leading a twenty-mule team.

As Freeman Dyson noted:

> "Oppenheimer was driven to build atomic bombs by fear that if he did not seize this power, Hitler would seize it first.

Teller was driven to build hydrogen bombs by the fear that Stalin would use this power to rule the world. Oppenheimer, being Jewish, had good reason to fear Hitler. Teller, being Hungarian, had good reason to fear Stalin. But each of them, having achieved his technical objective, wanted more. Each of them became convinced that he must have the political power to ensure that the direction of the enterprise he had created should not fall into hands that he considered irresponsible."

During World War II the controversy, petitions, and the like reflected a deep anxiety among the largely leftist, largely pacifist scientists. None considered that the bomb might usher in an era when the immense, destructive warfare that grew through Word Wars I and II was no longer really possible among the great powers.

We live in such an era. There are plenty of wars but none like World War II, which killed twenty-nine million Soviets alone, and more than sixty million in total, about 3 percent of the world population (more than 80 percent of them among the Allies, especially the Soviets and the Chinese). The prevailing postwar view of many of the nuclear scientists, and many intellectuals including Einstein, was simple: the United Nations should hold all nuclear weapons and prevent anyone else from getting them.

This view shows how distant we are from that time. No one knowing today's UN would think such a body could govern, much less use, such weaponry, or that such weapons could be somehow uniquely confined to the UN. The huge reduction in the death rate from nation-state warfare since 1945 did not come about through diplomacy alone; nuclear physics played a role too. So did the sobering lessons of Hiroshima and Nagasaki.

Perhaps the most lasting legacy of World War II is that these terrifying weapons made large-scale nation-state warfare impossible. (World War II's rate of battle deaths was around 300 per 100,000 each year. It has now declined to a historic low, about one per 100,000. See http://blog.nuclearsecrecy.com/wp-content/uploads/2015/06/ourworldindata_wars-after-1946-state-based-battle-death-rate-by-type.png.)

It is worth recalling that J. Robert Oppenheimer told his recruits at Los Alamos that these weapons might end *all* major war. The idea was afoot even then.

Karl Paley Cohen

He started playing the piano when he was eight and at one point considered becoming a professional concert musician. His role in the Manhattan Project moved from isotope separation when the centrifugal method lost favor.

Karl Cohen at age eighty-six

As Alvin Weinberg says in *The Second Fifty Years of Nuclear Fission*:

> Karl Cohen occupied an all-but-unique position in those early days since he was probably the only person at the time who possessed an intimate knowledge of both gaseous diffusion and nuclear reactors. He had participated in the development of the original theory of the diffusion cascade at Columbia in 1942 and, when Harold Urey was banished to Chicago by General Groves in 1943, Cohen also came to Chicago to work with Wigner on the design of heavy water reactors. Cohen therefore was the first to command a detailed understanding of both reactors and diffusion plants.

After the war, he moved into nuclear power for the rest of his life. From 1952 to 1955 he was a consultant for the Atomic Energy Commission, then a senior science adviser at Columbia University. He published *The Theory of Isotope Separation as Applied to the Large Scale Production of U235* in 1951. Karl was manager of the advanced engineering atomic power equipment department at General Electric, 1955–1965, then general manager of their breeder reactor development department, 1965–1971, then manager of strategic planning, nuclear energy division, 1971–1973. He became chief scientist of the nuclear energy group, 1973–1978. The Krupp Prize for his reactor work came in the 1970s. He retired to become a consultant professor at Stanford University, 1978–1981.

Karl cofounded and in 1968–1969 was president of the American Nuclear Society. In retirement he relished being the patriarch of his extended family, and especially sitting at the head of the table at holidays surrounded by his family—a doting grandfather and great-grandfather. In 2000 he was voted to be among the fifty most prominent American chemists of the twentieth century. He died in 2012 at age ninety-nine, rather distressed that he "could not last into three digits."

History is mostly about winners. It is also useful to consider those who did not win, but should have. Karl Cohen and the centrifugal method should have prevailed. As I argue here, that could have well have yielded a better world.

Marthe, Eugene, and Madeleine Malartre (top row, left to right); Elisabeth and Martine Cohen (below), 1946

Colonel Eugene and Madeleine Malartre

This colonel in the French army did indeed join his wife and hide on a farm in southern France from 1941 to 1945, as depicted here. I used Madeleine's diary for details of their lives, including the German soldier attack. They later moved back to Paris and in 1946 voyaged to visit the Cohens in New York, as shown here on deck as they arrived.

Some technical issues deserve discussion:

Centrifuges

To quote Karl Cohen in his contribution to the National Academy of Sciences biography of Harold Urey:

> In the summer of 1942 the reported experimental results on flow-through centrifuges were disappointing, showing only 36 percent of theoretical efficiency. Urey's protestations that countercurrent centrifuges would be easier to build and were more efficient were to no avail. Centrifuge work remained

at a low level. It is an irony of history that subsequent experiments in 1943 and 1944 proved that countercurrent machines could operate close to theoretical efficiency. At least six nations have at the present time [1981] operated countercurrent centrifuges with uranium hexafluoride, and it is the uranium isotope separation method of choice for five of them.

In November and December of 1942 there was a commitment to a full-scale diffusion plant, a smaller electromagnetic plant convertible later to full size, and heavy water plants.

The electromagnetic Oak Ridge Calutron plant supplied nearly all the U-235 in the Hiroshima bomb. The "full-scale diffusion plant" that cost so much and that General Groves chose over the centrifuge program gave only a few percent.

The purpose of building the reactors at Hanford, Washington, during the war was to produce plutonium, which had first been created in a UC Berkeley cyclotron. Because uranium was proving difficult to separate in the Oak Ridge diffusion plant, the Manhattan Project created Los Alamos, devoted to figuring out how to implode plutonium for a bomb. If there had been enough uranium, they need not have resorted to plutonium, which is far more difficult to implode to ignite a fission bomb.

Three engineering details, belatedly discovered in the early 1950s, made centrifuges work far better than gaseous diffusion:

A "point" bearing that allowed the centrifuge rotor to spin on the tip of a needle (like a toy top) with almost no friction.
The application of loose bearings and weak damping, which allowed the centrifuge to adjust itself so that it spun quietly on its center-of-mass axis without vibration, instead of trying to force the axis of rotation.
Driving the rotation using electromagnetic fields only, just as the armature of an electric motor drives its internal rotating shaft.

These points emerged from the work of Gernot Zippe, an Austrian physicist, who figured out with others how to fix the problems Jesse Beams had with his centrifuges. Zippe did this while being a prisoner of war in the Soviet Union! This led the USSR to drop their cumbersome gaseous plants (the USA used them, right?—so that must be the right path; until Zippe's light dawned).

The Zippe centrifuges came from working out the above engineering details that made the devices reliable and stable. There was no "secret," per se, no special materials, as historian Alex Wellerstein has pointed out. They just involved new features implemented by Zippe.

I estimate that another six months of work by Beams, maybe with a bit of insight from others and a bigger budget, would have done the trick by early 1943. These are clever engineering moves, that's all. These changes "solved essentially all the mechanical problems that had plagued Manhattan Project centrifuges," Scott Kemp of MIT writes. He argues correctly that it wasn't that fast centrifuges weren't possible in 1942. Jesse Beams just never figured out the right tricks. He never had enough time or funding.

The crucial turning points in this alternative history are the events early in the Manhattan Project, when the Urey group at Columbia could not get funding for centrifuge development. We forget the style of science in that era, when government did little research and corporations gave small sums for specific developments, all to acquire technologies useful in the short term. The entire style of Big Science came into being for the first time in the Manhattan Project's large laboratories and intricate coordination, invented chiefly by Groves, Oppenheimer, Fermi, and Lawrence. Karl Cohen once remarked to me that in 1939 he and Urey estimated that to develop fast centrifuges might take as much as $100,000—"so then we *knew* it was impossible!" At that time Karl was earning less than $2,000 a year.

Death Dust

In 1943 several American scientists proposed use of radioactive dust against Germany—Fermi, Oppenheimer, Teller, and others. They reasoned that the Germans could well be ahead in using the idea already. The documents quoted here about this are authentic. Strontium 90 seemed the best choice. Oppenheimer thought it was worth trying if it could poison the food of at least half a million.

They thought German battlefield use was possible. The USA Operation Peppermint to detect use of radiological weapons was widely dispersed among troops in the Normandy invasion. (My own father, who appears in this novel, was among such troops as a forward observer in artillery.) The army sent teams with Geiger counters and film to be fogged, to see if the Germans were using radiological dust as a weapon. Germany wasn't, of course. The German program never got the push Einstein gave the American program, in the way I've depicted. (Einstein did no work in the Manhattan Project, though he did some analysis of conventional explosives' effects.)

Werner von Braun had a continuous subscription to the magazine *Astounding* from the 1930s onward, having his copies delivered in wartime Germany via diplomatic pouch through Sweden. He knew of the radiological weapons idea invented by Heinlein, and so did the physicists in the German program. Taking the advice of Albert Speer, Hitler decided to drive ahead with the V-1, V-2, and jet airplanes, while the nuclear program hobbled along, accumulating uranium, without clearly understanding how to build a bomb or a reactor. The USA captured all their gear and scientists.

I have depicted John W. Campbell using his own words and those of the agents who interviewed him. He was well aware of the many possible uses of radioactive elements and encouraged his writers to explore them. I've also used the articles he wrote on the subject. He did say after the war that the strategic situation foreseen by Robert Heinlein in the death dust story was like "a duel in a vestibule with flamethrowers," anticipating mutual assured destruction and its acronym quite nicely.

Tolstoy famously thought that history in the large was not the fruit of individuals. Rather, he saw history as the outcome of innumerable, interconnected events, and so a product of its era and the work of millions. Certainly this describes much of World War II. But in the technical maze of the early Manhattan Project, the work of a few, and the judgment of even fewer (particularly General Groves) had great leverage. This novel argues that history has its pivotal fulcrums too.

Acknowledgments

For their contributions to the backgrounds of this novel thanks are due to the daughters of Karl and Marthe: Martine, Beatrix, Elisabeth; Ethel Paley; Karl Cohen. Photos of Karl Cohen are courtesy of Patrick Cashmore. Harry Turtledove added many useful historical points to my research and advised on an early manuscript.

For comments on the manuscript I thank Bart Kosko, Sheila Finch, Rick Wilber, Gordon Eklund, James Benford, Oak Ridge historian D. Ray Smith, John Rather, David Truesdale, Jon Lomberg, and the Cohen sisters. The sisters gave me many details about Karl and Marthe Cohen I have used in part, including much family correspondence and many memos. (Whenever possible I have quoted directly from these.)

I wish to thank for help and insights many who brought useful information about the era. On physics and historical matters, Garang Yodh was of great use. Michael Dobson contributed many useful insights and plot points. Albert Berger provided historical documents on the *Astounding* stories and the government investigation of those. Lydia Fletcher found documents galore. The late Bill Patterson advised on historical detail, plus the Heinlein and Cartmill stories. Alex Wellerstein provided through his site much useful insight.

I have used photos from the war era to show the look of the times. Most come from open online sources. ID badges are authentic Manhattan Project, including errors such as the typo in Groves's ID. Thanks to Alex Wellerstein for these.

I used many sources for this novel, including discussions with several of its principals. I read the biographies and autobiographies of them as well. In addition, these were especially useful:

Applebaum, Anne. *Iron Curtain: The Crushing of Eastern Europe, 1944–1956.* New York: Anchor, 2012.

Bernstein, Jeremy. *Hitler's Uranium Club: The Secret Recordings at Farm Hall,* 2nd ed. New York: Springer-Verlag, 2001.

———. *Plutonium: A History of the World's Most Dangerous Element.* Ithaca, NY: Cornell University Press, 2007.

Cohen, Karl. *The Theory of Isotope Separation as Applied to the Large Scale Production of U235.* New York: McGraw-Hill, 1951.

Dawidoff, Nicholas. *The Catcher Was a Spy: The Mysterious Life of Moe Berg.* New York: Vintage, 1994.

de la Bruhèze, A. A. Albert. "Radiological Weapons and Radioactive Waste in the United States: Insiders and Outsiders Views, 1941–1955." *The British Journal for the History of Science,* no. 25 (June 1992): 207–227. See also en.wikipedia.org/wiki/Radiological_weapon.

Kiernan, Denise. *The Girls of Atomic City: The Untold Story of the Women Who Helped Win World War II.* New York: Simon & Schuster, 2013.

Smith, P. D. *Doomsday Men: The Real Dr. Strangelove and the Dream of the Superweapon.* New York: St. Martin's Press, 2007.

Walker, Mark. *German National Socialism and the Quest for Nuclear Power, 1939–1949.* Cambridge, UK: Cambridge University Press, 1989.

Weart, S. R., and G. W. Szilard, eds. *Leo Szilard: His Version of the Facts: Selected Recollections and Correspondence.* Cambridge, MA: MIT Press, 1978.

I believe the best overall history of the Manhattan Project is Richard Rhodes's *The Making of the Atomic Bomb,* Simon & Schuster, 1986.

A useful website with much obscure background on this subject is blog. nuclearsecrecy.com. I thank Dr. Alex Wellerstein for many links.